A Taming
Season

~A Love at Lake George Novel~

CLAIRE GEM

www.EratoPublishing.com

Previously released from Lachesis Publishing as
Memories of You by Charlotte Daly

Dedication

I dedicate this book to the wonderful people in my life who have shaped and nurtured a seemingly impossible dream.

To my father, the late Frank Del Negro, who told me to "shoot for the stars, because if you don't, you'll never get off the ground."

To my daughter, Susanne Stich, who keeps right on telling me, "Don't give up, Mama. That's what puts you above the competition. You never give up."

And finally, to my husband Clark, who's been my most passionate champion for more than thirty-seven years. He holds me when I cry, listens when I complain, and cheers me when I succeed.

Acknowledgments

I want to thank a very special beta reader, Theresa Flynn, who read this story in its infancy, after multiple rejections, and said, "I love this story. I cried at the end—in a good way. I just can't believe you don't have a contract on this book."

There is no better editor—no—mentor, in this world than Joanna D'Angelo. Without her guidance, this book would never have been as good as it is. And it's damn good. Better than it could have ever been without her.

Claire Gem

Coming soon

A Love at Lake George Novel – Book 2

Anchor My Heart

A Taming Season

A Love at Lake George Novel
Book I

Prologue

One more summer of playing Princess of the Lake. Maybe her last. She was turning thirteen in the fall, and Zoe Anderson felt a little different already.

She was so glad her parents had sent her here to Lake George, away from their home on hot and humid Long Island. So glad that Aunt Delia welcomed her every summer, and treated her like a Disney Princess the whole time she was here.

From her perch on the front porch's swinging rocker, she could smell the aroma of something delicious baking, and giggled when her stomach let out an audibly embarrassing growl. Aunt Delia sure did love to bake.

She shifted her bottom on the hideous, floral printed upholstery of the cushions, trying to ignore how the plastic felt sticky and icky against her bare arms and legs. She flipped her book open to where she'd last left off. The Castle in the Attic, by Elizabeth Winthrop. She really liked the book, but the hero was only ten years old. That was just way too young for her reading tastes these days. Still, her aunt had been nice enough to buy it for her, and she didn't want to hurt her feelings. Aunt Delia seemed bound and determined to keep Zoe frozen in childhood as long as she could.

Massive rocks formed the jetty that divided Delia's

beachfront and that of the resort next door, and from the other side, Zoe heard laughter. Boys' laughter. She slid her bookmark back into place and laid the book down on the swing seat.

She tiptoed down the steps of the porch—as though anyone could hear her anyway. Motorboats whizzed up and down the lake, and the wind had kicked up, causing the wispy ends of her short, red hair to whip around, tickling her cheeks and ears. Her aunt always said she reminded her of a woodland sprite. Well, to be honest, she'd rather look like a sophisticated teenager, like some of the girls in her class—the ones taking modeling classes. She was too short for that though. They made a point of telling her so when she'd asked them about the classes.

Barefoot, she shivered as cold mushy sand squished up between her toes, soaked with murky lake water that was still, even this late in June, frigid against her skin.

Sneaking up to the jetty, she crouched low, listening. The voices—at least two boys, maybe three—echoed to her in intermittent snatches.

"Hey, Jay. How'd . . . lucky . . . snag these?

". . . your mom know?"

"Yup. Doesn't give a rat's ass . . . bigger problems . . . ."

It was then the wind switched directions and Zoe caught a whiff of cigarette smoke.

Yuck.

She wrinkled her nose.

Glancing up, she saw the dark clouds rolling in from the north end of the lake.

Storm coming.

She rubbed her arms as she began to shiver from the suddenly cooler breeze, turned and headed back toward the porch.

Her aunt was standing on the top step, holding a plate with something . . . As she drew closer, an enticingly familiar aroma reached her, and her stomach performed another noisy twist.

Yum.

Nothing better than Aunt Delia's homemade banana bread. Even if she did use rotten bananas to make it.

Zoe shuddered and tried not to think about the black-skinned fruits she'd seen heaped in a bowl on the counter when she'd arrived earlier that day. Surrounded by a cloud of tiny winged insects.

Ewww . . .

She shivered again. Aunt Delia always said, the blacker the banana, the sweeter the cake, so who was she to argue?

"And just what exactly are you doing, young lady?" Delia's scolding tone was one she reserved for the rare occasion when Zoe dared to stray from her reading spot on the front porch without permission.

"Nothing," she shot back, trying very hard to sound innocent and nonchalant.

One of Delia's brows arched and she cocked her head as the sound of the boys' laughter floated over to her from behind the jetty. She scowled at Zoe.

"Listen to me, Zoe Anderson. You don't need to have anything to do with that boy," she warned, pointing with one arthritic-gnarled finger in the direction of the jetty. "That boy, he's trouble with a capital T."

Zoe shrugged as she climbed the steps. "I thought I saw a cool shell wash up on the sand. That's all, Auntie." She reached forward for the plate. "Did you make this for me?" she asked through a smile. Her mouth had already started to water.

Chapter 1

Twenty Years Later

"They assigned me a new doctor. A woman this time."

Zoe took a deep breath and flicked her shoulder-length hair forward, draping the side of her face like a reddish-gold curtain. She sat across from her best friend, Medina, at a corner bistro table at Café D'Alphonse, one block off Broadway. It was oddly quiet at the posh French eatery, especially for a Friday.

"And? What words of wisdom did this new shrink have to offer?" Medina slammed one silk-sleeved elbow down on the checkered tablecloth, riveting her through narrowed eyes.

Zoe already knew how her friend felt about the help she'd been getting. In truth, she couldn't blame her for being dubious. It had been three years, and Zoe hadn't improved at all. She still had nightmares, even though the cops caught up with Conroe before he'd had a chance to wash the blood off his hands.

Since then some of her symptoms—the panic attacks, the fainting spells, the word scrambling episodes—had actually worsened.

Conroe was dead, but Zoe had found little comfort in the news the detective had delivered at the hospital, the morning after her life had fractured. The tragedy had seared indelible scars. On her face. On her mind. On her life.

"She says I need to reboot. Restart. You know, like you do when your computer gets fouled up with a virus. You restore . . . to an earlier time."

Medina arched a perfectly shaped eyebrow. "Honey, you're not a computer," she snapped. "It pisses me off the bitch even talks to you that way. What kind of a quack did they hook you up with this time?"

Zoe's eyes dropped to the napkin lying folded across her lap. "Someone I hope who can finally help me get through this." She hugged herself and met her friend's gaze straight on. "Dina, if I don't get my act together, I'm going to be out of a job. Barlow as much as told me that when she handed me the medical leave papers."

"But you're okay financially aren't you?" Medina asked. "David took care of you, right?"

"He did. He was very smart that way," she replied with a smile of remembrance. "But his life insurance isn't going to support me forever." She swallowed hard and sucked in a painful breath, dropping her gaze to the knotted fingers in her lap. "I can't afford to be crazy *and* out of work for the rest of my life."

Medina leaned across the table, reaching for Zoe's hand. "Look. I keep telling you, good little Catholic girl—you're not crazy. You've been through hell. You need to loosen up and accept that your life didn't turn out like a Disney movie. You've got three months. Go on vacation. Get a little drunk. Have a fling."

Yeah, right.

Zoe sighed and cut her eyes to the sweating goblet of Pinot Grigio next to her plate.

At least if I'm drunk, I'll have an excuse for babbling. For

5

sounding like my sentences come out of a blender.

Not to mention that the thought of a man even touching her still made Zoe's stomach lurch.

Rape. She'd read the word dozens of times on her clients' profiles, but never truly understood the victims' inexplicable guilt, disgust, and self-loathing. Now, she did. She would never forget those images, and the horror of watching her husband bleed to death while his murderer brutalized her.

Fling? Seriously. Give me a break.

She took Medina's hand. Its warmth was reassuring. She'd been such a good friend through all this. There at her bedside on the night it happened, holding her hand as detectives grilled her for the disgusting details. Through every one of the three reconstructive surgeries on her face. And at the other end of a phone call whenever Zoe needed her.

Keeping her voice low, Medina said, "It was a bad scene this time, wasn't it?"

Quick tears turned Zoe's glass of wine into a wavering, amber blur. She nodded.

"I was right in the middle of a session with a new client. Spousal abuse." She sought Medina's eyes. "I went from a social worker to a pathetic puddle in a heartbeat. I couldn't put five words together into any kind of logical order. It was like my brain froze." She leaned her forehead on her hand. "I'm supposed to be helping these women, Dina. Not scaring them even more."

She quickly discovered that news of yet another of her psychotic episodes had flown straight down the hall to her boss's office. Gladys Barlow had been nothing but supportive of her since David's death. They both knew how hard it was to get over trauma like this.

But Zoe knew that if her condition didn't improve, she couldn't possibly go on serving as a counselor at Family

Guardian Services. No matter how much her boss sympathized with her.

After the latest episode she'd spent three weeks—voluntarily—at Brockview Psychiatric Hospital. Group therapy, different medication, a new doctor. She'd been home less than a week, and was feeling stronger and more hopeful than she'd had since that horrific night.

"Honey, you're still too close to this thing," Medina said. "You're living the same life you lived before—working at the same job, with the same people. I think a few months off will do you good. But you've got to get out of here. Break your routine."

"This new psychiatrist agrees with you," Zoe said. "She says I need to get out of town. Go back home, or somewhere . . . someplace where I have happy memories before I met David."

Medina nodded. "Okay, so, are you going to visit your parents in Florida?"

"No way." Zoe rolled her eyes. Suffocating under Mommy's well-intentioned smothering was the last thing she needed. When her parents retired and moved to Florida, it had been the most liberating thing that had happened to her in recent years. "Remember I told you about the little cabin at the lake where we went every summer? When I was a kid?"

"At Lake George? I remember. Didn't you just inherit that place?"

"I did. Aunt Delia left it to me. The paperwork was in my mailbox when I got home from the hospital last week." She shrugged, and then forced a weak smile. "I never knew her very well. Delia was, well, a little eccentric. I quit spending summers there when I started high school, though we still talked on the phone now and again." Zoe sighed. "I'm sorry she's gone, but this inheritance . . . it came at a good time, I think."

"Who's going up there with you?" Medina asked.

"I'm going alone. I think I need some time by myself."

Medina's eyes flashed. "Alone? Are you kidding me? Is this another one of your shrink's ideas?"

"No," Zoe said. "This is my idea." She drew in a deep breath, and then took a sip of her wine. She sat up straighter and squared her shoulders. "If I'm going to reboot my life, I need to start inside my own head."

Zoe left the next morning, a beautiful sunny Saturday in mid-June. As she navigated up the Cross Bronx expressway, she noticed the traffic didn't clog the roadway nearly as bad as during the week. By the time her sporty Cadillac broke free of the tangled network of city roadways, she started to feel a little different. A little freer. It had been a long time—a very long time—since the city girl traveled to the mountains.

David never wanted to go 'up into the boonies,' his tag for anywhere there weren't streetlamps, five-star restaurants, and valet parking. Born and raised on Long Island, he was a city boy in the truest sense of the word. When he lost both parents in a car crash at nineteen, he'd inherited their money and invested it wisely. Vacations for David meant Paris, London, even St. Petersburg one year. But a quaint mountain village on the shores of a lake in the Adirondacks? Zoe had never been able to convince him to spend even one weekend there.

She switched to a classical station, the kind of music she seldom listened to. Once out of the exhaust-fume cloud of the city, she shut off her air conditioner and rolled down her windows. Mid-June in Manhattan could be stifling, but here, miles north of the city, the air was cooler, cleaner.

Reboot. Restore to an earlier time.

The words echoed in Zoe's head like a soothing mantra.

As much as she'd enjoyed her husband whisking her away to exotic locations, Zoe felt a pang of nostalgia now for the simplicity of her childhood summers. Her love for David had been so true, so heart-consuming, she'd never looked back from the day he'd asked her to be his wife. They both plunged toward their future with a united dream—a home on the outskirts of the big city, where they could raise a family but still be close enough to the excitement. They'd had their eyes on one particularly prestigious community in Great Neck.

They had almost made it.

Now, her future lay before her like broken shards of a shattered mirror. Somehow she had to piece it back together.

Her therapist was right. Zoe's only option was to rewind her life and start over again.

She exited the Thruway, where a clear blue, cloudless sky struck a vivid contrast to the lush green of the mountains on the horizon. As her car crested the hill, the lake opened up below her—a shiny, silvery blue ribbon at the mountain's base.

Zoe hadn't been back to the lake in almost twenty years. She knew she couldn't trust her memory to navigate, so she pulled off the road and fumbled in her purse for the attorney's letter, which had the cabin's address, and punched it into her GPS.

Although Zoe remembered the cabin was tucked up against some fancy resort complex, she couldn't remember its name. And how could she be sure if the place was even still there?

Ah, yes. Lakeview Lodge. It hadn't moved, but it did look different from the way she remembered. The elegantly scrolled sign at the entrance was new, as were the dozen or so log-faced A-frames that now lined the steep driveway leading down to the lake's edge. She spotted the wall of pines on the north end of the property and smiled. She remembered the driveway to the cabin wove down between those trees.

Something familiar, please. I need something to look the same, reassure me that not everything in my life has changed forever.

She slowed when she reached the wooded strip, but she didn't see a mailbox. Creeping farther, the mechanical voice of her GPS startled her.

Right turn here.

Where?

As she coasted slowly past, the computer warned: *recalculating route.* Zoe slowed and eased her car onto the shoulder. This couldn't be right. She knew her family's property was just north of Lakeview Lodge, the driveway winding down the hill between the tall trees.

Yet spread before her, on the north side, was another rolling lawn surrounding more A-framed cabins. A second, matching sign—Lakeview Lodge North—confused her further.

This had been another resort, something else back then. The Catalina or something.

Doubting herself as well as her trusty GPS, Zoe turned the Caddy around. She crept slowly back down the two-lane road, grateful there was no one behind her. When she got to the wooded strip dividing Lakeview's property, her GPS chirped again, insistently.

Left turn, here.

But there was no break in the wooden rail fence defining the entire length of the lavish resort's frontage. It was as though the driveway to the cabin had simply disappeared.

Guess I'll have to ask at the Lodge.

As her car wound slowly along the paved, serpentine

entrance to Lakeview, Zoe tried to locate something familiar. But everything about the resort was different. She remembered a cluster of clapboard cottages at the foot of the steeply sloping lawn, lined up like little white boxes at the water's edge. Now, elegant cedar and glass A-frames dotted the carefully landscaped grounds.

She finally spotted a smaller replica of the other buildings that wore a red neon sign—*Office*.

Zoe pulled into an empty spot in front, took a deep breath, and got out. A typical tinkling bell dangled from the inside knob and announced her arrival. Two wine-colored leather loveseats furnished the office. They were angled toward a massive, triangular wall of windows that overlooked the lake. Through a doorway behind the knotty pine counter, a smiling, white-haired woman appeared.

"May I help you, Miss?"

"Yes, um, I seem to be a bit turned around. I'm looking for my aunt's old cottage." She glanced down at her letter. "At 1334 Lakeshore Drive."

The woman blinked, and Zoe couldn't tell if it was surprise or curiosity that caused her straggly eyebrows to rise and inch a little closer together. "I was sorry to hear about your aunt. Quite sudden," the woman said.

Zoe nodded. "Yes, it was. Did you know Delia?"

"We did. But it's been several years since she stayed at the lake. Quite a few, in fact." A head tilt turned the woman's curious-surprised-pinched brow expression into one Zoe read as pity. "You don't plan on staying *there*." It wasn't a question, but a rather clipped statement.

Zoe sighed. She had to pee, and her back ached from the four-hour drive. And what business was it of this little old lady what she intended to do? Her patience with the Betty White clone was running out fast.

"Can you please tell me how to find it? It's been a really long time since I've been there, and neither I nor my GPS seem to be able to find the driveway."

Betty cleared her throat and glanced down at her registration book, picking up the pen and twiddling it between her fingers. Her voice grew tight, brittle. "There's no driveway . . . anymore. The only way to access the property is through Lakeview."

"Excuse me?"

"Your aunt sold the right-of-way to Mr. Rolland. About five years ago. The last summer she was here, I believe."

Now it was Zoe's turn to blink, raise her brows, and tilt her head. "And, Mr. Rolland is . . . ?"

"The owner. Mr. Rolland owns Lakeview."

Zoe paused, trying to sort out this new information. "So you mean I've inherited a house that's landlocked? No direct road access?"

"Oh, I wouldn't call that place a house, dear." Betty's facetious half-chuckle twisted around the words and irritated Zoe even more. Her expression must have given that away, because the woman pushed back from the counter and reached quickly for the desk phone. "Let me give Mr. Rolland a call. I think it would be best for you to discuss this directly with him."

While Betty made the call, Zoe used the office restroom. She emerged a bit more comfortable, but no less annoyed. And now, even more confused. True, she'd not been close with Aunt Delia. Neither were her parents. But she was sure her family had no idea that any part of the property had been sold.

The leather loveseat was incredibly comfortable, and felt good on Zoe's aching back. She tucked herself into the corner, kicked off her shoes, and folded her stiff legs up beside her.

The view of the lake from this spot was spectacular. The tiny A-frame replica sat about halfway up the steep hill that divided the winding two-lane road from Lake George. The new cabins had been placed so none, it seemed, blocked another's view of the water.

Ingenious architectural feat. Or amazing surveying. Or something.

There were whitecaps on the lake today, and Zoe watched as ski and pontoon boats zipped by. A single sailboat bobbed peacefully in the distance, idyllic against the backdrop of the lush mountains on the other shore.

Yeah, this is exactly what I need. Certainly a change from my window view at home.

Her Manhattan apartment, no way as posh as the one she'd shared with David, was in a lovely, but more modest stretch on the Upper West Side. Situated on the thirtieth floor, her living room had a great view, but the area was noisy and busy with constant traffic and people double parking to grab takeout from the Irish Pub across the street.

Zoe was tired and getting a little hungry. Thinking of the pub, a cool glass of wine sounded nice right about now, too. Where the hell was this Rolland guy, and why couldn't the old biddy behind the counter simply point the way to her aunt's— scratch that, her—cottage?

She was busy thumbing through a colorful flyer advertising local attractions when the glass door squeaked open. She looked up.

And all the irritation and fatigue of the day melted away into a single, warm, wet lump in her lower belly.

He was tall—quite tall, and somewhat lanky, but broad shouldered like a male model. His jeans fit his body as if the denim was enjoying every minute. His unbuttoned white polo shamelessly hugged a lean, sculptured torso.

This guy looked like he just stepped out of a Calvin Klein ad. Surely, this can't be Mr. Rolland.

She'd been picturing a man close in age to the woman she'd been trying to ignore for the past twenty minutes. But as he came through the door, the man glanced quickly at Betty, who nodded in Zoe's direction. Then he turned his eyes toward her.

Those must be colored contacts. I've never seen eyes the same clear, almost iridescent hue as a swimming pool. Maybe it was the contrast against the hair—jet black, stick-straight, and ornery. He'd tried to tame it with some sort of product, but with little success. One chunk hung defiantly over his dark brow.

"Hi. I'm Jason Rolland."

Jason extended his hand, his gaze scanning every inch of the shapely redhead in the bright, flowered sundress. What the hell was it made of? The clingy fabric outlined every one of her curves. The hem had inched up, gifting him with a view of an incredible set of legs.

So this is the woman I'm going to have to spar with over old Delia's property. I was hoping this would be a simple, long-distance real estate transaction handled by my attorney. This is going to be a little more complicated than I was anticipating.

Shit.

He cleared his throat as he watched Zoe untangle her legs and struggle to her feet.

Her naked feet. They were perfect too—two tiny, smooth-looking little bugs with pale pink toenails. Innocent little feet, shamelessly exposed. Her toes pressed desperately on the surface of the pristine white tile.

"Hi. I'm Zoe Anderson."

Breathless. Why did she sound breathless? Jason knew she'd been waiting for him, settled comfortably in the loveseat in the office, right? For at least the past twenty minutes while he'd dug through his file cabinet to review the paperwork he knew she would be here to discuss. So why should she sound breathless?

She must be nervous.

Jason watched as she tugged at the skirt of her dress, and then adjusted the neckline. She drew in a deep breath and hesitated for a very long moment before speaking.

"I'm Delia O'Reilly's niece, and I inherited her place." She straightened, apparently trying to stand taller. It didn't help much. Jason towered over her by at least a half-foot. She tipped her chin up to meet his gaze, and her silky, shoulder length, red-gold hair fell back, revealing all of her face. That's when Jason caught sight of the jagged pink line etched on her cheek.

Ouch. Where the hell did that come from?

Jason hesitated before answering. "Ooh, I'm sorry about that." He cleared his throat, and quickly slid his gaze away.

Damn my errant tongue.

"The cabin, I mean. I'm sorry, but I think you might be in for a bit of a disappointment. Do you know anything about the place?" He tried very hard not to sound condescending. But when it came to discussing the shack that Delia O'Reilly had held onto like a life raft, it was a challenge.

"Why?"

The single word sliced through Jason like a knife. Apparently, she was clueless. Had the situation been different, had the heir to Delia's property not been standing right here in front of him, looking like *this,* he might have been able to maintain his cool, business armor.

But one glimpse of the brutally scarred face of this softly rounded, vulnerable-looking creature caused Jason's macho shroud to dissolve.

Without a word, he reached out and took Zoe's hand.

Her eyes rounded like an owl's before slowly trailing from his face to their joined hands and back.

Had he offended her? No, she wasn't pulling away.

Jason squeezed her fingers in reassurance.

"Let me take you down to your aunt's cottage," he rumbled. Then he turned to the elderly desk clerk. "The Aspen is open, isn't it, Agnes? Late cancellation, from what Jade told me. Book Ms. Anderson in that chalet, would you please?" He turned back to Zoe. "You're a very lucky girl. The Aspen is one of our premier units. It's usually booked through the entire season."

Her clear, green eyes bore into his, as though she was trying to say something without opening her mouth. But she didn't utter a word.

"Come on. I'll take you down there," he urged.

"Don't forget your shoes, Ms. Anderson. The path to Delia's house has grown over quite a bit," the desk clerk called after them, sounding more like a scolding parent than hired help.

Thank you, Agnes. Shut up, Agnes. Jason bristled but kept the words inside his head.

He led Zoe down the hill toward the water, following along the edge of the pine wall. The grounds of Lakeview were meticulously mowed right up to the trees. But the soft green carpet ended in a tangle of vines that knitted the tall trunks together into an almost solid mat. The hill was steep and she stumbled once, the toe of her flip-flop catching in the grass. Jason reached out and reclaimed her hand.

"I wouldn't venture too far into the kudzu," he warned.

"The gardeners told me they've seen a snake or two sunning themselves along the edge."

Their hands still joined, he felt the shudder that ran through her. "Nothing poisonous," he added. "A garter, maybe a black snake. We don't bother them. We figure they keep the mice and moles under control."

The glance she slanted his way still looked wary.

Jason led her down close to the shoreline, to a corner defined by a tall privacy fence. The gate was almost invisible, blending into the solid, white wall. A small padlock hung from the latch. Jason fished a ring of keys out of his pocket and unlocked the gate. He pulled it open, revealing a weedy, overgrown path. He pointed to a small structure in the distance, obscured by the dense greenery surrounding it.

"That's your aunt's place. She hadn't been back here in years."

"You've got to be kidding, right?"

Jason cringed at the horror he heard so clearly in Zoe's tone.

"I'm afraid so," he answered flatly. "Delia wasn't very ambitious about keeping the place up. And she was too damned proud to let my crew even mow her yard for her."

Jason clearly remembered what the cottage had looked like twenty years ago. White clapboard siding, window boxes overflowing with bright pink flowers. He vaguely recalled peering through the trees now and then, hoping to catch a glimpse of the little girl with the carrot-red, pixie-short hair. The one always curled up on the front porch swing, staring intently into the pages of some book.

Jason cleared his throat, dragging himself back into the present. "Delia's place, sorry to say, had deteriorated into an eyesore. Detracting from the image I wanted for Lakeview."

Zoe stared at the abandoned shack in silence for what

seemed like forever. Then she turned to glare at him. Before she had a chance to say another word, Jason held both hands up in surrender.

"Hey, look. I tried to buy the place from her. Offered her the best money on the market. She wouldn't budge."

Jason watched as Zoe turned back toward what was left of her family's cottage. This had to be a cruel assault on her childhood memories. He couldn't help but feel a stab of pity for her.

He didn't follow as she picked her way through the brush toward the cabin, but stayed behind, leaning against the frame of the gate with his arms folded. He felt like he should say something—anything—to ease the shock for this fragile-looking woman.

The cottage was barely still standing. Most of the white paint lay in tattered shards on top of the mat of kudzu vine that now enveloped the entire foundation. On one end, the supports for the front porch had broken free. The planked surface now tilted at an alarming angle, making it seem as though the building might topple into the lake at any moment.

"Delia was getting on in years," he called. "She knew she couldn't keep the place up, but she was bound and determined not to sell it. I tried. I truly did. I was lucky she finally at least sold me the driveway—what was left of it, anyway."

Jason watched Zoe struggle with each step, her flip-flops catching in the vines. He winced as she swatted repeatedly—convulsively—at her bare legs and arms where deerflies or mosquitoes were no doubt feasting. She took only a few more steps before she gave up.

She turned and faced him, planting her hands on her hips. "How is that even possible? How could she sell you the right

18

of way, but not the property?"

Jason bristled and straightened. "It's possible, Ms. Anderson. It relieved Delia the responsibility of maintaining that dirt path she called a driveway. I provided paved parking for her here." Jason pointed to the small rectangle of blacktop behind him. "And for the record, I did Delia a favor. It was the only way she could hold onto this place. The county was about ready to condemn it."

Even from twenty feet away, Jason caught the flare of anger in her eyes. "So you took her right of way and forced her out. Leaving her—and now me—with a worthless piece of land."

He tipped back his head and squinted, studying her.

Not such a soft, vulnerable little thing after all. This one has a streak of wildcat, though quite ingeniously disguised.

"It's not exactly worthless." He spat the four words out, one at a time. "And I didn't take Delia's right of way, Ms. Anderson. I purchased it, fair and legal."

Zoe stalked back, stopping inches away and glaring up at him. She folded her arms across her chest. The action pushed her freckled cleavage into view.

He couldn't help it. He was a man, after all. His eyes sometimes had a mind all their own. They strayed down toward those luscious looking, speckled mounds. He also couldn't help the corner of his mouth twitching, just once.

Yup. Spotted mountain wildcat.

She caught him. When he lifted his gaze, her gold-flecked, green eyes had darkened to flint. She made a dangerous, guttural sound as her fisted hands dropped to her sides.

"My attorney," she said, stomping past him, "will be the one to determine exactly how fair and legal."

Chapter 2

Two hours later, Zoe pushed through the squeaky screen door of Lakeview's patio bar. She'd unpacked in the fancy chalet she'd had no intention of staying in, slamming drawers and snatching at hangers, muttering under her breath the entire time.

Who the hell does this Rolland guy think he is? And what am I supposed to do with a run-down shack on a piece of property without any road access?

She definitely needed a drink.

The patio bar was nearly empty. Mid-afternoon on a gorgeous, sunny summer day had drawn everyone, it seemed, out onto the lake or the beach. Zoe slid onto the end stool of the U-shaped bar, into one of their comfy, padded-backed seats, and ordered an Absolut and tonic.

The barkeep, a tall, slim woman with gorgeous skin the color of milk chocolate, stretched a healthy pour over ice and triggered tonic into the brim. She glided toward Zoe and set the glass down with a grin.

"There you go, Red."

Zoe blinked up into the woman's friendly eyes. Her gleaming, white smile was contagious.

"Thanks," she chuckled, "but it's Zoe. Quiet in here for a

Saturday afternoon, huh?"

"I'm Jade. Welcome to Lakeview." Jade kicked one foot across the other and leaned an elbow down on the bar. "Not surprising when the weather's so fine, ya know. Give it about, oh, another hour or so. Once happy hour starts, the place will be a mob scene."

Zoe sipped her drink and glanced around. The shiny oak bar looped out at a right angle from the restaurant, built above what used to be a boathouse, as she remembered. The elevated decking beneath her was bare wood, exactly like the docks below. A screen enclosure wrapped the deck to allow the lake's breezes to float through bug-free, and soaring high above her head, a dark green metal roof protected from the summer sun's beating rays.

"Where are you from? Is this your first time here at the Lodge?" Jade's deep voice and signature accent were syrupy smooth. Caribbean?

"I'm from the city . . . Manhattan. And I got a bit of bad news today, in case I don't seem too chatty. It's not because I'm a snooty city slicker."

Jade's grinned widened. "City girl, huh? Well, you couldn't have picked a prettier spot to get away. This resort has done nothing but improve every year it's been here."

Zoe grinned and dropped her gaze to the lemon and lime slices swimming in her glass.

"Yeah, I know all about this place. I mean, I know it's been here a long time. My parents and I vacationed at the lake every summer. Lakeview's different now, though. The bar and restaurant weren't even here."

Jade's perfect white teeth flashed a vivid contrast to her warm, brown complexion.

"Oh, yes, it's changed—a lot more since Mr. Rolland took the reins. It's been about . . . oh, ten years or so now."

The screen door behind Zoe squeaked open, and then promptly slammed shut. Two young men wearing nothing but colorful surf shorts scuffed barefoot across the plank floor, accompanied by three tall, willowy women in barely-there bikinis. They were followed by—who else?—Jason Rolland. He was still in his denim and polo casual chic uniform, and didn't even try to hide his obvious appreciation of the undulating ass of the girl striding ahead of him.

"Speak of the devil," Jade murmured, tipping her head in Jason's direction.

As the group headed for the far side of the bar, one of the beach bums snapped an obvious double-take over his shoulder at the sculpted leg Zoe had crossed over the other. Zoe caught the cynical scowl Jade flashed in his direction.

The barkeep shook her head, her lips pressed into a thin line. "It's too bad the lake has so many sharks." Then she turned back to Zoe, tapping her elegant fingers on the edge of the bar. "But not in the water. Let me know when you're ready for your next cocktail." Jade turned and headed in the direction of the newcomers.

Zoe watched Jade draw foamy tap into iced mugs for the two shirtless young men, shake up three pink martinis, and then mix a vodka with seltzer, apparently for Jason. As she plunked the glasses down, Jason leaned forward to whisper something to her, his mouth brushing close to Jade's ear. Zoe blinked at the woman's reaction. Jade rocked back, lifting her chin. Abruptly, she wheeled around on one heel. Then she glided, gazelle-like, through the swinging door into the restaurant.

Through the arched, tinted glass windows of the restaurant, Zoe could see black-and-white, cloth-layered tables lining the room's perimeter. She remembered when that space was an open-air loft above the boathouse. She'd

22

been nothing but a barefoot, scrawny little mass of freckles then, leaning daringly over the edge of the loft's open balcony, squinting against the sun's glare for glimpses of the jerky masses of carp in the cold water below.

I was so happy then. Not a care in the world. So innocent. So unspoiled. Happily ever after still meant something to me then.

Minutes later, Zoe snapped back into the present as Jade returned, carrying a serving tray balanced on one shoulder. When Jade clicked the etched glass plate of shrimp down on the bar in front of her, Zoe's eyebrows raised in question.

"I didn't order any—"

"The boss says, enjoy. On him." Jade's smile was gone, her tone flat and her movements brisk. Without another word, she turned and headed back into the kitchen, swinging the empty tray beside her.

Hmm. Jealous, perhaps? Maybe the pretty woman's more than just the barkeep.

Jade was right about the happy hour crowd. Before Zoe's glass was empty, the casual, comfortable bar transformed from peaceful to pandemonium. Jason's two tanned, half-naked surfer companions were soon replaced by an older, more sophisticated pair of couples. They all sported Ralph Lauren's best beachwear, and chatted easily with him.

Okay, so he owns the place. But this guy's his own most favorite celebrity here.

Little by little, the younger boaters and skiers trickled in off the lake, climbing the steps directly from the docks below. Some walked in off the beach, still dripping wet. Within an hour, throngs of people, glasses or bottles in hand, huddled close together, busy in conversation. The cacophony of voices echoed off the bare wooden floors. By five o'clock, the only empty seat left at the bar was right next to Zoe.

This second drink was surely stronger than the last. She kept hoping Jade would return to chat, but the slender, elegant barkeep was too busy. Or, perhaps, deliberately avoiding her. Another, younger girl had joined her to tend the bar. The newcomer's blonde mane and poppy-red lipstick reminded Zoe of a mannequin.

She'd always enjoyed people watching, and tucked into her corner seat, she had a perfect vantage point. Jason continued intermittent conversations with Jade, his ever-changing set of rapt companions, which now included one well-endowed brunette spilling out of her halter bikini top, as well as with the bleached bar-babe. Barbie divided her time between drawing beer from the tap into an endless stream of iced mugs, and flirting with the men—particularly Jason. But only when Jade's attention was drawn elsewhere, it seemed.

Apparently there was a brain underneath all that over-processed hair.

Zoe smiled as she watched what was turning into a soap-opera style sideshow. Every time any one of the guys down the other end of the bar glanced anywhere near the blonde, she struck a pose, and flashed a photo-shoot smile over her shoulder. Then her gaze returned to Jason, and she'd wink one mascara-laden eye. Her performance reminded Zoe of the sequin-wrapped models from that game show, *The Price is Right*. She wondered how many tubes of mascara Barbie went through in a week.

Zoe sighed and reached into her purse for her phone.

Probably should give Medina a call and give her the gruesome details about my cozy summer cottage.

She didn't notice Jason had changed seats until his velvety voice rumbled into her left ear.

"I see we share the same taste in recreational beverages." Zoe snapped around to stare straight into the man's unusual blue eyes. Jason had slipped silently onto the adjacent barstool, and Zoe couldn't help but notice how his jeans snugged as he sat, and in all the right places. Her breath caught in her throat, and then quickly relaxed to take in the musky scent of his cologne.

Was it cologne? Or just his scent? Zoe twisted her shoulders and sat up a little straighter.

"Look, Rolland, I'm not in the best of moods today. I'm sure you understand why." She shot him a sidelong glance, picked up her glass, and took a pull through the straw.

"Sure. I totally understand." He held her gaze for a moment, but then his eyes searched the bar until he caught Jade's attention. A quick nod and the next round of drinks was on its way. His gaze flashed back to Zoe. "And please, call me Jason."

Wow. This guy is cock of the block. Or so he thinks.

"So, I'm assuming you spent time at your aunt's cottage in the past. But have you ever stayed with us here at the Lodge?" Jason's voice was almost surreal. Warm, buttery. How could simply the sound of a man's voice cause her body to react this way? Especially since the very thought of a man getting any further than a goodnight kiss had been, for the past three years, all but repulsive?

Scratch that. Definitely repulsive.

Zoe cleared her throat and kept her eyes on her sweating glass. "Yes, and no. I never actually stayed here. But I spent a bunch of sunny afternoons on your beach, and in the game room." She shot him a mischievous glance. "I don't suppose you remember the way the boathouse looked before it got upgraded to what now looks like a five-star restaurant?" Zoe tipped her head in that direction.

Jason's smile spread over his face like an early sunrise. He leaned in a little closer, his eyes searching her face in a new way. "As a matter of fact, I do," he purred. "I grew up here. Lakeview is a family business."

Zoe cocked her head to one side as she returned Jason's intense stare. Those incredible, almost surreal blue eyes, lined by jet lashes thicker than any woman's fantasy. The inky black hair, thick and straight, and as defiant as his attitude. A memory stirred in the very depths of her mind . . . and then, a flash. Like a computer in search mode, her brain suddenly found a matching file.

The image of a lanky teen, shirtless, in faded, baggy jeans, even in the heat of the summer. A cigarette perpetually hanging off his lower lip. Almost every afternoon, the boy roosted on the edge of the dock for hours. A stream of smoke would trail away from his face as he squinted against the glare off the water, a pair of dark sunglasses perched uselessly on top of his head.

Suddenly, like a scent or a song that takes you back to the time when you first experience it, Zoe felt it again—that funny feeling in the pit of her stomach. Whenever the boy had glanced her way, she went all fluttery inside. She'd been twelve, a few years younger than him, but old enough for the hormones to have started stirring up all sorts of weirdness. Yet they never spoke, other than one time Zoe recalled venturing out onto the dock while the teen enjoyed his smoke, only to be chased off with a curt, "Get lost, brat."

Zoe blinked rapidly as the memory flickered. "How long has your family owned this place?"

A muscle tensed in Jason's jaw, but his eyes glinted with mischief. "Since you were just a little girl." He leaned one elbow on the bar, his body drifting closer to hers. "You sure have grown up. Sooo, pardon the cliché but . . . what have you been doing all of my life?"

The warmth in her cheeks spread lower, down over her

neck and into all the places that had been cold and lifeless for so long.

Damn it. A little alcohol and every barrier starts to break down.

"I live in Manhattan. I'm a family counselor," she stammered. "Social work." Zoe stopped short. She didn't want to go on, reveal any more details. She twisted her shoulders. "And you? I see you're still here at the Lodge . . . and given up that nasty nicotine habit too, I hope?"

Jason's broad grin of surprise revealed a row of white teeth so perfect, they looked fake. His eyes glinted with amusement. "So I guess you really do remember me, huh? Yeah, I quit. Got tired of having to wear those horrible tasting whitening strips on my yellow teeth all the time."

"Well, probably not the most admirable justification for quitting, but it works." A warm tingling washed over her. She wasn't sure whether it was from the vodka or from the connection she'd made. A real live connection with her past, sitting right here beside her.

Reboot. Restore to an earlier time.

Her new shrink may have been right. It did feel good revisiting old memories.

Of course the vodka lenses probably didn't hurt. But why did her first memory buzz have to come from this pompous ass, a guy whose ego was probably his biggest body part? The same guy who was holding her inheritance hostage?

He'd claimed the seat next to her, but was actually standing now between the stools, closer. He leaned one elbow on the bar. That stubborn lock of black hair dropped lower over his eyes, giving him a 'just got out of bed' look. Zoe's heart rate leapt up to a steady rat-a-tat as his scent surrounded her. She swallowed and leaned back.

Was that fluttery stomach a good thing? Or the prequel to

losing her shrimp appetizer? Now that would be embarrassing.

"Look, Rolland, I'm here for a little R and R. Guess it's pretty obvious it's not going be happening next door, at Delia's—or should I say—my place. I do appreciate you putting me up in your fine cabin, but—"

"So what do you think of what I've done with Lakeview? It's changed quite a bit since you were in pigtails and Swimmees, hasn't it?"

Does he actually remember me? Her chest muscles clenched then, that pre-panicky sensation that always preceded her episodes. She couldn't afford to start babbling now, or to faint. She knew that no matter how attracted she was to this man, she needed to remember that he was also her adversary.

She must get a call in to Medina, and then to her attorney, Xavier. Zoe needed advice on what she should do next.

Leaning forward, she wrapped both hands around her glass. The cool, moist surface was calming, grounding.

"Yes, apparently you have the same aspirations for your resort as Caesar did for Rome." Zoe turned to face Jason with a cool glare. "But I'm not giving up my little piece of turf just yet."

Slowly, but with deliberation, Jason reached out and placed one finger under Zoe's chin. Too shocked to react, she held his gaze, trying to ignore the electricity of his touch.

"Look, Zoe, I won't give you any line of bullshit about that property. I want the shack torn down. I'll pay you a handsome price for the little stretch of beach it sits on."

"It's not for sale. At least, not yet."

He tipped up her chin, and her hair fell away from the side of her face. With dread, she closed her eyes and jerked away. But as she did, she caught the flash of reaction in his eyes.

Recoil. Disdain. Horror. She'd seen it countless times before over the past three years.

"Pardon my curiosity, but what did a pretty girl like you do to deserve a beauty mark like that?"

"That would be none of your damned business, you pompous ass." Zoe snatched her purse and pushed back from the bar. Her stool clattered to the floor, and the conversation around her hushed. The air thickened.

Had everyone stopped talking?

Not now. Please. Not now.

She clutched her purse to her chest as she pushed through the screen door and skittered down the wooden stairs. With long though shaky strides, she headed straight across the parking lot toward the Aspen chalet.

Close call.

That's all Zoe could think as she fumbled with the key in the lock. *How could this man have such an effect on me? I've dated since . . . then. In fact, I've dated Xavier more than once. Of course, contact hadn't gone much beyond handholding. It can't. Maybe never again. Anything more than a chaste kiss and my body throws up a barrier and screams reject.*

Not to mention the time Xavier did kiss me goodnight, and I actually tossed my dinner after I locked the front door.

But now I've been in the same room with this perfect example of male asshole and my lady parts are threatening mutiny. How is this even possible?

No sooner had the screen door banged shut than Jade glided across the bar straight towards Jason, her eyes smoldering with anger.

"You've done it again, I see," she murmured, piercing him

with her gaze.

Jason dropped back into his seat after righting the overturned one. He lifted his glass and, seeing it empty, set it back down. He picked up Zoe's untouched drink and drained it by half.

"I've sure got a way with women, don't I?"

"You've sure got a way of chasing off every new female patron we have. Doesn't your brain have any bearing on what comes out of your mouth? Seriously—mentioning her scar? That kind of insensitivity isn't good for business, bub."

Jason swiped his hand down over his face. He glared up at Jade. "This one came up here looking for trouble," he snapped back. "She's Delia O'Reilly's niece."

He watched as realization caused Jade's eyes to widen, and then narrow. "So she's the lucky heir, hey?"

"Yup."

As Jason reached to finish Zoe's drink, Jade snatched both glasses off the bar. "Gonna get mighty interesting around here for awhile then, hey, Mon?" The glasses clattered none too gently into the wash bin underneath. Without another word, Jade turned and headed back across the bar.

Delia's heir is not at all what I expected.

He knew when he heard of Delia's passing that sooner or later, he'd be getting either a letter from an attorney, or some curious relative on his doorstep asking about the cabin. What he hadn't expected was a sexy redhead wrapped in floral print silk. One who made his blood pressure skyrocket, and the crotch of his jeans feel a little too confining.

Jason rested his chin on his hand and scanned the noisy happy-hour crowd. There were plenty of women—loads of sexy, bikini-clad sirens—practically tripping over themselves to talk to him every day of the summer season. So why, when he got near enough to this uppity bitch to smell her musky vanilla scent, did his jeans grow uncomfortably snug?

And why should he care how she got such a nasty scar on that angelic face? He couldn't explain it. But when he caught sight of the jagged pink line running from the edge of her gold-flecked green eye clear down to the corner of her peach, plump lips, his chest clenched with a sudden need to wrap his arms around her and protect her.

Sure, it could have been from a terrible car accident. A run-in with a mean dog. A nasty fall from a treehouse. But Jason's gut told him the scar signified something far more sinister. The mark was ominous, almost as though it had been deliberately etched there.

There was something, too, hiding behind the lady's cold, sharp glare. Jason had gazed into the eyes of a lot of women. He'd learned to read, fairly well, what was going on inside each pretty head—whether they were giving him the green light, or the stop-and-move-on rejection.

This one, though . . . he was perplexed. Her look was more than a brush-off. Not quite sure how to read the ice-shards she was shooting at him.

Yet there was also something familiar in her expression. He'd spent enough time in the woods, growing up in the wilderness of the Adirondack Mountains, to recognize pain and terror in the eyes of a wounded animal.

Zoe Anderson's most damning scar, he suspected, went much deeper than the line on the side of her face.

Thirty minutes later, Zoe was stepping out of the glass-enclosed shower in the master bath when she heard her cell phone singing from inside her purse. She padded out of the bathroom, a fluffy white towel twisted into a turban on her head. The hotel's monogrammed terry robe flapped open around her damp, nude form. Digging out the phone, she smiled when she saw the missed call's number. Flipping it open, she punched the speed dial and flopped down on the edge of the spacious king-size bed.

"Hey, Dina." Zoe pulled the towel off and ran her fingers through her wet hair. "I tried to call you earlier. You wouldn't believe the day I've had."

"What do you mean, Zo?" Medina's tone conveyed immediate concern. "Everything okay?"

Zoe proceeded to fill her best friend in on the details of her discovery, and the fact that instead of being tucked snugly into her childhood vacation cabin, she was lounging in the loft of a pricey resort chalet next door.

"No shit," Medina breathed. "You've had some sucky luck here, lately, haven't you?"

Zoe sighed. "It's all good. Fortunately, this Rolland dick had a cancellation on one of his premier cabins." She glanced around her at the sumptuous, luxury suite. The pitched, open beam ceilings soared high over the plush carpet of the loft bedroom. The bed was an acre of pristine sateen sheets and down comforter.

How could she complain, really? Would she have been more comfortable in the meager double size, iron-framed bed of her youth? Complete with leaky roof, mildewed everything, and questionable vermin for company?

"So what are you going to do, Zoe? Surely this guy has to deal with you, right?"

"Yeah," Zoe huffed out. "Yeah, he's gotta deal with me. I guess I need to call Xavier and ask him to start drawing up paperwork on this thing. Surely, there's got to be some way to get the right-of-way back from this guy."

Medina's response was delayed. "Hmm, I don't know, sweetie. I don't know a thing about real estate. I'm not sure X does either."

"He's a civil law attorney, isn't he?" Zoe's tone sounded screechy, even to her own ears.

"Civil law is way different than real estate law. But I'm sure Xavier at least knows somebody who can help you."

Zoe flopped back on the fluffy white comforter that smelled pleasantly of clean linen, as pure as the mountain air. She tossed one arm across her eyes. "Oh, Dina. Why couldn't this have been simple? Why couldn't I have just come up here, changed the sheets on the bed in the old cabin, and be lounging on the front porch swing by now?"

"Nothin's been too simple for you of late, dear friend." Medina's prolonged moment of silence spoke louder than her words. "You just gotta roll with it."

A bark of laughter burst out before Zoe could even think. "Let's just hope I can keep my heart from rolling over and playing dead around this Rolland dick by summer's end."

Chapter 3

After Zoe hung up with Medina, she lay sprawled across the huge, soft bed for what seemed like an hour. The whirling of a ceiling fan high above her in the open rafters had a hypnotizing effect, but she knew she'd never fall asleep. It was still broad daylight, and the grumbling in her stomach reminded her repeatedly that she hadn't eaten anything, except that shrimp appetizer, all day.

The bedside clock declared the time as 7:03. Time to go down and check out the Boathouse Restaurant. Zoe yawned and stretched, fanning angels with her arms and legs across the cool, silky bedspread. It felt good to be alive, a sensation she hadn't experienced in a while. She'd considered living and breathing a necessary evil in the years since David's death. For those first few months, she was unsure if she really wanted to go on without him.

But she was trying to get her life back on track and that included some enjoyment. Taking care of herself. With that in mind, Zoe bounced up off the bed and perused the generous collection of summer wear she'd brought with her.

Only a few hundred feet separated her chalet from the Boathouse Restaurant. The night was cool but still pleasant. Zoe chose a sporty outfit, crisp blue linen capris with a matching V-necked tank. At the last minute, she grabbed her white cotton knit cardigan, the one with the beads embroidered all down the plackets. She was glad she had, pulling it on as a puff of cool, moist air brushed her silky hair back from her face. She shook her hair forward again as she pushed through the oak-framed beveled glass doors into the restaurant.

The movement had become automatic, a reflex—a constant attempt to conceal her scar, and the unwarranted shame it carried. Conroe, the sick bastard, had carved the jagged line, from the corner of her eye to the edge of her mouth, with the knife still dripping with David's blood.

I want to be sure I'll recognize you if I ever see you again. My first piece of ass in five years. That makes you pretty damned special.

She'd only recently progressed to the point where the sight of her own face in the mirror didn't cause her stomach to roll over in disgust.

The Saturday night dinner crowd was almost gone. There were only three tables still occupied, and the parties at two of those were lingering over coffee. Zoe had noted the hours posted in gold script on the transom. She couldn't believe the restaurant quit serving at nine o'clock.

Wow, this really is the boonies.

In the city, dinner hour didn't even start before eight, and that was on weeknights.

The Patio bar, however, still bustled with activity. Zoe glanced through the door while she waited for the hostess, and noticed that Jade was gone. Instead, a tall, very blond, crew-cut man—or boy, actually—had joined the Barbie clone. He looked barely old enough to drink alcoholic beverages, let alone serve them.

A server finally appeared through swinging kitchen doors, and eyed her up and down. Her gaze strayed over Zoe's shoulder, as if in search of a companion.

"Will it be . . . only one? For dinner?"

Yeah, bitch, just one.

"Yes, thank you Ma'am. Can I have a table on the perimeter please? With a view of the lake?"

When Zoe had settled at the corner table with her heavy leather-bound menu in hand, she sighed and looked around her. Empty tables filled the center of the room. She remembered a pool table sat right there . . .

The memories started flooding back, and for a moment, a feeling of omnipotent melancholy overwhelmed her. Lake George had been a place of joy, freedom, fun-filled days, and starry nights. Sunny afternoons splashing at the lake's edge, and dreamy hours on the front porch, immersed in the adventures of *The Babysitter's Club* or the latest in the *Sweet Valley High* series.

Innocence, carefree childhood—gone forever. Suddenly Zoe felt very small, very alone. Moments later, when the black-and-white uniformed server returned to her table, Zoe's eyes were misty.

"Good evening. I'm Janine, and I'll be serving you this evening. Can I get you a . . . ?" The waitress paused, studying Zoe's face. "Is everything all right, Miss?" She was an older woman, and she looked tired.

"Yes, I'm fine." Zoe smiled, mentally regrouping and sitting up a little straighter. She glanced down at the wine list. "I'll have a glass of your best White Zin, and an order of oysters on the half shell. To start."

The waitress scribbled on her pad, and then paused for a beat with one eyebrow raised. In a clipped tone she asked, "Will you be ordering dinner as well?"

Zoe's eyes radiated anger. Seriously? First Betty White, and now an impatient, rude server intent on getting her in and out of the restaurant in a New York minute.

"Yes, I'll be ordering dinner," she replied in an overtly polite voice, topped off with a too-bright smile. "Eventually. The restaurant serves until nine, right?" Zoe made the exaggerated motion of checking the time, pushing the cuff of the cotton sweater above the diamond watch she always wore on her left wrist. Regardless of the early curfew of these mountain folk, she was here to slow down, relax.

The waitress's face fell.

"Yes, ma'am. I'll be right back with your wine and appetizer."

She had just disappeared through the kitchen doors when Zoe heard a commotion coming from the bar area. From where she sat up against the glassed perimeter, she could see almost the entire patio bar. The shrieking was coming from the bleached blonde Barbie, and it was directed at Jason Rolland.

Her frizzed mane looked more disheveled than before. She had come out from behind the bar to stand toe-to-toe with Rolland, her red-lacquered talons flailing in his face. He stood with his arms crossed and one hip cocked, glaring down at her. His eyes were narrowed, but his head tilt and half-hearted scowl certainly didn't convey anger.

Was that disgust? Humor? No, he actually looked bored.

The scene lasted less than a minute. Barbie screeched her finale in words Zoe couldn't make out before ripping off her black apron and tossing it in Jason's face. She spun on the heel of her rhinestone-encrusted flip-flop, and stomped out the door and down the steps toward the dock.

Zoe was so engrossed watching the sideshow she didn't notice the waitress return. She jumped when the wine glass tapped down on the glass top of the table. Glancing up, she saw it wasn't the older woman who'd taken her order. It was

Jade.

She almost didn't recognize her. No more bar apron. Jade's multicolored, jewel-toned dress wrapped her from shoulder to knee, allowing a view of her ribbon-laced ankles. She smiled down at Zoe with those arresting golden eyes.

"I see you've decided to join us for dinner. I must apologize for Janine. She's new with us here, and unfortunately I don't believe she's going to work out."

Zoe stared up at Jade in disbelief. Okay, she had figured that this elegant woman was one hell of a bartender, and someone probably important in the asshole owner's life. What she didn't figure was that she had such clout in the running of the whole establishment. For some reason, Zoe had assumed she was . . . simply a barmaid.

"Oh, no problem, Jade," she stammered. "I'm not in any particular hurry tonight. If you'd rather I take my dinner at the bar—"

"We wouldn't dream of it." Jade glanced down at the order pad. "Your oysters will be up shortly. Claude is shucking them as we speak."

When Jade left her, Zoe looked back into the bar, but the scene was over. The patrons had resumed their conversations. Jason was gone.

An hour later, Zoe was the only one left in the restaurant. She'd enjoyed a spectacular steamed and stuffed lobster dinner, and was getting ready to ask for her check when Jade reappeared.

"Would you mind if I joined you for a bit?" She didn't wait for Zoe to answer before pulling out the chair on the opposite side of the table. "How was your dinner? Was everything as you expected?"

"Everything was wonderful, Jade. Thank you so much."

Jade folded her arms and sat back in her chair, studying

Zoe with an appraising eye. "So, Jason tells me you're Delia O'Reilly's niece. Our new neighbor." Her mouth quirked up on one side, and Zoe couldn't tell if the expression was friendly or mocking.

Zoe straightened her shoulders. "That's right. And from what

Mr. Rolland tells me, I'll be needing a boat for transportation if I ever intend to do anything with the property."

"Now, that's not exactly true. Jason may have purchased the strip of land linking Delia's cottage to the highway, but the contract clearly states a shared right-of-way through Lakeview."

Okay, so the chic bartender also knows a lot about Lakeview's business dealings. Who the hell is she, really?

Zoe tipped up her chin and studied the woman's striking face. Her complexion was flawless, her hair as jet black and shiny as a raven's. It was impossible for Zoe to guess her age, but Jade's confident air alone made her seem older. Older, at least, than the cocky man who ran this place. "Are you a stockholder in the resort?" Zoe asked.

Jade smirked and cut her gaze to the side. "You might say that."

That was it. No further explanation, and the impish smile piqued Zoe's curiosity even more.

But it's none of my business. And why should I even care?

The arrival of a dessert tray interrupted the pregnant silence. A bald, stout man who could have been Popeye's younger brother appeared, balancing a tray on his cloth-covered forearm. His bushy mustache barely concealed a fleeting grin as his dark eyes flashed from Jade's to Zoe's and back, but he didn't say a word.

"Claude, I'd like you to meet Zoe Anderson." Jade's accent

laced her speech with smooth, cadenced grace. "She vacationed here at the lake with her family many years ago."

The burly man nodded and grinned sheepishly but kept his eyes down on the tray of sweet confections he held. He remained silent.

Jade turned to Zoe. "What can we get you for dessert this evening, Ms. Anderson? Our cheesecake is New York's finest, and our chocolate mousse is made with a touch of Bailey's Irish Cream."

Holding one hand to her stomach, Zoe shook her head. "I couldn't eat another bite. But the meal was fantastic."

As Claude disappeared through the kitchen doors, Jade studied her pensively. Then she said, "How about we both grab a Bailey's—on the rocks—and walk down to the docks? I'd like to show you the improvements we've made to the boathouse since you were . . . how old?"

Zoe chuckled as she replied, "Not yet thirteen, I think. A very long time ago."

Moments later, the two women were strolling down the steep sidewalk toward the lake's edge carrying plastic cups rattling with iced liqueur. The sun had set, and although it wasn't completely dark, the lake had already morphed into an oscillating pool of ink.

Jade pointed out a few improvements to the Lodge that Zoe hadn't yet seen or noticed. A colorful assortment of landscape lights lined the path to the docks. They illuminated outcroppings of rock and greenery in glowing shades of blue, green, and red. The cedar shakes on the boathouse were new, painted a serene shade of blue.

The building, though modern in its redesign, seemed to belong where it was, blending in with the natural surroundings. The entire resort wore an ambience of sophistication that Zoe didn't remember.

Not that she would have noticed any of these things at the age of twelve.

When they reached the water's edge, the two women stood on the planked length of dock bordering the entrance to the two-bay boathouse, sipping their drinks. Jade turned to face her, leaning up against the dock's railing.

"So what brings you up to the lake, Zoe? Just checking out your inheritance? Or were you planning a vacation?"

Zoe cleared her throat, shook her head and smirked as she glanced down at the weathered boards beneath their feet. "No, the timing of my inheritance was right on cue. I needed to get away from the city for a while."

Jade crossed her arms, resting the drink cup in the crook on her elbow.

"I'd imagine the bustle of the city can get to the mind after a while." Jade sipped her drink, studying Zoe with those unusual, golden eyes. "Personally, I've never been."

She chuckled. "It's pretty obvious you're not a Manhattan born and raised Yankees fan, Miss Jade. Is this place what's planted you here in the middle of Nowhere-in-the-Mountains of upstate New York?"

Jade's broad smile reached all the way to her eyes.

"Well, let's just say the business of vacationing is in my blood. Sort of runs in the family, ya know." She paused to sip her drink. "I was born in Jamaica. Guess you sort of figured out I was 'Island,' but definitely not Long Gyland."

Zoe threw back her head and laughed out loud.

"No, no, I figured you weren't, but I couldn't figure out why you might leave the idyllic island life for this." She swept her hand up toward the steep lakeshore, where the cabins' soft lighting glowed in the darkness. "I mean, don't get me wrong, this place is spectacular. There's no better place to 'get away from it all.' I just figure it must be even more idyllic in a place like Jamaica, no? Especially in the winter, when the snow shuts down much of the northeast tourist trade."

Jade's gaze dropped to the waters lapping softly against the sturdy round beams supporting the dock.

"I suppose. I spend the winters in Jamaica. Summers I spend here, at the Lodge with Jason." Jade paused to sip her drink, gazing out over the darkened surface of the lake. Then she turned to meet Zoe's questioning eyes. "We own another resort, down on the island. Lakeview, Jamaican style." Her grin shone in the darkness.

Zoe nodded. So they own multiple vacation properties. That would explain Jason's pressuring Aunt Delia to sell her tiny slice of upstate New York lakeside. A predatory land baron. A pair of them, perhaps?

How exactly are he and Jade connected? And what difference does it make anyway?

"Ya know, Zoe Anderson, I think you and me, we could become a sort of friends," Jade said, jolting Zoe back into the present conversation. "I don't usually get chummy with any of the guests. All I got's Jason. But I believe I would like to get to know you better. How long you plan on stayin' with us?"

She sighed. "I'll be here at least a few weeks. I need to work out this mess about the cottage, figure out what I'm going to do with it."

"Tomorrow," Jade said, "I don't work the lunch shift. Been itchin' for some shopping time. Jason . . . well, Jason is a poor companion for that sort of activity."

"Oh?" Zoe's questions simmered below the surface, and she struggled to keep them there.

"How would you like to join me for a little excursion down to Glens Falls?" Jade asked. "It's only a few miles down the road. They've a lovely outlet mall there. I have little time beyond the morning hours but . . ." She trailed off.

"I would love that, Jade," Zoe answered quietly.

What could it hurt?

"It's a date then," Jade replied. "I'll meet you at your cabin—the Aspen, I think you said? Around ten. No, nine. We'll hit the Yearling Inn for breakfast first. I'll let Jason know not to expect me in the bar until four."

Zoe's smile faded. Her curiosity was getting the best of her, regardless of common sense. Her next words popped out, bypassing her brain and reasonable logic.

"Are you and Jason . . . ?" But then she didn't quite know how to finish the question.

Jade didn't hesitate long enough for her to feel uncomfortable.

"Jason and I are very close." Jade's smile was full-blown Cheshire cat.

"I see." Even she could hear her own disappointment in her reply, though she couldn't explain why. She swirled the ice around in her cup. "I didn't realize Jason was attached."

It was Jade's turn to burst out laughing. Her brilliant smile gleamed in the darkness as Zoe stared at her, head cocked.

"No, no, no! Attached is not a word that applies to Jason Rolland. No, he's not attached—not to anything, or to anyone. Jason is, and always has been, attached to only one person. That be Jason Rolland himself."

The red digital readout flashed from 7:59 to 8:00 p.m., and a velvety baritone boomed from hundreds of home and car radios within a hundred-mile radius of Lakeview Lodge.

"Good evening, lovers everywhere, and welcome to Jason's Lair. I'm here tonight to take your requests and dedications, and to hear your heartaches. I'll play a song to soothe your pain. I'll find the right dose of melody to offer comfort to those whose love lives have landed on rocky shores."

Jason switched off the mike as he moved the soundboard slider slowly, and the moaning of yet another tired, classic love song began its umpteenth performance over the airways. He leaned one elbow on the studio desk and scrubbed his fingers through his hair.

How did I ever get into this business, anyway?

It was all Byron's fault. Okay, sure, Jason had a great voice—with a growling simmer reminiscent of Russell Crowe. And the winter nights on the shores of the frozen lake do get long. But the radio show ran year round, and in the summers when the Lodge was hopping, it was hard to climb those stairs to the studio. Four long hours, four nights a week really cut into Jason's summer fun.

He wasn't exactly sure how it had grown into such a hit, but it had been almost five years now since the show first aired. Byron, a good friend of Jason's father, was a media-marketing mastermind. He created Jason's Lair as a local dedication show, not unlike those of the talented Delilah and John Tesh.

Byron joked that if those two had ever gotten together and produced a child, the result would have been Jason.

At first, Jason thought of the whole idea as a joke too. But the show took off. The country folk who call the Adirondacks their home warmly embraced the idea of their very own, homegrown love guru. The local sponsors who found it difficult to advertise their wares or services once the tourists left town eagerly flocked to support the show. And Jason had a brand new identity.

The love guru, a completely different guy from the playboy everyone saw in action every summer season.

Jason rolled his eyes as all eight phone lines lit up before the Fugees had even started their last stanza. The tiny room on the top deck of his multi-level A-frame was outfitted with every piece of broadcasting equipment in the business, along with a switchboard-like display across the top of a multiline telephone receiver.

The studio door opened softly, and Jason glanced back over his shoulder. The ceiling in the loft wasn't quite full height, and the tall woman had to stoop slightly as she ducked in. She carried a small tray resting in the crook of her left arm. It contained a dome-covered plate, a steaming mug, and a small metal basket with a cloth-wrapped bundle inside.

"I brought you some supper, since I noticed you didn't take any with you earlier."

Jason's eyes scanned the lithe, female form wrapped in island bright colors. "You look a little homesick tonight."

Jade shot him a cynical smirk, and he cringed. Her sleek black hair was wet, and the smell of jasmine filled the loft. But the scent of fried seafood and warm bread quickly overtook her perfume.

Yes, he was definitely hungry.

"Thanks, darlin'. I wasn't in the mood before nothing sounded too appetizing." He lifted the metal cover off the plate to find a mound of steamed and deep-fried seafood confections. "You're too good to me, Jade, you know that?"

She set the tray down on the small table next to Jason's equipment, and then turned to pull up a bamboo chair.

"That's a fact, Mon. You sometimes don't appreciate how good your Jade is to you."

The Fugees had wailed their last line, and Jason held one finger up as he adjusted his earpiece. He pointed toward the telephone line indicators, all glowing bright orange, and rolled his eyes in Jade's direction before he picked up the first call.

"Good evening and welcome to Jason's Lair. What can I do for you this evening?"

"Hello. Uh, my name is Rachel. I'm calling, Jason, because I'm so lonely tonight. I've lost the love of my life . . . his name is Randy. We were together for almost a year and then, well . . . "

Jason glanced over and locked eyes with Jade as the caller rambled on. He stifled a laugh as Jade faked an exaggerated yawn. When the caller had finished with her request, Jason turned on the mike and purred his reply.

"Why, of course we can find you a tune, Rachel. It's truly a shame about you and Randy. I'll find something that speaks to his heart. Randy, if you're out there listening, this next song is especially for you—from Rachel."

Jason clicked off the mike and dropped his forehead into his hand.

"Geez, this gets harder every night, Jade. Is it just me? Or do some of these callers sound like pranksters? Sometimes I wonder if the joke isn't all on me."

Jade smiled as she reached over to pat Jason's arm. Leaving her long fingers curled warmly around his wrist, she replied, "There's a lot of lonely hearts out there, Jay. A lot of broken dreams and desperate people. You, of all people, should understand that."

He snorted as he picked one of the fried scallops off the mound of food on the plate. Popping it into his mouth, he replied cynically, "Well, if they only knew. I'm the god of love, all right. Heartfelt and trustworthy too. Little do they know, I'm vying for Stud of the Year Award, slaying innocent women's hearts on a daily basis."

Jade sighed, her eyes narrowed to slits as she glared at him.

"If you'd learn to think with your head instead of your

46

dick, you'd find there's a lot more to life that you might be missin'." Jade's bright red lips pressed thin. "You were two for two today, by the way—first, the redhead, and then, my best barmaid. How am I going to make it through the summer season without Tracy, hey?"

Jason slumped back in his chair in defeat.

"I'm sorry about that, Jade. I always seem to end up with my foot in my mouth—or with some woman's foot up my ass. Why can't I be as smooth a talker as I am behind this silly little microphone?" Jason knew Jade's silence meant she was thoroughly pissed with him. He smirked over his shoulder. "It's not like you don't warn me. What's that Island saying of yours? Talk and taste your tongue?" Jason grinned sheepishly.

Jade dropped her chin and glared through the still-dripping strands of black hair that had fallen over her forehead.

"You think you can hide behind the wild-boy façade. You're playing a role you haven't earned—only inherited. No one can see the real Jason Rolland who hides up here in this little room, night after night."

Jade reached into the basket on the tray and unfolded the black cloth napkin. Tearing off a piece of the crusty bread, she took a bite, chewing slowly, a thoughtful look in her eyes. "But I know who that boy is. You don't necessarily have to be your father's son, Jason."

He broke eye contact with her long enough to grab his fork off the tray, scooping a hunk of broiled haddock into his mouth. For a few minutes, he said nothing, chewing and watching the digital display on his DVD player, gauging how many seconds he had until the end of the next song. Then he raised his gaze to meet hers.

"I know you know the real me, Jade. Just don't tell

anybody, okay? I'm much safer staying right where I am—hidden in Daddy's shadow."

Chapter 4

The next morning, promptly at nine, Jade met Zoe in front of the Aspen. She drove them a mile up the road to the neighboring resort. On the outside, The Yearling Inn's restaurant looked like an ordinary Mom and Pop diner. Zoe was pleasantly surprised at the sumptuous spread inside.

The two ladies took a corner seat near windows that looked out into the dense forest covering the steep banks of the lake. As they sipped from steaming mugs and enjoyed fresh fruit and delicate omelets, Zoe was surprised at how quickly she was developing a kinship with her new friend.

As Jade poured them another cup of aromatic French brew from the porcelain pot on the table, she asked, "So tell me about Zoe Anderson. I don't know a thing about you, except that you're a city girl with extremely pretty eyes that drinks Absolut."

Zoe toyed with a stray mushroom with her fork, keeping her eyes trained on her plate. In her mind she could hear her new psychiatrist's advice: There's no reason for you to feel shame for what you've endured. Talking about this will help you to heal.

She took a deep breath and forced her eyes up to meet Jade's. "Mine is a Cinderella story with a tragic ending. City Cinderella. It's about what happens to good people who fight to protect the rights of other people. Even the ones who don't

49

deserve it."

Jade leaned her chin on her hand and studied her face as she spoke. Softly, she said, "I can imagine there are many dangerous games, especially in the thick of a big city."

"Yes," Zoe's sadness bled over her words, "very dangerous. My husband was a criminal prosecutor. One of his convicts got out. On parole. Broke into our apartment."

Jade's fork clattered to her plate as she lifted her hand to her mouth. "Oh." She reached across the table and gently laid her long, graceful fingers over Zoe's hand. "How long ago?" she asked.

Panic rose into her throat. This still happened, every time.

I'm going to get through this, now, without scrambled sentences. I can do this.

"Three. Three years. Ago."

"Were you . . . did you . . . ?" Jade stammered but Zoe knew exactly what she was asking.

She nodded slowly. The thoughts were getting sticky now, harder to arrange in her mind, let alone form into cohesive sentences. Better keep to a few words at a time. On a shuddering breath, she said flatly, "Knife. Blood. So much blood."

She could tell by Jade's expression that she understood the impact those horrific events had on Zoe's ability to function, to communicate. She held Jade's golden gaze and knew her new friend wasn't going to press her further.

Thank God. Somehow, that simple knowledge helped squelch the panic in her chest. Zoe reached out and took a deep draw from the straw in her ice water. She swallowed, and then squeaked out, "Raped me." Then she managed one more phrase. "I'm a w-widow."

There was a long silence, one when the sounds of rattling silverware and the clinking of porcelain plates seemed unnaturally loud and piercing. Jade held her hand, but avoided her gaze. Zoe was relieved. She'd had entirely too much of that look in the last three years. Shock, pity, and prying all rolled into one.

Finally, Jade patted her hand and pulled away. "I cannot begin to imagine your pain." Her words were soft, comforting. Jade's next words were a confession. "I almost feel guilty for having a life as carefree as I've had."

Zoe took a deep breath and dabbed at her lashes with her napkin. Suddenly, the vice-like grip on her throat fell away. The words came then, thankfully in a logical order.

"Life goes on. That's what my shrink keeps telling me. That's why I'm here—to learn how to go on. To return to the way I was before my . . . my glass slipper shattered." She raised her gaze to meet Jade's. Then she managed a small smile. "So tell me about this carefree life you've enjoyed. Make me jealous."

Jade's slow smile lit up her entire face. "I've got the best of both worlds. I spend summers here at Lake George, with Jason. When the autumn leaves fall I head down to my other home—in Jamaica, spend time with my mother, see good friends and family, and work at our other resort," she said quietly.

After breakfast, Zoe drove them down through the village, venturing on to the outlet mall a few miles south of the lake, in the little burg of Glens Falls. They spent a pleasant day shopping, bargain hunting, and sharing opinions on everything from fashion to home furnishings. By the time Jade stepped out of Zoe's car in the parking lot of Lake View, it was almost four o'clock.

"Are you coming in for happy hour?" Jade asked, a hopeful note in her voice.

"Of course. I've a few calls to make. Then I'll be down."

Zoe returned to the Aspen cabin and lounged in one of the two loveseats arranged before the massive stone fireplace. Should she call Medina first? Or call Xavier directly? Medina was his paralegal, but she was also Zoe's best friend. The law office would, of course, be closed now until Monday, but Zoe had his cell phone number.

She considered Xavier a friend, yet she knew he wanted more than that from her. But so far, she hadn't been able to think of him as anything other than a supportive ally. Someone to have dinner with once in a while. Someone to take her out and let her feel normal again. He didn't make her laugh though, like David always had. She swallowed around the sudden lump in her throat. But God knows, Xavier had certainly been patient with all her hang-ups.

Zoe didn't have the chance to make the decision. Before she'd flipped both of her Tory Burch flip-flops off her feet, her cell phone buzzed. She looked down to see the image of Medina, dressed in a way-too-tight, hot pink mini dress—her best friend's identifying pic on her caller ID.

"Hey, Dina."

"Whoa! Hey, chica. You don't sound like a woman who's rebooting her life in a childhood vacation rerun."

Zoe chuckled. "No. No childhood reruns here. I'm lounging in the luxury of a high-brow resort cabin." Zoe grinned to herself. "At a meager doscientos a night."

She heard Medina whistle through her teeth in a way Zoe had heard before. An expression that always made Zoe smile.

"Doscientos, huh? Better be pretty posh for that price."

Zoe cleared her throat. She knew Medina's personal financial situation didn't allow for extravagances like fancy resort cabins. What was she thinking?

"When are you coming up to stay with me, Dina?"

"I was actually thinking about weekend after next. What do you think?" Medina's voice sounded hopeful. Curious, but hopeful too.

"That sounds wonderful. I'm lonely for you already," Zoe answered. "But Dina, I've got to get in touch with Xavier. The property issues. I need him to file some papers."

"Don't bother with the X-man this weekend. I'll fill him in on Monday. Go into town, buy yourself a sexy dress—cut-too-low and way-too-short, in a fab color, and be ready to have a maravilloso time when I get there."

Zoe couldn't help but smile.

Oh, Dina. If I could only be as carefree a soul as you.

"I'm counting the minutes," Zoe replied.

By the time Zoe headed down toward the Boathouse, the restaurant's parking lot was filled to overflowing. As she pushed through the screen door to the patio bar, she could barely make her way past the crowd to order a drink. She headed down to the corner where the seats ended, to the empty space where the restaurant staff picked up their drink orders. As Jade slammed two mugs of beer down on the serving bench, her panicked eyes flashed to Zoe's.

"This is great, isn't it?' she hissed. "Thanks to Mr. Rolland's womanizing antics yesterday, I'm working alone. Again. In the height of the season. Such perfect timing that man has." She shot Zoe a desperate look.

Zoe blinked, another memory rushing her mind. Another enjoyable, almost-forgotten chapter in her past—before David. A part-time job. From her college days.

Reboot, restore to an earlier time.

"Hey Jade, I know how to do this, you know. I used to tend bar in Greenwich Village when I was in college." Zoe grinned at the shock on Jade's face. "I could come back there and give you a hand if you want."

53

Jade didn't waste time asking any questions. "Well, Red, get your cute little ass back here and grab an apron."

Mixing drinks is something you don't forget, even if it has been almost a dozen years. Yeah, the classic screwdriver might have morphed into a fuzzy navel, but whenever she was unsure, Jade was there to translate. Zoe had logged hundreds of hours working at the cozy Cellar Pub down on 8th Street. She didn't realize until now how much she'd missed it.

This is perfect. I'm not alone in my room. I'm out and about with people and music and fun, but I'm safe. There's a waist-high bar between all those people and me. The bartender's armor of anonymity protects me from having conversations linger beyond a few words.

By the time happy hour was over and the dinner crowd had moved into the restaurant, Zoe was actually having a blast. She quickly learned where everything behind the bar was located. She fell easily into the smooth rhythm Jade followed to keep the glasses washed, the ice bin filled, and every inch of the polished oak bar wiped shiny clean.

She and Jade were giggling about a young man who'd just staggered drunkenly out toward the cabins when Jason walked in.

Oh shit. Reality check. I'd almost forgotten about Mr. Hotshot Property Owner.

The look on his face, though, was priceless. He stared at Zoe as though she'd grown moose antlers.

No, we're going to have a little fun with this. Slyly, she turned her back toward him, then looked back over her shoulder, and mimicked the Barbie blonde whose place she'd taken. As Jason plopped into one of the empty seats, Zoe riveted him with a long, exaggerated wink.

She finished shaking a Cosmo and strained it into a frosted glass. After delivering it to the carefully coifed brunette snuggling up to her Al Pacino lookalike companion, Zoe turned on her heel and headed straight for Jason.

"And what can I get for you, Mr. Rolland?" Zoe slid her gaze up through her eyelashes as she wiped down the area in front of Jason. "Will it be your usual? I mean, our usual?"

"What the hell," was all Jason could muster. Before she could respond, Jade was standing beside her.

"Our new barmaid, Mon. No arguments. I can't do this alone night after night."

Jason never took his eyes off Zoe, who had folded her arms and was leaning on the bar directly in front of him.

Damn, he smells good. How does this guy always manage to look and smell like he just stepped out of the shower?

"Jade seems to be holding her own now," he said darkly. "Why don't you pour us both a drink and let's take a walk? I think we have some business to discuss."

Zoe hesitated three heartbeats, staring down at the coaster she'd flipped onto the bar before Jason. Then she glanced up at Jade.

"Go! Get the bastard outta here before I throttle him."

Interesting relationship these two have. Very interesting.

Jason strolled beside her in silence until they got down to the water. The clunking of the boat hulls against the docks struck a soothing rhythm. The breeze off the water sent a shiver skittering up Zoe's spine.

Or was it because she was standing so close to Jason? Better not ponder that one.

Zoe sipped her drink and leaned back against the cedar shakes of the boathouse. She glared up at Jason.

"Are you traditionally obnoxious and rude to patrons of the lodge? Or was your curiosity about my 'little beauty mark' yesterday so great you couldn't help yourself?"

Jason scrubbed a hand down his face, shaking his head.

He swore under his breath.

"I don't know what the hell is wrong with me," he grumbled. "Sometimes stuff comes out of my mouth all by itself." He stopped and turned to face her. "Listen, I'm awfully sorry. It was a dumb ass comment and completely inexcusable." He shrugged, his mouth twisting into a quirky, crooked grin. "You're right. It's none of my goddamned business."

Zoe's insides clutched. He looked like a repentant little boy. An image of the goofy teenager with the dangling cigarette flickered across her memory.

Is it possible to still carry a crush from when I was twelve years old?

"Can we start over?" he asked softly.

"That's exactly what I'm here to do," she retorted.

Jason cleared his throat. "So, where'd you learn to tend bar?"

She chuckled. "Surprised you, huh? It's how I paid for my rent and meals while I was in college." She smiled into Jason's eyes as he paused and leaned on the wall beside her. "I kind of enjoyed it. This was fun today, and Jade sure needed the help."

Jason swirled the ice in his glass. "Yeah, I guess it's my fault Tracy walked out on her. I need to try to keep business and pleasure a little more separate." He grinned sheepishly with a mischievous twinkle making his eyes sparkle crystal blue.

Zoe scowled. "Okay, you've got Jade. You obviously had Tracy too. Is that it? Or are there other members of the Rolland harem?"

She couldn't help her annoyance when Jason laughed out loud. "No, no. Tracy was only another one of the summer crew. She was nothing to me."

But no mention of Jade. Hmm.

Jason's smile faded and he slanted her a serious look. "You know, all the city girls come up here to play the summer away. Some of them like to work the bar, to meet guys. Some of them have it in their heads that they're going to snag a big fish. Not have to go back to work in the city come fall."

"And they see you as a big fish, I take it," she snapped. "The big, badass resort owner. Two, right? Jade says you own another chunk of paradise in Jamaica. As well as the little strip of land that used to be my driveway, I might add."

Jason dropped his gaze to the gray planks under their feet. "Look, I told you I'd be willing to work something out on that. Why don't you sell me the whole lot?"

"I'm going to let my attorney work on the issue," she said flatly. She didn't want to worry about that right now. She'd had a good time today, first getting to know Jade, then playing barmaid again. And the vodka she was sipping a little too fast on an empty stomach was helping that euphoria along fine.

No, I want to keep on having fun tonight. Maybe get a little reckless. Act a little like Medina.

She waited until she was sure he was watching, and then used the tip of her tongue to toy with the straw in her glass. His reaction delighted her. Shoving his hands in the pockets of his khaki shorts, he cleared his throat and shifted from one foot to the other. Before turning away.

"So how about you pay me tonight's wages by buying me dinner in that fancy restaurant of yours?"

Jason turned back to face her but his expression was somber. His head shake was almost imperceptible.

Zoe bristled. "I guess that's not in your plans, huh?" she snapped.

"No. I mean, no, I'd really love to take you to dinner, Zoe.

57

But there's someplace I've got to be in less than twenty minutes." He glanced down at his watch, and then threw back the rest of his drink. Leveling his gaze at her, he asked, "A raincheck?"

Ouch. Shot down. This isn't as easy as Medina makes it look.

"You snooze, you lose," Zoe shrugged as she drained her own glass noisily through the cocktail straw. It's better this way. The last thing she needed to do was complicate her summer. And her friendship with Jade. Whatever she was to this prick.

She raised her glass toward Jason in a salute, and then turned on her heel. Swaying only slightly, she trotted up the steps toward the restaurant.

Later that evening, as Zoe stepped out of the shower, she could have sworn she'd heard Jason's rumbling voice in the next room.

In my head? Am I seriously fantasizing about that asshole?

But it was only some talk show host droning out of the clock radio next to the bed.

Geez, I've got to stop this. This Rolland guy is nothing but a rich, pompous playboy. I need to avoid him like spoiled caviar.

On Monday morning, Zoe tried to reach Xavier at his office, but his assistant said he would be in court all day. She sighed, left a message, and decided there wasn't much else she could do about the cottage until she talked to the X-man. Or to some lawyer-friend of his who might know what her options were.

So Zoe spent the day turning back the clock. She sat on the back deck of the Aspen with coffee until almost noon, wearing nothing but the resort's cushy bathrobe. She whipped through half of the romance novel she'd bought last summer but never got around to reading. Then she took a long, hot shower, slipped on her bikini and cover-up, and headed down to the beach.

The early morning mist that habitually shrouded the lake had burned off, revealing a cloudless sky. Zoe managed to snag one of the resort's lounge chairs before they were all claimed. She dragged it down to the far corner of the beach, the area that bordered the slice of waterfront she now owned. A breakwater-style line of huge, granite stones still served as a natural fence between the properties. The rock wall effectively blocked Zoe—as well as any other Lakeview patron—from seeing what was on the other side.

Zoe considered climbing over the rocks to check out the condition of her beach. But she decided against it. She was feeling calm and relaxed for the first time in so long, she didn't want to risk spoiling the mood.

I would put on quite a show for the other tourists though, attempting to scale that rock pile in my bikini and flip-flops.

After slathering SPF 50 head to toe over her pale skin, she stretched out on the lounge chair. Digging her floppy sunhat and paperback out of her beach bag, she prepared to continue Operation Reboot.

She was totally swept away into the story when a dark shadow dimmed her page. A pair of bare feet had appeared in the sand right beside her chair. Male feet.

Zoe tipped her head up and folded back the brim of her hat. The glare of the midday sun turned the tall figure towering over her into a dark silhouette. Jason's voice rumbled low, washing down over her like a warm wave.

"Enjoying the amenities, I see," he said. Zoe could hear the laughter in his voice.

"That's what I'm here for," she shot back. She scrambled for her cover-up, feeling suddenly very exposed.

Why, oh why did she let Medina talk her into a bikini? She should have stayed with her safe, cute tank suit.

"Oh, don't do that. I was quite enjoying the view."

How could a man's voice—his voice—do that? Without his laying a finger on her, Zoe felt as though she'd been caressed. The oddity was that the sensation didn't turn her stomach. It didn't scare her. The sound of Jason's voice was almost hypnotic.

But she didn't like that feeling of vulnerability, laying flat on her back so close to him. She struggled into her cover-up, then to her feet.

"I couldn't get a view of my beach," she said. She swept her hand across to the line of boulders, nodding toward the security fence. "Ingeniously placed. You'd have to either be a mountain climber or twelve feet tall to see anything of my property from here."

Jason stuck his hands in the front pockets of his tailored shorts. "That was the general idea, Zoe. The cottage doesn't fit with the modern image I've created for this place." His tone was low and even, non-confrontational. He almost sounded a little sad.

Zoe fisted both hands on her hips. "And what were you going to do with the cottage if Delia had sold it to you? Bulldoze the whole thing? Build a few more modern marvels?"

Jason's gaze dropped to the sand between them. He nodded. "Probably, yes."

"Do you have any idea how many memories you'd be plowing under the sand if you did that, Rolland?" Zoe's annoyance was quickly accelerating into indignant anger. "That cottage has been in my family for almost thirty years. I

60

practically grew up there."

She felt the familiar tightening in her chest and heard her pulse thudding in her ears.

She had to remain focused. Stay in control. The last thing she needed right now was to lose control in front of the man who held her cottage—hell, the only remnants of her carefree childhood—hostage.

I have to be careful. If I get too upset, I'll start babbling. I'll be completely at his mercy.

He'd raised his eyes to meet hers. She studied them, knowing hers were still hidden behind her sunglasses.

God, they're so blue. A light, translucent, electrifying shade of blue.

There it was. That same tingling sensation in her core as the first time she laid eyes on him. But not just since that day in the office. Since almost twenty years ago.

He stared at her in silence as she waited for his reply. Surely, if he grew up here, the way things looked back then still held some nostalgia for him too, wouldn't it? Apparently not.

A bulldozer. The thought sent a shiver down her spine.

She was so engrossed in her own reverie, she was completely taken off guard when Jason, without saying a word, lifted his hand very slowly and slid her sunglasses away from her face.

"I can't tell what you're thinking if I can't see those celadon eyes," he said.

Celadon? Seriously? What man even knows that word?

"Your usual alpha male thing isn't going to work with me, Rolland. And by the way, they're not celery, or whatever you just called them. They're just plain old green." Zoe had started to tremble a little. She wasn't sure if it was from anger or . . . something else. Either way, she had to end this conversation soon before she turned into a sideshow.

She snatched her glasses out of Jason's hand and perched them on top of her head. Unfortunately, she forgot she had the beach hat on. The glasses tumbled into the sand, and she heard Jason chuckle as he bent to retrieve them.

He straightened, but made no move to hand them over. Slowly, he brought them to his lips and, staring into her eyes the entire time, blew gently on the lenses, one at a time, to free them of sand.

Christ.

Heat, coming not from the brilliant sun overhead but from a spot just above the line of her bikini bottom, spiraled up her body. As though she were stepping into a hot tub, she felt the tell-tale flush on her skin. She knew her cheeks were burning, bright pink. She felt her nipples strain against the lining of her bikini top. Thank God she was hidden beneath her cover-up.

She sucked in a quavering breath, and then let out a soft, exasperated growl.

"Give me those," she said, grabbing the glasses out of his hand.

I've got to get out of here. Now.

She reached down for the handles of her beach bag. She dropped the glasses in, and then her book. "I'm expecting a phone call. From my attorney. We'll discuss this matter later," she said.

As Zoe stomped away across the sand, Jason called after her.

"What were *you* planning to do with Delia's cottage, Zoe?"

She stopped short, but she didn't turn around. The tightness in her throat told her she shouldn't—and probably couldn't—form a reply. He was asking a good question. One she'd apparently not yet considered when she'd hopped in the car and headed up here.

Pausing long enough for one more shaky breath, she continued on her path toward the Aspen, her ankles working hard in the deep, white sand.

Jason watched her go, shaking his head and smiling. She looked like a pissed-off cat that had lost her balance and toppled down from some perch. She was struggling to keep her pace quick. But her flip-flops, and the sugary sand, made walking a real challenge. She obviously wasn't used to doing it every day.

Sure must be a little different from strutting down Madison Ave. in stilettos.

No, that image didn't quite fit. He couldn't imagine Zoe Anderson in stilettos. She seemed more like the sensible pump type. Pearls, maybe. A cashmere cardigan over a pretty, floral dress.

Jason shook off the ridiculous thoughts and combed his fingers through his hair. How am I going to handle this?

It was his father who'd started pressuring Delia O'Reilly to sell her land way back before Jason took over Lakeview. Dear old Dad, whose people skills ranked right up there with Charles Manson's.

He'd been away at college when his father decided he had to have the tiny strip of land next door. Jason couldn't understand why he hadn't concentrated on updating the cabins on his own property before worrying about what the neighbor's place looked like.

And he did remember what Delia's cottage had looked like back then. The quaint cabin mimicked the Adirondack-style bungalows that used to dot Lakeview's shoreline. The ones Jason had, as soon as he took over, bulldozed to make way for the Denver-style, modern glass and cedar chalets.

Jason knew it was a smart business move. He'd grown up at Lakeview. Seeing his own childhood home go down in a splintering billow of dust had been therapeutic for him.

But he could understand how for Zoe, it might be different.

For Jason, the way the Lodge originally looked only brought back ugly memories. Of seeing his mother's mind shatter into icy shards when she found out dear old Dad had been living a double life. With another complete family down in Montego Bay.

The same day Jason found out he had an older half-sister he hadn't known existed.

Chapter 5

When Jason slammed in through the bar's spring-loaded door, Jade was busy hand-washing martini glasses in a soapy basin behind the bar. She glanced up, unsmiling. He knew her better than to ignore that look. He froze.

"What happened? Did Troy forget to clean up after closing again?"

"Yup. That boy's an airhead. I warned you." She tilted her head in that condescending way that made Jason's gut twist.

He shook his head, but didn't reply. She was right. He was the one who had talked Jade into giving the guy a chance. Guess he should have listened to her after all.

"How did Zoe do? She seemed right in her element," Jason said.

"She did fine. She's a smart one, Red is." Jade slid the last martini glass onto the hanging rack over her head. "Don't be too hard on her about that property, Jason."

He'd slid onto a barstool and was checking his email on his phone, and only half-heard what she said. When a hand slammed down on the bar in front of him he nearly fell off his seat.

"Hey! What? I'm sorry . . . What did you say?" He looked up and she was glaring at him, her coppery eyes sharp on his.

"I said, don't be messin' with Red, Mon. She's carrying around more baggage than she carried in out of the trunk of her car."

Jason cocked his head and raised one eyebrow. Jade had a funny way of putting things sometimes, and this one went right over his head.

"What the hell does that mean?" he snapped.

She crossed her arms and leaned down on the bar in front of him. "Just you never mind. You and I, we've done fine without doing anything about that little cottage for all these years. There's no hurry to be causin' a fuss over it now."

Jason snorted. "Well, the sexy redhead's already got her lawyer on it. We may not have a choice but to deal with it. And probably pretty damn soon."

Jade's eyes narrowed, and she tipped her chin up. He was also painfully familiar with Jade's 'don't screw with me' look. He twisted his shoulders and picked up his phone again.

"I'm warning you, Jason. Red's a real nice lady. She's helpin' me out here for the next few weeks, too. I don't want you fucking around with her."

"I heard you."

"I mean it." Her long fingers curled around his wrist, her grip firm. He looked up to find her face inches from his. "Don't fuck with her," she breathed, "in any of the various ways you do."

Zoe waited until a few minutes before five before calling Xavier's office again. She was surprised when Medina answered the phone.

"Hey, you playing secretary today, too?" Zoe asked. Usually, Medina was busy sequestered in either the firm's law library, or down at city hall doing some kind of research for one of the partners. Medina had been a paralegal for X's firm for almost five years.

"No, Lana had a doctor's appointment, so she cut out a little early. What's up, Zo? Have you scouted out any hot fling prospects yet?"

Zoe laughed. That was Medina. Sex was right at the top of her list, about level with pretty pink cocktails and new shoes.

"I figure I'll let you scout out your own prey when you get here on Friday," Zoe said.

"Not for me, Zo. I'm talking about you. You know what your new doctor told you. Restore. Start over." Medina's voice lowered, and Zoe heard the click of a doorknob in the background. Medina continued in a conspiratorial hush. "There's no better way to start over than rolling around with somebody hot and fresh."

Zoe shook her head and sighed. If only it were that easy. "Hey listen, Dina, the X-man was supposed to call me back when he got in. Is he there? I need to find out what to do next on this property thing."

Her friend's voice returned to normal level. "No, Xavier didn't come back to the office this afternoon. Henri just got back. I guess court ran late today."

"Well, if he gets in before you leave, will you ask him to call me?"

"Will do. I am so looking forward to this weekend, Zo. Make sure you go buy yourself something short and tight. Girl, we are gonna parr-ty."

There was no use explaining to Medina that she'd probably be working behind the bar with Jade for most of Friday evening, and at least for happy hour on Saturday. There'd be plenty of time for that when she got there.

"What time do you think you'll be here Friday?" Zoe

asked.

"I'm taking the whole day off. Mani and pedi at ten, then I'll be on my way."

When Zoe hung up she smiled to herself. She and Medina were as different as two women could possibly be. Yet they had been best friends for years, ever since they met at an attorney social gathering Zoe had gone to. With David. Wow, how long had it been? Their wedding was right after college, not long after she'd gotten the job at Family Guardian Services. So, almost ten years.

Back in the Cinderella days, when she'd had her very own Prince Charming by her side. Her husband had been all that and more to her. In Zoe's line of work, she'd quickly come to believe men like David didn't exist. But she'd been one of the lucky ones, a fact that had made losing him all that much harder.

Medina had stood by her throughout the entire ordeal. She'd run interference between Zoe and the police, who hounded her incessantly after David's death. Medina acted as her liaison when Zoe was still confined to a hospital bed. Kept her company during those long, lonely nights she'd spent hiding in her apartment, through the pain and mental anguish after her plastic surgeries.

Being an only child, Zoe didn't have a sister, but Medina was as loyal and supportive as she imagined one might be. Even though in some ways, the two women were completely different.

Their definition of the word 'relationship' was one example, yet Zoe never questioned her best friend's lifestyle. It was simply none of her business. And Dina's life sure made for some interesting girls-night-out gossip.

Wednesday arrived and Zoe still hadn't heard back from Xavier. She called his office again, but his assistant said he'd gone out of town for a conference, and wouldn't be back until Monday. So although Zoe itched to get something started—make some kind of decision about the falling-down shack on the water—she couldn't do a thing.

She'd managed to avoid Jason all week. Or he, her. On Thursday, she casually mentioned to Jade that she hadn't seen him. Jade said he'd gone into Albany on some business, and wouldn't be back until the weekend.

Zoe blew out a sigh, unsure whether the news was a relief, or a disappointment.

She decided to stop obsessing, and forget about everything for a few days. Although her glance was drawn to that side of Lakeview's property each and every time she came out of the cabin, she resisted the urge to go back there. She could have, since Jason had handed her a key to the padlocked gate—her legal access through Lakeview's property—that first day.

But the possibility of deerflies, mosquitoes, vermin, and snakes made even considering that exploration easier to postpone.

Until late Friday morning, when curiosity, impatience, and a little bit of boredom overtook her. Zoe strolled down to the patio bar around eleven. She slipped through the screen door and thought it was abandoned until Jade popped up from behind the counter, a pencil clenched between her teeth, a pad of paper in hand.

"What are you doing, Miss Jade?"

"Inventory," Jade replied, after removing the pencil and sliding it behind her ear. "I always try to make sure we're good 'n' stocked for the weekends. What's up?"

Zoe rested against the bar and leaned her chin on her hand. "Jade, I wonder if I could ask a favor. I know it's probably not the wisest move I'll make, but I'd really like to

69

go over and at least check out my cottage. I mean, I haven't been within fifty feet of the place since I've been here."

Jade's eyebrows drew together and she cocked a hip. "I'm not so sure that's a good idea, Zo. Jason says there's all kinds of nasty creatures living over there."

"I know, I know. But I have jeans, heavy socks, and a pair of high-top sneakers I brought in case I wanted to go exploring in the woods. If I could just borrow a couple of things from your housekeeping staff . . . a bucket, maybe. A few sponges, and perhaps a pair of rubber gloves?"

Jade squinted at her and tilted her head. "You are one precocious little lady, aren't you?"

"I'd like to think I'm headed in that direction," she replied.

A half-hour later, Zoe headed for the fence at the end of the paved parking area, a bucket filled with cleaning supplies in one hand, the key Jason had given her in the other. Once through the gate, she slipped the key in her jeans pocket, hooked her thumbs in her belt loops, and sucked in a deep breath.

I hope I can do this.

The path was as hidden beneath vines as it had been days ago when Jason first brought her there. The early noon sun filtering through the trees was brighter, though, and somehow, the trek seemed less intimidating. Mustering all the courage she could, Zoe plucked up the handle of the bucket and surged ahead.

Navigating along the path wasn't nearly as difficult as it had been in her flimsy flip-flops. But as every step drew her closer to the cabin, her heart sank a little more. Mildew had woven a green tapestry on the siding, and the wooden frames of the windows had pulled away, curling on the ends like odd-colored corn chips. Even the glass was covered with algae, like the inside of a long-neglected aquarium.

What on earth would she find on the inside?

She clutched the rickety railing as she stepped up onto the listing porch and made her way to the front door. The hinges were rusted through and one had broken free from the frame entirely, skewing the door at an awkward angle. Setting the bucket down, she fished out the key, but realized there was no need. The lockset had long ago warped away from its setting. All Zoe had to do was turn the tarnished brass knob and the door swung open with a weary squeal.

A gust of stale air swept over her, as though the cottage itself heaved out a big sigh. Zoe blinked. For the briefest moment the smell of the place was . . . familiar. Cedar from the lining of the linen closet. Her aunt's pungent, flowery perfume. And was that . . . banana bread? She imagined the warm, cinnamony scent wafting from the tiny kitchen off to the right.

Memories flooded her senses.

"Auntie, how come you always use rotten bananas to make the bread?" Zoe asked.

"Not rotten, child. Just a little past their prime. Besides, those kind make the best. Come now. It's still warm—let me butter you a slice. There's nothin' better than warm banana bread with butter."

Zoe blinked again, and the pleasant aroma was gone, replaced by the tang of mildew and mold. Of wet wood and neglect. Of a place left behind and trampled by the forward march of time.

She stepped into the front room, a place she remembered as cozy and quaint, furnished with Aunt Delia's chintz-covered wingbacks and a corduroy loveseat. Now, it was empty except for the built-in hutch in the far corner where Zoe had stowed her stacks of summer reading. The once-cheery, lemon-yellow paint hung off the wall in blackened strips. With her next step, the floorboards groaned beneath her and felt spongy.

Probably unsafe to go any farther.

It was then she heard a faint buzzing sound, and her gaze settled on a massive web covering the hutch. The gossamer netting jiggled in spastic fits as a snagged deerfly struggled to free itself. Not fast enough. Zoe gasped as a hairy brown spider the size of a silver dollar zipped out from under the top shelf and pounced on its lunch guest.

She lifted a hand to her mouth and closed her eyes. Reality overwhelmed her. It was going to take a lot more than a bucket and a few sponges to resurrect this place. Swiping at her tears, she turned toward the door.

"I tried to tell you. Do you really think a good cleaning is gonna bring this old shack back to life?"

Zoe screeched and stumbled back a step. Just outside the door, Jason stood on the porch with his arms crossed. A muscle in his jaw worked, and his eyes were dark and flinty.

"You scared the hell out of me," Zoe snapped. "And you don't belong here anyway. You're trespassing. Get back on your own side of the fence." But try as she might, she couldn't keep the last words from garbling around a sob.

Jason's expression softened and he took a step toward her, reaching out to brush a tear off her cheek with his thumb. She swatted his hand away.

"It can be repaired. Surely, even up here in the boondocks there must be able carpenters. Who built your chalets?" She knew she was spewing nonsense—with her job in jeopardy, there was no way she could gamble with that much of David's insurance money. But she wasn't about to let Jason know that. Or find out just how vulnerable she really was.

He was shaking his head and wearing a sad smile. "It's a

waste of time, Zoe. Why don't you face facts and let the place go?"

Snatching the handle of the bucket she pushed past him and started down the steps, but he caught her arm.

"Zoe, sometimes it's best to leave the past behind and move on." His voice was deep and rumbling, and laced with something sounding more like empathy than pity.

But no, that couldn't be. This man had one goal—to take this property away from her. She needed to remember that.

Jerking her arm free she said, "Don't you understand, you self-serving bastard? That's exactly what I'm up here trying to do." Then, struggling to see her way along the path through tear-blurred eyes, she stalked back toward the fence.

Two hours later, Zoe was sprawled in a striped canvas lounge chair on the beach, berating herself for listening to her therapist's advice. How could she have possibly expected everything to look the same? Over twenty years had gone by, and Zoe knew Delia hadn't been back to the cottage since she went into assisted living five years ago.

Medina had been right. Her life was no Disney movie. Her childhood vacation memories were dead and gone, just like her fairy-tale life with David. Instead of feeling restored and renewed, she felt as though she'd visited a memory graveyard.

She was reaching forward for her tube of sunscreen when her cell phone started vibrating on the metal-top umbrella table.

"I'm here, Zo. Where the hell are you?" Medina sounded impatient, even a little annoyed. "I rang the doorbell at your mansion, but nobody's home."

Zoe hopped to her feet and peered up the hill from the lake's edge, shading her eyes from the sun. She could see a tiny Medina, standing on the steps of the Aspen, both hands on her curvy hips.

Well unless we're communicating telepathically, Dina must have that wireless thing in her ear again.

"I'm down on the sun-deck, Dina. Wait there—I'll be right up."

Zoe climbed the hill to the Aspen and had barely gotten to the parking lot when Medina wrapped her in a hug.

"How are you, chica? Besides pink and greasy?" Medina giggled.

Zoe tipped back her head and smiled up at her friend, clutching her sunhat to her head. Medina started out three inches taller than her, and then added four extra inches with crazy stilettos.

"How the hell do you drive wearing those things? There isn't a whole lot of asphalt up here, Dina. I hope you brought something you can actually walk in." Then she noticed the rental car parked in front of her cabin, right next to her sporty Cadillac.

Zoe burst into a fit of giggles as she watched Medina struggle her giant luggage out of the almost non-existent trunk of an electric blue Corvette. "For Christ sakes, Dina. I didn't even know you knew how to drive, let alone navigate something this fast!"

Medina dropped one hip and cocked her head. "Girl, I never said I knew how to drive—with this thing, I flew all the way up here!"

It was good to see her best friend again. Zoe was only a few years ahead of Medina, but eons older in every other way. At twenty-nine, Dina still acted like a hormone-charged teenager and was fun as hell to be around. Whenever she was with Dina, she felt almost herself again, even before she'd left the city for Lakeview.

Now, after a week of relaxation, she was much more centered, and looking forward to a carefree weekend with her pal.

After lugging Medina's monstrous suitcase, her garment bag, and an impressively heavy cosmetic case up to the second floor, they settled on the loveseats downstairs. Zoe fetched two tall glasses of iced tea from the kitchen.

"This place is sweet." Medina's eyes danced around the bright, modern space. "But when do I get to see your little *piece of paradise?*"

Zoe rolled her eyes. "I don't want to talk about it. It's in terrible shape, Dina. I don't know what I'm going to do about this whole mess, and I'm having a hard time thinking with Jason Rolland breathing down my neck."

"He sounds like a real asshole."

"He's a businessman." Zoe tipped her head and lifted one shoulder as she sipped her tea. "And we both know they can be ruthless when they want something."

Medina's laugh was a dark rumble. "You said that right. We work in a jungle full of men. Finding one with a heart is damn near impossible."

A jab struck Zoe straight through the heart. She knew that only too well. "I had one. Once," she whispered, lowering her head.

Medina leaned across the space between them and squeezed her shoulder. "I know. I'm sorry, Zo." When she raised her head she caught Medina's wink. "But this weekend, you're starting over. Getting a makeover. You're going to loosen up and learn how to hunt the jungle like a big cat."

This is why I love this girl so. Every time she sees me creeping too close to the edge, she snaps me back and spins me around.

"I did do a little shopping," Zoe admitted.

She told her friend about the day she'd spent down at the outlet mall with Jade, but as she glanced at the clock on the mantle she stood up in a rush. "Geez, I've got to change and get down to the bar."

Medina raised an eyebrow. "Meeting someone?"

"No, I'm tending bar with Jade."

"You're doing what?" Medina stared at her, eyes wide. She then commenced a tirade of colorful words Zoe couldn't understand, muttering in Spanish as she followed her up the stairs to her bedroom.

Finally, she lapsed back into English. "You knew I was coming up this weekend, chica. What the hell?"

Zoe thumbed through her closet. "I've been helping Jade tend the bar," she said, pulling a tee shirt over her head and tucking it into her shorts.

"I thought you were here to relax? Now you're working?"

She poked big, silver hoops through her earlobes as she leveled her gaze on her friend's in the mirror. "I tended bar in college, Dina. I told you that. It's kind of fun. The asshole owner of whom we were speaking? Well, he pissed off one of the barmaids the first night I was here. She stomped out right in the middle of the Friday night rush."

"So, like, you're abandoning me." Medina pushed out her full lower lip and slid her eyes to the side.

"Yeah, right," she snorted, "me, abandoning you. Imagine that."

Medina sighed and shrugged. "I can handle it. But you're mixing drinks, right? Make sure you pour mine full measure." She winked again.

It was almost four o'clock by the time the two girls left the cabin. Zoe knew that Jade would be looking for her. She handed Medina the extra key, pausing with a raised eyebrow.

"Now, I'm not going to tell you to behave yourself, because I know you better than that. But remember you're staying with me. You can't bring anybody home with you, okay?"

Zoe heard the noise of the crowd before they'd gotten halfway down the hill. The bar was busy as hell. Jade looked up in relief, greeting her with a warm smile. But she was so swamped she couldn't even come over to meet Medina.

"It's all good," Medina shouted over the noise. "You go on. Just mix me something cold and strong."

Zoe ducked under the bar and donned an apron.

She shook a Cosmopolitan for her friend, strained it into a frosted glass. She watched her waltz off, full hips undulating, gracefully balancing the stemmed glass even though she teetered on ridiculous needle heels.

Medina headed straight toward the end of the bar where a group of T-shirt clad young men in swimming trunks had convened, beer mugs in hand.

There she goes. Barely hit the water and she's trolling already.

Zoe had always been amazed at the way Medina played the man-crowd. She made the term 'free-spirit' seem conservative. But Zoe knew her friend was enjoying life while she could.

Medina still lived at home with her very traditional, very Hispanic family. And she was the youngest daughter. That birthright came with responsibilities.

They say that opposites attract, and that idiom certainly applied to Zoe and Medina's friendship. Dina was the totally modern, free-wheeling bachelorette, and Zoe was the good little Catholic girl. Yet she believed she had no right to judge her friend. She wondered sometimes if maybe Dina, deep down, actually dreamed of having a good man, a stable relationship, children. Zoe had, up until three years ago, come close to making those dreams a reality.

But it seemed neither she nor her friend were destined for

that kind of life.

Everything's changed now. Maybe it's time I shed the good little Catholic girl uniform, and cross over to Medina's side of the track.

Jason was sitting on the second floor of his own cabin, up the hill and off to the west of the patio bar. He'd gotten in from Albany exhausted and wishing he could just relax tonight.

Through his chalet's wall of glass, he watched Zoe and a curvy dark-haired woman prance down the hill to the door of the patio bar.

Wonder who the hell that diva is? Sexy body, but she doesn't hold a candle to the freckled one.

There was something about Zoe. Something that really made him nervous.

But it wasn't all about her body. No, it was something in her eyes. Something . . . vulnerable. He wondered what had happened to her, and couldn't help but feel as though he'd like to pummel whomever or whatever it was that slashed up her face.

Ever since he was a little kid, Jason had had a soft spot for wounded creatures. He couldn't remember all the times he'd carried a baby bird, fallen from its nest, or an injured bunny into the house, asking his mother to help him save it.

He didn't know Zoe very well, and most of the conversations they'd had so far had ended badly. So what was it? What was it about her that made him feel like taking her in his arms and just holding her?

Jason hadn't felt that way about a woman—about anyone—as far back as he could remember.

Maybe never.

He stayed in his cabin all of Friday evening, ordering

dinner to be brought up to him from the restaurant. His business in Albany had not gone well. Still active in the real estate empire his father had passed along to him, Jason had to admit that sometimes, he hated it.

The income could be amazing. But the process was so engrossing, so time and energy consuming. And there was so much ass-kissing to be done. Jason did not like to kiss ass, especially those of the stiff-shirted suits who flashed their portfolios around as if they were male appendages.

Jason had taken over his father's domestic business— Lakeview, and his corporate real estate connections—but he wasn't the same kind of man his father was. He didn't have an ounce of respect for his father's cheating, lying ways. What a shame, that in the world of business, those flawed traits sometimes made the most successful men.

After three days in Albany unsuccessfully trying to woo an Asian executive into buying a multi-million-dollar office complex, Jason was done. His ego was bruised, and he was tired. He'd come home without a sale, with no big commission ticket.

The last thing he needed at this point was to start having feelings—real feelings—for some redheaded bombshell who, in truth, was his opponent. Jason couldn't figure out what it was about her that turned his insides to sludge.

It's not like he didn't date. Dozens of attractive women, every summer season, flocked to him like fish to chum. He'd had his choice of where to take his pleasure since he was old enough to know what to do with his male parts.

About the only bright spot in his trip to Albany was when he discovered that Tracy—the barmaid who'd stomped out on Jade last weekend—was tending bar in the lounge of the Marriott where he always stayed. Apparently, she'd quickly rebounded from whatever he'd done or said to piss her off that day. She treated him like royalty when he'd eaten dinner at the bar, then took her forgiveness a step further when she knocked on his door a few hours later.

But trysts with women like Tracy were fleeting, meaningless pleasures. Like potato chips and beer, but without the calories. The blonde had moved on to another handsome young suit by Thursday, he discovered when he'd stopped in to say goodbye before he checked out. He'd had to order a beer to avoid sitting there by himself, looking like a fool when she brushed him off.

Now he was back home, in his own world, his own lonely cabin, sequestered in his tiny studio.

Jason wiped his fingers on the cloth napkin off the restaurant's tray, and pushed back his plate. The digital clock screamed at him—7:57. Only three more minutes, and he'd have to get his shit together. He'd have to transform into the all-knowing god of love who ruled Jason's Lair. Helping and healing the lovelorn through their broken hearts. Oh, the irony. He was the one causing the broken hearts in real life. But in his lair, he was every lonely lover's best friend.

"Good evening, and welcome to Jason's Lair."

Sincerity, even slight enthusiasm, was such an effort for Jason tonight. Good thing he was, at least, a pretty damned good actor.

He flicked the button for the first caller of the night. A tearful, whining voice came over the line. "Jason, I think I'm falling in love with my best friend's husband."

Oh, Christ. Here we go again.

A little before eight, the bar crowd had begun to thin out. Zoe filled herself a glass of seltzer from the trigger and leaned against the back counter.

Where the hell was Medina?

Jade joined her and grabbed a bottle of water from under the counter. "Where's your friend?" she asked, as if she'd read Zoe's mind.

Zoe shrugged. "Who knows? That's Medina. No doubt she's down at the docks checking out some guy's boat." She rolled her eyes. "Or in a boat, checking out some guy."

Jade chuckled, and then glanced at her watch. "Look, I got Troy comin' in at eight. Why don't you go find your friend? Have a little fun for the rest of the evening?"

"I could use a bite to eat," she replied. She untied her apron and tossed it under the bar. About then, a group of guys in island bright camp shirts bustled in through the restaurant entrance. They were carrying in some sort of electronic equipment. One of them had a guitar slung over his shoulder. She turned toward Jade and tilted her head. "Music tonight?"

"Yes. Jason thought it might help draw the restaurant crowd in after dinner."

"Where's Jason? I know he's back. I saw him earlier."

"It's Friday night, Red. Jason's in his lair," she said with a conspiratorial wink.

What the hell does that mean?

She was about to ask when Medina appeared on the heels of the musicians. She was chattering away with the tall, dark-haired dude as though they'd been best buds since high school.

Jade nudged Zoe with her elbow. "Go. This is supposed to be your vacation."

Zoe ducked under the bar and headed to the corner where the band was setting up. Medina was standing just a little too close to the tall guy, her fluttering hands and mobile hips making it plain she was on, what Zoe dubbed, high-a-flirt.

But before Zoe caught her friend's eye, a tall blonde with

waist-long, satiny hair slipped out of the crowd and headed straight for the band. She traveled like a torpedo. She wedged herself between Medina and the tall guy, whose grimace and quickly forced smile identified the blonde as somebody significant.

Zoe froze in her tracks. She couldn't clearly hear what the blonde said to Medina, but Zoe could tell by her narrowed eyes and jerky movements that it wasn't a friendly greeting.

Medina shrugged and turned to walk away, ignoring what came next out of the blonde's mouth, loud and clear.

"Catty bitch."

Without turning back, Dina raised one hand theatrically and flipped her the bird in reply. Then she spotted Zoe, and, grinning as though nothing had happened, swaggered toward her.

"How 'bout some dinner, Zo? I'm starving."

Inside the restaurant, another, smaller bar lined the far wall. Jade had told Zoe this was their winter bar, for when the weather got too cold to keep the patio bar open. It was humming tonight, manned by a tall, bulky man she hadn't seen before. He wore a Hawaiian print shirt, open halfway down to reveal several, heavy gold chains resting against a generously furred chest. His shaved head, and multiple tattoos covering his massively sculptured biceps, made him look almost threatening.

The minute she laid eyes on him, Medina growled like a wild animal. She leaned closer and mumbled, "I'm going to fetch us a drink, 'kay?"

Zoe realized how tired she was the minute she sat down at the table. Bar-tending was hard work. It had seemed easy when she was twenty-two. But that was ten years ago. She was yawning into her hand when Medina finally joined her, another martini in one hand and a glass of Pinot in the other.

"You're not going to poop out on me already, are you?" she asked. She spoke to Zoe but never took her eyes off the guy at the bar.

"I'm afraid I might, Dina. I spent the whole morning down by the water. I guess I'm not used to this much fresh air." Zoe opened the menu, but realized her appetite had already gone to sleep.

Medina was still staring toward the bar. She plucked the tiny plastic sword that speared a cherry out of her drink and began sucking on it. Zoe glanced from her friend to the bartender, who was admiring the performance.

Dina, oh Dina. She shook her head.

"Look, maybe I'll order a sandwich to go, and take it back to the cabin. Would you mind?" Zoe paused, but it was as though her friend hadn't heard her. "Dina?"

"Huh? Oh, that's fine with me, sweetie. I'll go eat something up at the bar." Her attention came back fully then, and she laid her hand over Zoe's. "Hey, you're feeling all right, aren't you?"

Zoe nodded, again in mid-yawn. "Yup. Just wiped out. I'll place a to-go order at the front. I'll see you later, okay?"

Medina didn't roll in until almost noon the next day. Zoe had worried some, but not enough to keep her awake. Once she'd showered, then devoured her turkey club sandwich, Zoe barely made it back up the stairs to that deliciously oversized bed. She slept so soundly she wouldn't have heard Medina come in if a team of horses had been dragging her.

The doorbell of her chalet chimed when Zoe was about halfway through her first pot of coffee and her second romance novel. When she opened the door, a raccoon-eyed Medina stood on the steps. Her voluminous cloud of dark hair framed her face like a frizzy halo.

"I thought I gave you a key," Zoe said, scowling. "You

83

didn't lose it already, did you?"

Medina's blurry eyes widened, and then she started fishing furiously in the outside pocket of her purse. "Damn. I forgot I had it." She produced the key, holding it up triumphantly. "Sorry. Did I wake you?"

Zoe grinned and shook her head, holding the door wide to let her friend shuffle in.

"You look like hell. Nice do. Sex hair?"

"My just-fucked look." Medina's smile wasn't the least bit embarrassed, but she did feign an attempt to smooth down her mass of kink.

"You're such a trip, Dina," Zoe said, heading back into the kitchen to refill her cup. "How was I supposed to know you didn't end up floating in the lake?"

"I was floating on the lake." Medina slipped her purse off her shoulder and flopped down in the loveseat. She smirked. "On Tony's boat. Got any coffee?"

Chapter 6

"Who the hell is Tony?" Zoe handed Medina a steaming mug—extra sugar, extra cream, just the way she liked it—and settled onto the loveseat facing her.

Medina blew across the top of the mug, sipping tentatively. Then she closed her eyes as a big smile lit up her face. "Ah, Zoe, you make the best coffee," she purred.

"Tony. Who's Tony? And what boat?" Zoe pressed.

"You remember the guy behind the bar last night? The big, hairy, gorgeous one?" Medina asked. "That's Tony."

"Well his head wasn't so hairy." Zoe snorted and shook her head. "Okay, Dina. Fill me in."

Medina set her mug down on the table between them. She stretched like a cat and yawned before answering. "Anthony Diali owns the charter boat company down in the village. He sometimes fills in at the bar for . . . what's his name? Jason? The asshole who owns this place."

"Is that so?" Zoe replied, one eyebrow raised. "Jade never mentioned him to me."

"Tony and Jade don't get along very well, apparently. In any case, Tony's *personal* vessel is named *The Crystal Mess*.

That's where I was last night, after he closed down the bar."

Alarm bells went off inside Zoe's head. "*The Crystal Mess.* So, doesn't that worry you a bit? Isn't that a bad wordplay on something you and I don't want anything to do with?" She tried not to sound like Medina's mother. But honestly, sometimes, somebody had to be. Just to keep her alive and out of jail.

"No, no, silly. Tony's not a drug lord. He paid for the friggin' boat with a bonus he got for busting a major drug ring a few years ago." Medina winked slyly as she lifted her mug again to her lips. "I think I may have hooked me a hot one here, Zo. Tony's some kind of bigwig with our own beloved NYPD. So big, he takes the entire summer off to stay up here."

A half-hour later, Zoe was waiting for her friend on the back deck while Medina showered and brushed away what she referred to as 'beach ball breath.'

How does she do it? She'd barely met the guy, and just like that, she jumped into the sack with him.

That was exactly the question she asked, once Medina was settled comfortably in a lounge chair, sipping her second cup of coffee. Dina's shapely curves were barely concealed under a short satin robe. Her long, wet hair sent rivulets of water snaking down the smooth surface.

Medina stared at her over her mug, pausing as if she were trying to figure out how to explain the theory of relativity. Then she tipped her head, her eyes narrowed.

"You almost sound jealous, Zo."

Zoe's lips pressed into a thin line. "Maybe I am. A little. I'm not sure whether the way you operate inspires or scares me."

"I have fun. I live life one day at a time."

"Well you certainly seem to be having more fun than I am.

86

In recent years, anyway," Zoe said. "I don't mean this to insult you, but—don't you ever feel . . . easy?"

A laugh burst from Medina, and she shrugged. "You and I come from different planets, Zoe. We were both raised in very traditional, if not different, families. Our life's course was sort of preplanned for us, right from the start."

"So if you were raised in the same traditional way, then how come you have no problem playing musical beds?"

Medina set down her coffee mug on the glass-topped table between them. She leaned forward, elbows on her thighs. "Zoe, I'm the youngest female in a strict, traditional Mexican family. There isn't any wondering how my future is going to turn out."

Zoe tipped up her chin. She'd remembered Medina telling her that there was no sense in her looking for a husband, because marriage was not in the cards for her.

"Dina, this is the twenty-first century. Are your parents actually going to insist you stay single and take care of them for the rest of their lives?"

Dropping back into her lounge chair, Medina turned away and didn't say anything for a moment. She crossed her legs, scratching one ankle with the heel of the other foot. She sighed. "Tradition is sometimes an unwritten law, Zoe." When her eyes met Zoe's again, they glistened with emotion. "Do you think I could honestly put my mother or father in a nursing home when the time came?"

A long silence made the air between them feel thick and heavy. Zoe was suddenly aware of the shouts of children echoing up from the beach. The sound, instead of being a happy one, seemed sad and lonely.

"So you're having a good time while you can. No strings attached. No hearts get broken," Zoe said softly.

"You betcha," Medina replied. Then a slow, mischievous

smile transformed her face. "And I know that's not the way you were raised. But with all you've been through, I think it would do you good to try my way. If only for a little while."

Zoe pinched the bridge of her nose between her fingers. "I don't know if I could. Hell, Dina, I've dated Xavier—sort of—for how long? And just the thought of getting naked with him turns my stomach."

"Maybe he's not the right guy for you. Maybe he wouldn't have been, even if what happened to you, hadn't. Look," Medina leaned forward again, stressing her point, "the right chemistry could make all the difference for you. Haven't you felt any attraction for any man since David?"

Zoe started to shake her head, but stopped. She was ashamed to admit—no, horrified to admit—how her body had reacted to Jason. Of all the men in the world.

Medina continued to stare at her, waiting for an answer. "Come on, Zo. Fess up. I can see there's been something stirring in that pretty red head of yours." One side of her mouth quirked up. Then she blinked and her smile fell away. "Oh, gosh, it's not Tony, is it?"

Now it was Zoe's turn to laugh out loud. "Hell no. Tony is definitely not my type."

"Whew. Good thing. Talk about awkward situations." Medina ran her fingers through her damp, rapidly kinking mass of hair. "So there's no reason, then, why you can't join me for the party tonight."

"Party? What party?" Zoe asked, shocked.

"Tony is having a cocktail party on one of his tour boats tonight." Medina held both hands up and tipped her head. "You know, sort of a pre-Fourth of July bash."

Zoe had completely forgotten that it was almost July. Had she really been here two weeks already? Damn, and she'd gotten no further in figuring out what to do with the mess she'd inherited than the day she arrived. She shook her head. "Man, I guess I've sort of fallen into a time warp since I got here."

"That's a good thing, Zoe. That's why you're here," Medina said. "You're not working the bar tonight, are you?"

She shook her head. "I guess Troy works happy hours on the weekends with Jade. I told her I'd stop by later on to see if she needed me."

"Good. Tony said the boat leaves the docks in town about six. So let's get upstairs and figure out what we're wearing to this shindig."

Four hours later, Zoe cringed and scrunched her eyes shut as Medina screeched the Corvette into a parking space near the Lake George Tour Boat docks. She knew this was a bad idea. She'd wanted to drive her own car, but Medina promised her that Tony could drop Zoe off at the Lakeview docks whenever she wanted.

The diesel exhaust from the huge boat's engine choked Zoe as she dashed across the parking lot, trying to keep up with her friend. Even though they'd had all afternoon to get ready, they were still running a few minutes late. Zoe's transformation, she thought ruefully, had apparently been a little more challenging than Medina had expected.

The tiny ticket booth stood right at the lake's edge and fortunately, the crowd that usually engulfed it had dissipated. Medina marched purposefully up to the hut in her four-inch turquoise heels. She didn't wait until the glass door had completely slid open before she accosted the old man inside.

"Hi there." She flashed her photo-shoot smile. "I'm Medina Flores. Tony Diali told me I could pick up my tickets here. Our tickets, I mean. I've brought a friend."

Tickets? How many people can you possibly fit on a private boat?

She wasn't sure if the man behind the counter was sitting on a stool, or if he was truly dwarf-sized. He also looked a little like a dwarf, with pure white hair that stuck out from the sides of his head in tufts. He blinked slowly, as though he'd just woken up from a nap.

He leaned forward to examine the girls through the glass, and both bushy eyebrows rose. Then he glanced down at a pad of yellow paper, shakily making two scratches with a dull pencil. Finally, he pushed two bright pink squares of cardboard through the opening.

"Have a good time, ladies," he said in a cheerful chirp.

Gosh, he even sounds like a dwarf.

Medina snatched the tickets off the counter and off she went, leaving Zoe to teeter behind her on stilettos that Medina insisted she wear. Between the needle-thin heels, the snug, elasticized mini that bound her thighs together like a girdle, and the stretchy tee strapped around her ribcage, she thought for sure she might pass out before they even made it aboard.

Zoe was concentrating so hard on keeping her heels from catching in the cracks between the planks, she almost plowed right into Medina when she screeched to a halt. Following her gaze, she looked up. Between two monstrous tour boats bobbed a smaller replica. A mirrored sign along the front of the second level shouted the vessel's name in neon: *The Crystal Mess*.

Medina planted her fists on her hips. "Well, what do you think?"

"This is Tony's boat?" Zoe gasped in disbelief. She'd been imagining a good-sized cabin cruiser, like the ones she'd seen coast up and down the lake since she'd arrived. "This isn't a boat. It's a freaking ferry."

Medina shot Zoe a wink over her shoulder. "I told you I

landed a big one this time."

The Crystal Mess was a three-level touring vessel, with the upper level open-air. The lower level was encased in glass, through which Zoe could see cloth-covered, round tables already set with crystal and porcelain. A crowd of people milled about, visible through the open sides of the middle deck. They were mostly clustered, drinks in hand, down the end where familiar Budweiser and Coors neon logos illuminated the back wall.

Zoe followed Medina to the boarding area and up the stairs to the bar. She whispered to Medina, "Did you say Tony owns this thing?"

"Yes ma'am," Medina answered. "And this is his personal vessel. He's a partner with the guy that runs Lake George Tours." They reached the top of the stairs and Medina combed the crowd with her eyes. "There he is. Come on. I'll introduce you."

The same burly man Zoe had seen the night before was leaning on one end of a highly polished wood bar. He was wearing linen shorts and a filmy gauze shirt, with the same hairy chest and gold chains peeping out between its half-buttoned front. Busy in conversation, he held a frosted mug in one hand and was gesturing with the other as he spoke. A profusion of gold and diamond jewelry glittered with every movement of his hand.

Zoe still couldn't believe that Medina was attracted to this guy. No way. Medina liked the tall, wiry ones—the ones who always looked too young for her—hipster guys fresh out of college. Guys that she could have fun with but not get too serious over. She knew Medina couldn't risk falling in love if her future was to take care of her parents. It broke Zoe's heart that her friend was bound and determined to never fall in love—to never think about having a significant relationship or even a family. At least she had experienced love with David. Even though she'd lost him so brutally, she would never regret meeting him and marrying him.

Tony was the exact opposite of every guy Medina usually went for. Not only was he broad, dark, and hairy, at least from the neck down, but he looked older than Medina. Not by a lot, but certainly by at least a decade or so.

As they drew closer, Tony stopped in mid-sentence, freezing when he caught sight of Medina. Zoe knew this was exactly what Dina was hoping for. She did look breathtaking in her turquoise sheath, one that wrapped her voluptuous curves from the ample display of her cleavage to a daringly bared mid-thigh. The color was magic against her rich skin tone.

Zoe couldn't help but feel a stab of jealousy as she watched Tony scan her friend from head to toe in awe. He plunked down his half-empty mug and opened his bulky arms toward her. Zoe was so caught up in the chemistry between the two, she didn't even notice who it was Tony had been talking to.

And then she realized it was Jason. Zoe knew the look of shock on his face mirrored her own. She hadn't seen him all week, not since the night he'd turned down her dinner invitation. As Tony wrapped himself around Medina and planted his lips on hers, Zoe stood frozen, staring speechlessly into Jason's eyes.

When Medina broke free, she fumbled with an apologetic introduction.

"Tony, this is my best friend, Zoe Anderson. I hope you don't mind. I brought her along tonight. She's the one who invited me up here to stay in her cabin."

"No problem at all, honey. My pleasure, Zoe." Tony patted Medina's behind and chuckled. "Have either of you met Jason

Rolland?"

Zoe reached a trembling hand to shake Tony's. Then she sputtered, "I believe Mr. Rolland and I have already met."

There he was with those eyes again, the ones that made her think of Edward's eyes in the Twilight movies. They were unnaturally blue. Supernaturally blue. And they grazed over her body in a way that made her feel as though he could see right through what she was wearing.

But when his eyes came back up to meet hers, there were creases between his brows.

"Nice to see you again, Zoe. You look . . . great," he said haltingly, but there was no smile, either on his face or in his tone.

Medina bounced out of Tony's embrace and grabbed for Jason's hand. Zoe caught Medina's appreciative perusal of Jason's tall and lanky form as she cocked her hip. "So you're the guy that owns Lakeview? The place rocks, man," she purred. "I didn't see you in the bar last night, did I?"

Jason cleared his throat. He seemed uncomfortable with the prolonged time she was holding onto his hand. "No. I've been out of town," he replied.

Tony must have sensed Medina's transfer of energy too, and didn't waste any time reeling her back in. Stepping beside her, he smacked her sharply on the butt, and then slipped his arm around her waist and pulled her to him.

"Come on, girls," he said, "let's get you both something to drink."

As Tony and Medina turned back toward the bar, Zoe could feel Jason staring at her again. She slanted her gaze toward him, and sure enough, he was.

"Is something wrong, Mr. Rolland?" she asked quietly.

Jason didn't reply, but only shook his head very slightly, which made Zoe even more uncomfortable.

93

She'd made a mistake letting Medina dress her up tonight. She felt exposed and vulnerable. Even though that's how her friend dressed all the time, the look just wasn't her. Now, Jason's scrutiny made her all the more self-conscious.

His expression said to Zoe that if he'd been wearing a coat, he'd have wrapped it around her and bustled her out of sight in a heartbeat.

She wasn't ready for that look in his eyes, one of concern and almost . . . possessiveness. Panic clutched at her throat, and for a moment she was afraid to even try to speak.

No. Not another panic attack. This is not going to happen to me again. I am stronger than this.

Zoe squared her shoulders, pushing her full breasts a little more firmly against the snug elasticized tee she wore. She took a deep breath, locked eyes with Jason, and said, "Well, are you going to fetch me a drink, or do I have to get one myself?"

Less than an hour later, *The Crystal Mess* shoved off. Jason didn't realize they were even moving until he glanced past Zoe's shoulder and watched a huge white sailboat drift by. The band had started to play, and he was finding it even more difficult to maintain an already awkward conversation with Zoe. Tony and Medina had drifted off into the crowd, virtually abandoning them.

He watched Zoe poking at the lime floating in her drink with the straw. Her eyes strayed through the crowd intermittently, and he knew she was probably looking for Medina. He reached forward and took a light hold of Zoe's elbow to draw her attention back to him.

"Let's go topside," he shouted over the noise, pointing up with one finger. "It'll be quieter up there."

The stairs to the upper level were steep and narrow. He

motioned for Zoe to go ahead of him, and then quickly realized his mistake. He spent the entire climb with his eyes within six inches of her firmly rounded bottom.

Okay, so he was human. And undeniably male. She was obviously having trouble keeping her balance on those spiked heels, which made her hips wiggle very enticingly.

Nice. Very nice. But why couldn't he just enjoy the view without wanting to whisk her away to a place where nobody could enjoy the scenery but him?

When they finally stepped out onto the open deck, he laughed as Zoe reached down and snatched off the stilettos. Huffing, she threw them down one at a time.

"Medina talked me into wearing these blasted things. I don't know how, for the life of me, she manages to navigate in them."

"You did look a little uncomfortable," Jason said. "Did she pick out your outfit too?"

Not so sure I like that look on you.

Zoe nodded and dropped her gaze to the floor. She folded her arms across her chest, probably in an attempt to cover up, but all it did was push the two rounded mounds up a little farther out of the scooped neck of her top.

Jason swallowed and looked away. He tried to keep his attention focused on the foamy stream of bubbles running behind the boat. The last thing he needed right now was to pitch a tent in the crotch of his dress pants. "You two been friends long?" he asked.

"Ten years or so."

Geez, it's harder to hold a conversation up here than it was over the band and the crowd.

He pushed on. "So, have you forgiven me for turning down your dinner invitation the other night?"

"What's to forgive? You owe me absolutely nothing,

Rolland." Zoe's tone was clipped and cool. "Nothing, at least, until we start discussing real estate."

Jason leaned back against the metal railing and searched her face. Her icy attitude was at least helping to keep his hormones under control.

"Well, I didn't want you to think it was anything personal. I had another obligation that night. I apologize."

Zoe's eyes snapped up to his. "Has it occurred to you that we've known each other less than two weeks, and you're always apologizing for something?"

Jason scrubbed his hand down his face.

Why, oh why can't I be as smooth in person as I am behind that microphone?

Zoe glared at Jason, waiting for his response. But she couldn't ignore the effect he had on her. The wind was ruffling his very black, very straight hair every which way. He looked like a tousled little boy who'd just woken up from a nap. And now, he looked frustrated and defeated. Was he really the arrogant, heartless real estate mogul his reputation touted?

There it was again. The fluttering, clutching feeling in her lower belly. Zoe tried to ignore the confusing, conflicting ways her body reacted to this man. She wanted to hate him, to blame her thrumming pulse and sudden lightheadedness on something other than pure physical attraction.

Maybe I'm getting seasick.

Then she realized that Jason was talking, and she hadn't heard a single word he'd said. She began to feel chilled as a mist of sweat coated her skin. She looked away, out toward the other boats zipping by on the lake.

Medina. He asked me something about Medina.

She breathed deeply and took a chance her answer would

make some sense. "Medina works for my attorney. She's a paralegal. I met her at a party I went to with m-my . . . l-late husband."

When Jason's eyebrows rose, she wasn't sure if she'd guessed wrong at his question, or even if the words had tumbled out in a sensible order. His next question, though, caused her throat to constrict.

"I'm sorry about your husband. How did you lose him?"

It will help you to heal if you talk about this. Open up and let the hurt out.

Zoe took a long draw from her drink, struggling to cool the tension in her throat. Then she drew in a shaky breath.

Here goes.

"He was m-murdered. Man with a knife, h-h-hiding. In our . . . our home." She squeezed her eyes shut as the images came rushing back into her mind, and had to swallow hard to abate the rising wave of bile. "Slashed. He slashed David's throat . . ." She choked on a sob. "I w-watched him bleed to death."

When she opened her eyes, Jason's wide eyes and open mouth only accelerated her panic. But it was as though a floodgate inside her had opened, and the words just wouldn't stop tumbling out.

"R-rape. Bloody blade . . . Held me down." She reached up and fisted a hand in her hair, then lowered it to her cheek, pointing with one trembling finger. "He cut me. M-my beauty mark."

The flash of shock in Jason's eyes pushed Zoe beyond her limit.

Jason watched as the plastic cup in Zoe's hand buckled in her clenched fist. It was only a heartbeat before the rest of her buckled, too.

The cup bounced on the metal floor and skittered off in the wind. Jason tossed his own drink over the side just in time to catch Zoe as her knees folded beneath her.

She seemed like such a little thing, but the weight of her limp form added to the sway of the boat, pitching Jason off balance. He searched the deck in panic, but there was no chair, no ledge, no place to lay an unconscious woman.

Now what?

Slowly, he sank to his knees, and then plopped down on a deck still slightly sticky with fresh paint.

He could feel the vibration of the music through the floor, and knew he could shout at the top of his lungs and no one would hear him. Jason pulled one hand free to feel the pulse in Zoe's neck. It thrummed steadily, if not a little too fast. He wasn't sure what had caused her to pass out, but doubted it was life threatening. He had no choice but to wait. Either she would come around on her own, or someone would eventually venture upstairs to find them.

Jason cradled Zoe's head and shoulders, shifting her so he could study her face. The breeze here on the upper deck was fierce, and it whipped Zoe's shoulder-length hair. The silky, red-gold strands smelled like honey as they lashed into his eyes and tickled his neck.

With her eyes closed, Zoe looked like a fairy child. Her pale, freckled complexion made her seem so young and helpless. Jason wondered if talking about her husband's murder had brought on this faint. She'd been there, witnessed it. And suffered an unthinkable violation by his murderer. He shuddered, his stomach turning as rage stirred deep within him.

Her scars, Jason realized, went much deeper than the one on her face.

But he didn't have too much time to ponder his questions.

Barely two minutes elapsed before Zoe's eyelashes fluttered. He found himself looking down into those eyes—the most beautiful pair of green eyes he'd ever seen.

Chapter 7

When Zoe opened her eyes, she wasn't at all sure where she was, or how long she'd been out. She was sprawled at an awkward angle, her lower half resting on a hard, vibrating surface. Her upper half was cradled in the warmth of strong arms. She blinked, confused.

When her vision came into focus, her first view was of the sky, clear and blue. Wind flipped her hair against her cheeks. Then she realized her face was only inches away from a pair of equally clear, penetrating blue eyes.

Before panic could take hold, as it usually did after one of these episodes, she tried hard to remember the face. She knew that angular jawline, and the straight, black hair whipping in the wind. David? No, it can't be David. He was blond. He's gone now. David is dead.

A painful clutching seized her heart. Struggling to draw in a breath, then blow it out, she tried hard to focus.

Her mind tousled with images, memories, reality for a few moments. Then, with equal parts relief and embarrassment, she remembered. *Jason.*

"So, what was that all about, pretty lady? Are you okay?" Jason asked with a nervous chuckle.

Although Zoe's every instinct was to struggle to her feet, she still felt a little lightheaded. The warmth of Jason's body, and the smell of him, comforted her. She found herself relaxing deeper into his embrace.

She sighed and closed her eyes. "I'm okay. I'm awfully sorry. This happens to me sometimes now. My shrink says it's some kind of panic attack."

When she opened her eyes again he was staring at her, his brows drawn together. He reached one hand up to brush a lock of Zoe's hair off her cheek. Then he stopped, feeling her stiffen.

"It's okay. I've seen it. You don't have to worry about hiding it from me."

His gaze flickered from her face down to her chest, then back to her eyes. "Besides, in your present position, there's lots more interesting views for me to concentrate on." A slow smile crept across his face as a devilish gleam lit up his amazing eyes.

Eyes the color of a sparkling pool. Eyes I could fall into and drown in.

A shiver skittered across her shoulder blades, but it wasn't from the chill.

The spell was broken as he frowned. "And how I'd love to keep looking. Except, my left leg has gone completely numb. And is starting to ache like hell."

It was then Zoe fully realized how awkwardly tangled their bodies were. Her legs were folded up underneath her butt at an almost impossible angle. Her miniskirt gripped her thighs together like a strait jacket, the hemline having hiked up to only inches below her crotch. Her boobs were literally spilling out of her tee. And both of Zoe's feet were also tingly numb.

She started to giggle.

Here I am, half undressed and on the floor with a man I hardly know. Medina would be so proud.

Zoe scrambled up onto her knees as Jason stood. He

reached out both hands to help her up.

"Are you sure you're feeling better?"

Zoe nodded. "Mortified, but I'm okay." She yanked down the hem of her skirt with one hand and hoisted up the neckline of her top with the other.

"Why? You've probably realized by now that I'm the kind of guy who likes women falling at my feet." He grinned, pinching her chin gently between his fingers.

A pang of fresh pain seared Zoe's heart. She'd never expected this kind of tenderness from the likes of a man like Jason Rolland.

"I do prefer it, though, when they don't take me down with them." He continued, holding out his arm.

Still unsteady on buzzing feet, Zoe latched on as the two made their way back down the steps to the middle deck. The band had taken a break, but the noise of the crowd was still deafening. She searched the mingling mass of bodies for Medina's familiar dark mane. Neither she nor Tony were anywhere in sight.

Jason kept glancing down at Zoe as though she'd melt away again at any minute.

"I'm okay now. I really am. I'm probably just hungry."

"What have you eaten today?" he asked.

Zoe cocked her head to one side, thinking. "Today is Saturday, right? Nothing, I guess." She shrugged.

"No wonder you're passing out. A recipe for disaster. Take one giddy redhead, starve her for a day, and hand her a double vodka." Jason snapped his fingers in the air. "Poof. She's out like a light."

Zoe started to laugh but then grabbed on tighter to Jason's arm as another wave of dizziness washed over her. She searched the room again for Medina. She huffed, "I don't know where the hell Medina got off to, but I don't care. I'm hungry."

"Then, pretty lady," Jason said, patting Zoe's hand, "we shall feed you."

Zoe kept a firm grip on Jason's arm as they descended to the lower deck.

The dining room was lit up in a kaleidoscope of color. Each round table was dressed in blue-checked cloth, a vase of red and white carnations in the center. Gold and silver streamers swayed from the ceiling beams. Some of the tables were already filled with guests, chattering and laughing over salads that were just being served.

In the center of the room, at the largest table, sat Medina and Tony. All the seats, except for two, were already occupied.

When Medina caught sight of Zoe she squealed and jumped to her feet. Zoe guessed by her friend's shrieks and flailing hands that she was drunk. Teetering atop her dizzying heels, Medina weaved her way towards them. She was impressed at how well, in her condition, Dina navigated between the close-set tables.

"Where on earth have you two been?" Medina shouted. She hadn't started slurring her words yet, but Zoe guessed it wouldn't be long before she did. "Tony and I have been frantic worrying over you."

Zoe glanced up at Jason, silently willing him to keep quiet about her fainting episode. He didn't betray her.

"I was showing Zoe the view from the top deck of this little dinghy." He winked at Tony. "It was pretty breezy up there. We seem to have lost our drinks over the side." He shrugged.

Tony grinned, a perfect white smile splitting his dark mustache and goatee. "Well, we'll get you another, then." He rose and pulled out a chair. "Why don't you two ladies have a

103

seat? Jason and I will make a bar run."

Zoe's memory of the next half-hour was fuzzy. Jason brought her a plain Sprite, and she was glad. The sugar boosted her in a hurry, and by the time dinner was served, she was almost back to herself.

By seven o'clock, she was enjoying her sumptuous meal of prime rib and skewered shrimp. She hadn't realized how hungry she was. Although she tried not to eat like a ravenous animal, she caught Jason's amused sidelong glances as she shoveled forkfuls into her mouth.

"How are you doing there?" Jason murmured, leaning close to Zoe's ear.

She nodded as she swallowed another bite of the succulent beef. "Good. Better now." Turning toward him, she smiled. "Thanks for your help up there."

She blinked, and something inside her stirred as she gazed into those impossibly blue eyes. He was studying her now with such . . . what? It seemed like genuine concern.

No way. Who am I fooling? He's probably just worried about the liability—for him or for his good buddy Tony.

Medina, she noticed, was beyond food. She'd pushed her shrimp around on her plate for a while, maybe even carved off a bite of the meat. But before Zoe finished eating, Medina had snuggled into Tony's armpit, dozing. He seemed to have no problem finishing off her plate after cleaning his own.

She noticed Jason start checking his watch about then, casting urgent glances Tony's way. *The Crystal Mess* had leisurely chugged all the way up the lake to Sagamore Island, navigated a wide turn, and was now headed back toward the village.

Jason was watching the shoreline intently. Zoe caught sight of the glass façade of Lakeview's Boathouse Restaurant at the same time he did.

"Tony, you've got to make a pit stop. Drop me off." Jason nodded toward his docks and stood, wiping his mouth with his napkin.

The minute Jason stood, Zoe panicked. It was the first time she'd not been physically connected to him all evening. She didn't feel faint anymore, just . . . vulnerable. He looked down and read the look on her face.

Reaching for her hand, he added, "And Zoe too."

Minutes later she and Jason stepped off the boat onto Lakeview's dock. As they said goodbye, Zoe hugged Medina, who was alarmingly unsteady. She locked eyes with Tony over Medina's shoulder and whispered, "Please, take care of her."

Tony nodded.

Time froze for a moment as they stood on the dock, watching Tony's luxury boat. The wind had abated some, and now the water rippled gently, sparkling against the long rays of the setting sun. *The Crystal Mess* chugged away, leaving behind a wide, undulating wake.

Jason said, "Come with me. I want you to see my place."

Zoe hesitated. She'd promised Jade she'd stop by to see if she needed help. But Jason was already off ahead of her, bounding up the steps beside the boathouse. He dragged her behind him, still clutching her hand. She gingerly tiptoed up the concrete steps on her still-bare feet, the horror-heeled shoes dangling from her free hand.

"Troy will stay if it's busy. I already texted him," Jason rumbled over his shoulder as if reading her mind.

Moments later, they arrived at the front door of Jason's cabin. Jason turned the key and the two tumbled inside, winded from the steep, uphill hike. Jason closed and locked the door behind them. Then he turned, taking Zoe's shoulders and drawing her to him.

He didn't hesitate long enough for her to resist, or think,

105

Claire Gem

or even complete another single breath. In one smooth motion, he pulled her body against his. He lowered his mouth to hers, his fingers tangling in her hair.

In that instant, time froze. She feared she might faint again. Out of breath from the climb, her heart already tapped against her ribs, but with Jason's warm breath on her face, it thudded even harder. His lips were warm and full, brushing softly against hers at first in a slow, back and forth caress.

He moved slowly, tentatively. Miraculously, Zoe's defensive instinct did not interfere. Not even when his tongue began a tender probing between her already parted lips. He deepened the kiss, his fingers trailing down her neck, over her back, to her waist.

Zoe's body reacted without her mind's permission. She arched against him, pressing her hips closer to his in an instinctive, feral reflex. Jason groaned, and the knot low in her belly caught fire. She moaned as his hands swept lower, cupping her bottom gently as he pressed his swelling groin against her.

She reached up then, stroking her palms over the hard muscles of his shoulders, warm and rigid under the crisp cotton of his shirt. His scent was intoxicating, spicy and new. Her body, frozen so long by fear and grief, was coming back to life, almost faster than she could believe. She literally vibrated with a hunger she thought she would never feel again.

How could this be? For so long, her heart had belonged only to David. He'd been her soul mate, her forever. The day they laid him in the ground, she swore she'd never feel that way about anyone ever again.

But this wasn't love. This was her body reacting, not her heart. A simple biological response to a physical need. Was that so bad? It certainly didn't feel bad. It felt . . . necessary.

106

Like water for thirst.

Even as her mind struggled with these new emotions, their embrace ended too abruptly. Jason pulled away, breathing hard. Panic and regret etched lines across his brow.

"I'm sorry," he gasped. "I know I shouldn't rush you."

"There you go apologizing again," Zoe said, the euphoria of these new sensations as addictive as a drug.

Don't stop.

She stroked her fingertips on the skin of his chest where his shirt buttons had come undone. "I think I'm okay with this, Jay."

But the panic in Jason's eyes didn't abate. He glanced down at his watch.

"I can't. Not now."

Zoe cocked her head. "Jade?"

"No," Jason said frantically. "Time. I only have seven minutes." He grabbed her hand and hauled her toward the staircase. "Come on. Hurry."

"Seven minutes for what?" Zoe had no choice but to stumble after him, up two flights of stairs.

She was out of breath and anxious when they reached the top, the final stairway ending before a narrow, closed door. Jason burst through the unlocked entrance. At first, she thought he was taking her to the attic.

Why the attic? This is weird . . .

She froze in the doorway as Jason reached forward into the dark. She heard a soft click.

A burst of colored lights scampered across a tabletop, flickering and flashing from stacks of rectangular boxes. The glimmering points brightened the dusk-darkened room with a carnival-like glow.

Zoe stood in the doorway, her jaw slack. Her eyes swept the tiny, cramped room. It looked like a storage unit for a defunct electronics store.

"What in God's name is this place?" Her question burst out before she could temper its tone. Jason turned, wearing the excited expression of a little boy with a secret.

"This is my hobby," he said. "I run a radio show. Dedications. You know, like Delilah, except nowhere near as popular as she is. Hell, I won't catch up to her fame for at least thirty years." He puffed out his chest and stood up to his full height, but ducked when he almost whacked his head on the ceiling beam. Reaching out his hand, he bowed theatrically. "Allow me to introduce myself. I'm Jason. Of Jason's Lair."

"Jason who? I thought your name was Rolland?" Zoe was confused, and for a minute considered the possibility she was having delusions.

He smirked but checked his watch again. "I'm a radio show host, Zoe. And my show starts in about forty-five seconds."

She watched silently as Jason rolled out the tall-backed leather chair and dropped into it. He grabbed a set of headphones off the table and pulled them down over his ears. He froze, waiting for the digital readout on his transmitter to flick from 7:59 to 8:00. Then he picked up the microphone. His voice—that incredible voice—rumbled into it.

"Good evening, all you lovers out there in the beautiful Adirondacks. Welcome to Jason's Lair." He reached forward to move a lever on the soundboard, and music rose to fill the tiny room.

Zoe burst out in hysterical laughter.

"Shhh." Jason spun to meet her eyes. His eyes twinkled, but he pressed his finger to his lips.

Zoe slammed her hand over her mouth, but she didn't fight him as Jason drew her down into his lap. She felt like a little girl again, full of wonder and surprise as she studied the bright lights and complicated buttons and levers on Jason's equipment.

"You? A love guru?" she whispered.

"Yeah, well, that's what all my fans think. In reality, I'm handing them a big old line of bullshit."

"So you're a love guru who doesn't have a clue about love?"

He chuckled, shaking his head as he rubbed one hand slowly up and down Zoe's back.

"Not a damned thing."

She nuzzled her face into the crook of his neck, breathing in his musky scent. This whole day had seemed like a dream. Minutes passed with Eric Clapton crooning softly in the air around them. Every muscle in Zoe's body melted to warm putty.

"Are you falling asleep on me, girl?" His voice was soft and deep. But he shifted upright in his chair and said, "My opening song is about finished, Zo. I'm gonna have to start taking callers."

Zoe reluctantly pulled herself to her feet, stretching like a cat and enjoying a good yawn. She was feeling content. She watched with smiling eyes as Jason donned his headphones and pushed another glowing button on one of the receivers. The light turned from red to green. Jason spoke in a low growl.

"Good evening, and welcome to Jason's Lair. What can I do for you this evening?"

To Zoe, the tinny voice echoing from the earphones sounded like a bug caught in a spider web. She couldn't make out the words, but Jason was staring straight ahead, listening intently to what the voice was saying.

For a minute, it seemed he'd forgotten Zoe was there.

She dropped into the empty chair in the room. The tiny attic space had been transformed into a full-blown radio studio, set up against a wall of glass. The view encompassed the entire southern lay of the Lakeview property.

The light of evening was fading, but Zoe could see all the cabins, her own Aspen, and the now inky surface of the water in the distance. A winding driveway that led to the restaurant, lined with iron lampposts. She blinked when, as she watched, the ornate globes flickered on.

Jason finished his call and moved the slider to raise the volume on the next song. He pushed back his earphones and swiveled his chair around to face her.

"I'm so sorry, Zoe. Terrible timing. But I have a boatload of paying sponsors. They wouldn't be too happy if Jason didn't show up in his lair on a Saturday night."

Zoe sighed and smiled. "Maybe it's better this way. Too much, too fast." Her smile was weak, convincing not even herself of her sincerity.

Jason reached for her again and pulled her into his lap. This time it was he who nuzzled into her neck. His hot breath fanned the fire within her, the stubble on his chin grazing her collarbone and sending electric shocks clear down to her core. He started planting chaste kisses on her skin, moving down along the neckline of her tee.

When his fingers traced the curve of her breast, she shuddered. But the tightening in her throat threw up a warning. The ghosts of her brutal violation—the ones that had kept Xavier's overtures to a single, chaste kiss—rushed up like foul smoke to choke her.

Center, she thought. Let go of the panic.

Reboot. Restore. Return to an earlier time.

She drew in a shuddering breath, but found herself grateful for the interruption of his radio show. Jason could only spend a few short minutes trailing his lips from her earlobe to the hollow of her neck and back before flashing his gaze up to check the clock. Zoe closed her eyes and tried to concentrate on the physical sensations. But the knot of panic in her gut remained.

Breathe. Feel. Live in the moment.

One muscle at a time, her body relaxed down into Jason's lap. His lips parted, and his innocent kisses became caresses from a warm, wet tongue. The tense ball in Zoe's chest softened, and then dropped lower. The tension reshaped itself, gradually melting into longing. Her breath quickened.

But the song was ending. Jason reached forward and pushed another button, releasing a pre-recorded string of advertisements. He pulled back, holding her shoulders. He was trembling, and beneath her, she could feel his arousal, hard and hot against her bottom.

"This is terrible, Zoe. I can't do a damn thing about this problem until after midnight."

Zoe giggled. "What problem? Are you a vampire, too?"

"I think you can feel my problem."

Zoe ran her fingers down over the sharp, angular lines of Jason's face. "It's been a very long time for me. And I don't know if I'm ready to—"

"I understand." Jason closed his eyes and slowly shook his head. He kissed her cheek, then her forehead. "Let's cool it down a bit. How about a cold bottle of water? I think we could both use one."

"Sure," Zoe replied. "In the kitchen?"

Zoe skipped down the two flights of stairs, slowing only when the dark space of the kitchen gave her pause. She fumbled along the wall until she found the light switch. A bright glow bathed the modern space from an elaborate trestle pendant hanging over the island.

Jason's cabin was a larger replica of where Zoe was staying. The floor plan was almost identical, but twice the size. His kitchen, like the Aspen's, sported stainless steel appliances and granite countertops. The contrast was striking against the knotty pine cabinetry. The wide, plank flooring under Zoe's bare feet felt like cool, polished satin.

She pulled open the fridge and squinted inside, searching through what seemed like a month's worth of Styrofoam take-out boxes for bottles of water.

"Well, good evening, Red."

Zoe shrieked and spun around, one hand splayed against her chest. Jade was leaning on the other side of the island that separated the kitchen from the living room. One eyebrow was raised. The entire front of her pale yellow sundress was splattered with something red.

"Oh my God, you scared me to death." Zoe's initial horror disappeared fast, because she knew instinctively the red splotches were definitely not blood. She'd seen the real thing, she new what it looked like. "What happened?"

Jade hesitated a very long moment before answering. Her golden eyes looked even more like a cat's now, narrowed and a little wary. "A little accident with the Bloody Mary mix bottle. But that's not the question of the moment, now, is it?"

Zoe swallowed, her heart still pounding against her ribs.

Shit. This is not good. What have I done? They're together. Even if it *is* an open relationship.

"Jason brought me. To see his studio," she began, but as the words left her lips, her brain began to scramble what she wanted to say next. She'd lost her bearings. It was all suddenly too much. Fainting on the boat. The attraction she felt to Jason. Her friendship with Jade. "Out. Passed. Faint. Thirsty . . . and, and . . ."

She started to tremble violently, and Jade was suddenly

around the island, right beside her, an arm around her shoulders.

"It's okay, Zo. There's no problem here. Come sit down. I'll get you some water."

Zoe sat on the couch hugging her middle, rocking, tears streaming soundlessly down her cheeks. Jade sat down next to her, uncapping the water bottle. She held it out to her.

"Drink this, Zoe."

Jade's hand rubbed up and down her back. Condensation almost immediately coated the plastic bottle, and it felt good as Zoe rubbed it across her brow. After a few more measured breaths, she glanced at the woman sitting beside her.

The angry gleam was gone from Jade's eyes. She looked at Zoe and smiled.

"Better now?"

Zoe nodded. "Sorry." She searched Jade's face, struggling to organize the words in her brain. "Friend. You . . . are . . . my friend." As long as she paused between each word, she was okay.

"That's right. And you are my friend, too. Nothing is going to change that." Jade's voice was calming, soothing. "I don't want you to get hurt here. You've already been hurt plenty enough for one lifetime."

Zoe drank from the bottle, draining it by half. "Better. I'm feeling better now."

"Are you sure?" Jade paused, frowning. Then she glanced down at her dress. "I'm going to change out of this mess. I'll be right back." She rose and disappeared behind a door beside the massive fireplace.

So she lives here with him. My God, how awkward. And here I am making the moves on her . . . what? Boyfriend? Roommate with benefits? No matter. I'm a pretty crappy friend to even consider what I'm doing.

By the time Jade returned, her heart had returned to a normal rhythm. She stood when she heard the door reopen.

"Jade, I'm so sorry. I never meant to—"

"There is nothing for you to be sorry about, Red. Jason and I have no secrets. He likes his women. It's you I'm worried about." Jade stepped close and held her shoulders, studying her face. "You sure you're okay now?"

"Yes, I'm fine. The episodes don't last long. But it's embarrassing when they happen."

"I'm sorry I brought it on. I didn't mean to startle you," Jade said. She glanced up at the clock over the fireplace. "I told Troy I'd only be a minute. I have to get back." She turned to leave, pausing in the doorway. "It's none of my business what you do, or Jason either. Share your body with him if you want. But don't trust that boy with your heart. He goes through women like a drunk goes through wine."

Zoe sat on the couch for a long time after Jade left. What a strange relationship those two have. There must be more to it than meets the eye. They can't possibly be lovers.

If they are, then I've just gotten permission from Jade to share Jason.

A shiver ran across her shoulder blades. That was plain weird, in her world. Maybe not in Medina's, but certainly in hers.

But maybe this was exactly what she needed. Causal, noncommittal sex. She certainly wasn't ready for anything more than that, and she'd felt frozen for so long. Would that free her?

Maybe. Her body had come back to life tonight. Her inner stirrings, longings, and natural instincts for coupling had been buried too long. But their revival scared her to death. Zoe had never had a casual sexual relationship in her life. She'd never simply had sex—she'd always made love.

What did Medina call her? The good Catholic girl. Yeah, well, she had been. And even in today's free sexual environment, she'd managed to hold onto her virginity until she'd met David, and knew he was the one. She didn't know how to have sex, just how to make love.

I need some time to think about this. I have to be sure this is what I want.

The rumble of footsteps on the stairs made her turn. Jason was wild-eyed.

"What happened? I was worried maybe you cut out on me."

Zoe stood and walked straight into Jason's embrace. "I'm sorry. Jade came in."

"Oh, shit."

"No, it's okay. We talked. She's okay."

Jason kissed the top of Zoe's head. "Look, baby, I hate to do this, but a three-minute song was the longest one I had."

Zoe chuckled. "I'll get your water. Go on up."

Jason tried to convince her to stay until his show ended. But she decided it was best for her to go back to her own cabin, rest, do a little soul-searching.

"Will I see you tomorrow?" Jason asked.

She sent him a sly smile. "We have some business to discuss. When's that conversation happening?"

"I'll come by and take you to breakfast."

Jason watched Zoe's silhouette fade and reappear as she strolled down the sidewalk in the darkness, moving from the light of one globe to the next. Those sexy shoes were swinging from her hand, and when she reached the steps to the Aspen, she stopped and turned, standing in a circle of light to wave. He waved back, even though he knew she couldn't see him.

An image flashed in Jason's mind.

A red-haired girl, swaying her straight, little-girl hips as she strolled down the docks past him, her flip-flops dangling from one hand.

Is there such a thing as fate? Is it possible that this woman was meant for me all along?

Jason hadn't been kidding when he told Zoe he knew nothing about love. In truth, he didn't believe he had the capability. His father didn't. Maybe that was why he had taken on this radio gig. He'd been looking for a way to experience the emotions without any of the risks. Maybe, by listening to other people's love stories, he could learn something about how love works. If it ever does.

More often, the callers and their situations only convinced him that in most cases, it doesn't. At least, not for very long.

Sex was easy. Fun. Rewarding, even if only for a few hours at a time. Jason never had time to get tired of one woman. Summers in upstate New York were short. Vacations ended. Women went back to their real lives, and likely forgot about him more quickly than he did them. Besides, he couldn't keep his foot out of his mouth long enough to secure a long-term relationship anyway.

But this one was different. This woman struck a chord inside him he didn't even know existed. Okay, so the foot-in-mouth syndrome was still there, but she didn't seem deterred by it. At least not yet.

Zoe was an enigma, sending mixed signals that messed with his head. On the surface, she was a spitfire, strong-willed and stubborn, but she was also sweet and very vulnerable. He wanted to spar with her and protect her at the same time.

But maybe there was something more to her allure. Was it because she was part of some lost childhood memory? Glimmers of a time in his life when he was carefree and happy, hopeful for the future? Maybe she brought back to him the boy he'd been before he witnessed the irreparable damage love is capable of. He saw what love had done to his mother.

Anything more significant than a fling scared Jason to death.

Jason watched as a tiny Zoe disappeared behind the door of her cabin. He realized that there'd been a tiny Zoe living in the depths of his memory all these years.

Somehow he also knew, no matter how this summer ended, there would be a tiny Zoe living inside his head for the rest of his life.

Chapter 8

Zoe was more than a little surprised when she stepped inside her cabin and the light was on in the upstairs hallway. She called out for Medina. Silence. But a moment later, the bulky figure of Tony Diali stepped out into the balconied hallway.

"I'm awfully sorry, Zoe. I figured I'd be gone by the time you got in. Medina needed some help getting up the stairs tonight." Tony started down the steps, his leather sandals clapping loudly on each wooden riser.

Zoe frowned and crossed her arms over her chest. "I could tell she was headed in that direction at dinner. She was having too good a time."

Tony reached ground level, and then sauntered over to lean on the kitchen island. "Tell me something, Zoe. You seem to know Medina pretty well. What's her deal? I mean, I like her. A lot. And I know she's a wild child, but I somehow get the feeling she's not as shallow as she puts on."

Zoe studied Tony, whose expression was almost fatherly. He was older than Medina, a certain switch for her since she tended to go for younger men. But hell, neither of them knew this guy very well. How much could she confide in him?

"I suppose the obvious question here is, why do you care?" Zoe tried not to sound bitchy. But Medina was her best friend. She was protective of her.

Tony cleared his throat, pulling on his short, dark beard.

"Look. I know you have absolutely no reason to trust me. We've only just met, and you don't know me at all. I can assure you, I'm a good guy. I'm a cop. A clean one. And I've got to be honest. Medina has about knocked me off my feet."

Zoe blinked. Soft words coming out of this large, tough-looking man. Disconcerting.

He dropped his gaze to the floor, and didn't say anything for a minute. When he looked up, his gaze locked with Zoe's. "If she's the woman I think she is hiding under that party-girl exterior, I've been looking for her for a long time."

Zoe paused. How does one describe the real Medina?

"Medina is a paradox. Her family is very traditional Hispanic. She's the youngest daughter."

Tony nodded. "Okay, that makes sense. She's sowing her oats while she can." Another long pause. "Does she always drink like this?"

"No, that's the strange part. I don't think I've ever seen her let loose quite like tonight. She likes her pretty pink cocktails, but she usually drags one out so long I'm afraid it'll evaporate before she gets it down."

Tony stared down at the floor, thoughtful, still tugging on his goatee. "Well, I've intruded on your privacy enough this evening. My apologies. But I wanted to be sure she got home safe."

"And I'm grateful to you for doing that."

"Tell Dina to give me a call in the morning. Once she's feeling up to it, that is." He said goodnight and quietly shut the door behind him.

After Zoe threw the deadbolt, she picked up her shoes and trotted up the stairs. The door to Medina's room was still open. She turned to pull it closed when she heard Medina's muffled voice.

"I'm sorry, Zoe. I know I promised I wouldn't bring

anybody back to the cabin with me, but it wasn't like that," she mumbled, her face half buried in the pillow.

Zoe stepped into the room and sat down on the edge of the bed. She laid her hand on Medina's arm. "Sounds more like *Tony* brought *you* back to the cabin. Got a little carried away tonight, huh?"

Medina groaned and turned her face farther into the pillow. "Yeah, guess I did. I don't know what's gotten into me. I usually hold it together because I know I have to stay in control. But Tony, he makes me feel so . . . safe."

"He seems like a nice guy. But don't assume too much, Dina. People act a lot differently when they're on vacation, out of their element. Believe me, if I could repeat some of the stories from my clients' lives, you'd be blown away."

After a few moments with no response, Zoe realized that her friend had passed out again.

Poor thing. She's gonna have one hell of a head-banger in the morning.

Zoe softly closed the door behind her and headed for her own room, turning out lights as she went. It was still fairly early, but she couldn't wait to shed her too-tight clothes, and step under the hot spray of her shower. Her romance novel lay on the bed where she'd left it.

Yes, that will be a great way to spend the rest of this evening.

Then she spotted the clock radio. She plopped down on the edge of the bed and turned it on.

There he was, humming out of the tiny speakers. So it *was* Jason she'd heard the other night. Zoe smiled and shook her head. Who would have ever imagined?

His voice was almost as sexy through those crappy little speakers as it was in person. He was offering condolences to some lovesick girl who was crying through the anniversary of her divorce. And he sounded different . . . like, genuinely concerned. Even sensitive, maybe.

Nah. Must be his radio persona. A really good acting job.

Still, Zoe was disappointed when the call ended, and music replaced Jason's purring growl.

She hurried through her shower, hoping she wouldn't miss his next call. She was anxious and giddy. Silly, like a teenager hoping for a glimpse of her favorite star. Still dripping but wrapped in a plush towel, Zoe padded out of the bathroom in time to hear Jason deferring to *a word from our sponsors.*

She slipped between the crisp sheets, still nude and slightly damp. The radio hummed quietly beside her on the nightstand. The glowing digital numbers reminded her of the ones in Jason's studio.

The memory of his touch came back to her then. His strong arms around her, cradling her body on the boat as she awoke from her faint. His firm grip on her bottom as he pulled her toward him, kissing her inside the door of his cabin. His insistent, searing-hot tongue exploring her mouth.

She shivered, imagining the way his jaw had scraped along her collarbone, and how the trail of his wet tongue had set her insides on fire. The hot ball of desire sat low in her belly. Between her legs, she throbbed for relief.

It had been a very, very long time since she'd felt this way.

She picked up the paperback, but the letters on the page might as well have been written in Latin. No, she wouldn't be sated from generic, erotic descriptions on a page. Not tonight. She snapped off the bedside lamp.

Zoe listened patiently for Jason's voice to rumble again over the airwaves. She turned the volume down low, so she could hear him, but not make out his words. She would indulge in her own private fantasy.

Her body was coming back to life. It was hungry. She needed to feed it.

Reaching down with trembling fingers, she found the warm silkiness between her thighs. Achingly sweet proof. Yes, she was still a whole woman. Damaged, perhaps. But obviously still capable of arousal.

The first time since before that night. She'd not felt this way since her last time with David.

The songs playing between Jason's conversations with callers were simply stepping stones, allowing her to climb very slowly. Every time she heard his voice, her heart tapped faster, her fingers moved more rhythmically. Yet seconds before her pleasure surged over the edge of control, another song broke the wave.

She could still smell him. The crisp linen of his shirt. The clean, musky scent of his body. How would it feel to have that stubble on his jaw scrape lower on her neck, on her shoulders, over her nipples? She ran her fingertips over her own hard peaks, one at a time. They were erect, taught and stippled. She gasped for breath, and small moans escaped from her throat.

Then, a soliloquy. She didn't know if Jason's lengthy talk was scripted, or freelance, or simply a clever ploy to steal time while he decided what song he would play next. It didn't matter, since she couldn't understand his words anyway. But her body heard him, loud and clear.

The wetness between her legs slicked the inside of her thighs, leaving the sheet under her sticky and damp. In her mind, she imagined Jason's face, felt his breath on her neck, tasted the hot sweetness of his mouth. She imagined his tongue, firm and demanding, dancing with hers. Teasing her nipples. Probing lower, and deeper.

Unable to contain the floodgates any longer, Zoe's hips

bucked against her hand. Her whole body tensed and shuddered as the wave crashed over her.

She climaxed with such intensity, by the time the pulsating pleasure subsided she was quietly sobbing.

Why? It went beyond physical relief. It was nice to know her sexuality wasn't beyond redemption. A little sadness pressed itself onto her heart, like a gauze pad blotting an open wound. The last time she'd experienced an orgasm was the night before her husband was murdered.

And the song on the radio played on. Marvin Gaye's classic, *Sexual Healing*.

Zoe awoke to the chiming of a bell she thought at first was her alarm clock. She opened her eyes, disoriented. Nothing was familiar. No, this was not her apartment.

Bright light leaked in around the edges of the blackout curtains she'd drawn the night before. The cabin. She was in the Aspen, the cabin at the lake. The ringing sounded again.

Doorbell. That must be the doorbell.

She pulled on her robe and shuffled barefoot into the hallway. Her mouth tasted like damp old newspaper, and she knew her hair probably looked like the Bride of Frankenstein's. There was no way she was answering the door in this state. But she was curious, and figured she might catch a glimpse of the visitor from the window.

Before she reached the stairs, she heard a muffled groan from Medina's room.

"You okay in there, chica?" Zoe knocked softly, and waited. In a second, another moan sounded. Then she heard Medina's muffled request.

"Zo, can you bring me some water? And some aspirin, please?"

By the time Zoe reached the foot of the stairs, the doorbell had quit ringing. She pulled aside the drapes a smidgen, and caught sight of Jason, trotting down the steps away from her cabin.

Damn. Breakfast. She'd said she'd have breakfast with him. What the hell time was it, anyway?

Zoe started a pot of coffee, and carried an icy bottle of water up the stairs. She'd have to retrieve aspirin from her cosmetic bag on the way. Medina's door was partway open. She slipped in, and heard the shower running. She left the water and the aspirin bottle on Medina's nightstand.

Might as well grab my own shower.

She turned on the spray and dropped her robe, standing in front of the vast expanse of mirror. Reaching up to lift her hair off her face, she yawned and stretched.

She felt good. As good as she could remember feeling in a long time. Leaning closer to her reflection, she took inventory.

Her body was curvy, rounded, but smooth and firm. Her breasts tipped upward still, her stomach still flat. She was thirty-two, but didn't feel like her body had yet yielded that admission.

No lines around her eyes or mouth. A good thing. The circles that had persisted under her eyes for the longest time now were suddenly . . . gone. Even the scar didn't look as angry this morning. Pale and pink, it resembled a gossamer ribbon cascading down the side of her face.

Almost . . . pretty.

Wow. Either this mountain air is intoxicating, or Jason slipped some kind of drug into my water last night.

A half-hour later, Zoe smelled the enticing scent of fresh-brewed coffee wafting up the stairs. She chose crisp, cream linen shorts and a Kelly green, silk tank. She almost never wore jewelry, since it drew people's gaze to her face. But today, she was feeling reckless. She chose a short necklace of polished stones in shades of coral and green, clasping it around her neck. She'd bought it on a whim the day she and Jade had gone shopping down in Glens Falls.

When she came out into the hallway, there was no sound coming from Medina's room.

She probably needs to let the aspirin take effect and sleep another few hours.

Her sandals made a soft tapping sound as she trod down the stairs.

A steaming mug in hand, Zoe was about to flop onto the loveseat near the fireplace when she spied a folded square of paper on the floor, apparently having been slipped under the door. She retrieved the note, scribbled in a typical male's messy hand on Lakeview stationary.

When you're up and about,
come down and join me for breakfast.

Jay

Zoe smiled.

If Jason knew about my fantasy last night, he probably wouldn't have waited until morning to knock on my door.

No harm in making him wait a little longer. She tucked her legs up on the loveseat and leisurely enjoyed her coffee.

She hadn't felt this good in years. Naturally, her session last night had relieved some pent up sexual energy. But Zoe didn't think she'd had any of that left to release. She'd crammed that part of herself into a dark closet three years ago, and hadn't freed it since. The thought of sex had, up until only a few days ago, made her physically nauseous.

Medina may well have been right. Living the same life, stuck in the same routine, hadn't allowed her to exorcise the ghost of her rape. In order to move forward, she had to go back and start over again.

When she rose to refill her mug, she poured one for Medina as well. She carried the cup up the stairs and knocked on Medina's closed door.

"Com'on in, Zo." Medina sounded a whole lot better than she had an hour earlier. When she pushed open the door she found her friend standing next to the bureau with a towel wrapped around her head. She was wearing nothing but a hot pink bra and bikini panties.

"Hey, thanks for the aspirin. It's helping my head already, I think. That and the long shower."

Zoe set Medina's coffee on the bureau. "And here's some java to help you along. You gonna be up to a trip to the outlet mall later like we planned?" She giggled, watching her woozy friend try to maintain her balance.

Medina was standing on one foot, trying to slip the other into the leg of bright red shorts. Failing for the second time, she grabbed the edge of the bureau, and then dropped the shorts to grab her toweled head with both hands. Wincing, she replied, "I should be all right in a couple of hours. It's still early, right?"

"Half past ten. I'm going down to grab some breakfast. Want something?" Zoe asked.

Medina winced again and scrunched her eyes shut, gingerly shaking her head.

"Noo, ma'am. Thanks for the coffee, though. I'd better start with that and see how it goes."

Jason sat at his usual corner table in the restaurant, a glass of orange juice on one side, steaming coffee on the other. He'd pushed his unused plate away to the center of the table and was riveted to the glowing screen of his tablet.

The Boathouse Restaurant was quiet, especially for a Sunday. The locals sometimes showed up on a sunny, summer morning for breakfast. But today, it seemed, everyone had made other plans.

Jason squinted at his list of emails. He had been playing monkey in the middle between a client from Germany who was interested in buying a vacant restaurant near the Albany airport and the property's owner. The negotiations had been going on now for almost two weeks. Jason pressed his lips into a line as he read the latest response from the potential buyer.

Not going that high. Offer firm.

He shook his head and swore, dropping his forehead against his hand. He closed the cover on the tablet and stared out at the lake. The water looked lazy this morning, undulating gently against an almost non-existent breeze. Jason blinked against the occasional flash of reflected sunlight.

He was anxious, but he knew it wasn't from worry over losing this deal. It was the woman. The one whose warm body had felt so good in his arms. Whose taste and smell had him thinking about her all last night. The one who'd caused the need for his cool shower before he could sleep.

He glanced down at his watch, wondering if Zoe would show up? Had he scared her off? Had Jade said something to warn her away?

And why the hell should he care? What made this one different from any other of his brief encounters over the past years?

Jason rose and carried his mug to the wait station, helping himself to another cup. It was nearing eleven o'clock. If Zoe didn't show up by the time he'd finished this one, she probably didn't intend to.

He turned and saw her then, standing in the doorway. She was scanning the few occupied tables, her brows drawn slightly together. She didn't see him. He watched as she eyed his usual table in the front corner, where his tablet and half-empty glass of juice remained. She approached the table and stood there, gazing out through the glass at the brilliance of the lake.

"Good morning," he said as he came up behind her. "Did you sleep well?"

Zoe turned, and when their eyes met, Jason's breath caught in his throat. She looked like a goddess. She was soft and curvy and glowing. The green color of her blouse matched her eyes, making them seem iridescent. The morning sun streaming in danced on her hair like it did on the water, sending flashes of gold light around her.

She was the most beautiful woman he'd ever seen.

A smile tugged at one corner of her mouth, and he couldn't tell if her expression was tentative or cynical.

"I slept very well," she answered, "even though I listened to your show until almost midnight." Her grin spread, lighting up her whole face.

Jason cleared his throat, blinking, feeling as though he'd just woken up. He looked down at the mug in his hand. He'd forgotten he was even holding it. He raised his eyes along with the mug. "Coffee? I'm on about my twelfth cup."

Zoe chuckled.

He pulled out a chair for her and motioned for her to sit.

"You look fantastic this morning. Certainly a lot more color in your cheeks than you had on Tony's boat last night."

Her smile grew mischievous. "I slept better last night than I have in a very long time," she said, drawing every word out very slowly.

Hmm. Wonder what that means?

"Mountain air, maybe?" Jason sat and grabbed his tablet, setting it down on the empty chair beside him. "So what will it be this morning? Are you the bacon and eggs type? Or something sweeter? Claude does amazing French toast."

Too impatient to wait for the sole breakfast waitress, Jason went back into the kitchen himself to put in Zoe's order. He brought back a tray holding juice, a bowl of chunked fruit, and a cup of coffee. Again, he found her staring out the window across the lake.

"I usually don't serve, so be prepared to move fast if I get clumsy," he said as he unloaded the tray. His hands were shaking, and he almost sloshed juice all over the white tablecloth.

What the hell is the matter with me? I feel like I'm back in high school. A goofy kid with a crush.

Jason fumbled through the rest of the order and plopped down in his chair. Zoe apparently hadn't noticed his jitters. She was still staring out the window.

"What's on the other side of the lake?" she asked. "It looks like all trees."

"The eastern shore is mostly privately owned. It's tough land to develop, since the shore is even steeper than on this side. It's mostly woods."

Zoe was studying him and it made him even more nervous. "You obviously must know all about developing land," she said. He heard that cynical edge in her voice again.

"I do. Besides running this place, and the radio show, real estate is the only business I've ever known."

Now why the hell did I tell her that? The last thing I want to do is bring up that sensitive subject this morning.

Before Zoe could react, Jason hurried on. "I know the guy that owns some of that land, on the other side," He nodded toward the window. "Why don't you let me take you over there this afternoon? I have an ATV. A four-wheeler. It's pretty fun."

Unable to keep his hands still, Jason picked up the bowl of fruit and scooped some out onto his plate. An errant chunk of pineapple rolled off the spoon and onto the table. "Shit," he mumbled. Then he held the bowl up toward her. "Fruit?"

Zoe nodded.

"So you'll go with me then? What time should I pick you up?"

"No," Zoe laughed as she reached for the bowl. "Yes to the fruit, but no to the ride in the woods. Medina and I are going shopping this afternoon."

Damn. But today is Sunday. The stores close early on Sunday.

"How about later, when you get back? It stays light until at least eight o'clock. Why don't you meet me at my cabin around six?"

Before Zoe could answer, their food arrived.

"Thanks, Rhonda. You're alone this morning. Callie call in?" Jason asked. The tall, painfully thin woman carrying the tray shot him a knowing look.

"How'd you guess?"

He arched an eyebrow. "Because she seems to call in sick lots of Sunday mornings, from what Jade tells me."

When she left them with their steaming plates, Jason slid his gaze toward Zoe. "It's so hard to get dependable wait staff. I guess Jade's told you all about that." He caught Zoe's smirk as she drizzled syrup on her French toast.

"She has. But Jade seems to think that's mostly your fault," she said.

Can't that woman stay out of my business and keep her mouth shut?

He sighed and pinched the bridge of his nose. "I guess I

do have sort of a track record."

"From what Jade tells me, you've got as many notches on your headboard as there are trees on that shore over there." Zoe's voice was almost singsong, and made Jason cringe.

He looked across the table at her. She was happily feasting on Claude's excellent French toast, her gaze fixed on her breakfast. Jason's appetite had vanished. He pushed his plate away from the edge of the table and leaned there on crossed arms, watching her eat.

After a long moment, her eyes shifted up to meet his. She stopped chewing and asked, "What?"

"I wish Jade would mind her own damn business sometimes."

"How does that work with you two, anyway?" Zoe asked. "I mean, I get the feeling she's pretty possessive of you. And that you two are . . . close."

"Yeah, we're close. But we're certainly not little kids anymore." He watched Zoe's head tilt, the tiny furrow appear between her brows.

Does she think . . . ?

Jason snorted. "You don't know?"

Zoe put down her fork and lifted her napkin to catch a drizzle of syrup at the corner of her mouth. She looked genuinely confused, and Jason started to laugh out loud.

"What's so funny?" she asked, her tone indignant.

He reached across the table and laid his hand over hers. She snatched it away. Jason shook his head, unable to extinguish his grin.

No wonder she's hesitant about getting involved with me.

"Zoe, Jade isn't my girlfriend. She's my sister. My older, half-sister."

Chapter 9

Zoe found Medina sprawled on the back deck with her coffee. She slipped out through the glass door and didn't even bother with a preamble.

"You are never going to guess what I found out," she said, settling into the chair beside her friend.

Medina lifted her sunglasses and peeked out from under them, squinting. Her eyes were bloodshot, and even though they were sitting in the shade, it appeared Dina was still experiencing some sensitivity to light.

"Do tell," she grumbled, not sounding very interested at all.

"Aw, come on, Dina. I know you must feel like poop on a stick this morning, but you know, that's all your own fault." Zoe leaned forward and propped her elbows on her knees. "You never did meet Jade last night. She was the tall, black chick tending bar."

Medina waited in silence for a moment. "Okay, so what?"

"I thought she and Jason were a couple in some kind of 'open relationship.' "

One of Medina's eyebrows quirked and she gave a little head toss, causing her to wince in pain and lower her sunglasses. She cleared her throat. "Okay. Something wrong with that?"

"Nothing. Except if that was true, and I decide that Jason

is my fling prospect, that puts me in a bit of an awkward spot, don't you think? I mean, I'm staying here pretty much the whole summer. And I'm working with Jade."

At this, Medina snatched off her glasses and stared at Zoe. "Did you just say what I thought you said?"

Zoe leapt up and started pacing back and forth along the bricked patio, twisting her fingers in front of her.

"So that's who's lighting your fire, huh? I knew when I got here you had your eye on somebody." Medina sat up too fast, but then grabbed at her head. "Oh, shit. My head is killing me."

Zoe grimaced. "Sorry about that. But guess what I found out? If I do decide that Mr. Asshole Resort Owner is my chosen fling material," she added air quotes to this part, "I've got no problems. Jade and Jason are siblings. She's his older sister."

Medina tilted her head to one side. "Huh? How is that possible?"

"Same dad, different moms. Jade's mom is full-blooded Jamaican." She couldn't hide her glee at this discovery. As much as she'd been attracted to Jason, she'd felt so guilty last night when she found out he and Jade actually lived together.

Now, that wasn't an issue. No longer an impediment.

"So, you're going for it, right?" Medina asked, flipping her hands up. "He's hot, Zo. You're lucky, actually, that you got here first."

Zoe stopped pacing and flopped down in the chair. Should she? Could she?

Now, her only barrier would be her own hang-ups. Her own ghosts. It still scared her a little even thinking about what it might be like to get naked with a man again. Would she start babbling again? Have a panic attack? Faint?

But then she remembered how it went down last night.

She hadn't even stopped to think at all.

She leaned toward her friend and sought her eyes. "Dina, he makes me feel alive again. I couldn't even let Xavier kiss me goodnight. But with Jason, it's like my body makes decisions without asking my permission."

Medina smiled slyly and sank back against the lounger. She crossed her arms. "You know, your shrink had a pretty good idea sending you up here. I haven't seen you this excited in years." She winked. "Go for it, girl."

Zoe was surprised when an hour later, Medina said she was ready to go shopping. Of course, she could have predicted that. Her friend's third favorite thing to do, behind breathing and sex, was shopping. She did let Zoe drive this time, though. They headed for the same outlet mall where she'd gone with Jade that first weekend.

It wasn't long before she realized that Medina was on a mission, and none too subtly—to outfit Zoe for her fling. Every time she picked up a sweet feminine sundress, a pale pink tee shirt, or baby blue shorts, the corners of Dina's mouth turned down. Pastels, she told Zoe, were out of the question.

"You don't want to look all soft and feminine, Zo. You aren't going in for a long-term catch here," Dina insisted. "You want to show off what you've got. Get in, have fun, and get out. Before you get hurt."

When she said that, Zoe's heart did a little flip in her chest. That's exactly what Jade had said.

Share your body with him if you want to. But don't trust that boy with your heart.

Can I even do that?

"I've never tried separating the physical from the emotional, Dina. I don't know if I can."

Her friend turned on her, planting one fist on her cocked

hip. "You can, and you will. You have to. You're not ready for anything else, and we both know it."

Zoe scowled down at the stretchy, jet-black tank Medina was holding out to her. "And what am I supposed to wear on the bottom? Painted on pants? It's too long to even put a miniskirt under it."

Medina slammed one hand against her forehead and muttered an oath in Spanish. "Sweetie, this is a dress, not a tank top."

Oh. My dear. Short. Very short. This thing will barely cover the cheeks of my ass.

"We're not talking love here. We're talking lust. Here, try it on." Dina thrust the hanger into Zoe's hand. "You can't catch a lover if you don't put your wares on display."

They left the mall two hours later with several bags between them. Zoe was lightheaded and giddy, feeling totally out of her element. She'd bought things she would never in her lifetime have picked out for herself. Medina's bags clunked as she tossed them into the trunk. They contained mostly shoes—not one or two, but three new pairs of those skyscraper stilettos she so loved.

As they pulled back into the Lakeview parking lot, Zoe gasped and brought a hand to her mouth.

"Oh, Dina. I'm so sorry. Tony asked me to tell you to call him when you woke up this morning. I totally forgot. Don't be mad, 'kay?" She slanted a look in Medina's direction. She had a hell of a temper, Zoe knew. She'd never been unfortunate enough to rile it, and she didn't want to start now.

Her friend snorted. "No biggie. I probably wouldn't have called him until now anyway. No use looking too eager. We kinda made dinner plans for tonight already."

She breathed a sigh of relief.

Medina turned in her seat. "What are you doing for

dinner? You could join us if you want."

"Actually, Jason is taking me on a tour of the east shore of the lake." She slowed the big car to navigate the sharp curves in the steep driveway. "On that thing, I guess."

She slowed the car near Jason's driveway and tipped her head toward his jet-black Hummer. The small trailer hooked behind it held a dark green, four-wheeled vehicle that, to Zoe, looked like a cross between a lawn tractor and an Army jeep.

Medina squealed. "Ooh, that sounds like fun. Have you ever been on an ATV before?"

She shook her head. "Nope. You?"

"Nope. You'll have to fill me in on the experience. Make sure you wear those long pants you bought, though. The mosquitoes in those woods are as big as dragonflies," Medina said.

A surprised chuckle escaped Zoe. "How the hell would you know that, Miss New York City girl?"

Pulling up the hem of her red shorts, Medina pointed to a half-dozen, raised pink spots on her thigh.

"Tony owns a bunch of land over there. He took me on a personal walking tour that first night we met." Medina's grin was completely and totally evil.

They parked and tumbled in through the front door, tossing their packages down and flopping onto the loveseats. Zoe kicked off her sandals and reached down to rub her sore heels. Medina grabbed her phone and hit a button before holding it to her ear. After a brief conversation, she ended the call and smiled across at Zoe.

"Hey," she said. "Tony's not picking me up until five-thirty. We've got about an hour to kill. Why not break open that bottle of cold Zin we picked up?"

Tall mountains bring early sunsets, Zoe soon realized. The Aspen faced the lake, which meant the back patio faced west.

It wasn't even five yet, but the sun was already rimming the tops of the tall pines behind her cabin when she and Medina headed out with their chilled glasses.

When they'd settled in their chairs, Medina asked, "I guess I made a fool out of myself last night, huh?"

"You didn't do anything too bizarre," Zoe began, pausing. "But what got into you, Dina? It's not like you to get so drunk."

Medina sipped her wine and stared off into the darkening woods. "I dunno. I'm wondering that myself. Tony makes me feel so, I don't know, comfy," she said. She smiled across at Zoe. "I let down my guard. I guess that's not such a smart thing to do, huh?"

Zoe studied her friend's eyes. She saw something new in them. Something she'd not seen before. "I like Tony fine. Don't get me wrong. I just don't like to see you lose control like that."

Medina drew in a deep breath and sighed. "You know, Zo, I'm not getting any younger. I've been enjoying this free-spirited life for at least a decade now. But time's running out for me. I guess I'm starting to feel a little bit desperate."

"You aren't even thirty years old yet," Zoe said. You've got your whole life ahead of you."

Medina glared at her. "I know what life ahead of me holds. I don't have the options you do."

Zoe's shoulders slumped. Her friend's words stung, but no sooner had they left her lips than Medina covered her mouth with her hand. "Oh, Zo, I'm so sorry. I'm being so damned selfish here."

"Dina—" she began.

"This, I'm certain, is something you can understand. I'm scared, Zoe. I'm scared half to death. I think I might have met the man of my dreams, the man I want to spend the rest of my life with." Sudden tears glistened in Medina's eyes. "But that's not an option for me."

The buzzing of Medina's cell interrupted them. She glanced down at the display and scowled, then cast a helpless look toward Zoe before she answered.

"Hi, Papa."

Zoe felt like a little kid getting ready to climb on a carnival ride. She stepped up into the front seat of Jason's Hummer, studying the helmet he'd set on the floor between them. She chattered nonstop with questions.

"How fast does this AVT thing go? Is this a place where other people ride too? There's no chance we'll get lost, right?"

Jason laughed and held up one hand as he turned the key and the Hummer rumbled to life. "Whoa, whoa! Let me answer the first question before you fire out numbers two and three."

Zoe clamped a hand over her mouth, feeling foolish. "Sorry. I guess that glass of wine I had with Medina made me giddy."

"How is Medina, anyway? I'm assuming she got home okay."

"Tony brought her home. He was leaving when I got in last night. I think he probably had to carry her up the stairs," she said, shaking her head. She looked over at Jason. "Is Tony a good guy? You know him pretty well, right?"

"I do. In fact, it's his land we're going to buzz around on tonight. And yes, he's a very good guy. And it's ATV, by the way. All-Terrain Vehicle." He flashed one of his megawatt smiles, which zapped her like a taser. A most pleasant kind of taser.

Jason deftly navigated his huge vehicle, trailer in tow, through the downtown village of Lake George. In order to reach the east side, they had to follow the lake down to its south shore, where Tony's boats were docked. From there, they turned left on the road that hugged the east side of the mountain lake.

Zoe was amazed at how different the shore on this side was. "There's nothing here," she said as they followed the winding road through the dense woods.

"There are a few private homes in these first few miles."

"Where?" she asked. Although a mailbox or paved driveway dotted the roadway intermittently, no houses were visible from the road.

"I say homes, but they're really mansions. The driveways either snake down through the woods to the shore, or up into the steeper terrain on the other side of the road."

They had traveled about five miles when he slowed down and put on his left turn signal, though Zoe hadn't seen another car on the road with them. She also couldn't see where he intended to turn.

"Uh, where's the driveway?"

He slid his gaze toward her, one side of his mouth quirking. "You have a problem finding driveways, don't you?"

She narrowed her eyes, but before she could come up with a retort, the truck lurched. She gasped and grabbed for the strap over the door on her side. Jason had turned onto what appeared to be a widened path, thick with pine needles. The huge Hummer sank on the soft surface, and bounced when the wheels of the trailer dropped off the pavement.

"What the hell," she squeaked.

He shifted the truck into low gear, and they crept slowly down a steep hill along a trail she swore wasn't wide enough for his massive vehicle to fit on. She hung onto the ceiling strap with both hands now, squeezing her eyes shut when Jason zigged and zagged around a huge tree standing right in the middle of the path. The brakes whined as he braked. When she opened her eyes they were parked in a small clearing.

"We're here. Tony's land covers almost fifty acres on this side of the lake. C'mon. Let's go for a spin."

She stood aside and watched in awe as Jason climbed up onto the trailer, unfastened a strap or two, then lowered the tailgate to the ground. She giggled as he scrambled onto the four-wheeled monster, looking a little like a nimble monkey. The engine roared to life, and in one smooth motion he shifted into reverse and backed slowly down the ramp. Pine needles sprayed from under the tires as the rear wheels struggled to gain traction on the soft surface.

He grinned at her, and then twisted and patted the seat behind him. "Grab that helmet, Zo."

She retrieved the helmet out of the truck and brought it around to where he was standing next to the idling ATV. He took it from her and fiddled with the harness.

"Here. This should fit well enough now."

"Where's yours?" she asked as she slid the shiny black helmet over her hair.

"Tony borrowed it last weekend. I forgot to get it back from him." He bent to help her fasten the chinstrap, and she scowled at him. "Don't worry. When I ride alone, I usually don't bother with one anyway."

Although the seat didn't look like it was designed for two people, Jason showed her where to step up, on the foot rack on the side of the rumbling vehicle.

"You have to get on first. Then slide back and I'll get on."

She had to wrap her arms snugly around him to keep from sliding off the end of the slick leather seat. Her butt barely fit. And although she'd heeded Medina's warning about wearing long pants, she realized now that the thin, linen slacks she'd chosen didn't give her enough traction on the seat. They also didn't offer much insulation against the evening air, cooler in the shadowy pine forest.

The next hour, for Zoe, was surreal. She'd never experienced anything like this before in her life. Growing up in a crowded suburb on Long Island, riding anything smaller than a full-size car was dangerous. Bicycles were best confined to the trails and parks. That, and since she was an only child, she didn't have the advantage of tagging along on a big brother's escapade. As pine-scented air blew in her face, Zoe wondered if she'd ever felt this alive.

Jason navigated the sure-footed vehicle along a trail almost obscured beneath a thick layer of needles and dead leaves from last winter. In some places, the tall, narrow-trunked pines grew so close together that the light was all but blocked out. In other areas, broad-trunked maples stood farther apart, allowing more sunlight to filter to the ground. Here, where the underbrush grew thick and matted, they traveled through a leafy tunnel.

In the midst of one of these clearings, Jason turned the key and the engine died. They coasted a ways down the slope before he brought the four-wheeler to a slowly rolling stop. Silence fell over them like a heavy blanket. He didn't say anything, and made no move to dismount. Zoe, reluctant to give up the warmth of his body against hers, sat still and gazed at the scene around her.

The few, long bands of golden light from the setting sun slanted through the branches, falling to the leafy carpet in bright, scattered patches. Dust particles kicked up by the knobby tires floated in the shafts of light, sparkling like glitter. The scent of pine mixed with the dusty scent of dead leaves.

What a change, from the ever-present cloud of diesel

fumes choking the streets back home.

After a few quiet minutes, she whispered, "My God, Jason, this is breathtaking."

Jason reached down and grabbed her hand at his waist as he softly breathed, "Shhhh." Then Zoe realized why.

Ahead, at the edge of the clearing, Bambi stood staring at them. The fawn was tiny, her sides still splotched. She was so close to them, Zoe could almost count the white spots. It appeared she'd staggered to her feet from a dead sleep. She stood like a statue except for a slight swaying, like a statue someone had bumped into. Her eyes were huge, black pools rimmed with a lush, golden fringe. She blinked at them, her velvety muzzle quivering at their strange scent.

Zoe stared, holding her breath, but the frozen moment didn't last long. Two larger deer bounded out into the edge of the clearing with no more sound than a single twig snapping. The largest carried a huge rack of antlers. They didn't stop, but bound past the baby fawn, who turned and followed. In an instant, all Zoe could see were three white tails disappearing over the tops of the bushes.

When Jason turned, she gazed up at him, her eyes brimming with unshed tears.

"These woods are filled with deer. Tony doesn't allow any hunting. He actually brings sacks of corn down in the winter to feed them," he said. With one finger he caught a tear that spilled onto her cheek. "What's the matter, pretty lady?"

"They're so incredibly beautiful. The only deer I've ever seen were in a zoo. It's not the same."

Jason smiled and kissed her cheek. "No, it's not the same." He turned and started the vehicle. "Let's go down to the water before we lose the light."

The terrain near the water's edge was very steep. She squeezed her eyes shut and clung tighter around him as the big tires slid sideways in places where the needled bed was thick. When they finally reached the bottom, Jason pulled up beside a wall of rock, one that appeared to shoot straight up out of the ground about six feet from the edge of the water. He climbed off first and turned to help Zoe down.

They were standing on solid granite. It seemed as though a giant knife had cut the rock cleanly in an L-shaped step right at the lake's edge. Jason unsnapped her helmet and slid it off, propping it on the seat of the four-wheeler.

Reaching for his hand, she crept closer to the shoreline and peered over the edge. The water was crystal clear, and she couldn't tell if it was a reflection she was seeing, or if the rock actually continued down in a flat wall beneath the surface.

"This is a stone wall that goes down at least thirty feet before leveling off," Jason said, as though he'd read her mind. "Amazing what the glaciers did all those years ago. When I was a kid, I used to snorkel over here. The granite under the water is as smooth as a polished countertop."

Small schools of fish darted silently just under the surface. The only sounds were the soft lapping of water against the rock, and an ever-increasing chorus of crickets from the woods behind them. Her hand felt warm in Jason's, even though the air was rapidly chilling. The sun began to dip beneath the trees of the opposite shore.

Reboot. Restore to an earlier time.

It was happening.

Jason turned, cupping her face. His hands smelled vaguely like leather and oil, a strangely appealing, masculine scent. She tipped her head back, unafraid now her scar would show.

I've seen it, he'd said. You don't have to hide your scars from me.

His eyes glittered in the last rays of the sinking sun. They were clear and blue and intense, probing deeply into hers and sending a thrill through her that made her knees wobbly. Very slowly, he lowered his head and covered her mouth with his.

This was a very different kiss. Gone was the hungry urgency of last night. Zoe melted into the warmth of his breath, the softness of his lips on hers. He seemed in no hurry to taste her. With chaste, tickling brushes of lips against skin, he pressed his mouth to her cheek, her chin, the edge of her jaw. His hands smoothed over her shoulders and down her back. Zoe's breath and heartbeat came faster as the moment stretched out, as though time itself was slowing down.

She swayed, and Jason pulled away, his eyes filled with concern.

"You okay?"

She smiled, nodding. "Very okay."

Tipping his head, furrows appeared between his dark brows. He trailed one finger along her jaw to tuck a strand of hair behind her ear. His blue gaze, so intense on hers, reflected more than desire. One corner of his mouth twitched, and he swallowed.

This is Mr. Super Ego? He looks more like an uncertain, worried little boy rather than a heartless playboy.

When his hands slid back down to rest on her shoulders, she felt him trembling.

"Cold?" she asked. Although she'd been thoroughly chilled when they first stopped, her entire body flushed now with warmth that radiated from the inside out.

He shook his head, never taking his eyes off hers. "Far from it. I don't know what you do to me, lady. You undo me." His voice rumbled so low she almost hadn't heard him. As though he didn't mean for her to hear.

144

Zoe wasn't sure if or how she should respond. The moment, for her, was intensely physical. There was no denying the clutching in her chest when she looked into his eyes. But the ball of heat dropped steadily into her lower belly, one she recognized and welcomed like a long lost treasure. Her intense sexual attraction to this man, combined with newly opened floodgates on her comfort level, was like gasoline on a campfire.

Medina's words echoed in Zoe's mind.

We're not talking love here. We're talking lust. You're not ready for anything else, and we both know it.

A shudder of anticipation chased between her shoulder blades. The sun had dropped below the trees now, with night falling fast. Jason pulled her against his hard, muscled chest and ran his fingers through her hair.

"You're cold, though. And we'd better get out of these woods before dark."

They rode in silence back up the steep bank. She kept her face buried against his back, her arms in a death grip around his waist. She held her breath, swaying with the motion as the knobby tires slipped and spun in the loose footing. By the time they reached the truck, the woods were almost full dark.

The lights of the Hummer created a haloed oasis in the blackness. Jason worked fast, driving the ATV up the ramp and securing the straps. She stood watching, her arms wrapped around herself. Her skin was cool, but inside, a slow simmer made her anxious. Her breathing was still rapid and shallow.

Could she do this? Dare she even try?

In her mind, she bundled all the fear, all the pain and anguish she'd suffered into a big, knotted ball, and then pushed it into a pit with a heavy, metal lid. She almost heard the cover clang shut.

145

When Jason got into the truck she slid across the bench seat to snuggle into his side. Once they were out on the paved road, he lifted one arm and wrapped it around her.

"That was so much fun," she whispered. "Thank you for taking me."

He cuddled her closer to his side. "We'll do it again."

When she laid her head against Jason's chest, the steady, rapid beat of his heart told her he wanted her as much as she wanted him. She trailed her fingers down his chest, toying with the chest hair peeking out from the open placket of his shirt. He growled deep in his throat.

"You keep that up and we might not make it all the way back to the cabin."

The five-mile trip seemed like a hundred. Finally, he pulled into his driveway and killed the lights, and then the engine. He paused long enough to take a deep, shuddering breath. Then, he shifted in his seat and pulled her into his arms.

Chapter 10

Jason buried his face in her hair. She smelled like the forest, piney and fresh, mingled with the scent of his own shampoo from wearing his helmet. A little thrill gripped his throat, smelling something of himself on her.

Like she was his. He wanted her to be his.

He kept his kisses slow and gentle, starting on her cheek, following the line of her scar from her temple to her lips. Brushing across her mouth, he trailed his tongue along her jawline to her other ear, nipping at the lobe. Shudders ran through her when he nuzzled her neck.

She was breathing fast, and her pulse tapped rapidly against his cheek. His restraint was wearing thin. Her hands were moving through his hair, down his shoulders, across his chest. When his lips found hers, his control evaporated. He slid his tongue between her parted lips and began his exploration of this woman who had, somehow, woven a spell over him.

The kiss was long and warm and wet, and she tasted familiar, yet excitingly brand new. Their tongues tangled in a dance of tenderness touched with the urgency he sensed building in her. Her eagerness set his loins on fire.

"Let's go inside. Before I can't walk anymore," he gasped,

147

pulling away and gazing into her eyes. They glowed in the light from the porch lamp, twinkling with mischief.

"Do you mean, because of this little problem?" Her hand strayed to the throbbing bulge in his jeans. "Oh. Not such a little problem at all." Her fingers began an agonizingly sweet dance against his erection. He shifted and moaned.

"I'm not kidding, Zo. If I don't get this damned denim straightjacket off, I'll explode, right here under your hand."

He pushed open the car door and dragged Zoe out the driver's side behind him, one arm hooked around her waist. When they got to the door, he pulled his keys from his pocket, dropping them twice in his attempt to fit them into the lock with fumbling fingers. She started giggling.

By the time they stepped inside and locked the door behind them, they were both laughing. He turned toward her and put a finger to his lips, and then checked his watch. He called out, "Jade? You home?"

Silence. He tiptoed across the room and tapped on Jade's door. No response.

He dragged her behind him, still giggling, up the stairs and into his room. In one smooth movement he kicked the door shut and wrapped his arms around her, lifting her clear off the floor and spinning her around.

"Stop it, silly. You're making me dizzy."

He silenced her with an urgent, explorative kiss.

She met his aggressive tongue with her own, dipping, sucking, biting gently on his lower lip. Her fingers began working the buttons on his shirt as he peeled her sweater back off her now sweat-dampened shoulders. One strap of the silky tank she wore underneath fell to her elbow.

Jason groaned at the sight of that one, freckled mound. He started at her chin, his tongue on a journey with a definite destination. With two fingers, he grasped the stretchy fabric and pulled the tank down farther, taking with it the strap of her bra.

He stopped and studied her face. She was gazing up into his eyes with an expression he wasn't sure he could read. He knew she wanted him. But he also knew he needed to progress carefully.

She'd told him already that she'd not been with a man since that night.

He hesitated, asking with his eyes what his body was afraid she might deny. Her slow smile brought his blood to a boil and his skin misted with sweat. She reached up and pulled down the lace of her bra, exposing one very full, very freckled breast, the nipple hard and stippled and bright pink.

Very slowly, he lifted a hand and cupped the warm flesh, tenderly running his thumb over the stiff peak. She dropped her head back and moaned, arching toward him.

"More," she groaned. "More, Jason."

But he was, in his condition, in tight denim, in serious pain. He fumbled to unbutton his jeans.

Why the hell didn't I wear zippered ones tonight?

"I'm sorry. Gotta get these things off or I'll end up with gangrene," he mumbled. Finally, his erection sprang free, and he closed his eyes and whimpered with relief.

When he opened them, Zoe was pulling her tank over her head. She unfastened her bra and it fell to the floor. In another moment, everything covering the incredible body before him was gone. She stood before him, naked, with pleading eyes.

"More. Please."

He gathered her to him, reveling in the sensation of her soft, hot skin molding against him. Her nipples poked into his bare chest as though they were begging for attention. Deafened by the rushing of blood in his own ears, he knew he was rapidly reaching a point of no return.

Too fast. Way too fast. I'm not a virgin teenager anymore. Slow down. Let the lady make the next move.

He dragged in a shaky breath as he waited, and his heart sank like an anchor when she placed both hands on his chest and gently pushed him away.

God, please. Don't stop the momentum now.

When Zoe dropped to her knees in front of him, his heart leaped and his cock twitched.

Come on man, you're far from a green teen. Control. Maintain control.

Her breath was hot on his skin, and when her cheek brushed against his cock, his desire flared to a higher level, much more difficult to control. He began to tremble as she placed soft, chaste kisses along his length. When she took him into her hands, she looked up and licked her lips.

No. Won't be able to hold it back. I'll come in her mouth before she gets me fully inside.

He staggered back a step and croaked, "No, Zoe. Please. I want to be inside you."

She blinked, and for an agonizing moment she said nothing and didn't move. He couldn't read the expression on her face.

Uh-oh. She was raped, you asshole. Maybe all she wants is only oral sex this first time.

Finally, she rocked back on her heels and clambered to her feet. She wrapped her arms around him and the touch of her warm skin against him made him shudder.

"Okay," she murmured in a voice so sweet, and so demure, his heart clutched in his chest.

He reached down and lifted her, carrying her to the massive king-size bed. After she was settled back against the pillows, he lay down beside her, stroking her body with his gaze.

"You are incredibly beautiful, Zoe Anderson. I'm honored you're sharing your lovely body with me."

But he was struggling to control his own needs with more intensity than ever before. This felt like more than a roll in the hay. There was something . . . precious, almost sacred about this joining. He wanted to be sure the experience was one she'd never forget. One that would overwrite anything in her past.

Good or bad.

He kissed her deep and long before his tongue followed the graceful line of her neck to her freckled breasts. The peaks stood high and stiff, and when his mouth covered one, she arched up and cried out. He suckled her, his fingers covering her other breast. Cupping the warm, soft mound in his trembling hand, he used his thumb to trace patterns over her nipple, keeping rhythm with the tip of his tongue on the other.

She writhed beneath his touch, moaning and thrusting her hips against him.

"Yes, Jason. Yes."

His fingers wandered lower, finding the warm wetness between her legs. She moaned again, and her breath quickened into shallow panting. His fingers stroked her once, danced in a tiny circle around her clit, and slipped deep inside her. She climaxed immediately, bucking against him as she completely lost herself in the orgasm.

Her screams of pleasure almost brought him to spill himself all over her thigh.

Give her time, bro. Take some deep breaths, and think about the latest baseball stats. Are the Yankees on a winning streak? Who's pitching tomorrow's game? Who the fuck cares?

He laid his head against Zoe's chest and felt the pounding of her heart against her ribs. It was almost as though she were purring, basking in the afterglow of her climax. He wanted her to enjoy this, savor the feelings. Brand these moments into her memory.

But he was achingly grateful she rested for only a minute.

Her fingers raked through his hair, gathering a handful of it to gently lift his face to hers. Her intense green gaze was almost threatening.

"I assume you have a condom? I hope to God you have one. I haven't been on the pill in years, and you do have a reputation, my boy. Lots of partners."

Ouch. She's right, but ouch all the same.

He nodded dumbly, and then fumbled in the drawer of the bedside table. When he produced the foil packet, he tore it open and started to apply it himself. She reached over and snatched it out of his hand. He blinked.

Don't want to come in the lady's hand, either.

"No, Zoe. You won't get it on. I'm too . . . close."

She studied his face with a measuring look before handing it back to him.

Nothing exciting about putting on your own condom. I can hold on a little longer this way.

When he was finished he swung one leg over her hips, bracing his weight on his hands. But she didn't spread her legs. Her body tensed beneath him, and her eyes rounded. He froze.

Not this way. Okay. She needs to be the one in control.

He rolled off immediately and lay on his side next to her, his fingers tracing circles on her stomach. But not for long.

Zoe pushed him down until he was lying flat on his back. In one smooth movement she swung over him, sliding her searing slit over his throbbing erection. Slowly, she lowered herself onto him. She was tight and hot. He gasped and struggled for control.

"Can't hold this much longer, Zo. Sorry."

But she was sitting perfectly still. Smiling, she ran one finger along his jaw, her eyes locked on his.

This is sweet, incredible torture. With a woman who seems to have sprung out of one of my most exciting, erotic dreams.

Slowly, she started to rock. Jason reached up to cup those swollen, freckled mounds. One at a time, he brought his thumbs to his mouth, sucking on them. When they returned to their destination, properly lubricated, they began a slow circling around the hard peaks. Her gasp caused his cock to twitch inside her.

Control, dude. Maintain control. She has to come with me. I want her cresting the wave right beside me.

And she did. At the moment he knew he couldn't hold out any longer, her core pulsed rhythmically around him and she screamed his name. The convulsive waves around his swollen shaft brought him powerfully, mind-explodingly over the top.

She collapsed on top of him, sobbing into his chest.

Sobbing. Oh no.

"Are you okay?" he asked, running his fingers softly up and down her back.

"Yes. Yes," she said. "Really okay."

They fell asleep side-by-side. She nestled close, her face buried in the crook of his neck, and he loved the way her body fit against his. He wasn't sure how long they slept. But they both started when the front door slammed.

Jade was home.

Fifteen minutes later, Jade heard Jason racing down the steps. She glanced away from the open refrigerator.

His hair was still dripping wet from the shower, and he was barefoot, wearing only jeans.

"Hey, Jay." She grabbed the quart bottle and poured herself a glass of milk.

"Hey, Sis. You all done down there?"

"Yeah. Kinda slow tonight. Troy's closing for me." She took a long swallow of milk, and then gave her brother a knowing look. "Needless to say, I'll have plenty to clean up in the morning."

Jason pulled a bottle of water out of the fridge, twisted the cap, and chugged half of it. She caught his sheepish grin, and the way he shifted his eyes ever so slightly toward the staircase. Jade heard the flow of water from the upstairs shower clunk off.

"Another liaison, huh?" She shook her head. "You sure have a high turnover rate." She drained her milk glass, stored it in the dishwasher, and headed for her room. "I'll try not to spoil the mood."

"It's all right, Jade. It's Zoe."

Jade closed her eyes and blew out a breath as her heart sank. She turned on him, glaring. "Now what are you doing messing with that nice lady, baby brother? She doesn't need any more heartache."

Jason held up both hands in front of him.

"I know that. It's different this time. Zoe is . . . she's different."

She stared at him. He did have an odd look about him lately, ever since that one arrived. Almost starry eyed. But she knew him too well. Knew the kind of life he'd—they'd both—come from. Her brother was not what Zoe Anderson was looking for. God knows, he certainly wasn't what she needed.

And he was just standing there, one hand on his hip, with that goofy I-just-got-me-a-piece grin. She sighed, sliding her gaze away. Too late now. What's done is done. Obviously no use for a big sister lecture now.

Without another word, she turned away and pulled her bedroom door closed behind her.

A few minutes later Zoe came down the steps and found Jason with his head on his hand, leaning against the counter. She didn't have to ask what had transpired, since she knew it was Jade she'd heard come through the front door minutes ago.

"Is she upset?"

He nodded, and then startled her as he pounded his fist on the counter. "She has no business being mad, if she is. This is my house."

She reached a hand up and laid it on his shoulder. "She's my friend, Jay. I think she's worried I'm gonna get hurt. She thinks I'm looking for . . ." She hesitated. "Something more permanent."

At that, Jason's gaze snapped to hers. He studied her eyes for a long moment, and Zoe couldn't help but wonder what was going through his head. He turned away, frowning. His sigh was more of a huff. "I guess she's got good reason to worry about that. Jade thinks a lot of you."

Relief washed over her. Medina was right—this truly was the perfect man to get her past her issues. His sister's reaction had proven that. His reputation didn't lie.

Then what was that strange expression on his face just now? He'd almost looked surprised when she acknowledged the nature of their relationship. Nothing permanent.

It didn't matter. Her protective wall was firmly in place, and this was about her, not him. She blurted, "I'm starving."

Jason turned his head slowly toward her, an impish grin spreading across his face. "You can be so adorable sometimes, you know that? Like some little kid who can't properly prioritize what thoughts pop out of her mouth."

She shrugged and held up both hands. "Can't help it. My body is hungry? I feed it."

"It's nine-thirty. The kitchen doesn't close until ten on Sundays, but we'll have to eat in the bar. Do you mind?"

"I'm so hungry I'll eat in the parking lot if I have to," she said.

Zoe walked with Jason down to the restaurant, arms linked around each other's waists, and sat at the end of the abandoned bar. Troy made them both a vodka and tonic, and started busily cleaning up behind the bar and reorganizing bottles, occasionally glancing over his shoulder at Jason.

Maybe with the boss in the house, Jade wouldn't come in to quite such a mess in the morning.

But Jason's attention wasn't on Troy. Jason was turned toward her, holding one of her hands in both of his, and wouldn't take his eyes off her face. She tried to keep her gaze forward, neutral.

I'm enjoying myself. Just a drink and an evening meal with a sexy guy. Nothing romantic. A nice epilogue to a fantastic session in the sack.

But he obviously wasn't happy she wasn't mooning all over him. His hand wandered up her arm to brush back a strand of her damp hair and tuck it over her ear. When she didn't turn toward him, he asked, "Hey, where'd you go?"

Like a puppy nudging me for attention. I guess he's used to being worshipped after his performances. A temporary state before he turns back into the big bad wolf.

His words interrupted her thoughts. "You okay, pretty lady?"

"I'm fine. Great, actually. Better than I've felt in a long time." She turned and met his gaze. "Hey, look," she said, pointing to her own lips. "Complete, coherent sentences. I like what this therapy is doing for me."

Jason's brow furrowed. "Is that how you're thinking of us? Therapy?"

She looked away. It was too hard to keep looking into those clear, blue eyes and not imagine some kind of emotion in them.

"Yes. Therapy." She took a deep breath and rested her chin on one hand. "You see, Mr. Rolland, I've had a major problem all of my life. I've never been able to separate two, very different concepts. Sex, and love."

To her surprise, he reacted as though she'd slapped him. His head tipped back, eyes narrowed. "You mean, like your friend Medina seems to able to do."

Anger flared in her chest. "Yes. Like Medina. And the problem here is?"

He blew out a big breath, and then leaned forward on crossed arms, staring off into the distance. "I guess you've got no reason to believe I'd be interested in anything more than that. With you. My reputation precedes me."

Troy interrupted the moment, laying a platter heaping with fried food on the counter between them, followed by two empty plates and rolled silverware.

"Can I get you anything else?" he asked.

Jason shook his head with more vigor than necessary. Troy rocked back, raised an eyebrow, then turned and walked away.

Zoe watched Jason reach forward and snatch a fry off the top of a still simmering pile. He got it as far as his plate before he dropped it, swearing and shaking his hand.

"Well that was pretty stupid. You can see they're still sizzling hot," she chuckled.

His stony expression held for only another moment

before the embarrassed smile forced its way through. "My reputation includes an inability to resist things that are sizzling, smokin' hot."

He sure knows his lines well. Delivered with that deep, rumbling voice of his, and capped off with that crooked smile, he's practically irresistible.

She chose not to respond as she rolled a wing off the pile onto her plate. These weren't nearly as hot, so she picked it up and pulled the first bite of spicy meat off with her teeth. "As long as I'm around, you won't have to worry about that. I mean, about keeping your hands to yourself."

His reaction startled her as he laid a hand on her cheek and drew her to face him. "Don't make it sound like I'm some kind of dog in heat. I want you, I won't deny that. But with you, it's different, damn it."

She dropped her gaze and turned away, Jade's words echoing in her head.

Share your body with him if you want. But don't trust that boy with your heart.

He was persistent, she'd give him that. He kept talking as he stroked her arm with the back of his hand. "Everything feels different with you, Zoe. I'm honored you trusted me like you did tonight. I was hoping I'd healed some of your hurt."

Jade was so right. He was pretty convincing when he turned on the charm. Zoe had to keep reminding herself that although Jason truly did seem to like her, she shouldn't attach any significance to it beyond a physical relationship. Eventually, he would move onto his next conquest.

She turned toward him then, her resolve solid. "Jason, you've helped me to revive a part of myself I thought was dead, and I'm grateful for that. But I've told you, three years ago my life took a side trip through hell." She closed her eyes and sighed, then met his gaze. "Look. I'm just not ready for anything but . . . this. Let's enjoy the next few weeks while I'm here, okay?"

He blinked, the furrow between his brows deepening. Then he leaned back in his seat and raised his hands in surrender.

"Okay. I get it. I'm sorry."

He reached out to place two fingers under her chin.

"I mean it. I'm sorry. We'll go at your pace."

His voice was soft, and so damned sincere. A little chink of her heart's armor fell away—

Oh boy, I really need to be careful.

It would be so easy to let him wrap himself around her heart, and then what? She knew all too well—Jason Rolland wasn't the forever kind.

The next week passed by in a flash. Medina left to go back to the city Monday morning, but said she'd return the following weekend. Tony had invited her to come up for the big Fourth of July celebration. Apparently, her friend couldn't resist. This was completely out of character for Medina, who usually didn't revisit one of her trysts two weekends in a row.

Hmm. There must be something in this mountain air.

Jason left early on Monday as well, heading to Albany. Business, he'd said, with regret oozing all over his words when he announced he wouldn't be back until Thursday. Apparently, this happened fairly often. He handled real estate deals during the week, and then came back to the lake and managed the resort and his radio show on the weekends.

She breathed a sigh of relief when she peeked out her window that morning. His Hummer was already gone from his driveway. But what was that twinge of disappointment?

Jason's eyes had held hers a bit too long after he'd kissed her goodbye the night before. But he had lots of experience

159

convincing girls they were his one and only. Lord knows how many night visitors he brought back to his hotel room while he was in the city, 'doing business.'

Now what was that little flare in her chest? Surely not jealousy?

This is a fling. Purely physical. Don't let your heart get in the way.

That afternoon, she headed down to the beach. She'd pulled a filmy, sheer sundress over her bikini, and was stocking her bag with all the necessities for a leisurely afternoon—bottled water, sunscreen, magazines, another paperback.

Oh, and my hat. Where did I leave my sunglasses?

She heard her cell phone buzz from where it lay on the granite counter, plugged in to charge, and snatched it up.

Xavier. Finally.

"Zoe, my love. How are you? Are you enjoying your vacation?" As usual, the X-man stitched closed a three-week gap of non-communication with practiced charm.

It's the French accent. Must be the accent that gets to me.

"I am now," Zoe said, "but it got off to a rocky start. Did Medina fill you in about the cottage I inherited?"

There was a pause, and she heard muffled murmuring. The rude bastard had covered the phone to talk to someone else.

He finally came back on the line. "I'm sorry, ma chère. The office is always crazy on Mondays. So, the cottage is lovely, yes?"

He hadn't even been paying attention. "No, Xavier, it's not. It's a pitiful shack that looks like it's ready to fall into the lake. And there's no driveway anymore."

This time the pause, she knew, was Xavier absorbing this information for the first time. "So, where are you staying?

Didn't Medina come up to spend the weekend with you?"

She spent the next few minutes filling him in on the disappointing details of her predicament. She paused when she realized there was silence on the line. "Xavier? Are you still there?"

"Yes. Yes, Zoe, I am. I've been flipping through my files while you told me this story. I have a friend who specializes in real estate law." She heard the tapping of fingers on a keyboard. "Ah, here he is. Arlin Clarke. I'm sending him an email as we speak. Arlin will know how to handle this situation."

Great, he's handing me off. Another delay. She ran a hand through her hair and started pacing back and forth between the kitchen and living area. "Xavier, I've already been here three weeks. I've only got until the end of August to get this thing taken care of."

"Why don't you just sell it?" His tone was flat, disinterested. "Doesn't the guy who bought the right of way want it anyway?"

She flopped down in the loveseat and dropped her forehead onto her hand. "You don't understand. There are a lot of memories here for me. I'm actually thinking about having the place fixed up."

A groan in her ear, followed by a resigned sigh. "Why don't I come up there and take a look? Let you know what I think. I have a meeting with a colleague in Albany coming up. It's not far from there, right?"

"No, not far. When?"

"I'm not sure just yet, love. Let me make some calls and get back to you."

When Zoe hung up the phone, she wasn't sure whether she felt better or worse. It was a good idea to have a neutral, outside person evaluate the situation. Not smart to make decisions based on emotions. He was her attorney, after all. She should trust his judgment.

But Xavier, here? In what he surely would consider unexplored wilderness?

An image popped into her brain. Aristocratic, stiff-backed Xavier Le Blanc, wearing one of his finest Armani suits and blindingly polished Italian leather shoes, picking his way down the tangled path to her dilapidated shack. She imagined the disgusted lift of his closely-shaven lip as a deerfly landed there, and he swatted at it, his profanities almost musical in their French lilt.

She rocked back in her seat, giggling.

Jason had been making the trek to Albany almost every week now for the past four months, but today, the road didn't seem to want to end. His usual favorite top four stations on Sirius couldn't keep his mind from wandering back to Lakeview Lodge. To the events of the last twenty-four hours.

To Zoe Anderson.

What is the matter with me? I'm too young for a mid-life crisis. Hell, I'm not even forty yet. And it's not like I've had a dry spell in the bedroom.

What is it about this particular softly rounded, liberally freckled, unpredictable spitfire that has my guts wound up in knots?

Jason glanced at the clock on his dash, quietly swearing. He still had plenty of time to make the eleven o'clock closing at the title office. The trip never took more than an hour, but it seemed he'd been on the road half the morning. Everything around him, even time, had slowed, stuck in a sweet thickness, the honey of Zoe's memory.

He had a hell of a day in front of him. A closing at eleven, finally, with the persnickety Asian client he'd been trying to sell to for at least three months. After that, he was meeting with a prospective new buyer. A neurosurgeon from Buffalo, moving to the state capital and looking for a mansion to suit his not-so-easy-to-please wife. Jason hoped that by four o'clock he would be standing under a hot shower in his usual suite at the Marriott.

It was actually almost six by the time Jason was finished with the day's business and headed down to the hotel's restaurant for dinner. He'd considered room service. Eating dinner in his boxers, in front of the TV, his feet propped up on the bed sounded pretty damned good.

But he feared lying on that bed would only bring back steamy memories of how he'd spent last night. With Zoe.

Her beautiful face kept popping into his head. She was there, everywhere. In the scent of his shampoo, shaking her gorgeous hair free after lifting off his helmet. In the light flashing off the copper trim of his window, the same color as those silky strands. He sat on the edge of the bed and lifted the phone to order dinner. Then he replaced it.

There was something missing. The king-sized mattress, wrapped in crisp white linen, seemed vast and cold and empty without her next to him.

Jason pulled on khaki trousers and a white polo, and slipped leather loafers onto his bare feet. He headed downstairs for a drink, a meal, and, maybe, a little distraction.

He was relieved to see Tracy was not working the bar tonight. Hell, knowing her, her latest fling with *this* restaurant's manager had probably already burned out, and she'd moved on. Jason settled in a corner booth with a good view of the TV, where ESPN was airing one of the World Cup soccer games.

Jason didn't recognize the waiter. He should, since he

spent two or three days here almost every week. But staff turnover at this place was unbelievable. He ordered a rare T-bone and loaded spud to go with his double Absolut.

Turnover. That was the word Jade had used last night. She'd criticized his revolving bedroom door more than once. But why, all of a sudden, had the comment stung?

He'd always assumed there was no other way to be. Following in Daddy's footsteps. Emulating the only male role model he'd ever known. Big talk, big money, big ego, living fast and hot and furious.

A thin layer of super-hot flames licking across the surface of life, but without much substance.

Living that way made Jason feel like a colorful autumn leaf. A few fleeting, but temporarily bright moments. Afterwards, he always fluttered to the ground, spending the winter cold and alone.

Over the last few days, for the first time in his life, Jason had felt different. Zoe touched a nerve in him, stirring emotions he not only didn't know existed, but he didn't believe in. At least, he'd never believed in them before.

The closest he'd ever come to that elusive four-letter word was as the Love Guru of Jason's Lair. A complete act. Feeding a line of bullshit to a sappy, sentimental audience who believed he actually possessed a heart.

Did he? Until last night, he didn't believe his heart was capable of more than simply keeping his body alive.

Now, he was mortally terrified that it wasn't made of granite after all.

Jason had tipped back his head to drain the last of his vodka when the flash of color slid into the booth across from him.

"Hey, tiger, I was hoping to catch you here tonight."

Chapter 11

For Zoe, the week passed in a flash. She slept in every morning until the sun had burned the morning mist off the lake. Then she lounged down by the water or on her back deck most of the day.

But one can only spend so many hours playing beach bum. By four, she was stir-crazy, and more than happy to head down to help Jade serve the happy hour crowd.

With Fourth of July weekend looming ahead, Lakeview's quiet serenity quickly evaporated. By Thursday, every parking space on the entire property was occupied. Jade had cordoned off the restaurant lot, along with her and Jason's parking spaces, with orange cones. The peaceful, serene resort was reminding Zoe more and more of the city.

Which wasn't such a bad thing. She hated to admit it, but she was getting a little homesick for the hustle and bustle of Manhattan. The influx of people and activity, though, had an opposite effect on Jade.

"I've got to get out of here for a few hours. I'm getting boathouse fever," Jade murmured to her on Thursday night.

"Isn't Troy back tomorrow? How about shopping?" she asked. "I finished that last book I bought. How about it?"

Jade hesitated, considering. "It's crazy to think I could get out of here the Friday before the big weekend. We'll have to

165

see how fast the place fills up tomorrow."

The next day dawned gray and drizzling. The air was unseasonably chilly, and Zoe felt that way inside too.

I'm getting cabin fever, too. I've got to get back into civilization for an hour or two.

But moving her car meant she probably wouldn't be able to park anywhere near her cabin when she got back. Holding a giant umbrella over her head, she snagged one of the parking cones from the entrance to the restaurant lot. She marked her space, then spotted Jade heading down the hill from her and Jason's cabin. She wore a red slicker with a giant hood that almost obscured her face.

Zoe pulled up beside her and rolled down the window. "Headed to Bolton's Landing for an hour or two. Wanna join me?"

Jade pushed back the cuff of her raincoat and checked her watch. "I suppose Troy can handle the lunch crowd for a little while. This rain's going to keep the numbers down, I think." She flashed a wide smile. "And exactly what we needed to sneak away."

She slid into Zoe's car, wincing as she watched water stream off her coat onto the leather seats.

"Don't worry about it, Jade. Can't be helped. Nasty morning, huh? I hope it quits by tomorrow or the fireworks show will be a real challenge to pull off. What do they do when it rains on the Fourth?"

"Postpone it. Really screws things up. The restaurants and bars fill to capacity and by midnight, it's like being in the middle of a herd getting ready to stampede."

"Great. Let's pray the rain wears itself out today, then."

Zoe pulled the car out onto Route 9N and headed north. She remembered Jade telling her about all the cute little gift shops in the next town. She squinted between the slaps of the wipers, taking the sloped curves slow. When they hit a straightaway, she glanced over at Jade, who was staring at her.

"What? Why are you looking at me like that?"

"Heard from Jason?"

She nodded and rolled her eyes. "He texts me about five times a day. You never warned me how needy that brother of yours can be. In fact," she slid Jade a look, "what you told me about him is just the opposite of how he's acting. With me, anyway."

She heard the crackle of Jade's raincoat as she shifted in her seat. "Usually, he is. The opposite, I mean," Jade murmured.

"Does he go to Albany every week?"

"Yes. During the season, anyway. Not so much in the winter, from what I know."

"You mentioned you go home for the winter?"

Jade nodded. "I head back around the first of November. Right after the Halloween party." She flashed a grin. "The Big Haunt. It's the last big shebang of the year."

"That sounds like fun. Maybe I'll plan a weekend up here around then."

Jade was silent for a few moments, and then asked, "What's it like in Manhattan? You said you've got an apartment down there, right?"

"I do. You know, Jade, you ought to come visit before you head back to Jamaica this year. I've got plenty of room. I'd love to take you around, show you the big city."

"I might just do that, Zoe. Thanks."

They passed the black-lettered sign announcing *Welcome to Bolton's Landing*. Zoe slowed the car, searching for an empty parking spot on the street. "Wow, I guess we weren't the only ones with this idea."

167

"When it rains, they shop. And if it keeps raining, later, they drink."

Oh, lucky day. One of the cars ahead came to life with brake and backup lights. Zoe stopped and flipped her signal.

After maneuvering the big car into the tight space, she shut the engine and turned to Jade. "Now you remember, I probably won't be down to work with you tonight until about five. Xavier should be here by three or so." Inwardly, she winced. The property was a sensitive subject both she and Jade tried to avoid at all costs.

And the thought of dragging her attorney along that tangled forest path in this weather was even more unpleasant.

Jade nodded. "This guy's your attorney, right?"

"And my friend. Medina's worked for him for a long time. Of course, the X-man, as Dina calls him, would like us to be more than friends, but so far," she shrugged, "that hasn't happened."

Zoe popped open her huge umbrella when they got to the sidewalk, but it was only a slow, miserable drizzle coming down. Most of the shops had awnings, and she and Jade were able to dart from one to the other along the street. She helped Jade pick out a pretty, art-glass necklace from one of the shops.

"The gold flecks in this match the ones in your eyes, perfectly." She grinned as she adjusted the slab of sparkly glass against her friend's throat. "It'll go perfect with that yellow sundress you have."

As they left the shop, Jade said, "This is quite a treat. I usually don't do much other than work and watch Jason flit around the whole time I'm up here."

"I know," Zoe exclaimed. "You work so hard. Is it easier in the winters when you're in Jamaica?"

One side of Jade's mouth lifted. "I like working. Keeps me

168

out of trouble. But yes, it's easier in Jamaica. I have more friends there, and don't work nearly as many hours."

As they strolled up the street under the cover of the awnings, Zoe said, "Ooh, a bookstore," and pointed across the street. She popped open her umbrella. "But we will need this to get across."

The morning went by way too fast. Zoe almost couldn't believe what time it was when Jade said, "I've got to get back. And won't your X-man be here any minute?"

"Holy crap, you're right. Let's get going." Their fun run had ended, but Zoe felt glad she'd been able to give Jade a break from work. And maybe, cement a friendship for her, here in Lake George.

Zoe swore as she pulled into the Lakeview driveway. Cars jammed every single lot, and lined the serpentine drive almost halfway to the road.

"Damn. I borrowed one of those cones to mark the spot in front of my cabin, but looks like somebody decided to move it aside and park there anyway."

"Park up here by our place. They haven't gotten to moving our cones aside yet, fortunately."

Zoe parked, thanked her friend, and headed down the hill toward the Aspen. The rain had stopped, but the sky was still a dull, heavy gray. The air was warmer, though, and the humidity made her collar feel sticky on her neck. She started digging in her purse for the key, mentally flipping through her closet trying to decide what to wear to work tonight, when she reached her cabin.

The car parked where hers ought to be was a gleaming black Mercedes, and there was a man sitting behind the wheel. Zoe walked around to the driver's window, and was greeted by the stony face of Xavier Le Blanc.

"You're early," she said as the window whirred down.

"Hello to you too, ma chère," he replied. One of his perfectly shaped, blond eyebrows lifted. "Why on earth are you even considering keeping property this far from the civilized world?"

Zoe stared into his cool, gray eyes for a beat. "You haven't even gotten out of the car yet, and you're hassling me already." She nodded toward the Aspen and lifted the keys. "Come on inside and see this lovely chalet I'm staying in."

A few minutes later they were facing each other on opposite loveseats. Zoe had brewed herself a cup of coffee, but X had opted for the glass of wine she'd offered. His eyes flitted around the room and disdain twisted his features.

"You can't tell me you like this kind of place," he began. "I mean, the whole log cabin concept was in vogue about twenty years ago, but this place is almost . . . archaic."

She set her mug down on the glass table between them with a sharp crack. "This place is gorgeous, Xavier. It may not be your style, but for a vacation spot—"

"No, it's certainly not my style. Now, a condo on the Riviera, maybe—"

"Look, this was probably a waste of both our time. If you think *this* place is too rustic, I don't even have to take you to see the property I inherited," she snapped. "You obviously don't understand my sentiments. I grew up here. Every summer. Picnics. Sandcastles. Toasted marshmallows."

His brows drew together and he leaned forward. "Zoe, how's your . . . condition? You seem to be lapsing into single word sentences again. Are your new meds not working?"

She groaned.

This is exactly why you and I are never going to be more than attorney and client.

"You just don't get it, Xavier. It's okay. I understand why. You grew up in the city." She picked up her mug and sipped, studying him. As usual, he wore an impeccably tailored designer suit. "I hope you brought a change of clothes. I don't think Armani will enjoy traipsing through the woods."

He scowled. "My bag is in the car. Let's get it over with. Then we can meet Arlin down in the restaurant."

She blinked. Arlin. Oh yeah, his real estate attorney friend.

"You brought him?"

"I told you, Zoe, I know very little about real estate law. Besides, I didn't want to drive halfway across the state alone."

"Where is he?"

Xavier clinked his wine glass down on the table with an impatient sigh. "I just told you, Zoe. I dropped him off at the restaurant. He hadn't eaten anything today, and he wanted to grab a sandwich and a cocktail while we waited for you."

She arched a brow. "If he's the real estate attorney, shouldn't he be the one going to look at the cottage?"

"I said he knew real estate law, Zoe. He looks at contracts and blueprints and lot plans. He very seldom visits individual properties. Besides," he leaned forward to peer out the windows toward the woods, "there's no need for the two of us ruining a good suit of clothes."

A half hour later, Zoe led him across Lakeview's grounds to the padlocked gate. The grass, though neatly mowed, was still wet. Zoe wore her beach flip-flops, not caring if her toes got a little damp. Unfortunately, Xavier didn't have that option.

He lagged behind her. She turned to find him stepping with odd, jerky movements, as though trying to avoid land mines. Xavier had changed into his ultra-casual wear—a pair of starched khakis and a silk linen shirt. Apparently, at the moment, preserving his new Finley loafers was his primary concern.

She shook her head and stifled a smile. When he finally made his way to the gate, she slipped the key Jason had given her into the lock while he used his handkerchief to dry his precious shoes.

"This," she said as she pulled the gate open, "is my country mansion."

Although it had stopped raining almost an hour earlier, water still dripped from the heavy tangle of branches hanging over the path. Xavier peered into the gloom, his face twisted.

"It's a veritable jungle," he said in disgust. "Is it even safe to walk through there?"

"I don't think the mice or moles are dangerous. I'm told, though, there is the possibility of snakes."

A complete waste of time. She was certain there was no way he was going down that overgrown path, let alone anywhere near the house. Why had he even bothered to come? Why had she thought it was a good idea in the first place?

Xavier had no interest in any property that had more than six square feet of natural lawn around it. He didn't know how to navigate on anything but concrete sidewalk or granite flooring. He lived in one of the most expensive sections of uptown Manhattan in an apartment that looked more like an art gallery than a home. The one time he'd invited Zoe in after they'd gone to dinner, every word she said bounced off the smooth, polished surfaces and echoed back to her.

He refused to take one step beyond the pavement, and turned toward her. "What you've inherited, sweetheart, is an albatross. You'll be lucky if you can give this dump away."

Her annoyance flared to anger. She folded her arms and narrowed her eyes. "This albatross used to be my childhood vacation home. I tried to explain to you, Xavier, that there are a lot of happy memories for me here."

He patted her arm and spoke with such condescension her hand itched to slap him. "This fellow—the resort owner—who wants to buy the property is a fool. My advice is to take the first bid he offers and run, very quickly, to the bank." With that, he brushed past her and headed back toward the Aspen.

Pompous, insensitive asshole.

Yet through the fury burning in her chest, realization jabbed an even sharper blow. She'd known the truth since the first day she saw what was left of the cottage. Tears stung her eyes as she followed him, watching as he tiptoed through the wet grass like a persnickety cat.

An hour later, Zoe dressed for her evening behind the bar. Xavier had insulted her, spoken down to her like she was a child, and made fun of the way she'd been raised. But she was done crying.

Let's handle the hurt Medina-style, by scabbing it over with a bitch-from-hell attitude.

She stared into her closet. Originally, she'd decided on a feminine, colorful sundress paired with pastel ballerina flats. Instead she snatched out the clingy, too short, and too low-cut black dress Medina had pushed her to buy.

She spent an extra few minutes layering on smoky eye shadow, and rimmed her eyes with thick, Cleopatra-style liner. She pushed aside her usual sheer pink gloss, deciding instead on the siren red lipstick—another Medina-inspired purchase. And although she knew it would kill her to work in them all night, she chose her tallest, shiniest, patent leather stilettos.

Tonight, it was all about the entrance. Xavier and his real estate expert friend—what was his name? Marvin something?—would be waiting for her in the bar. It was obvious once the X-man got a glimpse of her country-girl roots, he didn't care for them. He couldn't possibly understand the sentimental, softer side of Zoe Anderson.

Tonight he was going to see the new one. The stronger, bolder woman she was struggling to bring to life.

Like the bride of Frankenstein.

Jason recognized Tony's BMW pulling in off the highway and waved him into the private lot near his cabin. There wasn't a spot left anywhere else on the property. Cars were lined up along the driveway all the way to the road. He smiled when he spotted Zoe's car nestled in the space close to his.

They all got out at the same time, and while Tony and Jason were shaking hands, Medina was hanging out of the passenger side of Tony's car, pulling on another pair of her trademark, four-inch heels. Bright yellow snakeskin this time.

Ah, now there's a subtle fashion statement.

Tony followed Jason's gaze and scowled. "Dina, I told you not to wear those blasted things tonight." He stepped to the side of the Beemer and pulled her into his arms.

Jason turned away but still heard him say, "Why don't you save them for a private showing? Later?"

Could have gone all day without hearing that little comment.

"Hey, I'll see you two at the bar in a minute," he said.

Medina looked up. "No radio show tonight, Jason?"

He shook his head. "My buddy Brandon covers for me from his studio down in the village. Two weekends for sure—Fourth of July and Halloween."

She smiled as she stood and latched onto Tony's arm. "We'll see you down there, then."

Jason knew Zoe was working the bar with Jade tonight. He'd been gone all week, and had texted her a bunch. But she'd only answered once or twice. He couldn't wait to see her. "I want to change out of these work duds. Save me a seat, will you?"

The outdoor globes had just flickered on twenty minutes later when Jason pushed in through the patio's screened door. The place was jammed. It took several minutes for him to wade through the crowd, since a three-person-deep barrier separated him from the bar.

It didn't help that his progress was hindered multiple times. Friends called his name, but he managed to get past most with a wave and a smile. Until he found himself face-to-face with an old flame who was obviously already tipsy. She wrapped her arms around him, planting a disgustingly wet, wine-drenched kiss on his mouth.

So nice to see you, but I don't even remember your name, sweetheart.

When he finally reached the bar, he snatched a cocktail napkin to wipe his mouth before even greeting the hulking mass of Tony, who'd obviously bullied his way into claiming a seat for his woman. He stood behind Medina, one hand on her thigh, the other on an iced mug, guarding an area free for Jason to slip in. He grinned and gripped Tony's hand.

"Hey, thanks, man."

But the words had hardly left his lips when he caught sight of Zoe, and his smile disintegrated.

She wore no bar apron. Her dress could best be described as a flimsy piece of black Spandex that barely covered her, revealing every contour of her body. Three inches of freckled cleavage spilled out from the top, and the hemline barely covered her underwear.

If she was wearing any. What the fuck?

Making matters worse, she was deep in conversation with a man sitting at the far end of the bar. Way too deeply. He was preppy looking, with short-cropped blond hair, and wearing a silk shirt he'd left unbuttoned nearly to his waist. His tailored jacket, though definitely out of place here, screamed money.

At first, Jason was sure the man was gay. Until he watched the way his eyes were drifting back and forth between Zoe's eyes and her cleavage. Then he realized she was also conversing with the man sitting next to him, one with ebony skin and exotic features. One whose eyes and quick smile were following unabashedly the movements of Jade nearby.

His sister. What the holy hell?

Tony's big hand landed with a bang on his shoulder. "Slow down, cowboy. She's just doing her job."

Medina shifted around in her seat. "That's Xavier, Jason. He's Zoe's attorney."

Gasoline on a campfire.

Jason surged in that direction but Tony's hand clamped down on his upper arm, hard.

"Don't be going there, bro. We don't need any scenes in here tonight. Get the lady's attention, and take it outside."

But Zoe had spotted him, and flashing an apologetic smile toward her guest, glided across the bar. She wore her polite, generic work smile.

"Can I get you your usual, boss?"

Boss? Seriously? Have you forgotten what happened between us last weekend?

"What the fuck do you think you're doing?" He struggled to keep his tone low, but the pressure from Tony's death-grip on his upper arm made him realize he wasn't keeping his volume down as low as he'd thought.

"What? I'm tending bar for you, helping out Jade. I've been doing the same thing all week," she answered sweetly, as if she were addressing an agitated child.

This can't be happening. Did I imagine the entire two days we spent together?

He searched her beautiful green eyes—even though they were buried in so much black shit he almost didn't recognize them—for some glimmer of emotion. He saw . . . nothing.

An icy fist clenched around his heart. And his rage stepped in to defend it.

"Why the hell are you dressed like that? And who the fuck is the blond prick across the bar?"

Zoe rocked back on one spiky heel and tipped up her chin. "I'm sorry if you don't approve of my attire, Mr. Rolland. I wasn't aware the establishment had a dress code for bartenders."

There it was. The icy, smartass tone he'd heard from more than one of his sexual conquests. After they'd realized, or had decided, their fling was over. But somehow, on Zoe, it didn't fit. He never expected that kind of attitude from her.

Like a knife slicing into his gut.

Jade appeared beside her, carrying two blended drinks. "No drama tonight, Mon," she grumbled his way, and then delivered the drinks to the two women beside him.

He locked gazes with his sister as he spoke.

"Zoe, I need a moment with you. Outside. Now."

Zoe practically saw the flames shooting out of Jason's eyes. She ducked under the end cap of the bar and stomped after him as he pushed through the crowd toward the rear screen door. It slammed and he was gone, but she knew that route could take him to only one place. Down the steps and into the boathouse.

The door leading into the boathouse creaked eerily as it swung open, and Zoe blinked as her eyes struggled to adjust to the dark interior. A pale stream of light leaked in from the window to the supply room, but it didn't help much. The air reeked with a strong, fishy odor. Two of the Lodge's boats were tethered to wooden posts, and the only sounds came from the sloshing and thumping of their hulls as they bumped on the padded docks within.

After a moment, her eyes adjusted, and she located the dark figure standing in the far corner.

"Jason Rolland, what exactly is your problem tonight?"

He stepped forward, his silhouette gradually emerging as a shadowy figure less than a foot away from her. She could smell him. That piney shampoo and the musky scent of his skin surrounded her. The aroma made her heart rate kick up.

Infuriating her. Her body had apparently decided to override her brain.

"You're dressed like . . ." he said, then paused to scrub his hands through his hair. "Like Medina dressed you again." His growling voice was laced with pent-up fury.

She struggled between her old self and the new one. The old Zoe was crushed, embarrassed, ashamed. The new one was just plain pissed off.

Let's go with the new.

"And your point is?" she snapped.

She heard his sharp intake of breath. The air between them crackled with tension. It was a full minute before he said anything else.

"Who's the preppy asshole who couldn't take his eyes off your tits just now?"

She tipped her chin up and stepped another foot closer to him.

It's too dark in here, dammit.

She wanted to see his eyes, his reaction to what she had to say.

"He's my attorney. I've also, for your information, dated

178

him a time or two. He's here with his friend, Arlin, to help me sort out this mess with my inheritance."

She heard a sound escape from him, almost a growl. "This Xavier guy seems to have a lot more interest in your personal real estate than any piece of land." Jason took a wide stance and fisted both hands on his hips. "And his buddy seems to have taken an unnatural interest in my sister."

Seriously? He's jealous of the attention *both* of us are getting?

She spun on her heel and started walking away. He was acting like an asshole, and she was completely over it. "Please, Jason. Stop embarrassing yourself. Arlin is from Jamaica. He and Jade have some things in common. And it's about time you cut your sister some slack. All she does is work. Get your head out of your ass and realize you're not the only one allowed to have fun."

She took two long steps, but stopped short when strong fingers wrapped around her arm. And none too gently.

But suddenly, his voice was softer. "I'll do anything you want about the property. That's not what I care about."

Zoe drew in a deep breath, and then blew it out. She turned to face him. Although she couldn't see his face very well in the dim light, his eyes were clearly glistening. A tiny crack raced along the wall of ice she'd wrapped around her heart.

No. Surely, I am mistaken. This is a playboy. A man completely incapable of anything deep and meaningful.

"Jason, let's get something straight. I'm a big girl. I've earned the title. I may have played Cinderella once upon a time, but my glass slipper shattered. About three years ago now."

He stood there, frozen. A long moment of silence sent crackles of tension she could almost feel sparking into the air between them.

Why is he so upset? Jealous? How can the playboy of Lakeview Resort possibly be jealous? But he sure as hell seems to be.

She stepped towards him, trying hard to soften her tone. "I'm here trying to start my life over." She lifted one hand and laid it on his cheek, searching eyes that had gone dark and stormy. "I'm working on mending the old me. This is the new one. Like her, or not."

She expected him to pull away, flinch, or lash out. He didn't. He simply stood there, as if he'd turned to stone.

She went on, her tone more adamant. "Don't try to own me. Don't tell me what I can and can't do. Or wear, for Christ's sake. That little girl in pigtails you remember? Well, she died the night my husband did, right in front of my eyes while his killer raped me, then carved open my face."

Zoe faltered as the pained look in Jason's eyes, combined with unthinkable memories ripped open the scab on her heart. She dropped her hand and choked back a sob. "You're the playboy, remember? Free and easy sex, no commitments. What the hell difference does it make to you how I dress?" As she turned away she muttered, "I thought, of all the men I've known in my life, you would be the least likely one to care."

Chapter 12

For the next three hours, Jason sat at his usual corner table in the restaurant. Alone. He could see the bar clearly through the glass wall, but he knew Zoe couldn't see him. He waved away the menu the waitress offered, ordering a double vodka instead. She delivered the tumbler of ice and clear liquid and left him alone. Thank God.

He watched Zoe as though he'd never seen her before. In truth, he felt as though he hadn't. This wasn't the same woman whose eyes had fluttered open as he held her, the night she'd fainted on Tony's boat. Or who'd gazed up at him in childlike wonder on their trek across the lake in the woods. All of that softness, the tender femininity he'd found so gut-wrenchingly tempting, had disappeared.

Or maybe it was simply out of view, buried under tons of black makeup, her sweet smile hidden behind a heavily painted mouth. It was as though she were acting, putting on a show for . . . who? For this attorney asshole that looked as though he could easily swing either side of the sexual arena? Or was he seeing, for the first time, the real Zoe Anderson, a city girl he really didn't know at all?

And why did he care? She'd made it clear. All she wanted was a fling.

Jason drained his glass and motioned to the waitress for

181

another. He was glad when he saw Tony had finally claimed his seat next to Medina, studying menus. They'd decided to eat dinner at the bar. A good thing. He didn't want any company right now. He was confused and angry and . . . what? What was that aching feeling deep in his chest?

The pain twisted his gut as he watched Tony and Medina laugh and cuddle, sharing a plate of seafood, taking turns feeding each other. Mr. Tough Guy Tony didn't look so tough tonight. Apparently, this Medina really had him by the balls. Jason had known Tony for years, and he'd never seen him act like this.

And yet, Jason couldn't ever remember seeing Tony this happy.

The androgynous attorney continued to flirt all night with Zoe. Even though the prick nursed the same glass of red wine the entire night, every time Zoe passed by he reached to grab her hand. Once, he pulled her across the bar to brush his lips on hers. Jason almost threw up in his glass.

His Jamaican friend demanded a lot of Jade's attention, too. During lulls in the drink orders, Jade returned again and again to lean her long, elegant frame on the bar in front him. Her normally masked smile was open and genuine, and she seemed much more animated tonight. He'd never seen her act like that before.

What the hell did these men do? Spray pheromones into the air around the two women?

By the time Jason's fourth vodka was half-gone, he started drifting in and out. He was watching Tony and Medina share a dish of bananas foster one minute, but he blinked and they were gone. The crowd thinned, but attorney-boy and his buddy remained.

Great. Abso-fucking-lutely-great. Zoe and Jade now had more time than ever to stand by them and flirt.

A stack of papers appeared on the bar in front of the two men. Zoe leaned over, studying them, listening intently to whatever legal advice the two men were fabricating. Meanwhile, neither man hid their admiration for her freckled breasts at close range. Jason feared one would pop out onto the bar any minute.

The smiles and nods told Jason that whatever was on those papers, whatever the two men were persuading her to do, they were succeeding. Attorney-boy finally pulled a gold pen out of his shirt pocket and handed it to Zoe.

Jason drained his glass and slammed it down on the table. He waved at the waitress, who hesitated when she spotted him. She cast a worried glance over her shoulder, and then disappeared into the bar. A few moments later, it wasn't the waitress, but Jade who rounded the corner and appeared next to him, glaring down.

"What the hell is the matter with you, Mon?" Her hands were rolled into tight fists on her hips. Standing over him as she was, Jason could swear she'd grown to nine feet tall. And she seemed to be wavering a little. Or was that his eyes? Yes, perhaps it was.

The flowers on her blouse are . . . moving. Swaying in the breeze. But there's no wind in here.

Jason chuckled and swiped a hand down over his face.

I think four double vodkas might be my limit.

"So how are Zoe's real estate negotiations going? You'd think . . ." he hiccupped, "you'd think as the other interested party in this venture, I'd have been involved, wouldn't ya?" Jason found it difficult to make the words come out without spitting. His tongue felt lazy, swollen.

Wow, vodka is a wonderful anesthetic. Makes talking a little challenging, though. But it's a very effective painkiller. I don't feel nearly as bad now as I did earlier.

183

Jade was scowling at him, shaking her head. "You're drunk on your ass, bro."

"Don't you look at me like that, big sister. I'm a grown man. I can drink as much as I want." With his head tipped back, struggling to keep his eyes focused on Jade's face, he was feeling a little dizzy.

Wow, she's *really* tall tonight.

He tried to stand up. Jade's hand came down on his shoulder and slammed him back into his seat.

"No scenes. This is my place of business too. You keep your sorry ass right there in the chair." She turned and motioned for one of the waitresses. "Go tell Claude we need some help out here," she murmured.

"I'm not hungry," Jason sputtered. "What the hell do I need Claude for?"

But there he was, appearing as if out of nowhere right beside Jade. The man, whose mass he'd always found intimidating, looked even bigger tonight.

It's like I've been dropped into Alice's Wonderland. Everybody is either bigger or taller.

He chuckled at the thought, and was struggling to form the words around his lazy tongue when Jade said, "Claude, Mr. Rolland isn't feeling well tonight. Can you please help him up to his cabin?"

Claude reached to untie his stained, cook's apron, but Jade laid a hand on his arm.

"Better leave that on. We'll get you a clean one when you get back."

"I'm not ready to go to my cabin," he began, struggling to make the words come out in an unscrambled, intelligible sequence. "Besides," he planted both hands on the table and tried again to stand, "I need to have some words with our pretty little barmaid before I go."

But before the words were out of his mouth, Claude's bulbous arm hooked around his rib cage, painfully, and lifted him to his feet.

Man, this guy's strong. And fast. We're moving way too fast.

The whole room was swaying now, and the movement made Jason's stomach lurch. He couldn't seem to keep his feet moving fast enough to keep up with Claude's pace. His toes kept scraping along the floor, bumping over the doorstep, and then thumped down the steps to the parking lot.

He made it as far as the driveway before the nausea overtook him. When he gagged Claude stopped, allowing him to belch the contents of his stomach into the grass at the edge of the pavement.

Oh, that's a little better.

He grabbed Claude's arm and tried to push him away.

"I'm okay now. I don't need you to . . ."

But the hairy tree trunk coiled itself around his rib cage again, nearly lifting him off the ground.

"The lady says I'm to help you to your cabin. That's what I mean to do," he said.

The next conscious thought he had was—pain. He blinked back into awareness as Claude dragged him up the three concrete steps to his front door. Since he wore no socks with his loafers, his bare ankles scraped on the rough edge of each riser before banging into the next.

In the next moment, he was reclining on his sofa. His ankles were stinging, but he was afraid to look down to see if he was bleeding. His head was pounding, and the shadows on the ceiling kept spinning around and around and around.

Zoe untied her apron and tossed it into the busboy's tub

under the bar. She swept back a lock of damp hair off her face and looked around for Jade. It had been one hell of a night. When Jade said the Fourth of July weekend drew a hefty crowd, she wasn't exaggerating.

Her watch said it was almost midnight, and there were still several stragglers sitting at the bar. About time for last call. But where was Jade? She'd disappeared a while back and it seemed like she'd been gone for hours.

Jade whisked in moments later.

"The kitchen still open? I'm gonna grab a bite before I turn in," she asked.

Jade nodded. "Claude's still here. He got back a few minutes ago."

Got back . . . from where?

She pushed through the door into the restaurant.

They were already closed, but several of the waitresses were still bussing tables. The only one she knew by name, Nora, headed her way.

"Get you something from the kitchen, Zoe?" she asked.

She nodded, and then glanced over toward Jason's customary corner table. "Have you seen Mr. Rolland tonight?"

Nora's eyes widened and she cleared her throat. "He was here for a while. Almost all evening, in fact. He left about an hour ago."

Hmm. Odd reaction.

"Did he leave alone?"

Nora couldn't seem to meet her eyes, and started shifting from one foot to the other. "Not exactly."

Ah. Another tryst. Well, guess I should have figured that. Especially after our war of words down in the boathouse earlier.

Zoe glanced down at the menu she'd picked up at the

hostess stand. "Why am I not surprised," she said, more to herself than anyone else.

"It wasn't like that," Nora said, a little too quickly. Then she stepped closer to Zoe and murmured into her ear. "Claude had to help him back to his cabin."

She leaned back in surprise. "Claude? Why, was Mr. Rolland ill?"

"No, ma'am." The waitress dropped her gaze to the floor, as if afraid she was saying too much. "Mr. Rolland had a little too much to drink tonight." She cleared her throat, and when she raised her head, worry had etched lines between her brows. "I've never seen him quite like that before."

Zoe closed her eyes and sucked air into her lungs in a slow, controlled breath. Then she opened the menu and scanned it.

"Nora," she said, "I'd like you to brew me a pot of good, strong coffee. Put it in one of those insulated carafes we use for large tables." She met Nora's eyes. "Is Claude still here?"

Nora nodded.

"Okay, ask him to heat one of those loaves of French bread he baked this morning. Bring that to me, wrapped in cloth, in a basket. Can you do that for me?"

Nora blinked, hesitating. "Of course, Ms. Anderson. But didn't you want to order some dinner?"

Zoe shook her head. "My appetite seems to have taken a hike. The bread and some coffee will be just fine."

On her way up the hill, basket and carafe in hand, Zoe stopped by her cabin to retrieve her trusty bottle of aspirin. She also snagged the key Jason had insisted she use, the one that opened his front door. She headed toward his cabin.

Of course, there was no response to her ringing of the doorbell, twice. Knocking didn't work either. Finally, she set down her load and fished the key out of her bra where she'd slipped it. The skimpy black tank dress she wore didn't have any pockets.

The door creaked as she pushed it open to complete darkness. Zoe stood in the doorway for a moment, allowing her eyes to adjust. The blinds on the living room window were open, so a tiny amount of light from the driveway lights slivered through between the slats.

I wonder if he even made it upstairs?

But that question was answered with Zoe's next breath. The living room reeked of vomit. She squinted and made out a long, lanky form stretched out on the sofa.

She crept past him toward the kitchen, giving the sofa a wide berth. Lord knows what she might end up stepping in. She reached for the switch over the range, figuring the bright, overhead fluorescents might be a bit cruel. She grabbed a bottle of water out of the fridge.

Zoe cautiously tiptoed toward the sofa, searching the surface in the dim light for any possible land mines.

Well, at least he didn't barf all over this beautiful hardwood.

Apparently, the unpleasant miasma wafted from the man himself. Dark spots showed plainly on the front of his white shirt.

She kneeled down on the floor beside him. The dim light from the range hood, along with what little seeped in from the window, illuminated the contours of his face. With his eyes closed, he looked like a boy. One suffering from a bad stomach flu. His inky hair stuck up and away from his head at odd angles. Only one stubborn strand fell across his brow, and Zoe couldn't help but notice how long his lashes looked, feathered across his cheeks.

You don't smell very good, but you certainly are a very good-looking man.

188

Zoe reached up to brush away the errant lock of hair, but he didn't stir.

"Jason?" She kept her voice soft, quiet. "Jason? You okay?"

He groaned and his dark brows drew together, but he didn't open his eyes. After a moment, he lifted one hand to his head, while the other reached out to slide in her hair. She instinctively recoiled, but stopped herself.

Hope there's no stinky stuff on those fingers. But I have plenty of shampoo.

"I brought you some aspirin, Jason. And some coffee."

He groaned again, his eyes fluttering open to slits.

"I've got some warm bread here too. You'll feel a lot better if you try to get some of this in you."

He brought both hands up to cover his face. "Oh, I am never, ever drinking vodka again, little girl." He raked one hand through his hair, wincing at the contact. "Even my hair hurts."

"I'm not surprised. From what I heard, you raised the Wall Street Index on stock for Absolut tonight."

Jason tried to smile, but even that seemed to cause him pain. And he was still slightly slurring his words.

He is going to feel like pounded shit come morning.

He opened his eyes, at least as much as he could, searching her face.

"You still mad at me?" he asked.

She scowled. "I should be, even more now. What a dumb ass thing for you to do. Over a damned dress."

As he lifted himself onto one elbow, she handed him the water bottle, and he took a few sips. He winced as he swallowed.

"But are you? Mad?" he asked. His voice was husky.

Something deep inside Zoe's heart clenched. It was

painful. Agonizing. Where was that armor? She took a deep breath, and imagined inhaling liquid ice, drawing it down into her chest. Around her heart.

He's fling material, nothing more.

There. That's better.

"I'm not mad at you. But don't ever again think you've got any right to criticize what I choose to wear, or how I choose to act. Or who I choose to talk to."

She rose and fetched a mug from the kitchen. Then she filled it with coffee from the carafe and handed it to Jason. He had managed to push himself to a sitting position. She sat down next to him and poured some of the coffee from the carafe into the mug.

"You smell really bad," she said, wrinkling her nose. "Puke a la vodka."

Jason sipped from the mug and grimaced as he swallowed. He hung his head and ran his other hand through his wild hair. "Stupid. Just plain stupid."

She studied him. "So this isn't a regular occurrence, I'm guessing? The title of alcoholic isn't a fixture on your list of other dubious character traits?"

His eyes rose to meet hers, his brows drawn together. "You've been talking to my sister too much. She sees me six months a year. Jade may think she knows everything about me, but she doesn't."

Zoe opened her mouth, but then closed it and nodded. Jason was holding her gaze with such emotion, her breath caught in her chest.

If he is the man he'd like me to believe he is, then . . . what? I'm not ready for that kind of relationship.

No, he's a fox. He knows all the right things to say to a woman. No denials, but enough information to mislead—possibly.

"You still going with me tomorrow night to see the fireworks?" he asked, his gaze never leaving hers. "Should be really pretty out there on the water."

She hesitated only a few seconds before nodding. She was here to relax, have fun. What was Medina's advice? *Get a little drunk. Have a fling.*

"Yes, but tomorrow night, it's my turn to get tipsy," she said, releasing a slow smile.

Jason set his mug down on the table and shifted toward her. He reached out and took both of her hands, gazing intently into her eyes. "I'm sorry if I embarrassed you tonight. I promise, it will never happen again."

Another chunk of ice around her heart melted.

It would be so easy to fall in love with this man. I'm going to have to be very careful to keep my heart out of this.

Zoe awoke late the next morning. The Fourth of July had dawned hours earlier, revealing a clear, blue sky reflecting off the placid surface of the lake. The storm had passed, leaving behind milder, less humid air. Perfect for the summer holiday celebration.

She showered and was flipping through her closet when her cell rang. When Medina's sunny voice blasted in her ear, she smiled. Medina had always been the most carefree person she'd ever known. But Zoe had seen a change in her since she'd met Tony. Now, even her voice glowed.

"Hey, kiddo. What happened to you last night? Tony and I went down by the water around eleven, but when we came back Jade said you'd left. Everything okay?"

"I'm fine. But I'd be willing to bet there's a certain resort owner whose head feels like a lead-filled balloon this morning."

"Uh oh. I didn't know Jason was a big drinker."

191

"Apparently, he's not. Usually. So, you know how you felt the morning after cutting loose?"

Medina groaned. "I'd rather that entire six hours or so would disappear from my memory."

"I'm sure Jason will too. I went up to check on him. Aside from being covered in a vodka and vomit cocktail, he was alive."

"So what was his deal last night, anyway? What was he so pissed about?"

"He basically told me I was dressed like a whore. And I think he was jealous of Xavier."

"He obviously hasn't seen you around the X-man long enough to realize he doesn't do it for you." Medina laughed. "So, what'd you decide about the cottage? I saw him and that Arlin guy going over some paperwork with you."

"I'm signing Arlin on to research the property value. Then we'll set a price and offer it to Jason, I guess." Zoe sighed. "It's like letting go of my childhood. But maybe it's time for me to leave all that behind and move on."

Medina was silent for a moment. "I suppose that's probably best."

"So, are you and Tony still joining us tonight for the fireworks? Jason said his pontoon boat is like a floating living room with a bar."

"Sounds awesome. What time?"

"Well, if our captain can fit his head out of the door by seven, we're supposed to start out then."

As Zoe hung up the phone, she heard the doorbell. She was still wrapped in a towel, but she crept to the window and peeked down. There on the doorstep, looking rumpled but at least wearing clean clothes, was Jason. He was holding a long-stemmed red rose.

Zoe fumbled with the latch on the window and slid it

open. She stuck her head out and called down to him.

"Hey, what are you doing up so early? I didn't expect to see you venture out of a darkened room for another few hours."

Jason squinted up at her, shielding his eyes from the noonday sun. A broad grin spread over his face.

"It's all thanks to you, milady. Without your ministrations, I may have been permanently pickled."

She grinned. "I'll be right down."

Her hair still dripping, she answered the door barefoot, wearing nothing but the towel and a smile. Jason's eyes grew wide and his mouth fell open.

He stepped in and shoved the door shut with his foot, then dropped to one knee. He held out the rose. "I hope you'll forgive a very foolish man."

She snatched the rose from his hand and tossed it on the coffee table. Then she reached up and loosened the towel from its knot between her breasts. It dropped to the floor.

In an instant she was in his arms, his mouth closing hungrily over hers. She parted her lips and his tongue darted and teased her own. His hands slid down and cupped her bare ass, and he pulled her against him. The quick, growing thickness of his erection pressed insistently against her lower belly. She ground her hips against him.

"You certainly smell better than you did a few hours ago," she said between kisses.

"You, my girl, smell absolutely wonderful. And taste even better."

"Do I? How can you be so sure?" Zoe tilted her head to the side and fluttered her eyelashes.

Passion flared in his surreally blue eyes, making them almost fluorescent. He kissed along her jawline until his breath tickled her ear.

"You know, you're right. How can I be certain you taste as good as you smell?" he growled. His tongue flicked against the sensitive skin of her neck. "I'm afraid I'm going to need proof."

While his hands smoothed over her hips and up to cup her breasts, his tongue started tracing a trail to meet them. He kissed first one hardened nipple, then the other with soft, chaste presses of his warm lips. Then he took one into his mouth and began to suckle her.

Zoe's thighs began to tremble and she feared her knees would buckle out from under her. Her breath quickened and she moaned as hot, moist desire spread though her like wet fire. She wobbled and Jason caught her, sweeping her into his arms. He crossed to the sofa in two strides.

It felt strange to lie on this piece of public furniture naked. Its texture was smooth and rough at the same time. Soaring windows above the closed blinds had allowed sun to stream in, warming the damask.

But the blinds were definitely, thankfully, closed.

The loveseat wasn't quite long enough for Zoe to stretch out entirely. Jason knelt on the floor beside her, lifting one of her legs to rest over the cushioned arm. Then he pulled her other leg toward him. She heard him gasp as she opened up for him.

First, his hot breath on her open slit sent shock waves through her, and a tensing in her core that made her squirm. Then he drew back, starting at her knee, first with his lips. He pressed warm kisses against her skin in small steps, one following the other up her thigh. Their path was straight and sure.

She began to tremble uncontrollably as the stubble on his cheek grazed her inner thigh. He drew back, retreating to her knee. Now, his tongue came out to play. He traced a path, hot and wet, wandering from knee to thigh. Then he stopped. Again, he returned to her knee.

Her body quaked all over and the need in her core pulsed with a maddening rhythm. She couldn't wait much longer. When he made his second trip up with his tongue, she captured his head in her hands. She pulled him toward her, pleading.

"Please, Jason. Take me."

His tongue found her then, licking and sucking and circling her stiff clitoris with such sudden intensity, she lost control. Her climax, wave after wave of indescribable pleasure, claimed every cell of her consciousness. As her pleasure peaked and waned, he softened his touch. Eventually, he sat back on his heels, running his hands up and down her thighs.

She felt the tremors in his hands. He was struggling to maintain his own control.

"Spots. Upholstery," she managed. Yet it wasn't some psychotic episode that reduced her sentences to single words. It was the overwhelming afterglow of her orgasm.

"I've got a great housekeeping crew." His words tumbled out on a panting breath. "Now's let's hope they're as good on upholstery as they are on carpet." But like a dark cloud passing over his face, he suddenly closed his eyes and grimaced. "Oh, no. No protection. I have no protection."

She grinned. "You don't need any."

Dropping to her knees in front of him, her hands began an explorative journey, stroking his lightly furred chest, his slim hips, and followed the trail of dark hair down from his navel with one finger.

"Stand for me," she whispered, and then giggled. "Not you." She stroked his throbbing erection. "You're already standing at full attention." Her eyes met his. "You."

He did as she asked. She took his stiff penis into her hands, reveling in its velvety smoothness, the heat, and the throbbing weight of him.

She'd never been very good at this, and had never really enjoyed it much. But in this moment, she felt wanton and powerful, and there was nothing she wanted more. Hands, lips, and tongue, she worshipped him. His breath came faster and he ran his hands over the top of her head. When she took him into her mouth, opening to surround as much of him as she could, Jason moaned and tangled his fingers in her hair.

"I can't hold on much longer, Zo."

In a smooth, regular rhythm, she ran her lips along the length of him, flicking her tongue before plunging him into her mouth again and again.

He was panting now, moving with her, and meeting her strokes with desperate thrusts. As he drew close to his release, he fisted her hair in both of his big, strong hands. Tightly.

Flashback.

She sucked in a gasp and squeezed her eyes shut against the memory. The horror and disgust. A feeling of helplessness, of being trapped. The pain of being held down by a fistful of hair . . .

No. This is Jason. My choice, my pleasure, on my terms.

Using all of her senses, she anchored her mind in the moment. She opened her eyes and looked up, watching as he tipped his head back, his gorgeous face rapt in ecstasy. She tasted him and breathed in his musky scent. Reveled in the way his pubic hair tickled her nose. Her hands slid around to grip his hard buttocks, slicked now with a veil of sweat. She dug her nails in as he climaxed, shouting her name.

I'm winning, getting stronger every day. I will not let the past dictate my future.

A Taming Season

Chapter 13

When Zoe peeked in through the screen door at three o'clock, the Patio Bar was packed. There was no way she was muscling through that crowd. Instead, she ducked into the restaurant and, scooting around the smaller crowd waiting for tables, entered the bar through the adjoining door.

Jade turned and spotted her, her shoulders sagging with relief.

"It's been like this since lunch," she said, nearly shouting to be heard over the clamor of conversation. "I sure am glad to see you."

Zoe donned an apron and got to work. Nearly an hour passed before no one was holding up an empty glass, and there was a lull. Jade leaned up against the back counter next to her, crossing her arms.

"How's my brother? Still alive?"

She nodded and looked toward the floor. "Oh yeah. Definitely still breathing."

She could feel Jade's steady gaze studying her. "You have a bit more color in your cheeks than you did when you arrived at the Lodge. Country air doing you good, huh?"

She felt the blush creeping up her neck. "That too," she said, and grinned.

She lifted her face and met Jade's eyes. No trace of reproach or worry, like she'd seen there when she first found out about her fling with Jason. Her expression now seemed almost amused.

Jade shook her head. "Don't know what it is you're doing to that brother of mine. Whatever it is, seems to be rockin' his world."

"Hey, chica!" Zoe heard the familiar shout echoing over the din of voices. She turned and saw Medina, hooked firmly to Tony's massive arm, pushing through toward the bar. She was waving her free hand in the air, and there was something colorful dangling from her fingers.

"Look what I found in the village, Zo!" Medina sounded like a sugar-rushed kid when she and Tony finally made it to the bar. In her hand were two strands of miniature twinkling lights. The tiny bulbs were red, white, and blue. "They're necklaces. Battery-powered. We can wear them tonight on the boat. This way we can find each other."

Zoe laughed as she poured the ingredients for Medina's traditional Cosmo into a shaker. "I don't think finding each other will be a problem. Jason's boat isn't quite as big as Tony's."

"So what's this about Tony's being bigger than mine?"

Zoe jumped when Jason's voice rumbled into her ear as his arm encircled her waist. She glanced back over her shoulder. "You helping tend bar tonight?"

He squeezed her before letting her go. "No, but I did bring in reinforcements."

Zoe turned to see a young, very pretty woman standing next to Jason. Her long hair was pulled back in a ponytail, and she wore a Yankees ball cap.

She doesn't even look old enough to serve drinks.

"Collette's been working down at Murphy's, in the village, on her college breaks. I'm borrowing her for the night," Jason said. He smiled and winked at the attractive young woman.

Zoe felt the slightest wave of . . . what? Jealousy? Indignation? But it vanished when Jason turned back to her and flashed one of his gut-melting smiles.

"Collette's gonna help Jade while you go with me out on the boat later." His voice was low and growly, as if he meant the words to be heard by only her.

Jade had joined them, and was standing with her hands on her hips, scanning the girl from head to toe. "You look young. Do you know anything about mixing drinks, Collette?" she asked.

She bobbed her head. "I'm in law school. Been tending bar at Murphy's for about six years, every time I come home on a school break.

Jade scowled. She reached up and lifted the ball cap off the girl's head and said, "Lose the ponytail."

Collette did as she was told, shaking her straight, honey-red hair free. Jade pointed to her baggy white tee. "Knot that up around your waist." When the girl did, a couple inches of her flat midriff showed between the shirt and her tiny, very short denim cutoffs.

"Better," she said. Her eyes slid to Jason, and then to Zoe. "You two go on. We'll handle it from here."

Jason held Zoe's hand and led her down the steps toward the docks, where his pontoon boat was bobbing against the bumpers.

"You looking forward to this?" he asked. He lifted her hand and kissed it, searching her face.

"I am," she said. "I've never seen fireworks like this before. In the city, there's always a ground-glow going on. I'll bet the mountains make a gorgeous backdrop."

But she seemed distracted. Distant somehow. Her eyes flashed to his face once but didn't linger as she turned to look

200

for her friend.

Medina and Tony were a few steps behind, practically joined at the hip.

"Hey, Dina, come on. You two can do more of that later," Zoe called, laughing.

She won't meet my eyes. She looks everywhere else but into my eyes. Probably just excited.

He stepped onto the boat, and then turned to steady her as she followed him. Tony did the same for Medina, giving her ass a gentle smack as she made her way on board. She swatted his hand, and stuck out her tongue at him.

"Come on, you two. This is my little dinghy we're taking tonight. I get to make the rules. Nobody gets naked." Jason said in mock seriousness. "Maybe I ought to make you drive, Tony. That way at least one of your hands will stay occupied and out of trouble."

"I'll do it," Tony said, dropping down into the captain's chair and firing up the twin outboards. Medina stood behind him, her arms encircling his shoulders.

Jason led Zoe to the curved corner of the leather bench seat. He sat close beside her, settling one arm over her shoulders while his other hand laced fingers with hers.

There were already dozens of boats on the lake. Although the air had remained calm all day, all the boats' wakes had the water kicking up whitecaps. The pontoon boat hardly rocked on the waves, but Medina, still teetering behind Tony on another pair of her ridiculous spiked shoes, stumbled and giggled. Tony swiveled his chair around and patted his thigh, and then pulled her onto his lap.

Jason watched as Tony leaned in and whispered something in Medina's ear. Then they gazed at each other long enough to where Jason was worried about the direction of his boat.

"Hey you two. Let's not crash my boat tonight, okay?"

Tony grinned and turned his attention back to the water.

Jason had never seen him like this with a woman. His buddy was the burly, tough-guy city cop. Warm and fuzzy? Never. Not even with women he wanted to sleep with. At least not in public.

What is it about these two women? Are they secretly witches who've cast spells on both of us?

Jason leaned in to breathe the sweet, vanilla scent of Zoe's hair. He scooted his butt away from her, angling so he could rest his head on her shoulder. Zoe tipped her head against his, but kept her eyes trained straight ahead.

After a few minutes, he grasped her chin between two fingers, drawing her face to him. "You okay?"

Zoe nodded and smiled. A polite, sincere, but banal smile. He tried to look into her eyes, try to read what she was thinking, feeling. But after a brief glance, she slid her eyes away.

He buried his face against her neck. Yeah, she smelled like heaven, not only her hair, but her skin. Not some fragrance she slathered or sprayed on. This was the scent of her that moved him, and not only his man parts. When Jason held her in his arms, he wanted to own her, body and soul.

He'd never wanted a woman like that before in his whole life. The need shook him down to the core of his being.

"Yo, Jay. Didn't you hear me? The anchor, bud. We're gonna drift right over those buoy lines."

Tony had positioned their boat within a dozen yards of the huge, flat barge, the launching pad for tonight's fireworks. Buoys were strung in an irregular line around the craft creating a floating fence. Somehow, Tony had managed to claim a spot right up against the boundary.

Jason scrambled to his feet and released the anchor line.

He let the rope slide through his fingers until it stopped, then tugged to secure it. "Got it. All set."

"We've got at least another hour to kill," Tony said. "Let's get the girls a cocktail."

Zoe jumped to her feet. "I'm the bar bitch. Let me."

He watched in amusement as Zoe found her way around the tiny wet bar hidden in the front corner of the boat. She pulled open the cabinet doors underneath the sink and rummaged through for plastic cups and an ice scoop. He had a rather excellent view of her firmly rounded ass from where he sat, and had to shift, crossing his legs to disguise the growing bulge in his shorts.

When the drinks were made and handed out, Medina lifted one of the silly lighted necklaces she had looped around her neck and handed it to Zoe.

"Almost dark, Zo. Time for some bling."

The expression of childish glee on Zoe's face made Jason's chest ache. What a wonder this woman was. A unique combination of soft and spitfire, innocent girl, and strong-willed woman. The feeling was new to him, exhilarating and terrifying at the same time.

Is it possible I'm falling for her? Is this what love feels like?

When darkness settles over a mountain lake, it falls like a brick. The heavy woods swallow more than their share of light, so dusk is a brief whisper between daylight and complete blackness. One minute Jason was watching Tony and Medina cuddle across the boat, and in the next all he could see was the glow of Medina's silly necklace.

Like stars winking on in the night sky, marker lights flickered on all around them. The tiny amber and green globes seemed to hover in the darkness, bobbing on the water like tipsy fireflies. The air cooled fast once the sun disappeared. Jason sighed as Zoe snuggled up to him.

When the pop and whistle of the first launching rocket sounded, Zoe jolted in his arms. He squeezed her tighter against him. "Now, the fun part begins," he whispered in her ear.

To him, the fireworks were nothing new. He grew up in the village. Every summer, year after year, he'd watched the display from different vantage points. They marked many of his life's milestones.

As a little boy, he'd watched them from the dock, munching on a hot dog and cramming popcorn into his mouth until he was sick. When he'd gotten older, he and his buddies would stake their claim in a corner of the city park. There, with contraband cans of beer concealed in paper bags, they'd laugh and shout the night away as the sky over the village turned into a sparkling fantasy.

Once his dad gave him his own boat at the age of sixteen, it became his floating bedroom, and hiked his popularity way up. Jason Rolland's Fourth of July parties on the lake were wild, teenage orgies, where the fireworks had nothing to do with the thrills.

Tonight, though, was different. Something magical was happening, and Jason wasn't sure if he should embrace the emotion or run like a startled deer. This simple, familiar experience, with Zoe beside him, became brand new.

As each stream of fire streaked up into the night sky, Jason gazed in wonder—not at the starbursts of red, green, gold, and silver—but at the reflection of those colors dancing in Zoe's shining eyes.

She was mesmerized, he realized. Was she going back in time in her mind too? To those Fourth of Julys on the front porch of the cottage? She blinked, and smiled, and oohed and aahed, clapping her hands like a little girl.

No wonder she was so devastated to see her childhood cottage in ruins. He suddenly realized that after the hell she'd been through, this is why she was here. To return to a safe, happy place in her childhood with innocent, carefree memories. He winced, remembering how she'd reacted the day he talked of bulldozing the place. How could he ever think of taking that away from her?

I will make it new for her. I will do the impossible and turn back the clock. No matter what it takes, I will rebuild Zoe's cabin. It will be my gift to her.

The stillness that settled over the lake was almost deafening after the show's brilliance. Zoe heard an occasional hoot of laughter echo across the water from the closest shore, or from another boat. She leaned back against Jason, their bodies spooned on the cushioned bench seat. She heard Medina giggling from the other end of the boat, some twenty feet away. But her friend's glowing necklace was all she could see.

They floated that way for nearly an hour, watching the lights of the other boats gradually fade into the distance. Medina's giggling had ceased, and Zoe wondered if she'd fallen asleep, or if they were quietly making out. Finally, Tony cleared his throat and spoke into the darkness.

"You guys ready to head in?"

"We're ready. Thanks for driving, Tony. You're so much better with these things than I am," Jason said.

"This was fun," Zoe breathed, nuzzling against his neck. "Magical. Thank you."

She leaned her head back and watched the stars winking overhead, enjoying the feel of the wind in her hair as they traveled back to the docks. Jason held her, one arm around her waist, the other stroking up and down her arm. Once or twice, he lifted her chin with two fingers, trying to get her to meet his gaze. Every time he did, her lids fluttered closed.

I need to keep this experience all about the physical, enjoying the moment. Flings aren't supposed to involve gazing lovingly into each other's eyes.

The air was much cooler now, and with the boat moving, the wind chilled her until she was shivering.

"Cold?" Jason asked.

"A little. But I'm sure you can take care of that once we get home."

Jason helped Tony dock the boat and tie it up while she and Medina watched them. Her friend had come up to sit next to her as they'd approached the shore.

"Did you have fun, Dina?"

Medina turned to face her, but didn't answer. Although it was dark, the lights from the docking area shone in her friend's eyes. They were filled with tears.

"What's the matter?" She reached out and touched her arm.

Medina sighed. "I can't ever remember feeling this content. So totally, completely happy."

Zoe reached out and hugged her. "It's very different up here. Not what we're used to. Like a dream."

As they headed up the steps from the dock, Jason leaned in and whispered in her ear. "Jade will be home by now. Your cabin?"

She nodded. "Hmm."

They walked Tony and Medina to their parked car, and after hugs and goodbyes, headed toward the Aspen.

They headed up the path to the front door, listening to the thunderous serenade of crickets from the woods beyond. She reached into her pocket for the key, but Jason stopped her. He held his fingers to his lips. Dragging her by the hand, he led her around the outside of the cabin to the secluded backyard.

The way this cabin angled out from the serpentine drive, its backyard was the most private of any on the property. A very shallow patch of grass separated it from the dense woods. The landscape sloped off sharply from each side, so no other structure had been built there.

The moon hung like a monstrous, celestial globe, illuminating everything to near daylight. But the trees and the cabin itself cast certain areas of the backyard in shadow. He led her there, with the crickets screaming their riotous cacophony in her ears, and the smooth grasses spread under her feet like a lush carpet. When they'd reached a particularly deep patch of shadow, Jason stopped and turned, folding her into his arms.

His kiss was firm and insistent, his hands suddenly roaming all over her body in a hungry frenzy. She parted her lips and he thrust his tongue inside, cupping her head and angling to go deeper. She leaned toward him, pressing her heavy, swollen breasts against his hard chest. He moaned and pressed his hips closer, his hard arousal pulsing against her belly.

When she pulled away and dropped to her knees, she heard him gasp.

Jason had always considered himself a normal man with normal physical responses. He wasn't a teenager anymore, and had long since outgrown the jackrabbit syndrome. He prided himself on his self-control in the bedroom. But with Zoe, all bets were off.

This woman held an invisible, double-edged, sword over him. He couldn't get enough of her, and her touch drove him to heights of pleasure he'd never known. But there was something deeper, stronger in her power over him. Something that dissolved every last ounce of his macho armor.

Zoe dropped to her knees in the grass before him and reached up to lower his zipper. Passion flamed inside him, and he knew that tonight, he couldn't let her set the pace. There was simply no way he could hold on that long. The minute her hands began their sensuous dance around his stiff erection, the pressure began to build. Fast. Too fast. When he felt her hot breath against his skin, he instinctively took a step back.

"I can't. Not tonight, Zo. I'll come all over you in seconds. Please. Let me please you first." His voice was rough and raspy, punctuated by panting breaths he'd already lost control over.

He knelt down in the grass facing her, taking her face into his hands. Moonlight reflected off her creamy pale skin, the golden glints in her hair, and her shining eyes. She was like some ethereal fairy creature, the most beautiful he'd ever imagined. He traced one finger gently down the irregular path of her scar.

"Don't ever think you're damaged. In any way," he said. "You are the closest thing to perfection I'll ever be blessed enough to touch."

For one fleeting instant, she met his gaze, and he felt as though their souls collided in a wondrous union. In the next breath, she slid her eyes away.

"Then touch me, Jason. I want you to touch me, everywhere."

Her body was there, every gorgeous part of her, except her heart. Why was she hiding herself from him? It hurt him, frustrated him, and made him all the more determined.

How can I reach her heart? How can I show her how

much she means to me?

His breath shuddered in his chest and his hands trembled as he slid them down Zoe's sides to her waist. He grasped the edges of her silky tank and lifted it over her head. Underneath, she wore a piece of satin and lace that strained to contain her full breasts, the taut peaks clearly visible.

He felt himself trembling on the edge again. He dropped his hands. "You do it," he rasped.

Her smile was sweet as she reached up and unclasped the front clip of her bra. It fell away, revealing generous curves punctuated with stippled, dark points. Jason cupped them, running his thumbs over her hard nipples. He drew in a shuddering breath and looked away.

Take control, dude. You can't come now. You have to please her first.

But her hands were on his face, drawing his mouth to hers. Her lips met his in a hungry tangle of tongues, and he pushed her down, laying her on the cool, damp grass. His fingers trembled almost uncontrollably as he fumbled with the foil packet he'd snagged from the back pocket of his shorts. He stood, dropped his clothing to the ground, and applied the protection himself.

No way in hell I can let her do it. Not tonight.

He gazed down at the heavenly vision beneath him. Zoe lay nude on the grass, moonlight glinting off her tawny hair, spread now around her head like a halo. A wood nymph, from one of his most intense fantasies.

She's like a dream. I am so not living this.

He wondered for a moment if he should straddle her. He knew she had ghosts. But there she was, lying there, knees bent and thighs spread open so invitingly. When she reached her arms up for him, he knew it was okay.

He settled between her thighs, but entered her first with

his fingers. She gasped when he pushed first one, then two fingers inside her. She thrust against him and moaned. When he began circling her hard clitoris with his thumb, her moans became strangled screams.

She came hard around his fingers, pulsing and throbbing and writhing. He almost came apart and couldn't wait another moment. Before she was through, he grasped her hips and lifted her, pushing into her hard and deep. He thrust once, then twice into her pulsating center before he lost control himself.

They lay on the grass together until their sweat cooled and chilled. When she started to shiver, he helped her to her feet and led her to the back door of the cabin.

"We're lucky the key fits both front and back," he mumbled, chuckling.

They slipped inside, still very naked, dragging their now damp clothes in one hand, firmly connected by the other.

Later as they lay in her bed, Jason held her close and stroked her hair until she drifted off. He listened until he heard her breathing grow slow and steady. When he was sure she was asleep, he whispered aloud into the darkness.

"I've had sex with dozens of women in my life, Zoe girl. But until tonight, I never knew what it meant to make love."

Xavier's phone call on Tuesday morning lurched Zoe back into reality.

"Arlin's done his research on this, Zoe, and it seems the right-of-way transaction was perfectly legal."

She scowled into her mug of coffee. Still in her bathrobe, she was sprawled out on the loveseat downstairs. She was getting to the good parts of her latest novel, and almost resented Xavier's intrusion.

Plus, the X-man's voice in her ear when she was right in

the middle of experiencing a lustily written sex scene made her empty stomach a little queasy.

"Okay," she said after a moment. "Okay, well, where do we go from here?"

She heard papers shuffling. "It's probably best you discuss this directly with Arlin, but he's away at a conference this week, so he asked me to update you."

"Did he have any advice on what I should do next? If the transaction was legal, then it sounds like my property is worth next to nothing." Zoe sat up and clunked her mug down on the table. "Unless I want to rebuild and drive through Lakeview every time I come up here."

"Not exactly next to nothing, Zoe. Especially to this guy who owns Lakeview. I think if we play our cards right, we might be able to soak this guy pretty good for the lot. I'm sure that old shack doesn't reflect well on his upscale resort." Xavier chuckled. "And I do use that term loosely."

We? Since when are *we* making this decision? And since when are we considered a *we*?

Zoe shook her head and leaned it on her hand. "Look, Xavier, I need some professional advice here. I'd love to restore the old place and keep it, for nostalgic value, if nothing else. But at this point, I don't even know if I'll have a job to go back to in August."

"Now, Zoe, I've told you. You have no worries there. I'll always be here to take care of you. I understand your issues, and I can be a very patient man. I've always been willing to wait for you. Until you're ready."

Yes, this is the Prince Charming who's been waiting patiently for me to get over my husband's murder, and my rape. So I can consent to be his perfect, socialite, trophy wife. Ugh.

Not that X was that much older than Zoe. But he'd

explained, in very clear, logical terms, why he'd been interested in her on their first date. She'd met Xavier a year after David's death when she'd stopped by Dina's office to pick her up for lunch. Dina had been working for Xavier for two years at that point and had told her all about her sophisticated but stiff-necked boss.

The X-man had claimed he'd been captivated by Zoe at first glance. Of course, she'd been in no condition to even notice him let alone date him, so Xavier had waited a very respectable six months before asking Zoe out on their first date—and six months after that, to marry him.

And like the knight in shining armor that he aspired to be, he'd kissed the back of her hand and promised to take care of her, honor and cherish her, if she would consent. Nothing about love, which at the time, to Zoe, had almost seemed a manageable arrangement. Almost.

Xavier Le Blanc was a high-profile Manhattan attorney and had endless social events where she would, he'd said, look marvelous on his arm. He promised to whisk her away to every exotic location the world had to offer. He could afford to wardrobe her to the nines. One of his very good friends was one of the best plastic surgeons in all of Manhattan who, he was certain, could fix that little problem with her face.

He'd made it clear he wasn't interested in having children, and was a simple man when it came to sexual needs. Zoe had interpreted that to mean he either had a mistress in every borough of the city, or was a closet gay. Every time they'd gone out for dinner, he'd always left her at the door with nothing more than a chaste kiss goodnight.

In any case, Zoe had managed to put off giving him an answer to his proposal for the better part of a year.

Zoe hung up with X's promise that his buddy Arlin would get back to her as soon as he breezed back into town, sometime later that week.

She wanted to call Medina, but knew her friend was working. Right there in Xavier's office, no less. She briefly considered calling her parents, but spilling her problems on them usually only made them worse. Could she talk to Jade? Probably not about this particular issue, since it had to do with the resort.

What scared her most was how she yearned to talk to Jason. But he'd left for Albany that morning and wasn't expected back until Thursday.

Now that's a dumb idea. He's the last one I should talk to. He's my adversary on this issue.

Her phone pinged and she glanced down to read the text lighting up her screen.

In between meetings. Missing you already. Call later. Love you.

Jason. Zoe's breath caught in her throat. The very last thing she needed right now was to see those two words. Did he actually mean them or was it just part of his charming way of keeping his fling-of-the-moment captivated while he was out of town.

Yet, she couldn't deny the way her heart clenched when she read them. And that fact terrified her to the core.

Chapter 14

For Zoe, time over the next several weeks seemed to evaporate as she fell into a pattern that suited her well. She was alone most of the week, since Jason left every Monday for Albany. Even when he returned on Thursday, his radio show obligated his evenings from eight o'clock on.

A nice, regulated separation, making it much easier to avoid getting too attached.

Well, partially separated, at least. Her chalet was booked beginning July fifteenth, so she had reluctantly moved in with Jason. Since he wasn't home half the time, or in his studio a good chunk of the remainder, she found the situation comfortable. Exactly what she needed.

Zoe slept late and usually stayed in her bathrobe until noon on the patio reading. She played tourist, dozing under an umbrella, listening to the happy chatter of children playing in the sand, and to the soothing sounds of the water swooshing back and forth along the shoreline. Afternoons, she tended bar, only occasionally having to field off the flirtatious advances of some guy looking for some summer fun.

I've wrapped my head around this fling thing, but one man at a time is enough, thank you very much.

She and Jade took several day trips, shopping, sightseeing. They even went to Fort Ticonderoga, forty miles or so north of the lake. Although a great historical site, that trip did nothing but give her the creeps.

Apparently the museum's curators felt that crumbling stone walls, ancient cannons, and cases filled with muskets and swords didn't tell the story of the Revolutionary War with enough gripping detail, so they made sure to offer gritty, realistic exhibits as well. Zoe cringed viewing the morbid displays of partially dismembered mannequins, blood-stained wooden tables, and the eerie sounds of fake moaning prisoners chained in the dungeons. She left Ticonderoga with a much more memorable impression of war than she recalled from American History class.

"Next time let's stick to happy places," she told Jade on the way home. "I know history is important, but there's so much sadness oozing out of those stone walls. Too much for me."

Jade glanced over at her. "How are you doing, Zoe? I mean, really?" Her expression was warm with compassion.

She sat up straighter and threw one arm over the top of her steering wheel. "I'm doing extremely well. No more word blender episodes. I think the combination of this mountain seclusion, along with my new meds, are actually working."

Not to mention the incredible sex I'm having with your brother. Or that he follows me around like a lost puppy every minute he's home.

Jade, of course, already knew that. But Zoe's relationship with Jason wasn't one she wanted to discuss with his sister. Heck, she didn't even want to consider it a relationship. Although she enjoyed the friendship she and Jade were developing, when it came to Jason, she'd rather Jade think of her as just another one of her brother's summer romps.

Safer that way. Much, much safer.

Medina became a regular weekend visitor, though she

didn't stay at the resort. Tony's summer place on the other side of the lake sat plumb in the middle of what Medina distastefully referred to as 'the uncharted wilderness.' But that didn't keep her from driving up after work every Friday afternoon, and getting up at the crack of dawn on Monday to drive back.

This thing with Tony has got her whipped.

She'd never—ever—seen Medina stay with a guy this long. And to rent a car and make that four hour drive every weekend? No doubt, Tony was paying for the rental. Medina didn't make that much working as an assistant to Xavier. But there was something motivating her, very strongly, to take that trip every single weekend. Was it possible that her friend was actually falling in love?

No way. Not Medina. Tony was the big, hunky alpha-male type—definitely not the type her friend would put up with for long. The sex must be incredible.

Zoe was quite enjoying her own sexual reawakening these days. She loved how Jason could barely wait to get his hands on her every Thursday afternoon. She'd wait for him in his cabin, and was having quite a fun time playing the siren. They had the cabin to themselves for those few hours, while Jade worked the bar. And Jason didn't have to climb the stairs to his studio until eight.

She was feeling particularly frisky today. She and Jade had been to the outlet mall, and while her friend had gone in to browse at the Coach store, she slipped in to a lingerie boutique that specialized in spicy.

Zoe had never bought bad girl undies.

So later that afternoon, as she waited for Jason's Hummer to pull in the driveway, she couldn't wait to show them off.

Jason had never been crazy about the time he spent in

Albany. He was a country boy at heart, and although the city offered lots of excitement and choices, it also exhausted him. Business had been especially difficult this summer. Was it the financial climate? Or had it been his distracted, indifferent attitude toward the importance of making that final sale?

From the minute he checked in at the Marriott until he checked out on Thursday, all he could think about was Zoe.

What the hell is happening to me? Surely, I didn't intentionally leave my testicles back at the lake.

But somehow, it seemed as though he had.

Tracy was becoming a bleached blonde, perfume-doused albatross. A grim reminder of the guy he once thought he was. She'd maintained her job at the bar in the hotel's lounge, though Jason questioned how that was possible since he'd chatted once or twice with the restaurant manager. His little fling with her had lasted all of three days. But he kept her on, knowing that peak season would wane soon, and then he'd have the perfect excuse to let her go.

She stalked Jason. She knew when he'd be coming in, and knew his favorite suite. Although the hotel's excellent security didn't allow her any information, still, she showed up night after night in the lounge, seeking him out, even if she wasn't working. Jason used to plant himself with his laptop in the lounge for hours every night, handling business. Now, he retreated to the privacy of his room to avoid any uncomfortable confrontations.

He was relieved to hand in his key and sign the credit card receipt on Thursday morning.

"Hey, Josh, how's it going?" Jason was surprised to see the hotel manager behind the front desk. "Got you actually doing some work today, huh?"

The short man with buzzed, dark hair chuckled and shook his head. "Gotta get out here sometimes to see how things are being handled. Don't want it to end up like the restaurant situation."

Jason cocked his head. "Problems in the restaurant?"

"Not really. You knew your castoff, Tracy, had a thing going with Brian, right?"

Jason rolled his eyes. "Ask me if I'm surprised."

"Well, that fire burned itself out pretty quick, since Brian said all she could talk about was you. Anyway, her last day is today."

"Well I can't say I'm sad about that." Jason scanned the printed bill Josh handed him. "She's been almost stalking me lately."

Josh's eyebrows drew together. "Now why didn't you say something about that, Jay? I could have—"

"Don't sweat it, man. It's good she's leaving, though. I've got somebody I'd love to bring with me next time, and bumping into Tracy would definitely not be cool." He signed the invoice and slid it back over the counter. "Same suite, next week, okay? But I'll be coming in Monday afternoon. Can you have a bottle of champagne on ice in the room by, say, three?"

Josh slid him a knowing look, and then winked. "Gotcha. Done. See you then."

A little thrill clutched in Jason's chest. He couldn't wait to bring Zoe here. His schedule next week was wide open, and he intended to keep it that way. He knew she was a city girl, and Albany certainly couldn't hold a candle to Manhattan. But the state capital was a neat city, with lots to offer. He wanted to show her that although Lake George was rural, civilization—as she defined it—wasn't very far away.

As he turned from the counter, briefcase in hand, he saw the valet drive up with his Hummer outside the lobby doors. Distracted, he was digging in his pocket for the valet's tip, and looked up just in time to avoid colliding with a woman.

Tracy. Shit.

Her last day, and just his luck, she was working the lunch shift.

"Hey, Tiger," she purred, throwing one arm around his waist as she dragged him back into the lobby. "Where you been? I've been missing my Jay-Jay."

"Good, Trace. Kind of busy. Gotta run." He glanced down at his watch. "I've got a meeting before I head out this afternoon."

Her hands went to her hips, and she cocked one hip, glaring at him. "What's up with you? You're over me?"

He straightened his shoulders and met her glare. "Look, Tracy, it was great. We had a thing. A summer thing, and it was great. But it's done now, and I hear you've already moved on anyway. Brian, right?"

Her eyes narrowed and he cringed. Her too fluffy, unnaturally golden hair, at that moment, got bigger. She puffed up, like a cobra.

Oh, shit. Not good.

"Yeah, I tried moving on. Didn't work. I couldn't get you out of my mind. I was hoping it would be the same for you." It actually sounded like she was hissing. *Hissing.*

Holy fucking shit.

Jason tugged on the collar of his button-down shirt and glanced around. Josh had disappeared into the office. No help there. It was a little early for any new check-ins, and late for checkouts. There was no one else in the lobby.

He looked at the floor between them and shook his head. "I'm sorry Tracy, but it's not. I've moved on. It's just how it is."

The air between them crackled, almost visibly, with electricity. But not the good kind. He dragged in a breath and

219

blew it out.

"Gotta go. See you around, 'kay?"

He turned, gripping the briefcase handle so tightly his palm hurt. With long strides and no hesitation, he headed out the lobby doors.

Once I'm out of here, I can leave this all behind. Like it never happened. It never should have.

He was almost to the sidewalk when he heard Tracy's shrill words vibrating through the closing door.

"I guess you've forgotten about that little equipment malfunction we had, haven't you?"

He froze and whirled, glaring at the wild-haired blonde through the glass. His heart crashed like a block of ice on granite. He couldn't exactly hear what she said next. But he easily read the words her blood-red lips formed as she patted her flat abdomen.

"I'll be in touch, Tiger."

The drive back to Lake George was the longest he could ever remember. Was it possible the crazy bitch was telling the truth? This couldn't—could *not*—be happening. What a horrible twist of fate it would be if Tracy ended up pregnant with his child.

Sure, in today's world, DNA testing could easily determine the truth. But Jason didn't know how that worked, and whether the test could even be done before the baby was born. And although he was certain he was in a sizable pool of possible fathers, he could very well be facing up to nine months—possibly a lifetime—of veritable hell.

Why, after all these years of living this carefree way, did this have to happen now that he'd met Zoe?

Carefree my ass. More like careless. My whole life, trashed because of one tiny piece of flawed latex. Or plastic. Or whatever the hell those things are made of.

And how could he possibly hope to nurture his relationship with Zoe now? He already knew her opinion of him. Hell, this was proof. He was a player. Fling material. Nothing more.

That may have been true before, but not since Zoe.

Once on the highway, Jason watched a mass of purple and gray storm clouds creeping over the Adirondacks ahead.

Yup. Describes my life right about now. Perfectly.

A frightening image flashed through his mind. Tracy, propped up in a hospital bed with a blanketed bundle in her arms. His stomach clenched, and then rolled over. What a horrible sentence to strap onto a brand-new, innocent life— Tracy for a mother. It was enough to make a man impotent.

But as he drove up the last, long stretch of the Northway, his thoughts drifted back to Zoe. Soft, warm, sweet, fiery, freckled Zoe. The one who'd been so brave in coming up here to claim her inheritance, even after all the trauma she'd been through. The one who'd been so concerned about him the night he'd gotten drunk, even though she'd had every reason to be furious with him.

At that moment, Jason wanted desperately to bury his face in her hair, and smell himself on her skin. He yearned to see, in her deep green eyes, a glimmer of what he was starting to feel about her. Not only smoldering passion, but something deeper. Something more enduring.

His disturbing daydream about Tracy floated back in, casting a shadow over his thoughts, matching the storm clouds up ahead. But gradually, the image shifted. The woman in that hospital bed was red-haired, with speckled, peachy-pale skin. One cheek was clearly etched with a brighter, zigzagged line. Her minty eyes were wide with wonder as they shifted from the bundle she clutched tenderly in her arms back up to meet his.

When he imagined her smile, the highway outside the windshield washed into a watery blur. And not a drop of rain had yet fallen.

The skies opened up over the Adirondacks about a half hour before Jason finally got back to Lakeview. Although the digital numbers on his dash claimed it was only four o'clock, he could swear twilight had fallen. Even with the wipers frantically slapping at the relentless sheet of water, he could barely see the road. It was dark enough for headlights, but still too bright for them to do any good at all.

Finally, home. The golden glow from his second story window told him where Zoe was waiting for him. His heart skipped a beat, and he sat for a few moments watching the light in the window as the rain thrummed his car.

That's what it's like to be with her. She's a glowing light that makes all the bullshit of daily life fade away. There's no doubt—I'm in love with her. And I'm scared to death this life-changing summer is going to end.

The dash from car to door was barely seven steps, but enough to drench Jason head to toe. He stepped inside and slipped off his squishing loafers, leaving them on the doormat. The living room was dark, the only light coming from the tiny bulb under the range hood in the kitchen. He didn't see her at first. But as his eyes adjusted to the dimness, he realized someone was stretched out on his couch.

Jason raked his hand through his dripping hair. "Zo?"

Without saying a word, she rose and came toward him. For a moment, he thought he was dreaming. Like an angel, or a specter, she was surrounded by a cloud of something sparkly and pale, and it flowed around her wrists and ankles as she moved. She stopped less than an arm's length away, and he wanted so badly to reach out and fold her into his arms. But his clothes were soaked and icy.

Then he realized he could see right through the diaphanous cloud of fabric that continued to move around her, even when she stood still. She wasn't naked underneath, and although he couldn't clearly see what she had on, he knew he couldn't wait to explore. She was gazing up at him with a spark in her eyes that shot him straight in the groin.

"Oh, Zoe," he breathed. "Let me get this wet mess off me . . ." His fingers were shaking as he fumbled with the buttons on his shirt, peeling it off and dropping it on the mat. She reached forward and grabbed his wrist.

"There's another wet mess you need to take care of," she murmured, and guided his hands between the folds of fabric and straight to her wet slit. He groaned and dropped to his knees, replacing his fingers with his tongue.

Her patch of tawny hair tickled his nose as he tasted her. She was sweet and clean and slick. His own arousal pressed painfully against wet denim as he slid his hands under the gown and realized she was covered with patches of lace that were somehow ingeniously designed to allow access to all the best places. He gripped her rounded bottom and licked her hard clitoris. Her fingers twisted in his wet hair and she tensed, exploding under his tongue within seconds.

"You've missed me," he said, rocking back and looking up at her. She smiled and reached out for his hand.

"Come see my new things."

Jason followed her up the stairs to his room. He realized that the golden light he'd seen from outside came from candles. They were everywhere, bathing the entire space with a flickering, magical glow.

She turned and pulled on a ribbon between her breasts, and the billowing gown slipped from her shoulders and puddled around her feet. His breath caught in his throat. The patchwork of lace underneath skimmed her curves, but hid

223

nothing. Creamy, speckled skin peeked through everywhere. Ruffles cupped the curves of her breasts, but her taught, upturned nipples were in plain view, beckoning him.

"Oh, Zoe." His throat was thick with longing. "You are the most beautiful creature I've ever seen."

A seductive goddess, yet somehow, soft and innocent. How is that possible?

Her slow smile made him feel flushed, breathless. His blood pounded in his ears, and his erection throbbed.

Painfully. Tight, wet denim. Get it off, stupid.

She watched, silently, as he struggled out of his jeans, and then rolled his drenched underwear down off his hips. His stiff cock sprang free, and he moaned.

"I need you," he said. She stepped forward and into his arms.

Her body molded soft and warm against him, the lace a little scratchy, her nipples hard nubs pressing into his chest. He covered her mouth with his and she opened for him. Their tongues began a slow, teasing dance that had his cock pulsing against her belly. Her hands were everywhere, tangled in his hair, tracing the sensitive skin behind his ear, down his neck, across his chest.

Then she pushed him away. "If you don't slow down, Tiger, this isn't going to last nearly long enough," she said.

The nickname sliced through his heart like a hot blade.

I'm not that man anymore. Not since you.

He could think it, but couldn't form the words. She wouldn't believe him anyway. If not now, surely when . . .

I'm not letting this moment go. I'm not letting you go, my love.

He took her hand and led her to the bed. Sitting on the edge, he pulled her close and rested his cheek between her breasts. There was so much he wanted to say, but he didn't know how. This woman had broken through his armor, seeped into his soul in a way he'd never imagined possible. She was a drug he couldn't live without.

They stayed that way for a long moment, Zoe's hands combing through his hair. Finally, she cupped his face in her hands and met his gaze.

"Take me," she pleaded.

The flames inside his chest and his groin flared again as she stepped back and peeled the lacy patchwork off, one piece at a time. Jason reached for her and pulled her down beside him. He ran his hands over every inch of her body, worshipping her with his eyes. Then he covered one nipple with his mouth.

He loved the way she gasped, her hips writhing as her tight, stippled nub relaxed under the warm slickness of his tongue. It swelled and throbbed in his mouth, as he suckled her gently. He moved to the other one, continuing to stroke the wet peak with his thumb. Zoe moaned and rocked her hips.

"Now. I need you. Please."

Still teasing one nipple with his tongue, Jason slid his fingers to her slit, slipping first one finger in, then two. Zoe groaned and pushed against him, thrusting in an accelerating rhythm. When he pressed his thumb against her hard clit, she cried out. He circled it once, twice, three times before she came apart, her core pulsating around his fingers and drenching them with her sweet pleasure.

She held him, her hands pressing his head to her chest. Her heart thudded against his ear, very fast, but then slowed, little by little. After a moment he heard her whisper, "Now you."

Jason's hands shook as he rolled the condom down over his throbbing shaft. His control was nearly gone. He knew he wouldn't be able to hold on very long once inside her.

He threw one leg over her, but then stopped, remembering. Instead, he rolled onto his back. She climbed on top, hovering teasingly over his stiff cock. She smiled down at him, her mouth quirked in a devilish half grin.

"Zoe, please," he moaned.

Very slowly, she took him in, sliding down over him until he was completely inside.

One with her.

She sat still, gazing down at him, her smile fading. Something chased across her face, some emotion Jason couldn't read. Almost . . . sadness. In the next moment, it was gone, and she dropped her head back and began to rock her hips.

Jason felt the pressure building so fast he couldn't take in enough air to keep up. He reached up and cupped her breasts, stroking his palms over her nipples. She rocked faster, and then reached down to slide her hand between them where they were joined. As he watched her using her own finger to please herself, his control began to crumble.

He gripped her hips with his hands and stilled her for one heartbeat, then two. Zoe opened her eyes and met his gaze.

Jason's throat was thick. The words came out gruff.

"My Zoe."

She blinked, and he saw it again. Some unnamed emotion that skittered across her face for the briefest instant, and then disappeared. She closed her eyes, dropping her head back. When she thrust her hips against him again, he lost himself in his release.

Later, as they spooned, dozing on the bed, Jason asked quietly, "Come with me to Albany next week? Please?"

Chapter 15

Zoe couldn't sit still as Jason drove them to Albany on Monday afternoon. As much as she'd been enjoying the slower pace of the mountains, there was a little city girl inside crying for some bright lights, concrete, and crowds.

The Albany Marriott, Jason had told her, was smack in the middle of downtown. Lots of everything close by.

"Restaurants, the Capital Building, the Palace Theatre, two different museums. All within two or three blocks. What do you want to do this week, milady? Your wish is my command." Jason flashed that perfect smile and her heart melted. His eyes were radiant today, mirroring the translucent blue of the sky.

She bounced up and down in her seat, fully aware she was acting like a child. But she couldn't help it.

"I . . . I don't know. I'm so excited to have choices. Don't get me wrong. Staying at the lake has been the best tonic in the world for me. But," she twisted her fingers together, "I've missed the faster pace of a city. Just a little."

The valet loaded their luggage on a cart while Jason tossed the keys to the concierge. "Don't plan on moving her much this week, Donny. Park her wherever she won't be in your way."

Sleek, shiny, and modern. Those were the first words to

pop into her mind as they made their way through the lobby to the desk. Dark, polished woods, chrome, and a touch of whimsy in the bright colors of the patterned carpet screamed elegance. She brought her hand to her mouth, and then glanced toward Jason.

"Civilization," she whispered. He blinked, and his brows drew together ever so slightly. "And I'm here with my mountain man. How perfect is that?" She stood on tiptoe and kissed his cheek.

"Still in the honeymoon suite, Mr. Rolland?"

Zoe's eyebrows shot up when the desk clerk spoke. The thought flashed through her mind—*Still*? I wonder how many other temporary Mrs. Rollands have shared the same suite.

"You've got three, right? Switch me out this time, Gary. Something different." He turned and smiled down at her. "A new start," he said, holding her gaze.

As they rode the elevator to the top floor, Jason linked his arm through hers. She studied him suspiciously, but said nothing. "I always ask for the honeymoon suites because they're the best in the house," he explained. "Plus, they're almost never in use during the week. For what I pay here, I want the cream."

Once she stepped through the door of the suite, she understood. The suite was more of an apartment than a room. The sleek, modern decor mirrored that of the lobby, with romantic touches like cozy loveseats and flower-filled vases. The king-sized bed perched at the top of a spiral staircase over the living area. A green, wired bottleneck stuck out of a stone chiller on the bar, with two flutes sitting beside it.

Zoe arched an eyebrow. "Do you always have a bottle of bubbly waiting for you in your honeymoon suite?"

A pained look flashed across his face. He shook his head,

his expression that of a hurt little boy.

"No, Zoe," he answered quietly. "I did this especially for you."

"Oh . . . T-thank you . . . That's very thoughtful." Why did she feel all muddled? It was only natural she assumed he'd entertained women in hotel suites before.

Jason popped the cork and poured them each a glass. Raising his, he said, "To new beginnings."

Zoe blinked. Was there a subtext here? Did he mean . . . ?

No. He's right. That's why I'm here—to reboot my life.

She clinked glasses and sipped, nodding. "Yes. To new beginnings."

When he stepped close to nuzzle her neck, she giggled and backed away. "Stop it, silly. I want to drink this, not spill it." She wandered toward the wall of glass overlooking downtown Albany. The sight of that city skyline had her heart thumping.

"Are we going out before dinner? I mean—I'm not hungry yet. It's early, right?"

Jason laughed and ruffled her hair. "Put on your comfy walking shoes. We'll walk around the city as long as you like, and then decide what to do for dinner."

When they stepped out onto the street, Zoe breathed in the smell of the city. She was back in the forest built of concrete and steel, a place she'd known as home for most of her life. Of course, Albany wasn't nearly as big as New York. But it was a lovely city, a mix of old architecture and new. They walked hand in hand through the weekday-quiet streets, passing the Capital Building, then Times Union Center.

"Did you want to stop and see anything this afternoon? We've still got some time before the museums close down," Jason squeezed her hand and smiled down at her.

She shook her head. "It's so nice to be here. Thank you for bringing me, Jason."

Yes, it was good to be back in the city. But it had never felt this good. The hollow, aching place, the chunk missing inside her, wasn't there anymore. But what was filling the hole instead? Surely, this man beside her—and how wise a decision was that?

Jason stopped suddenly, and she lurched as she was firmly attached to him at the elbow. "You have to know," he said, "I'd do anything for you. Anything within my power."

His eyes were so intense on hers, and she so wanted to believe him. Desperately. How could she be sure that his words and actions weren't just part of his usual, summer fling routine. And even if they weren't—was she truly ready for more?

She drew in a deep breath of the cooling, early evening air and drew her ice-shield around her heart again. Then she slid her eyes away.

"What's for dinner?"

The Marriott's restaurant was as sleek and modern as the rest of the hotel. Zoe ordered a fancy martini instead of her usual vodka and tonic, and giggled at the waiter's anguished face as he struggled to deliver the over-full glass, sans spill, from tray to table.

A small, frosted glass candleholder cast a soft glow over Jason's features. He hadn't taken his eyes off her since the minute he tossed the car keys to the valet. He also hadn't shaved today, and the rough, dark shadow caused stirrings low in all her special places. That same stubborn lock of inky hair continually tickled one eyebrow.

A beautiful man, no doubt. And he knows exactly how to make a woman feel special.

They enjoyed chateaubriand and a medley of roasted vegetables, along with the bottle of Pinot Noir Jason ordered to go with dinner. Conversation was hushed, laced with laughter and smoldering glances. Zoe knew the alcohol, and the magical setting, was starting to melt her barriers.

Could it be so bad to go with this for a while? Maybe he really is different with me. Maybe . . . okay. Three days. Let me pretend for three days that this romance is real. That the tenderness in those achingly blue eyes is the real thing. That maybe, there is a future in love for me. A future with this beautiful, impossible man.

Two days flew by in a flash. A virtual honeymoon. She and Jason spent metered time during daylight hours touring the city, visiting the Capital and the Albany Institute of Industry & Art. On Tuesday night, they heard a local symphony orchestra perform at the Palace Theatre. And every minute they weren't out on the street or dining in one of the area's five-star restaurants, they were sharing their bodies.

Zoe had never realized how exciting sex could be. The lofty, elevated bed, by the end of their stay, was a last resort. They coupled in the shower, on the bureau, on the carpeted floor in the dark, the lighted cityscape as a backdrop. He took her against the wall, holding her hips as she wrapped herself around him when they became one.

By the end of that second day, Zoe's resolve was slipping. Jason was weaving his sensual charm around her like an enchanting spell.

On Wednesday, they went shopping. Jason called a cab and they rode the few miles to Crossgate Mall. They'd barely walked fifty feet inside the building when Jason spotted Frederick's, and gripped her shoulders to steer her toward the colorful displays of sexy lingerie. Later, Zoe picked out an invitingly soft cashmere sweater for Jason at Macy's. It wasn't until he slowed his pace as they passed Littman's Jewelers that her carefree mood began to slip.

231

"Let's go look. I'd love to see what kind of things you like," Jason pleaded.

She shook her head, her feet planted firmly.

Not a chance.

Yet she couldn't ignore the hurt look in his eyes. Or the longing in her heart.

That night, they ordered dinner in. Jason took the tray at the door, dressed only in a pair of comfy, plaid sleep pants. He arranged the plates on the tiny bistro table in the corner of the suite. But when Zoe waltzed down the spiral stairs wearing only a push-up bra and thong panties, Jason quickly lost the pajamas. Dinner cooled a bit while the rest of the room heated up.

They ate afterward, on the floor, and although the broiled seafood tasted heavenly, Jason couldn't take his eyes off her. She wore his rumpled shirt pulled over her shoulders, but underneath, she was still delectably nude. Her skin was flushed from sex, tinted pink as though she'd come back from a morning run. Jason picked at his own plate as he watched her eat. Her eyes glowed bright green in the flickering candlelight.

I've never, ever been this content in my entire life.

When Zoe's cell began ringing inside her purse on the sofa, their cozy cocoon began to crack.

"Let it go to voicemail," Jason pleaded. But he knew Zoe had only a few days before she was due back at work in the city. The real world had begun to creep into their paradise. He closed his eyes and took a deep breath as she got up and answered the phone.

When he heard her say, "Hey, Xavier. What's up?" he stiffened.

A long pause preceded her next words. "Yes, I'll be home

next weekend." He watched her walk toward the windows overlooking the city.

I'm losing her. Right now, in this moment, I'm losing the only woman I've ever loved.

"I'm good . . . Yes, I got the papers Arlin sent . . . I agree. I think that's the best decision."

Xavier's voice floated out from the phone as she listened to whatever smooth line he was feeding her. She walked slowly toward the windows.

"Me too. This summer has been good for me. But I'm looking forward to getting back into a routine."

Jason wasn't prepared for it. He'd never experienced the sensation in his entire life. But the stab of pain in his chest was worse than any heart attack could ever be.

Her final words drove the stake clean home. "I'll be home late Saturday. I'll give you a call when I get in."

When she hung up and gazed out the picture window hugging her arms around herself, she already seemed so far away.

He got up and went to her. "Zoe, we can't end it this way. I'm not ready to let you go." He searched her face, but she kept her gaze trained on the skyline.

Toward the city. Toward her escape.

Laying a hand on her cheek, he gently turned her to face him. "I love you, Zoe," he murmured, unable to control the thickness in his voice. "I know you have plenty of reasons not to believe me, but I swear it's true. For the first time in my life, I'm in love . . . With you."

She blinked rapidly, and his heart swelled to see tears brimming in her eyes. He swallowed hard against the lump in his own throat.

"I've never felt for a woman what I feel for you. You've stolen my heart. You own my soul."

With his thumb, he brushed away the single tear as it leaked from her eye. She held his gaze, her eyes shining.

"Damn it. I never expected th-this . . . with y-you," she began before squeezing her eyes shut. Slowly, she shook her head, as if trying to fend off an inevitable emotion, one that was obviously pushing her backward in time, toward a weaker, more vulnerable point in her life.

His heart clutched with confused emotions. He couldn't bear to hurt her. But he couldn't bear to lose her either.

As she melted into his arms, a sob escaped around her words. "Da-da-damn you, Jason Rolland. I think you've m-made me—"

"Love me, Zoe. Because I love you with my whole being. And I know in my heart that I will love you for the rest of time," he said.

Zoe awoke to Jason's cellphone ringing at nine o'clock the next morning. She untangled her arms and legs from around his body so he could grab the device off the nightstand.

"Yeah? Oh, hi. Yeah, I'm still here," he grumbled.

A long pause followed, and she watched as Jason raked his fingers through his hair, shaking his head.

"It's got to be today?"

She knew he'd managed to postpone every other appointment he had until the following week, but apparently, this one couldn't wait. After agreeing on an eleven o'clock meeting, Jason hung up. He turned and drew her into his arms.

"I'm so sorry, baby. The client is flying back to Japan tomorrow morning. He wants a second look at the plaza I showed him last week. If I don't go, I've got no chance of making the sale."

Zoe ran her hands up and down his warm, muscled back

and searched his eyes. There truly was regret there. Could it be true? Had she really found love again? She buried her face against his neck, reveling in the prickle of his unshaven jaw against her cheek.

"Not a problem. We've had three glorious days. What's a couple of hours?"

They made love again, with the brilliant morning sunlight streaming across their bed. Zoe had never felt so cherished in her whole life. Physical pleasure was one thing. But the joining of their eyes as they both climaxed together—that's what broke through to Zoe's soul.

As he held her before walking out the door, he whispered into her hair.

"I love you, Zoe. I know with my reputation, it might be hard to trust that I'm telling you the truth. I almost can't believe it myself. But you've found a trapdoor into my heart. Please." He took her face in his hands and pressed his lips tenderly against hers, then gazed deeply into her eyes. "Please give me a chance to prove I'm worth taking a chance on."

She lounged on the massive bed until almost noon, filled with the dizzying elation of new love. How had this happened? It was like a miracle. All she'd wanted this summer was to free her tortured soul. Heal her damaged sexuality. She'd really thought Jason was the perfect candidate for that.

Somehow, fate had smiled on her a second time. When Zoe buried David, she was certain she'd never find love like that again. Yet against all odds, this wild, reputedly untamable man had handed his heart over—to her. And deny it as she tried, deep down, she knew the truth.

She loved him, too. Deeply, truly, desperately.

Slowly making her way out of bed, she yawned and stretched. It felt good to be complete again. Not only complete, but totally in love.

Zoe gazed out at the incredible view from their top-story suite, the sunlight glinting blindingly off the windows of the surrounding buildings. She did love the city, but much of those memories tangled with a life she'd left behind. No—those memories were bound to a life, and a love, that had been taken away from her. Now, images of her days with Jason in the wilderness on the mountain beckoned to her, warming her soul.

This was right, and true, and such serendipity. Aunt Delia had left her what turned out to be a falling-down shack on the water, but in reality, what she'd given her was a whole new life.

Zoe was getting ready to jump in the shower when there was a knock on the door.

He has a key. Had he forgotten it? And housekeeping knows better than to knock before checkout at one.

Zoe pulled on the plush terry robe the hotel provided and made her way to the door. She squinted through the peephole. A woman? In street clothes . . .

Oh my God, I hope nothing's happened to Jason.

Zoe pulled the door open and came face to face with a feeble memory. Her brain thumbed through the files for several seconds before she found the connection. Tracy. The blonde, Barbie bombshell from the bar the first night she'd arrived at Lakeview.

Today, though, Tracy's wild facade seemed subdued. She wore conservative dress jeans and a lacy, fluttery pink tank. Her cottony hair was pulled back in a ponytail, and she didn't appear to be wearing any makeup at all.

Zoe was surprised she'd even recognized her.

"Oh. Hi," she stuttered. "Uh, Tracy, right?"

The blonde nodded solemnly and riveted Zoe's eyes with a

deep searching gaze. "Can I come in for a minute?"

Tracy flounced in. She'd obviously not expected such an easy entry. Zoe raised one eyebrow and motioned toward the sofa.

"Can I get you something? Coffee?"

Tracy shook her head, although her hair didn't move. "We have a problem, you and I," she said. Ominously.

A half-hour later, Tracy left, and Zoe clicked the door shut behind her and fastened the chain. Then she stepped under a shower spray so hot it could have caused first-degree burns. Wielding a loofah sponge, she lathered up and scrubbed. Again and again, she scraped her pale skin with the rough ball of netting, trying to wash away the poison of the last three days.

Like a worm into her soul, Jason had found his way into her heart. No amount of soap, or hot water, or salty, streaming tears, could wash his memory away.

Two hours later, wearing her sunglasses to cover her red, swollen eyes, Zoe rode the elevator down to the lobby. She'd called a cab from the room, and explained it would be a long-distance fare. To Lake George, over an hour away.

"What do you mean, she's gone?" Jason clutched the room phone in his fist and shouted into the mouthpiece. "Gone where? Didn't she leave a message?"

He'd returned to his suite at three o'clock to find the room empty. Zoe was gone, as were her clothes and luggage. All that remained was her scent, her enticing, heart-melting aura that at the moment made Jason want nothing more than to bury his face into the pillow where she'd last lain her head.

He threw the phone down on the floor, tearing the cord free from the receiver. He stalked from one end of the suite to the other, searching for a reason. The rumpled bed was still spotted with evidence of their last coupling, but the closet had been cleared of everything she owned. He burst into the bathroom and with one stiff-armed thrust, sent everything remaining on its surface clattering to the tile floor.

He'd called her cell, and he'd texted, multiple times. No response.

What happened? Why had she done this to him?

A knock on the door of the suite sent his heart to a gallop. She was back. She'd simply been out shopping, or sightseeing, or . . .

Jason yanked open the door and found Tracy standing outside. Same poufy hair, with enough black crap around her eyes to pave a driveway. About three inches of cleavage struggled against a laced-tight top that looked more like lingerie than a blouse.

"Hey, Tiger."

"What the fuck do you want?"

The cab slowly wove its way down the serpentine drive of Lakeview. Zoe directed the driver to Jason's cabin, praying Jade wouldn't be there. She paid the fare, and then turned to wheel her luggage toward her Caddy.

Gotta make this quick. Band-aids need to be yanked off fast.

She swore when she turned the key in Jason's door and realized it was unlocked. Jade was coming out of her room as she stepped inside.

"Zoe. What's the matter? Where's Jason?"

Her resolve had held strong for the entire, excruciating, seemingly endless seventy-three-mile cab ride. She'd allowed herself one good cry after Tracy had hugged her, mumbled her apologies, and left their suite.

But this was Jade. In the past life-changing weeks of the

summer, this woman had become Zoe's good friend.

The floodgates opened.

Sobbing, Zoe explained that after an idyllic three days with the man she was certain was her true love, Tracy had shown up. She'd been elusive, but stated she thought she was pregnant. Tracy basically claimed that Jason was the father of her unborn child.

"If she's telling the truth," Zoe blubbered onto Jade's shoulder, "then he was fucking her in Albany at the same time he was sleeping with me here. I'm so disgusted. I feel so used."

Jade's strong arms held her, patting her back. "My brother, he's a shallow being, Zoe. I warned you from the start."

"I know. I know. I was such a fool."

"No." Jade pushed Zoe away and gripped her gaze. "Not a fool. You were sowing your wild oats. You were doing exactly what your doctor, and your friend, Medina, told you to do. You were freeing your soul."

Zoe searched Jade's eyes for comfort. Such a strong, vibrant being. So independent. So self-assured.

"How can you be so strong, Jade? What made you that way?"

Jade drew her again into her embrace. "Ah, Zoe girl, it's because of the way I was raised. I knew from the beginning that men don't always hang around." She held Zoe at arm's length and smoothed her hair away from her brow. "You've had hard lessons too. We both learned hard lessons. It will make us stronger for the knowing, no?"

She had all her things packed into the Caddy. Zoe checked her watch, and knew she had to get out of town before Jason got back. But she had to go see it one more time. Her childhood idyll. Her former perfect refuge.

Zoe drove down to the paved spot Jason had made for her aunt Delia, clutching the gate key in her palm. She'd pulled on a pair of jeans, donned socks, and laced up her Nikes for the dicey venture.

She had to see it, just one more time, up close.

Zoe unlocked the gate and pulled it closed behind her. The late afternoon sun streamed in through the branches. She could hear the crickets chirping already, even though it was barely four o'clock. She hugged herself, and then began making her way toward the cabin.

She smelled the stagnant, fishy odor of unkempt beach before she even reached the front porch. The beach was buried under decades of neglect. Where the sand peeked through between patches of rotting leaves, its surface glimmered with the slimy, green growth that quickly overtakes unkempt waterfront properties. Zoe hunched her shoulders and shuddered.

This is my life. Stagnant, neglected, wasting away.

When she reached the front porch, she rested her foot on the bottom step but knew she couldn't go any farther. She'd tried that when she first arrived.

Her first instincts that day had been right. There was no going back—no reclaiming the happy innocence of life before David. No redemption of a happily-ever-after, even though Jason had almost succeeded in deceiving her into thinking it was possible. Like that spider on the hutch, he'd snagged her in his net, and nearly devoured her.

Now she knew the truth. True love comes around only once. She needed to let the past go, and move on.

There is nothing for me here but painful, useless memories.

Zoe made her way back to her car and turned the key with tears streaming down her face.

Gotta let it all out now. Gotta get over this lame, Disney fantasy today. I've got a four-hour drive to get over this dream.

By the time I cross over into Manhattan, I'll be a whole woman again.

Jason drove the Hummer at breakneck speed up the Northway. He hadn't been able to reach Zoe, or Jade, on his cell since he discovered Zoe had left. Nobody was answering.

Oh God, don't they know how my guts are twisted up inside me? Why won't anybody answer the fucking phone?

He made the 70-mile drive in less than an hour, grateful a highway patrolman hadn't added any more time to his trip. As he turned into the drive, his heart clenched in agony. Zoe's car was gone.

Jason checked the time on his dash, and then passed his own cabin, driving straight down to the restaurant. He knew that's where he'd find Jade.

When he burst in through the screen door to the bar, happy hour was just beginning. Jade was drawing tap for a boisterous group of young men on the other side of the bar. Her back was to him.

He waited until she'd served them before calling her name. She turned on her heel and froze.

One of her dark eyebrows rose, and she glared at him. "You know she's already gone. I'm not sure why you'd be surprised."

Jason swore and snatched his phone out of his pocket, holding it in the air. "She won't answer my calls, Jade. Can you call her from your phone? Please? I have to talk to her." Fury flared in his sister's eyes. He knew he was shouting, that he was making a scene. But he didn't care. The hole in his chest ached so badly, the pain obliterated every other logical thought from his mind.

Jade tipped her head toward the door. "Outside."

He followed as she ducked under the end cap and went out through the back door. He caught up with her at the bottom of the steps.

She wheeled and planted her hands on her hips. "What the hell do you think you're doing? You got yourself into this mess. It's a crying shame you dragged that innocent lady down with you. She's way too good for the likes of you." Jade threw her hands in the air. "Now you want to smear your shit all over this place. You're a fuck-up, Mon. You're exactly like our father."

Sucker punch. The air left his lungs with such force he almost grunted. He shoved his hands in his pockets and turned away, his eyes trained out over the water.

He heard his sister's footsteps on the stairs, the screen door squeak open and bang shut. He didn't know how long he stood there, but the pain inside him made him afraid to move. Afraid, like cracked glass, he might splinter into shards.

She was right. This is what their father had done to Jade's mother, and to his own. Dear old Dad couldn't keep his dick in his pants. Even with an exotically beautiful wife who worshipped him. Who diligently stayed on the island and kept his resort in Montego Bay running smoothly. Who'd taken his name, even in defiance of her family's warnings, and given him a baby girl two years later.

No, none of that stopped Ryan Rolland from playing. Jade was five years old when he decided he couldn't resist Jason's mother, who worked for him at his other resort in Lake George. A woman, he imagined, not much different from Tracy.

Daddy screwed around, and the odds finally caught up with him. He lost.

And I was the booby prize.

"Hey, Medina. It's me. Wanted to let you know I'm home. I decided to come home a few days early. Give me a call when you can, 'kay?"

Zoe hung up the phone and pinched the bridge of her nose between her fingers. The four-hour drive, and then fighting rush hour in the city, had left her with a massive headache. The crying probably hadn't helped either. She dropped down on her most comfy, overstuffed chair, the one that faced the windows.

Darkness hadn't completely claimed the skyline. But in the city, it never does. Zoe watched as lights winked on in windows of the apartment building a few blocks over. The neon outlines of the new bank building flickered to life, standing out against the sky like a cartoon cutout. Somewhere from the street below she heard a horn honking. It was a sound she'd learned to tune out, hardly notice.

But she hadn't heard it in a while. She was home. It suddenly occurred to Zoe that after just minutes of stepping in her door, she was surrounded by more people within a few blocks than she had been in the entire past five weeks.

So why do I feel more alone than I ever have in my entire life?

She'd felt alone, and desperate, and damaged, in the weeks after David's death. But David hadn't been responsible for what had happened. And he'd paid the ultimate price, just for doing his job. No, David hadn't been the one to abandon Zoe. Fate had.

This pain was more personal. This was a betrayal. A breach of trust. The mental image of Jason sleeping with that tramp week after week, and then coming back to her bed within hours, made her want to vomit.

243

The thought revolted her. Almost as much as the rape.

Chapter 16

Medina panicked when she got Zoe's message. Tony had picked her up at the office and they'd gone to dinner. Her phone, buried in the bottom of her impossibly crammed bag, was still on silent. She didn't think to check it until they'd gotten back to Tony's apartment.

"What happened? Are you okay?" She could tell by Zoe's one, simple word—hello—that she'd been crying.

And she also knew that the prolonged silence would be followed by a strangled sob.

"Yeah. Home." Zoe let out a short, cynical laugh. "Had enough."

Medina leaned forward, casting a worried glance over her shoulder toward Tony. "Hey, you're having trouble again, aren't you? I'm coming over."

She heard Zoe blow her nose, and then heave a big sigh. "No, Dina. Really. I'm fine. Just enjoying a good, old fashioned crying jag."

"What happened, hon? I thought things were going pretty good with you two."

Zoe hiccupped. "I've had enough of living in a dream world. It's time for Cinderella to come back down to earth."

"Are you sure you don't want me to come over?" she asked, watching as Tony nodded in agreement.

"No. Let's do lunch tomorrow, okay? Maybe things will

look a little clearer by then. And hey, Dina?"

"Yes?"

"I'm going to need you to give me a refresher course on that Jezebel thing you're so good at. You know, sex with no strings attached? I think I might have flunked the first time around."

Medina closed her eyes as an arrow shot straight through her heart. She'd pushed Zoe to this. Thought it would break her free. Instead, it seemed, all it had done was break her into tinier pieces.

When she rung off, she slid her gaze toward Tony. "Why couldn't Jason have turned out to be for Zoe what you have for me?"

Tony snorted and shook his head. "Jason? Jason Rolland? You've got to be kidding. Zoe had to know what she was getting herself into. Nobody's ever going to tame the tiger of Jason's Lair."

Zoe met with Arlin at his office the next day. She wanted to get the real estate contract finalized, signed, and in the mail. The money from the sale of the property would come in handy, since she knew her paycheck was about to take a hit. When she went back to work on Monday morning, she intended to ask Barlow to move her to the administrative office.

She was better, much better, than last spring when she'd fallen apart in front of a client. The new meds seemed to be working well, and there was no doubt that the last six weeks had been . . . good for her in many ways. But Zoe knew in her heart that she wasn't ready to sit down and help other broken women try to mend.

In some ways, she was more broken now than ever.

"That should about cover everything," Arlin said as he

initialed the last page of Zoe's contract bid. "I'll have these overnighted to Mr. Rolland first thing Monday morning. I see no reason why he should refuse the property for this price."

Zoe cleared her throat, feeling a stab of pain at just hearing Jason's name. "Well, if we have to negotiate, I'm willing to do that. The place is a lost cause. I don't think there's any bringing it back."

Was she talking about the cottage? Or herself? The Zoe *before*? Both, surely.

Arlin slid his glasses off and leaned the tip of the earpiece on his chin. His dark eyes searched her face. "Zoe, are you doing better? Xavier is worried about you."

She nodded. "I'm fine. Much better. This summer was good for me. A temporary change of lifestyle. A great getaway." She stood and reached out to shake Arlin's broad hand. "I appreciate your finishing out this contract for me on such short notice."

As she turned to leave, he said, "Zoe, would you mind if I asked you a question?"

She looked up as he came around the desk, tilting her head.

"The woman you worked with up there, in the bar. The Jamaican lady," Arlin began. "I never got the chance to speak with her, privately, that night. Do you know if she's married, or in a relationship?"

Zoe closed her eyes. Ah, the ultimate irony. Perhaps her failed romance with Jason had a purpose after all. A chance meeting. Like a phoenix, from the cinders, another love would rise to take its place.

She shook her head, a small smile creeping in. "No. Jade isn't in a relationship. She's a wonderful woman, though. A pure spirit. I'm hoping she holds out for the right one."

"Do you think she'd mind if I contacted her?" Arlin leaned

a hip on his desk and folded his arms. "At the resort, I mean."

"I don't think she'd mind at all. In fact, I'll be calling her this weekend. I'll be sure to mention you were asking."

On Saturday night, Zoe consented to have dinner with Xavier. Already, the loneliness was eating her alive. But going out with Xavier was safe. She knew she could trust the X-man to keep his distance and not ask too many questions. He was way too stiff-shirted for any conversation that even hinted at emotions.

Which is exactly what I need right now.

"So, your meds are working. You seem much more relaxed, Zoe." Even though the candlelight softened Xavier's sharp jawline, it couldn't mellow his expression. He studied her with cold and clinical eyes. Strictly business. "But I completely agree with your asking for the transfer at work. You should take all the time you need." He reached across the table and patted her hand.

Why did it feel like he was being condescending?

She stiffened. "That's not exactly true. The salary is a third less than I'm making now. And even if Jas . . . the property sells for the asking price, that money won't last forever."

Xavier leaned forward on crossed arms. His eyes, like Jason's, were blue. But his were a pale, almost gray hue. Cool. Like light passing through an ice cube. "Perhaps, after a while, you'll consider allowing me to take care of you," he said. "I believe I could make a very happy life for you, Zoe."

She dropped her gaze to her lap, where her hands had retreated moments earlier. "Xavier, I don't love you. The kind of relationship you're asking for is archaic. Like an arranged marriage."

He nodded. "True. But I believe, in time," he said, his voice a little softer than she thought he was capable of, "you might develop a fondness for me. Like I have for you."

Fondness. *Fondness?* Could she ever settle for that, now? After this summer? After falling in love with a man who didn't know what love was?

But Xavier's offer sounded safe. A relationship like that wouldn't involve her heart. Never again would she have to worry about hurting like she was right now.

"Give me some time," she said, so low she wasn't sure he'd even heard her.

I have to wait until the bleeding stops before I can move on.

The days after Zoe left dissolved into a numbing blur for Jason. He'd given up trying to call her. She wouldn't even respond to any of his texts. If only he could explain the truth to her. Tracy had played her—played them both—and destroyed the seed of something very beautiful.

There was no way Tracy could be pregnant with his child. When she'd come to the suite the day Zoe had left, he'd confronted her.

"So, you're sure I'm the guy, huh? You'll of course consent to DNA tests."

Tracy had stiffened. "I'm not even completely sure if I'm pregnant yet. I'm a little late. I've been afraid to do a home pregnancy test." She lifted her mock tear-filled eyes to meet his. "I wanted to tell you first. I thought you might be . . . happy."

"Happy, huh?" Rage flared in Jason's chest. "You're not sure, yet the last time we were together was over six weeks ago. And the *equipment malfunction*, as you call it, happened months ago."

Tracy blinked and took a step back.

"Yet you found it necessary to share that information with

Zoe. What did you think that would accomplish, Tracy? Did you think you could force me to marry you?" He spat the words.

Tracy began wringing her hands. She took another step back. Tears were streaming down her face, leaving black streaks of mascara in their wake.

"I thought we might have a future together." She clutched her handbag to her chest and lowered her head.

Jason chuckled darkly and swiped his hand over his face. "Another city girl wanting to snag a big fish," he mumbled.

It was his own damn fault. He'd played the game, and now it was time to pay up. Even if she wasn't pregnant, she'd accomplished what she set out to do—destroy Zoe's faith in him.

"Look, Tracy," he said, his tone cold, robotic, "if you're pregnant with my child, I will take care of you and the baby. But there's going to have to be proof, and one thing is for certain." He waited until she'd met his eyes. "I won't marry you. And I will never, ever love you."

Three days later, when the FedEx truck pulled up to Jason's cabin, he already knew what would be inside the thick manila envelope. A real estate contract for Zoe's property. It was the final twist of the knife in his heart.

She's letting go of the past. All of it. And that includes me.

Medina and Tony continued to make regular trips to the lake throughout the months of September and October. Tony's tour boat company didn't officially close until after Halloween, a big holiday at the lake. Medina was so wrapped up in Tony, and in getting her family to accept the idea of her being in a relationship, she didn't see much of Zoe. She called her almost every night, though, and kept tabs on her through Xavier.

She hadn't seen Jason since that last weekend when they all had breakfast at the restaurant.

"I ought to give Jason a call," Tony said to Medina as they drove back to the city one Sunday night. "Lakeview usually hosts a huge costume party on Halloween. But I haven't heard from him. I wonder if he's even having it this year."

"The Big Haunt? Yep, it's on. Zoe told me. She's been in touch with Jade."

"Any news on what Jason is up to?" Tony asked.

Medina shook her head. "I don't even mention his name to Zoe. But she did tell me one interesting piece of information she got from Jade. That Tracy chick he was screwing? She wasn't pregnant after all. False alarm."

"Well that's good for him. And for the almost-kid. If it's one thing I can't imagine, it's Jason as a father."

"I should have known better than to encourage Zoe to get involved with him, Tony." She leaned her forehead on her hand. "I should have realized she's a forever kind of girl. She's not like me."

Tony reached over and took Medina's hand. His eyes were glittering in the glow of the dash lights, and it struck Medina, as it did over and over again, how lucky she'd been to meet him.

"Does that mean there's no chance I'll ever change you into a forever kind of girl?" His voice was low and rumbling.

Medina blinked back quick tears. "I think you already have."

Halloween fell on a Saturday night. Medina brought her luggage to work the Friday before, and Tony picked her up early. They still hit terrible traffic. A four-hour trip stretched into almost six. By the time they got to Tony's cabin it was after seven o'clock, and Medina was exhausted. Their original

251

plan to grill steaks seemed like too much trouble.

"Let's go to Lakeview for dinner. I need to see how Jason is doing anyway. I've only spoken to him once since the summer, and he doesn't sound right," Tony said, checking his watch. "He doesn't go on the air until eight. Hopefully, we'll catch him in the restaurant."

They found Jason sitting alone at the restaurant's bar. The Patio had been closed down now for at least three weeks, ever since the first frost. He was tucked into the last seat, hunched over a glass empty except for ice and a lime wedge.

Medina almost didn't recognize him. Jason had always been lanky, his height making him seem even more so. But his clothes hung on him and were rumpled. He looked as though he'd either decided to grow a beard, or forgotten to shave for a week.

"Hey, buddy, how the hell are ya?" Tony reached for Jason's hand, and then the two briefly embraced in that stiff, awkward way men do. "What the hell you been up to? Is the caveman look part of your costume for tomorrow night?"

When Jason embraced Medina she could feel his shoulder blades protruding through his shirt. His hair had grown longer, and the shaggy layers hung around his ears in defiant clumps. He smelled like vodka and . . . what? Smoke? She frowned.

"You been sick, Jay? You look a little weather-worn," she asked.

Jason slid his gaze briefly across her face, and then dropped it to his glass, which he had taken in both hands, clutching it like a buoy. "Nope. Just getting lazy. End of the season and all." Jason nodded toward Todd, who grabbed his glass and turned to refill it. "Some drinks for my friends here too."

"Where's Jade tonight, Jay? She left for the island

252

already?" Medina asked.

"No. She'll leave this week, though. She's got tonight off so she can pack and shit. She never was one for all this costume stuff."

When they all had a fresh drink in hand, Jason took a huge swallow before asking, "How's the winterizing on the boats going? All set for the big chill?"

"Yeah, we're about done. Next week we'll finalize everything." Tony took a long gulp from his mug of beer, wiping the foam off his mustache with two fingers. "What's up with you, man? You've been pretty tough to get hold of these past few weeks."

Jason shook his head but kept staring straight ahead. "Been busy. Got winterizing stuff to do here too, you know."

"You gonna help me check the big boat down at the dock in the morning? Medina won't be much help," Tony smiled and winked at her, and she smacked his burly arm.

"Yup. Glad to." Jason drained his glass with the third swallow, to Medina's surprise. She glanced up at Tony, and then back at Jason.

Tony slid his gaze from Medina's. He cleared his throat. "Sooo, who's your date for the party tomorrow night?"

Jason stared into the maze of bottles at the back of the bar, and shook his head slowly from side to side. "Nobody." He motioned with his glass again to Todd.

He swiveled his seat to face them. Those electric blue eyes that Zoe had so mooned over weren't so sexy any more. They were sunken, laced with red lines, with purple half-moons underneath.

Jason's smile didn't reach his eyes. "Who knows? Maybe that'll change by the time the party's over." He picked up his full drink and nodded to Todd, and then at them. "Gotta run. Show starts in a few minutes."

A rattling gust against the window woke Jason. A cold snap brought Saturday's dawn whistling in under heavy, gray skies with a biting wind. He was still wearing his clothes from the night before, sprawled out on top of the comforter on his bed. It was freezing in his room.

He sat up, swore, and barely made it to the bathroom before belching up the sour dregs of his last drink from the night before. His head, surely, was going to explode. He splashed cold water on his face, and then reached for the pack of cigarettes on the counter.

By ten o'clock, the time he was supposed to have met Tony down at the docks, three cigarettes and a hot shower had made him feel almost human. Jason pulled on thermal underwear and his heaviest jeans, a plaid flannel shirt and his Carhartt jacket. His phone rang as he was grabbing his keys from the hook near the door.

"Sorry. Running a little late. Be there in ten."

He found Tony adjusting the ice-flow propellers on the dock in front of *The Crystal Mess.*

"I still don't see how those things keep the ice from crushing that hull like a soda can," Jason said, shaking his head. Tony grinned up at him, his face all but obliterated by dark sunglasses, a knit cap, and his dark goatee and beard. All Jason could really see were teeth.

"Kinetic energy, my man. As long as the water keeps moving, it can't freeze. It's a much cheaper option than pulling these big mamas off the lake and storin' them." He nodded toward the Ticonderoga and the Minnehaha, the two, much larger tour boats Tony owned with a silent partner.

"Where's Medina?" Jason asked.

Tony nodded toward Murphy's Bar and Grill, one of the few year-round businesses at the lake, sitting on the shore above them. "She's waiting on us for lunch. Come on. Let's go get your pontoon pulled out."

In less than an hour, Jason's pontoon boat sat dripping on a trailer in the lot of Sam's Marina across the street, where it would be wrapped in plastic and stored for the winter. He and Tony headed back toward Murphy's. The wind had picked up, and Jason swore it was ten degrees colder than when he'd first gotten out of his truck.

"Aren't you cold?" he asked Tony, who had unzipped his jacket as he guided Jason's trailer back to the ramp.

Tony looked him up and down. "You haven't got any meat on you anymore, dude. You're nothing but a bag of bones. And those bones, I might add, don't smell the best. What's up with you?"

"Fuck you," Jason barked as he pulled his corduroy collar higher up. He'd forgotten his own ski cap, and his ears were paying the price. He couldn't decide whether they were simply numb or had frozen and snapped free from his head. "You and Medina seem to be getting on pretty good." A gust of wind snatched the words from his mouth, and Jason wondered if Tony had even heard him.

But Tony nodded, "Dina's something special. She's gotten to me. Think she might be a keeper."

"What the fuck does that mean? I didn't think you knew the meaning of that word."

Tony stopped and faced Jason, a smile splitting his mustache and goatee. "We all gotta give in sometime, bro. Ain't none of us getting any younger."

They had reached the last set of railroad-tie steps leading up to Murphy's lakeside entrance. Tony nodded and Jason led the way. He heard his friend's words behind him, even over the whistle of wind in his half-frozen ears.

"I have never known you to go more than a day or two

without some hot thing stuck to your side. What's going on, man?"

Jason shook his head and dropped his gaze to his feet. But he couldn't speak. His throat was too tight for him to make any sound at all.

In upstate New York in late October, dark falls early and hard. Jason would have driven his Hummer the short distance down to his own restaurant, but the parking lot was already filled to overflowing. This late in the season, there wasn't much left for people to look forward to as far as social events. That's why the resort always did so well for the Big Haunt. Jason usually looked forward to it, too.

Tonight he wished he had an excuse to cut out early, retreat to his lair, hide in his studio. But his buddy had been covering the broadcast on this night for him for over ten years. If he'd suddenly decided he didn't need Brandon's help, questions would be raised.

He never bothered with a costume. In past years, whatever outrageously sexy costume his date for the night was wearing usually drew enough attention for the both of them. But tonight was a special occasion. Jason didn't have a date.

He dressed carefully in the tuxedo he had pulled out of storage. After several attempts and multiple, generous dollops of gel to tame his ridiculously stubborn hair, he gave up. It reached his shoulders now, jagged and choppy in uneven layers. One thick hank fell forward over his brow. It was so long it almost obscured his vision. He added the finishing touch, pulling it down awkwardly over his head.

A black, plastic headband with two, bright red, sparkly horns.

He definitely looked the part. Dark, purple crescents

under his eyes, the whites of which he hadn't seen clear in weeks. Sunken cheeks and a deathly pale pallor. The classic, undead look.

Yeah. This is me. I'm alive, but not. Still breathing, but slowly, steadily rotting from the inside out.

And there's no doubt I'm hell-bent and sure to reach my destination.

Chapter 17

Zoe's mother called her on Halloween.

"We can't make it for Christmas, Zoe," she said into her ear. "We're taking a Caribbean cruise with Allie and Dan Sutherland this year. You remember the Sutherlands, don't you, Zo?"

Oh yeah, I remember the Sutherlands. Allie the airhead and Dan, her creepy-weird, UFO-obsessed 'better half.'

Her mother continued. "But we'd like to come visit for Thanksgiving. Do you have plans yet?"

Zoe sighed and rested her forehead on her hand. It was Halloween, and this was such an apropos trick-or-treat. Yes, it would be good to see Mom and Dad again—treat. No, I don't want to put them up and try to keep them busy enough to stay out of my business for what will probably turn into a very long week. Nasty-ass trick.

"No, actually, I don't. I hadn't made any plans at all," Zoe said, trying with everything she had to sound cheerful. "When will you be up?"

Her new role at Family Guardian Services was boring enough to anesthetize a patient scheduled for amputation. Zoe had stacks of files waiting on her desk every morning that she had to read through, input into the online filing system, and sign off on.

Basically, from 8 a.m. to 5 p.m., every freaking day of the

workweek, she was alone in a little room with a blinking cursor and a stack of files.

Yes, it protected her from any drama. Kept her off the emotional roller coaster of interacting with abused and troubled women. But was this the best role for her now?

No. It didn't keep her from riding her own emotional thrill ride, again and again and again, as though she had an all-expense-paid, non-expiring ticket to never-ending hell.

In many ways, Zoe was more alone than she'd ever been. She'd essentially lost not only Jason, but Medina as well. Between her family and Tony, her friend simply didn't have much time left to babysit a lovesick disaster. In a small way, Zoe felt let down by Medina. Wasn't she the one who boasted about sex with no emotional ties? Wasn't she the one who'd encouraged her to have a fling in the first place? Now Medina was bringing Tony home to meet the family.

Zoe had also kept in touch with Jade, which probably didn't help any. But she loved Jade. Kind, caring, so elegantly proper in every way. It didn't change the fact that every time she spoke with the woman, her gut ached with memories of the summer. Jade was careful not to mention Jason, but inevitably, his name came up in conversation.

He wasn't, as it turned out, a father-to-be. Zoe wasn't sure if that nugget of information made her feel better or worse. It didn't change the basic fact: Jason had probably been sleeping with Tracy, and her, at the same time. She had to keep reminding herself of that.

She had to keep her ice-armor solid and strong.

Her worst moment, without a doubt, had been the day Arlin had called her, three weeks after she'd gotten home. Jason had signed the real estate contract, initialed it in all the umpteen necessary places, and sent it back—Priority Overnight—along with a bank check for the full asking price.

No hesitation, no questions asked. No note, no accompanying documentation.

Zoe had literally handed over the last bit of her childhood—her memories of innocent carefree days, her belief in a happily-ever-after—for a bank check. She'd stared at the computer-generated document, her eyes filling at the sight of Jason's loopy, slouchy signature at the bottom. His words that first day she'd met him echoed in her head.

I didn't steal the right of way, Ms. Anderson. I purchased it, fair and legal.

Now he'd bought the rest of her little girl dreams, fair and legal. Just freaking wonderful. She signed the check, deposited it in her bank, and walked away.

Trick-or-treaters don't visit high-rise apartment complexes. Not, at least, unless they're attached to the friends or relatives of the occupants therein. Zoe knew she'd be sitting there, all alone, all night.

She'd never been one much for television. That TV-eating amoeba, football, had engulfed every channel anyway, at least the ones not smeared with blood from some Halloween horror movie. And the only books she had in the house were romances. Definitely not the kind of reading material to lift her spirits.

Medina had left with Tony yesterday for the lake. For the Big Haunt, as Jade called it. The last big shebang before the resort closed down for the winter.

Jade hadn't asked if Zoe wanted to come up for the event. She did, however, mention that Arlin would be making the trip. And staying the night, ironically, in the Aspen.

"I'd like to come visit you in the city before I head out to the island, Zoe. The week after Halloween. Is that a good time for you?" Jade asked.

Zoe had to wonder if Jade was coming to visit *her*, or to bring herself a little closer to Arlin. Xavier had already told her he'd made reservations at Daniel, one of Manhattan's most beloved French restaurants. Reservations there, especially on a weekend, were a premium luxury.

"I know the maître d'," Xavier had said. "I've secured their best table for six, first Friday in November, seven-thirty." His self-satisfied grin mimicked the sickly green visage of the Grinch.

"I'll take you shopping before then, Zo. Buy you something nice. I want you to look dazzling."

The Boathouse Restaurant was packed to capacity with all sorts of strange characters when Jason came through the door. The small, local band he'd hired had already started their set, and were well into their rendition of Monster Mash. All of the tables had been moved to the periphery of the room to make room for dancing.

Jason spotted Jade, tending bar along with two local girls he'd hired to help her for the night. To his surprise, Jade was in costume. She was dressed as Cruella de Vil.

She'd sprayed one side of her jet-black hair with white costume paint. The bright red, stretchy tank dress she'd chosen set off the rich color of her skin. A shawl of faux, white fox covered her shoulders. And every now and then, when her hands were free between mixing and serving drinks, she picked up her extra-long cigarette holder and flicked it.

Perfect. My sister rocks. What a good sport. Too bad she doesn't know me for who I really am.

Then again, how could he expect her to? All she's ever seen him do is exactly what their father did—play around without a care for anyone else's feelings but his own. Hell, even he believed he could never be any other way.

261

Until Zoe. She'd touched a part of him he didn't know existed, and then trusted him enough to offer her scarred heart. Unfortunately, playing Dad's role for so many years cost him the most precious gift he'd ever been given.

I've totally fucked my only chance for real happiness. I wonder, after the crappy way Jade's seen the men in her life treat women, if she'll ever risk her own heart.

But he saw him then, the man sitting at one end of the bar. In Jason's usual seat. He was deep in conversation with Jade at the moment. His sister's smile, Jason noted, had never looked as vibrant as it did tonight.

Maybe my sister will get lucky in love. Of anyone I know, she certainly deserves it.

He recognized Arlin from when he was here in the summer giving Zoe advice. The man whose signature had graced every one of the forty-seven pages of the real estate contract from Zoe that Jason signed not two months ago.

Zoe. The thought of her brought her unique fragrance back to him, the sight of delicate freckles on her creamy skin. The way her eyes had reflected the colors of lake and forest the day they rode the four-wheeler through the woods. The knife in his chest made another slow, agonizing turn.

How could he have hoped she'd be here tonight? In his heart, Jason knew better. Thanks to sneaky, gold-digging Tracy—no, thanks to his own cheap, sleazy self—there was no way Zoe Anderson would ever give him another chance to win her affection. Not ever.

Another jab hit his heart as Jade's words floated in his brain: *She's way too good for you. You're exactly like our father.*

Friendly greetings, slaps on the back, and a few sloppy, lipstick-smeared kisses followed him as he made his way through the crowd toward the bar. He caught sight of Tony, though if not for his friend's unusually massive physique, Jason wasn't sure if he'd have recognized him.

Zorro, Jason guessed. Black mask, cape, and sheathed, fake sword at his side. Although on Tony's hip, the plastic sword looked more like something that should be spearing a cherry and floating in a martini glass.

Medina clung to Tony's side, draped in voluminous purple and black folds of fabric that seemed alive. They moved with every breath of air. Her pointed wizard's hat was spangled with gold and silver foil stars that glinted in the muted light. She must have used steroid shampoo. Her hair was normally wild and huge on a good day, but tonight the dark curly mass was downright intimidating.

If only she was a witch. I'd ask her to cast a love spell on my Zoe.

The screech came from behind him and to the left somewhere, and Jason instinctively cringed. Two seconds passed before a pair of arms wrapped around his torso, and for a moment, he thought he'd been caught in some black widow's snare.

Almost. It was Tracy.

"Hey, Tracc. Long time no see," Jason said, peeling her fingers from around his chest as he turned. "How've you been?"

He'd barely gotten the words out of his mouth when she gripped his face with both hands and planted a wet one right on his lips. She smelled of wine and smoke and something earthy and feral he chose not to dwell on.

"Whoa, whoa. It's good to see you, but not that good," he sputtered. But Tracy was drunk on her ass and not to be dissuaded. She locked lips with him again, going for it with her tongue this time.

Jason fought back the gag reflex.

263

But by the time he managed to push Tracy away and wipe his mouth on his sleeve, he caught sight of Medina, who'd witnessed the entire scene. Her lips, painted a strange, purplish black color, were pressed in a thin line. She shook her head slightly as she turned away.

Jason was relieved to hear Jade's voice coming from right behind him. "Is the lady paid in? This event is by advance ticket only."

Tracy thrust out her Wonder Woman costumed chest and stuck her chin in the air. "I'm paid in." She snatched a folded, orange rectangle of cardboard from between her barely concealed breasts and thrust it in Jason's direction. He stepped back and threw up both hands.

"Jade's in charge of all that."

The rest of the night, for Jason, deteriorated into a bad nightmare. He hugged people he didn't recognize. Was kissed—on the mouth—by women he wasn't sure he'd ever met. Tony and Medina floated somewhere in his periphery, but he never managed to make it back through the crowd to actually converse with them.

And Cruella de Jade remained, for the better part of the evening, hunched over the extreme end of the bar, batting her eyelashes at Arlin.

Jason didn't even drink. He didn't have the stomach for it. There was so much about this night that was wrong. Everything was so fake, so superficial. Yeah, he was probably making a lot of money. But when it came right down to it, what the hell good was money?

The scary part was, this party reminded him of his life up until this night. Nothing but a shallow, artificial charade.

The party was winding down by around midnight. Jason had managed to find a quiet corner near the table where he and Zoe had dined together so many times this past summer.

Memories filled the air so thickly he could almost smell her, and the pain in his heart skyrocketed.

Okay, now I need a drink.

He had the barmaid pour him his first vodka and tonic. Leaning into the shadows, Jason sipped his drink and gazed out over the blackness he knew was the frigid water of the lake. Not frozen yet, but cold enough to stop a heartbeat in a matter of seconds.

He wished he could become invisible. He wanted to disappear.

That's when Wonder Woman took him down.

Quite literally. Tracy was beyond drunk, and came careening across the dance floor toward him, staggering on ridiculous spikes, like the ones Medina wore. He didn't see her until the very last moment. Thank God. If he hadn't thrown down his glass and held both hands out to catch her hurtling body, they might both have crashed through the glass and ended up in the icy water below.

Tracy was unconscious when he first caught her, and Jason made every attempt he could to hold her body up off the floor without touching any exposed body parts. It was a formidable challenge, as there were plenty of them. In her tumble, her ill-fitting costume had come undone. Most of one rubbery, silicon-enhanced breast bulged above the strapless bodice. Jason grappled for purchase on the slippery, plastic-coated fabric with the flying W plastered across her boobs, trying to keep her head from hitting the window. Reaching lower, his hand slid up under the skimpy skirt and ended up planted squarely on one cheek of her ass.

Of course, that's right when the song the band was playing ended, and all eyes turned in his direction. As Tracy's eyes fluttered and she looked up at him, a broad smile played across her face. Her gold tiara hung halfway off the side of her head but was ensnared in her lacquered hair. She looked ridiculous, and Jason struggled to contain his disgust.

"My hero," she blubbered. Then her eyes rolled back in her head, and she was out cold.

Zoe had just gotten in the door from work when her phone buzzed inside her purse.

"Zoe, it's Jade. How are you?"

"I'm good. How about you? Are you still coming down this weekend?" She walked through her apartment as she spoke, flicking on lights everywhere. The sun set so early now, she longed for the brightness of summer . . . she longed for something else too but she would not allow herself to go there.

"I am. My flight out of La Guardia leaves Monday, three o'clock. I'd like to come Friday afternoon, if I may. I've arranged a limo to bring me down," Jade said.

"That would be great. I'll call Medina and we'll go shopping on Saturday. Did you know about the dinner Xavier and Arlin have planned?"

Zoe could hear the grin in Jade's next words. "I do. I'm really looking forward to it."

A twinge of—what, jealousy? Yes, that must be it—spread behind Zoe's breastbone. She tried to keep it out of her voice as she gave Jade her street address, and they agreed on a time for her arrival. When she ended the call, she stood in the fluorescent glare of her kitchen for a long moment.

She'd wanted so badly to ask about Jason. Would he be all alone now that the resort was closed up for the winter? Or was Tracy living with him? Medina told her all about the scene at the Big Haunt last weekend. It sounded as though Jason and Wonder Woman had gotten pretty cozy.

Zoe opened the refrigerator and grabbed the quart of

milk. Then, sighing, she put it back and reached instead for the bottle of white zinfandel.

She poured herself a glass, took a sip, and set it down on the counter. She paused, looking around her. One by one, she turned off the lights in her apartment, until the only light came from the tiny bulb of the range hood. She picked up her glass and raised it in salute.

Huh. I guess that part of my psychosis is gone now too.

For the first time in three years, she wasn't afraid to be home, alone, in the dark.

The Manhattan cityscape was fully illuminated, and through the massive windows, almost looked like a neon mural. Zoe flopped down on the floor in front of her sofa, leaning back against it, and sipped her wine.

She knew it was foolish to worry about Jason. If there'd ever been a man capable of taking care of himself, it was the tiger of Jason's Lair.

Jade arrived late Friday afternoon by limo. Zoe had called down to the security desk earlier and told Arthur, the concierge, that she was expecting company, and to please ring her through.

A light tap sounded on the door five minutes later and Zoe found herself wrapped in the long, willowy arms of her friend.

"I'm so glad you decided to make a pit-stop here before you left," Zoe said. She chuckled as she watched the doorman place Jade's two meager bags inside the door. "You certainly do travel light, though, if you're not planning on coming back to the states until spring."

Jade laughed. "I shipped a crate of things out last week. Jason teased that it was heavy enough to hide a body."

Stab. There it is again. Just the mention of his name was like a hot spear through her heart.

I guess this is inevitable, if I'm going to be spending three days with the man's sister.

After her things were settled in the guest room, Zoe poured them both a glass of wine and joined Jade on the sofa. She was staring out at the city skyline in awe.

"Such a view you have, Zoe. I'll bet the sunsets are gorgeous."

She nodded as she sipped her wine. "But I'll bet they can't hold a candle to the sunsets in Montego Bay."

"You must promise you will return the favor, and come visit me on the island," Jade said. She lifted her glass, then paused and held it out toward her. "To new and everlasting friendships."

They clinked and smiled. A bittersweet bubble rose in her chest. How was it possible that Jade and her brother were so different? Yes, they were only half-siblings. One could not ignore the obvious racial difference from having two different mothers. But over the summer, she'd seen them interact. Hell, for a while she'd actually suspected they were lovers before she found out they were related. Could they really be so morally different? Or was it a case of like father like son? After all, Jade's father abandoned Jade and her mother. Was Jason like that too?

Yes, of course he was. He was exactly like his father, sleeping with two women in two different cities at the same time. Tracy and her.

Zoe sipped the wine and let it trickle down over the fresh wound on her heart.

The next morning, the three girls met at the Starbucks a block from Macy's downtown. As they sipped lattes and munched on croissants, Zoe relaxed in a way she hadn't been able to since being at the lake months ago. Medina and Jade were getting along great, even though they hadn't really chatted until today.

"So we're all going to Daniel's tonight, I hear," Medina said, sipping gingerly through the foam of her steaming hot latte. "Tony's taken me there once. Have you ever been, Zo?"

Zoe shook her head, her mouth too filled with flaky pastry to answer right away. Her gaze shifted from Medina's to Jade's and back. She watched Medina's conspiratorial smile envelop Jade. "I hear Arlin's joining us too."

Jade blushed, smiling with a twinkle in her eye. She nodded. "He's called me, once or twice, since the Big Haunt. He's a nice man." But she dropped her eyes to her cup as a silent signal that no further details were forthcoming.

Zoe swallowed, and then cleared her throat. "Does everybody have a fancy-enough-to-eat-at-Daniel's outfit picked out?"

Both of her friends' heads shook emphatically. They both spoke at the same time, in jumbled words Zoe interpreted as, "That's why we're shopping today." Then Jade and Medina looked at each other and burst into laughter.

They scoured every inch of Macy's before moving on to some of the smaller, pricier boutiques along Broadway, dipping into a few side streets along the way. By two o'clock all three had crinkly sacks in hand. Medina looked ridiculous trying to keep the hem of her dress, draped in plastic and swinging from a hanger, from skimming the sidewalks as they headed for the subway.

"We need a taxi, Dina. No way your dress is surviving the subway system."

So they hailed a cab and all three girls piled in. Zoe slumped back against the seat, twisting her stiff neck from side to side and drawing in a deep breath. She wished she were looking forward to tonight more.

It was easy to get caught up in the excitement of the day,

the feminine thrill of having brand-new, sexy outfits to wear to a fancy dinner date. But Zoe wasn't exactly feeling the magic.

Unlike Medina's siren red, and Jade's neon tropical, the dress Zoe chose was black. Simple, uncluttered. Something she might have easily worn to a business meeting. Or a funeral.

Because in reality, that's how Zoe felt. As though she were in mourning. Not for David. She'd made her peace with losing David. It had been a tough, long three years, but she was finally healing from that agony.

No, she was grieving for someone—something—she wasn't sure had existed outside her imagination. For a love she swore she'd never give in to. For a man she wasn't sure was even deserving of her love.

So many times in the past months she'd been tempted to read his texts, listen to his messages without spastically hitting the 'delete' button. But every time her finger hovered over the key, Tracy's face popped into her memory, like a ghoulish ghost in a Halloween horror flick.

And even if Tracy hadn't been involved, if she'd given her heart to a man who'd been nothing but a player all his life, how long before he would have tired of her? No, she'd been through hell these past three years, and she was finally putting her life back together. She might dress like she was in mourning for the rest of her life, since there's no such thing as second chances for true love.

They had just finished getting ready when Medina's cellphone rang. It was Tony, and Zoe watched Medina's eyes grow wide as she answered.

"Okay, then. We'll be right down." Medina turned to face her friends, her eyes glittering. "Our knights have arrived. In a white stretch limo."

Zoe rolled her eyes. "You've got to be kidding."

Why is Xavier turning this into such a big deal?

And a big deal it was. The three men were waiting for them in the limo with champagne glasses in hand.

"We thought Jade might want a little tour of downtown before we head to dinner," Xavier said.

Zoe knew she should be grateful for Xavier going out of his way to show her friends a good time. But she couldn't help feeling patronized, and that he was showing off. This must be his new tactic.

If he shows my friends how wonderful he is, they'll help convince me that I can't live without him.

The entire evening did seem like a dream to Zoe, but not necessarily the good kind. She went through the motions, playing the city socialite just the way she knew Xavier wanted her to. Smiling at all the right moments. Letting him order for her off the menu, since of course it was in French and he spoke the language fluently. She even steeled herself and managed to swallow a bite of his escargot without gagging.

Zoe felt like an actress in a low-budget off-Broadway play. This, she knew, would be her life if she married him. She'd be dressed to the nines, wined and dined, primped and pampered. Like some fancy French poodle with a diamond-studded collar. Most women would give anything to be standing in her stilettos right now.

As they lingered over coffee, Zoe glanced around the table. Medina cuddled with Tony as he fed her a spoonful of his crème brûlée. She'd never seen her so happy in all the years she'd known her. There was no doubt about it—Medina was in love, and Tony worshipped her.

Jade was leaning, chin in hand, so close to Arlin they were sharing the same air. Her golden eyes danced and skittered over his face as he talked. His dark eyes seemed to be

271

memorizing every feature of Jade's beautiful face. Zoe felt sure the man would be planning multiple trips to Jamaica throughout the winter.

Xavier, his eyes trained on his cellphone screen, might as well have already left the building. He'd been texting with some associate on and off throughout the meal. His dessert remained untouched next to a cup of coffee that had gone so cold, the cream was separating into clotted clouds on the surface.

Occasionally he'd remember Zoe was there. He'd look up and smile, lifting her hand to brush his lips over her knuckles. Then his thumbs would go to the keyboard of his phone. Zoe wasn't sure if she wanted to burst into tears or run out of the restaurant screaming.

So she simply smiled sweetly, dabbed her lips carefully on the white linen napkin so as not to smear her lipstick, and tried not to focus on the steady, aching throb of her bleeding heart.

Chapter 18

By the time Zoe padded out into the living room late Sunday morning, Jade was already up. She'd brewed a pot of coffee, and was standing before the expansive windows, mug in hand, dreamily studying the skyline. She turned when Zoe's slippered feet scuffed the hardwood.

"Good Morning, dear hostess. I hope I didn't wake you."

Zoe shook her head as she headed to fill her own mug. "I've so enjoyed having you visit, Jade. I only wish you had more time to spend here."

"Me too. But I booked my return flight when I came up in April. I've already changed it once, to fly out of La Guardia instead of Albany." Jade sipped cautiously from the steaming mug, and then smiled. "It sure has been nice, though."

Zoe shuffled across the room and flopped down on the couch. An awkward silence followed, as time was running out for both of them to acknowledge the elephant in the room. They'd spent the entire weekend together and Jade hadn't mentioned Jason's name except for that first day. She knew his sister had been careful to avoid saying anything about him at all.

But she had to ask. She couldn't let Jade fly out without knowing.

"How is Jason? Will he be staying up there at the resort all winter? Or does he go to Jamaica too?"

Jade shook her head, but didn't turn from the window. "He's only been to Montego Bay once. It's not his thing. He loves the mountains. That's where he grew up, ya know."

Zoe swallowed and closed her eyes, struggling for the courage to ask the next question. "It must get terribly lonely up there in the winter. I mean, just about everything shuts down, right?" She let a short bark of laughter escape to cover her nervousness. "But I guess Jason isn't ever lonely, is he? I'll bet Tracy's already moved in by now. Or whoever came after her."

Jade's mouth pressed into a thin line, one dark eyebrow lifting. "I don't know what Jason's deal with Tracy is."

She blinked. Could that be true? Jade was his sister. She lived with him, for at least half the year. "Didn't she accuse him of getting her pregnant?" Zoe pressed.

One of Jade's lips curled up in distaste. "Tracy is a cheap, lying slut. She wasn't pregnant. Why Jason ever got tangled up with her, I'll never understand. I thought he was done with her the day she stomped out of the bar, that first day you arrived." She looked away, shaking her head. "The bitch showed up at the Halloween party, half-naked. By the time the night was through Jason had his hands all over her."

Zoe swallowed, clutching the sides of her mug, almost enjoying the scalding heat searing her fingers through the ceramic. "And the property? Has he . . . ?"

Jade turned back toward the window with a sigh. "I'm sure the cottage is already gone. He was going to get a guy in this week with some heavy equipment to demolish it. By now, I'm sure he's scraped the place clean off the face of the earth."

The blade that had thrust through Zoe's heart made a slow, agonizing turn.

Later that afternoon, Zoe hugged Jade as they stood on the curb by her taxi.

"Will I see you next summer? At the Lodge?"

"Of course," she said, though her answer was hollow and a flat-out lie. "I'm sure I'll be up with Medina and Tony—if they're still together, that is."

When she got back up to her apartment, her phone was ringing. It was Medina.

"Oh, I was hoping to catch Jade in time to say goodbye. Has she already left?"

"Her taxi just left for the airport. She had a great time, Dina. Thanks for helping me take her around town."

Medina was silent for a long moment. "Zoe, are you okay? You were awfully quiet at dinner last night. Did Jade say something to upset you?" She paused. "About Jason?"

"Only the same thing you told me about him and Tracy at the party last weekend." Zoe swallowed the tight ball of emotion that was rising in her chest. "Nothing more."

"It's for the best, Zo. That asshole wasn't right for you."

She swallowed hard and stared down at the busy street below. Even on a Sunday afternoon, the traffic never stopped. "No, you're right. Getting involved with Jason was a mistake. One I do not intend to make again."

The day Jade's limo came and took her away, Jason dug out the wooden *Closed for the Season* signs from the storage shed. He climbed the hill to Lakeview's sign and snapped the first one onto the hooks hanging from the sign's bottom edge. Then he hiked the half-mile up the highway and did the same for the Lakeview North sign.

There was still plenty to do before Old Witch Winter showed up. The housekeeping staff would be deep-cleaning every cabin over the next week, shampooing rugs and upholstery, and bringing him lists of any repairs that needed doing. He had a local handyman coming by later that morning to start turning off water and draining pipes, since none of the chalets were winterized except for his.

He was on his way back to his cabin when he spotted John Barber's pickup truck turning in off the highway. He waved, and John stopped. John was the best handyman in the Lake George area, and someone Jason hired on a regular basis to do work around the property.

"Hey, that time of year again, huh?" John said, reaching through the open window to shake his hand. "Seems like summer flies by faster every year. I like the caveman look, by the way. Almost didn't recognize you."

Jason chuckled and looked down, moving gravel around with his toe. "Listen, John, do you know anybody who does demolition?"

John's eyebrow shot up. "Thinking of razing the place and starting over? Again?"

He shook his head. "No. Not yet, anyway."

"Don't tell me you finally talked Old Lady O'Reilly into selling you that broken-down shack."

He cleared his throat. "She passed. Earlier this year. I finally managed to convince her niece to sell it to me."

Quickly changing emotions played over John's face. "No shit. I hadn't heard about Delia. But it's good you finally got the property, huh?"

Jason looked away, down the hill and off toward the lake. "Yeah. It's fucking wonderful. I want the whole goddamned lot scraped clean, as though nothing had ever been there."

Zoe was actually looking forward to cooking Thanksgiving dinner. She would never give Jamie Oliver a run for his money, but for a big occasion like this, she applied herself. The day before her parents were due to arrive, she went shopping.

She spent an entire morning wheeling a grocery cart through Jubilee Marketplace, carefully picking out individual, perfectly shaped sweet potatoes, artisan bread for the stuffing, and a compact but very fresh, hen turkey.

It took her three trips from the parking garage up to her apartment to bring up all the bags. With the perishables safely crammed into her suddenly inadequate refrigerator, Zoe poured herself a cup of tea and strolled to the window.

The sun had slipped behind the tall buildings to the west. One by one, the streetlights flickered on, casting a neon glow on the few small trees sprouting from their tiny soil islands in the concrete. They were still struggling to celebrate autumn, bravely hanging on to the sparse, remaining leaves of brilliant red and orange, waving them in the breeze like bright, tattered flags.

I bet fall in the mountains is gorgeous.

The parks on Long Island, where she'd grown up, lit up every September in an almost neon palette. But other than photo calendars or film documentaries like Aerial America, Zoe had never experienced the mountain wilderness in autumn.

She allowed herself to imagine, for a moment, what it might be like to ride through the kaleidoscope of color on the back of Jason's four-wheeler. She could almost smell the dusty, papery haze the wheels would kick up as they crunched through the fallen leaves. The contrast of those warm, sunny colors against the cool blue of the lake and sky must be breathtaking.

He wafted back into her memory then. The feel of his lean, taut body. The way the inside of his helmet enveloped her with his unique scent, a combination of his shampoo, the woods, and clean male sweat. The way his muscles rippled under her fingers as she'd hung on to him, shutting her eyes when the rear tires skidded and spun.

The streetlights grew misty halos. The knife made another agonizing turn. Zoe dropped her face into her hands, and tried to purge some of the pain with a good, old-fashioned crying jag.

She sat there a long time, allowing herself the luxury of self-pity. She'd been a fool to let her heart get involved with a man like Jason. What made her think she could just have sex and not eventually fall in love? She wasn't like Medina. She just wasn't built that way.

But heck, Medina wasn't that way anymore either. She and Tony were practically joined at the hip now, and it was obvious they were very much in love. Even Medina had finally let her guard down and given her heart away.

She should have known better. Should never have let her hopes and dreams get involved in what was meant only to be a casual, summertime fling.

When she finally looked up, the sun was gone. Street lamps glowed beneath her window, and far off in the distance, she heard the lonely echo of an ambulance siren. The sounds of the city. So different from the peaceful sounds of nature in the mountains. She'd had a good cry, so she should feel better now, right? Then why did her chest ache as though that ambulance should be on its way for her?

Her parents arrived two days before Thanksgiving. They'd flown in, and when Zoe got home from work on Tuesday afternoon, they'd already stowed their luggage in the guest room. When she opened the door to her apartment, her dad was watching the news station, and her mom was in the kitchen fussing over a pot of something that smelled an awful lot like her childhood.

"I didn't want you to come here to cook," Zoe began, hugging her mom as she peeked over her shoulder into the boiling pot. "Mmm. Chicken and dumplings." She kissed her mother on the cheek.

"I don't get a chance to cook for my little girl too often. And you've already banished me from the kitchen for turkey day." Her mother held her out at arm's length. "It's good to see you. But you're too skinny. Are you sick?"

Zoe closed her eyes and shook her head.

Here we go. Mother-smother.

"No, mom, I'm fine. Really." She turned to hug her dad, who'd left the news long enough to greet her and grab another beer out of the fridge. "Hey, Daddy."

"Your mother's been fussing here in your kitchen all afternoon. I hope you're hungry."

Knowing she'd go crazy if she took off the entire week to be with her parents, she explained there was no way she could be away from the office both Wednesday and Friday. Her parents were retired, and were used to an uncluttered routine. Zoe had satellite TV, so she knew her father would be happy. And Mom had already given her a list of supplies to have in for homemade apple and pumpkin pies. She would be busy baking up a storm.

The apartment smelled like a bakery when Zoe got home on Wednesday afternoon. They left the pies cooling on the counter while she took her parents across the street to the Irish pub for dinner.

Sid was forking up his first bite of shepherd's pie when he said, "So the sale on Delia's cottage went through okay?"

Zoe tried to push back the wave of bile that rose unexpectedly in her throat. "Yes. A done deal. I put the money in CDs. Are you sure you and mom don't want some of that for—"

"Don't be ridiculous, sweetheart," Karen cut in. "Your father and I have been very fortunate with our investments over the years. We've got all we need. You hang onto that. For your own future."

Zoe rested her fork on the edge of her plate, her appetite suddenly gone. What future? The kind of future she wanted was one like her parents had—love, a home, a family. The kind she'd dreamed was possible sitting on the front porch of that homey cabin up at the lake all those years ago. "It was so sad to see our old place in that condition. All those memories, rotting away."

And now, all those dreams bulldozed into an early grave.

"Delia was my sister," Sid began, wiping the foam from his beer off the stiff brush of his salt-and-pepper mustache, "and God rest her soul, I loved her. But she was a quirky one. Never did understand why she didn't sell the old shack years ago." Her father's tone was so matter of fact he might have been discussing the latest community improvement project.

Karen blotted her mouth with a napkin. "Is the fellow who bought it going to fix the place up?"

Zoe's throat closed. She couldn't talk about this, not now. Not when the wound was still raw.

Fate came to her rescue. At that moment, a wailing toddler distracted the waitress who was delivering drinks to the next table. She inadvertently tilted her tray a little too far. Three mugs of beer came sliding across in their direction, clanking together and crashing to the floor within inches of Zoe's chair. Beer splattered the entire side of her tailored trousers.

She'd never in her life been so happy to have a pair of good slacks ruined. By the time the mess was cleaned up and order restored, the subject of the cottage in Lake George was completely forgotten.

After the meal, they were chatting over coffee when Zoe announced they would be having a dinner guest for

Thanksgiving.

"I don't know if I ever mentioned him to you, but Medina has worked for him for years. He's a civil law attorney. Xavier Le Blanc."

Both her parents' eyebrows rose, as though they'd rehearsed the synchronized reaction.

"French?" Her father's eyebrows proceeded to crawl toward each other, making a funny little bulge appear between them.

"Yup. Born there, but grew up here. Trust me, he isn't nearly as impressive in the flesh as his name suggests."

Her mother reached across the table and patted the back of her hand. "That's great, Zo. It's about time you got out and started dating again."

"Another lawyer, hey?" Sid asked, one eyebrow raised. "You've got a thing for those attorney types."

Zoe caught the angry slash of Karen's eyes in Sid's direction. Then she turned back to her with a pained expression. "Your father and I both want you to go on with your life. Leave the past behind and move forward. We look forward to meeting Alexander."

"Xavier, Mom. It's Xavier."

Thanksgiving Day began very early for Zoe. By five in the morning she was rinsing a naked turkey in the sink, salting down its insides, and slathering butter all over its skin. Once Mr. T was in the oven, she started on the dressing. By six, her mother had joined her, helping peel potatoes and trim green beans. The goal, Zoe hoped, was to have everything prepared before Xavier got there at noon.

And then the fan dance could begin.

Zoe showered and changed into her most conservative sheath dress, in an autumnal but rather boring shade of nutmeg brown. She spent extra time patting makeup over her scar, dreading that the X-man would make some offhand comment about his talented friend, the plastic surgeon, in front of her parents. Simple gold balls on her earlobes and a tiny, plain cross on a chain around her neck completed the look.

She studied her appearance in the mirror. A perfect Stepford wife.

This is what my future looks like.

Precisely at twelve o'clock, the doorman buzzed and announced Xavier's arrival. Xavier was always on time. He came through the door with his arms loaded with a bouquet of the finest red roses and a bottle of expensive white wine. French, of course.

Xavier was in his casual uniform today. Crisply pressed khaki trousers, a pale yellow Ralph Lauren shirt, and no tie. She knew his Ferragamo Python loafers probably cost more than her parents' plane tickets.

Python. How fitting.

As introductions were made, she noticed how her mother scanned the man head to toe as he stood inside the doorway.

Yes, Xavier was a good-looking man. Pale blue eyes, golden blonde hair always trimmed super short and tamed with product. A sharply angled, strong jaw and a straight, aristocratic nose. But Zoe couldn't help but notice these things as though she were admiring a statue of some Greek deity.

Xavier was nice to look at, but underneath the enticing exterior, he was as cold as a stone sculpture. At least, that's how she felt about him. He didn't stir a fire in her, not even a spark. Not like Jason had.

Stop thinking about Jason. Especially today. It's Thanksgiving and I am thankful for what I have. I will not dwell on what I've lost.

The day progressed smoothly, but rather stiffly. Conversation remained benign and superficial. Food was passed around Zoe's small dining table in bright Fiesta ware bowls, and every dish had turned out delicious. There was enough laughter and toasting to make it feel like a family event.

Sort of.

Zoe could remember more relaxing afternoons spent at the dentist's office.

Xavier hit it off quite well with Sid, causing her increased concern. Thankfully, football seemed to be the common denominator, and she hoped it would stay that way. She dreaded the X-man doing something stupid before the day was out, like asking Daddy for her hand in marriage.

The panic of that thought sent her stomach tumbling. Although she politely heaped one small scoop from every bowl onto her plate, Zoe barely ate a bite of her dinner.

At seven, in between games, Xavier finally got up to leave. He kissed Zoe chastely on the lips, and then grinned over her shoulder at her parents.

"Your daughter is very special to me. I'm hoping to see both of you again, very soon."

Dad retired to watch the rest of the game in the guest bedroom shortly afterward, leaving Zoe and her mother alone on the couch.

"Xavier is a very nice man. He seems to be very fond of you."

There it was again. That word. *Fond.*

Zoe sighed. "You're right. In fact, he's told me that a number of times. He's very *fond* of me." She choked out a cynical laugh. "So fond, in fact, he's asked me to marry him."

Her mother's eyes widened, but Zoe was impressed at

how well she suppressed her shock. "How long have you two been seeing each other?"

"A little over a year. On and off." She met her mother's gaze, and then rolled her eyes. "It's not exactly the romance of the century."

"I could tell that. I'm old, but not completely blind, Zo." Her mother choked back a laugh. "He acts as though his underwear is too tight."

She chuckled. Her mother might be a bit overbearing at times, but she did have a sense of humor. And a keen sense when it came to judging people.

Zoe dropped back against the couch and gazed up toward the ceiling. "My brain says, go for it. He's a good catch. He's smart, has a great job, makes a lot of money, and runs in all the best social circles. And he's decided I would be the perfect Mrs. Le Blanc to flaunt on his arm."

"But you don't love him." Karen's words were not a question, but a statement.

Zoe shook her head, hating that tears were welling up in her eyes. "No. I definitely don't love him." She leveled her gaze at her mother. "I'm not even sure if I can bring myself to share his bed."

Karen reached across and gathered Zoe in her arms, and she finally let the floodgates open. She sobbed against her mother's shoulder for what seemed like hours. It felt good to let it out, at least some of the hurt. But she dared not tell her mother the real reason for her pain.

"Zoe, some people's lives only rock a little on the waves. Yours got hit by a tsunami. You were well on your way to a wonderful lifetime cruise with David. But unfortunately, the ship sank. Ever since then, you've been floating around in a lifeboat, lost and alone." Karen tucked Zoe's hair behind her ear and looked into her eyes. "Don't feel like you have to grab the first man who shows up to rescue you. Even if he is driving a fifty-foot yacht."

Her mother's reference to a boat made Zoe cry even harder. "What if you think you've found the right one," she sobbed, "but his boat is battered and scarred, and might have a leak or two in the hull?"

Karen studied her face with that knowing, mother look. Without meaning to, Zoe had just emptied the story of her entire, sorry summer. But instead of an interrogation, or any judgmental lectures, her mother's eyes simply grew soft and misty.

"When I met your father," she said quietly, "he had quite the reputation. He made Captain Jack Sparrow look like a monk. But Sid fell in love with me. And I with him, even though he's definitely no Johnny Depp." Karen chuckled. "When it happens, love—real love—can change anything. Anyone. Even a rogue like Captain Jack. Or your father."

"But it can't happen more than once, can it?" Zoe whimpered. "I had that kind of love with David. Do you get a second chance? And if so, how can you be sure it's real?"

Her mother lifted Zoe's chin with one finger. "Anything is possible. If you can't find any other way to wrench the knife out of your heart than to be with him, then you know it's real. You've gotten lucky, again. And, if he truly loves you," she swept a tear off Zoe's scarred cheek with one thumb, "the rogue will find some way to make you believe it."

Jason's Thanksgiving dinner consisted of a turkey sandwich he washed down with a beer. Any restaurant that did stay open year-round in the village was closed for the holiday. Not that Jason felt like going anywhere, or being with anyone. As long as he had a case of beer in the fridge and a couple packs of cigarettes on the counter, he was perfectly content to stay home and watch football alone.

Besides, he had boxes of pictures to go through. First thing that morning, he'd climbed up into the attic and retrieved two plastic tubs labeled with masking tape. He swallowed hard at the sight of his mother's loopy handwriting.

Photos.

How he'd ended up with these, he wasn't sure, and until today, he'd avoided them. Avoided even thinking about them. The memories on the scraps of paper in those boxes were simply too painful.

But somewhere, in the foggy depths of his mind, he remembered his mother taking a snapshot on a day they'd spent out on the water. Her old Nikon camera, he remembered, was so big and heavy, like a bowling ball when he'd carried it down to the boat for her.

He pawed through the stiff, curling squares of Kodak paper. The colors on most of them had faded appreciably already.

Really gotta get off my ass and get these things scanned and digitized. Before they fade away completely.

Jason sat cross-legged in the middle of the living room floor, snippets of his life scattered all around him. His chest tightened when he came across images of his mother, young and vibrant, her smile exuding enough energy to light up an entire room. There were very few shots with both his parents together. Dad wasn't home very much. Always flying off to some distant site to close yet another real estate deal.

Or to his other family, the one down in Montego Bay that nobody knew about.

There were hundreds of pictures of Jason. Mostly black and white. His mother's hobby was photography, and when she wasn't busy overseeing the running of the resort in her husband's absence, she was taking pictures. He remembered she even had her own darkroom, closeted by black drapes in one corner of the creepy basement of the old clapboard house.

All Lakeview's cabins were old, Adirondack-style bungalows back then. The wood-frame cottages wore white siding with forest green shutters they would latch closed when the resort shut down for the winter. Like now, the only structure on the site that was built to withstand the cruel, upstate New York winters was the family home.

But not one of the original buildings remained. All of it was gone now. He'd made sure of that. The clapboard cottages, and even the two-story family home. The house he grew up in.

The place where his mother, six months after finding out about his father's other family in Montego Bay, had gone down into her darkroom and hung herself from the rafters.

Jason swiped angrily at the tears he hadn't realized were streaming down his face and scrambled to his feet, heading into the kitchen for yet another beer. He leaned back against the counter, taking in the scene. The entire living room floor was covered with pictures. His life, his history, fragments of time frozen and printed with his mother's loving hands onto light-sensitive paper.

Immortalized? If only. The images were steadily fading, from the paper as well as from his memory. Slowly decaying, like so many fallen autumn leaves.

That's when he spotted it, peeping out from the edge of the layered mass. He slammed the beer bottle down on the coffee table and dropped to his knees, sliding the warped and faded image out from under the others. He tried to hold it still, but his hands were shaking so badly, the details looked even more fuzzy and out of focus than they actually were.

Jason rushed to the phone hanging on the kitchen wall. He punched the numbers in and waited, hoping his friend the architect was eating Thanksgiving dinner at home.

The third, then the fourth ring buzzed in his ear.

Dammit. Why don't I have Ethan's cellphone number?

But someone picked up, and a few seconds passed when all he heard was background noise. Then Jason made out the sweet, tentative greeting of a very little girl.

"Hewwo? Happy Tanksgibbing. Robertthan rethidence."

What was his daughter's name? Teresa? Tamara? No. Tabitha.

"Is your daddy home, Tabitha? This is Jason Rolland."

Jason heard conversation and laughter in the background, along with the droning echo of the same football game as he had on his own TV. After a minute or two passed, he wondered if the tot had laid the phone down and forgotten him. But then Ethan Robertson picked up.

"Ethan. I'm really sorry to bother you on the holiday. But I'm so excited, I had to call and let you know right away. I found it."

Chapter 19

Zoe planned on spending Christmas at home, alone. Her parents were off on their cruise. Medina had some traditional, big family gathering with her parents and umpteen siblings and their kids. It was also Dina's big chance to introduce Tony to the entirety of the Florez clan.

And, thank God, Xavier had headed out the week before for San Francisco, where his parents lived in some fancy mansion overlooking the Pacific Ocean.

He'd begged her to join him. No, begged wasn't the right word. Xavier was not a man who groveled to anyone for anything. Persistent, yes. He could even be described as patient, sort of in the same way a rattlesnake will lie in wait, utterly still, until the moment is perfectly right to strike.

But Zoe had used her aversion to flying, along with a flurry of paperwork at her job that simply had to be finished up before the last day of the year, as irrefutable excuses.

Christmas fell on a Monday. Since the X-man was flying back the following Thursday, Zoe promised they could celebrate their own little Christmas that weekend. The entire city would still be lit up with decorations, as Manhattan refused to allow the festive mood to wane until after the ball dropped in Times Square on New Year's Eve.

Last year, Zoe had dug out her tiny, tabletop tree from her

storage space, pulled the wire branches down into position, and simply plugged it in. Voila, instant Christmas. But for some reason, this year, she hadn't had the energy to do even that.

Her office closed at noon on Christmas Eve. Zoe walked home, her progress slow through the throngs of last-minute shoppers rushing along the streets of Manhattan like ants stirred up out of their mound. The air was bitterly cold, but no snow had fallen. A dense gray cloud cover seemed to weigh heavy on her shoulders.

Zoe was surrounded by all the excitement, from the chatter of the shoppers bustling along to the music being piped out into the streets by the larger department stores. But the bubbling happiness failed to ignite anything inside of her. Like glowing cinders landing in a snow bank, only to be extinguished by the cold, wet snow. Even in the midst of hundreds, probably thousands of people, she felt utterly and truly alone.

She was nearly home when she spotted a vendor on the corner selling Christmas trees. He couldn't have had many to start, as the space he'd claimed wasn't much bigger than her bathroom. There were only two or three trees left. But there, half-fallen over in its makeshift pot stuffed with dried moss, was a perfectly shaped, two-foot high pine.

Zoe blinked, not sure if the hot tears rushing to her eyes was from the sting of the icy wind or a sudden memory. Without hesitation, she approached the vendor, took some cash out of her purse and handed it over. Then, cradling the tiny tree in her arms like a baby, she made her way the remaining short distance to her apartment.

Since she didn't own a tree stand, she made do with a heavy pottery vase she found on the top shelf of her linen closet. She placed a heavy-bottomed tumbler with some water in the vase, and placed the tree in that. The brush of its lower branches resting on the lip of the stone-like container kept it steady.

Zoe wasn't sure how long she'd been fussing with the tree when she realized she hadn't even taken the time to shed her coat and stocking cap. When she did, she caught a glimpse of herself in the mirror, and did a double take. She'd almost forgotten her trip to the hairdresser yesterday afternoon. Her sheet of shoulder-length hair was gone. She'd decided she'd been hiding her scar long enough.

Besides, the longer hair had been driving her crazy. She'd been a pixie girl ever since she was a kid.

So it was time to take it all off. She wasn't afraid for people to see her scar anymore. The long strands of carrot-colored silk had fallen to the floor around the salon chair, and when Zoe emerged, she felt almost—but not quite—like her old self again.

Zoe was showered and in her comfy sleep clothes by five o'clock that afternoon. She placed the tiny tree on the floor beside the TV cabinet. Then, she clicked through the channels until she found that wonderful station that aired nothing but a Yule log crackling in its hearth.

She spent the entire evening right there, on the floor, with her pillows and blanket. Breathing in the spicy scent of the pine, she listened to traditional old carols from her childhood until, eventually, she cried herself to sleep.

The next days passed in a fog. It was hard to feel the usual letdown that struck the day after Christmas when Zoe was sure she couldn't get much lower. Back to work on Tuesday, she listened to the excited chatter of all her coworkers, showing off their special gifts, and retelling funny or touching stories of their family holidays.

She stayed in her office and a few times, considered

closing the door. But that's not how things were done at Family Guardian Services. Doors remained open all up and down the halls of the administrative offices, a subtle but significant symbol of their openness to help one another.

Right before she broke for lunch, a light tap on the doorjamb drew her attention. Medina was standing there, looking like an over-excited little girl with a very big secret.

She rose and crossed the room to hug her friend. "How was your Christmas, Dina? Was the family nice to Tony?"

But her friend remained oddly silent. When Zoe pushed her away and studied her face, Dina's dark eyes were filled with tears.

"Uh-oh. Not good?"

Medina pressed her lips together and shook her head, obviously unable to speak for a moment. A fat tear trickled down her cheek.

"Dina, honey, what happened?" She took Medina's hand in both of hers.

But she shook her head again, choking back a sob. "I'm not sad, Zoe. On the contrary. I've never been so happy in my entire life."

She held out her left hand, and Zoe spied the ring. The center stone, marquis-cut, had to be well over a carat. Surrounding the solitaire were countless baguettes that caught the glow of the fluorescent lighting overhead, spraying sparks of fiery light everywhere.

"Oh Dina," she breathed, and hugged her friend again. Then her own tears came, and the two of them stood locked in a shuddering embrace.

Part of Zoe—the better part—was so happy for her friend she couldn't put her feelings into words. Medina had met the man of her dreams when she believed her destiny had been set in stone.

The other, lonely, hurting part of her wanted to reel back and bitch-slap her.

Wasn't Medina the one who told me a summer fling would be my best remedy? Who'd said Jason, with his revolving bedroom door, was the perfect target?

All true. But her friend also warned her about letting her heart get involved. With Jason, that was the biggest mistake Zoe could have ever made. Obviously, Medina had gotten luckier with Tony.

She led Medina over to the small couch in her office and grabbed the box of tissues off her desk. "So how are your parents taking this? What happened to *I'm the youngest daughter, and it's my obligation—*"

"Tony," Medina paused to blow her nose, "is one in a million. He completely understands the family tradition thing. His parents are Italian. Like, they both live in Italy. They moved back there after Tony's dad retired. His sister still lives with Mama and Papa. She's forty-three."

Zoe shook her head. "Okay, but I still don't get it. How does that help your situation?"

The smile that spread across Medina's face made her look like a teenager again. "Tony bought the brownstone right next to my parent's house. He's promised them we'd both be there for them. Only a few steps away, no matter what."

Zoe leaned back in amazement. "Tony did that?" She shook her head and blew out a breath. "I know I never got to know him very well, but I figured he was just another rich playboy. Just like . . ."

The ball of pain rose up in her throat again then. She turned her eyes away. Even hurting as she was, she refused to be selfish enough to bring down her best friend on the happiest day of her life.

Medina reached out and took her hand. "Hon, I know this

summer didn't work out for you. I can't tell you how sorry I am that you got hurt. I feel like it's my fault."

Zoe struggled to maintain control, swallowing the big ball of pain that made her throat ache. "It's okay, Medina. It's my own fault. I was supposed to jump in the sack with the guy, have a good time, and then walk away." She choked out a laugh. "It certainly was fun while it lasted. But I guess I wasn't Jason's kind of girl. Tracy was."

Medina squeezed her hand in sympathy. "I don't think so, Zoe. I mean, I know it looked like the two of them were all at it on Halloween, but Tony said Tracy was sloshing drunk that night. He was actually the one who called a taxi for her. After she passed out in his arms, Jason didn't want to have anything to do with her."

Zoe lifted her eyes to her friend's, struggling with a tiny ember in her chest that almost felt like hope. She swallowed. "So they're not living together?"

Medina shook her head. "No. He's alone. Tony gave Jason a call to wish him a Merry Christmas yesterday, and he says he sounds awful."

"Awful," Zoe repeated, blinking. "What did he mean *awful*?"

"Jason told Tony he knew he'd lost you forever when you didn't call him on Christmas. He said he had hoped the gift he'd sent you might have changed your mind. Prove his feelings for you." Medina tilted her head, her brows drawn together. "You didn't tell me Jason sent you anything."

"He didn't," Zoe said flatly. "I got a box of stuff from my parents. But nothing from Jason."

After Medina left, her curiosity pushed her to dial her apartment's office.

"Arthur, this is Zoe Anderson. Are there any packages down in the office for me?"

She heard the desk clerk shuffling through the pile of boxes she'd seen growing behind his desk all week. Lots of the people in her building had gone home to family for the holidays, and their packages had piled up in the office until they returned to claim them.

After a moment, he picked up. "No, Ms. Anderson. I don't see anything here for you. I'm sorry."

Should she call Jason? Tell him his package never arrived? She shook her head. What difference could any gift possibly make? A piece of jewelry, a shiny bauble, or scrap of designer silk would only further prove the point that Jason Rolland was a rich, shallow man who believed he could buy any woman he wanted.

He'd never understand what was important to her. And money wouldn't buy her heart.

Although the Christmas season in Lake George Village was usually the slowest time of the year, some places stayed open. Like Murphy's Bar and Grill, where Collette Delgado worked summers when she was home from college. Now on winter break, she was glad when she'd called the day after Christmas, and Kathy said, "Sure! Come on in this afternoon. I'm ready to go bonkers here talking to myself."

Collette arrived just after whatever sparse lunch crowd had dispersed. After a quick hug from Kathy, she wandered behind the bar as she tied on her apron.

"Hey, it looks like you've got some homeless guy on your porch." She stood on tiptoes to peer through the window looking over the back patio.

Kathy didn't even look up from the register. "Nope. No homeless guy. He comes in here a couple times a week. Orders a burger and a couple of beers."

"Does he stay out there? It's freezing."

"Can't smoke in here. He'll smoke half a pack while he waits for his burger, and then lights up again right after he's done." Kathy walked up beside her. She shook her head and frowned. "I don't know what his deal is. You can take him his burger when it comes out if you want. A fresh ashtray, too. It's worth it. He tips pretty good."

A few minutes later, Collette hurried down the steps to Murphy's coveted screened-in porch, a favorite fair-weather hangout for lake-dwellers and tourists alike. Today, it wasn't the most pleasant place to be. She hunched her shoulders against the biting wind, hurriedly pushing through the spring-loaded screen door. On her tray she balanced a plate holding a cheeseburger, a bottle of beer, and a clean ashtray.

The man didn't react when the door slammed shut behind her. She quietly set his food and beer on the round metal tabletop in front of him, and then asked if he needed anything else. He shook his head, but didn't say a word. He never even looked up.

When Collette came back inside her shoulders were quaking.

"My God it's cold out there."

"Well, you went and cut off all your winter insulation, kiddo. Where did all of that pretty hair go, anyway?"

"Oh, you know, I'm getting ready to graduate. Gonna be taking the Bar exam soon . . . They tell me I gotta start looking the part. All grown up and professional. Do you like it?"

Collette had finally parted with her long, honey-red hair on a monumental day about a month ago. No more long ponytail. Now, the ends of her blunt-cut bob barely skimmed her collar. She was still trying to get used to having to brush it back off her cheeks. Like, constantly.

"Yeah, it's cute. You do look older." Kathy raised her

eyebrows and drawled dramatically, "Very sophisticated, dahling!" They both giggled.

Kathy set to wiping down tables as Collette watched the man on the porch wolf down his meal. He was tall and lanky, his cheeks sunken, and he looked like he hadn't bathed in weeks. Black hair hung in stringy strands nearly to his shoulders. She couldn't guess his age, but the gray flecks throughout his straggly beard definitely dated him. He looked very sad.

"Are you sure that guy has a home to go to?"

"Yeah, he lives somewhere on up the lake. He usually comes down here on his four-wheeler over the ice, like he did today. Believe it or not, I think he's got money."

Collette was amazed at how fast the man's burger disappeared. She printed off his ticket and folded it into a leather binder, hurrying out to the porch just as he pushed the empty plate away from him.

"Can I get you anything else?"

The man shook his head and mumbled, "No thank you."

"I'll leave this here then. No hurry."

He reached for the folder and looked up for the first time. Doing a double take, his eyes narrowed, and he studied her intently for a long moment. As his gaze wandered over her face and hair, she noticed his eyes were the most incredible shade of ocean blue.

She blinked, feeling awkward. "Are you sure I can't get you anything else?"

The man looked away and shook his head. "I'm sorry," he mumbled. "It's your hair. You reminded me of someone I used to know. Sorry."

When she hustled back inside with her tray, Collette slammed the door behind her against a gust of frigid wind. Then she leaned back against it, staring into space.

That guy looked familiar. But who was he? She sifted memories through her brain, like a computer scrolling through a contact list looking for a name to put to his face.

Kathy came out of the kitchen and stopped in her tracks. "What? Did something happen?" She sounded concerned.

Collette shook her head, still staring, as if in a trance. "No, nothing happened." She lifted her gaze. "I think I know that guy," she murmured. "His eyes . . . you just don't forget eyes like that."

Shrugging, Kathy went back behind the bar and started rinsing glasses. "I've no idea who he is," she mumbled.

It took another thirty seconds, but when Collette's brain found the matching file, she bolted toward the window. "That's . . . Jason Rolland. The guy who owns Lakeview Lodge."

Kathy turned toward her with one eyebrow raised and disbelief written all over her face. "That guy? No way. I've only seen him a time or two—he hardly ever graces the doorway of *this* place. But the Rolland-dick I know is Mr. Ladies' Man. No way he'd go out anyplace looking like that poor sap."

"No, no, that's him. I'm sure of it," Collette fairly shrieked as she hustled back to the window. "I worked for him this summer. But he sure as heck didn't look like that."

Collette peered out the window, but the man was gone. The black leather folder lay on the table, money sticking out from under the edge. She heard a muffled roar from down below where the steps led onto the frozen lake. An engine. She watched as the man in the bulky, Michelin-man style coat scooted away across the ice on a monstrous ATV.

"I'm sure that was Jason Rolland," Collette muttered. "I wonder what happened to him?"

Kathy joined her at the window. "If that really was

Rolland," she said, "something way bad happened to him."

When Collette went back later to clear the table, what she found inside the leather folder, for a burger and two bottles of beer, was a crisply folded fifty-dollar bill.

Xavier breezed back into town Thursday morning on the red-eye, but he made a point to call Zoe at work. She'd completely forgotten he was due home so soon.

"Don't forget, love. Tomorrow night, five-thirty sharp. Cityscape Cafe."

"Five-thirty," Zoe repeated, shocked. "Isn't that kind of early for dinner?"

"I'm sorry, chérie, that was the only time I could get. Holiday weekend and all. I promise, it will be magnificent. Our table has a wonderful view of the skating rink."

Zoe got home the next day weary, and running a little late. She was standing in front of the elevator, waiting for the doors to open, when the desk clerk came out of the mailroom and spotted her.

"Ms. Anderson," he began. "Wait."

He ducked back into the office and returned carrying a thick manila envelope.

"I'm terribly sorry, Ms. Anderson. I found this at the back of the pile of packages I'd been storing for the residents all week." He shot her his most apologetic look. "It must have fallen down behind the stack."

The return address was Lake George, New York.

Zoe rode the elevator to her apartment, unlocked the door, and laid the package on the table near the door. She glanced up at the clock. Xavier would be sending a car for her in less than fifteen minutes.

She would wait. She'd wait until she was home and showered. Comfy and relaxed. There was no telling what was inside the thick envelope. For all Zoe knew, it was probably copies of the real estate contract she'd signed to surrender the chunk of upstate New York that represented, in her mind, what remained of her old life.

She would deal with that final blow later, alone.

The view of the lavishly decorated skating rink at Rockefeller Center was absolutely breathtaking. One entire wall of the Cityscape Cafe was glass, floor to ceiling. Flanking the long side of the iced oval and one story above it, most any table in the restaurant was guaranteed a spectacular view.

But the X-man was right. They did have the best one in the house. The concierge led them to a cozy table for two, tucked into the far corner of the room, right up against the window.

Zoe leaned her chin on her hand and gazed out over the sculptures below. Tiny trees took the place of hedges in the huge stone planters, and their multicolored lights twinkled in the early darkness. White fairy lights rimmed the entire perimeter of the rink, where couples holding hands and laughing groups of teenagers glided across the ice.

What a wonderful painting Norman Rockwell could make of this.

A waiter appeared promptly and asked for their drink orders. Xavier was poring over the wine list.

Zoe glanced from the stiff-backed waiter, to Xavier, and back again. She covered her mouth with her hand to hide her smile. The X-man, with his formal black suit and bright red bow tie, was dressed almost identically to the waiter.

"Would you like a bottle to share, my love? What's your fancy?" He beamed his best, most well practiced smile at her.

She reached for the wine list. "Can I see?"

Quickly, Zoe scanned the list from top to bottom. The selections were arranged in order by price.

Hmm. No Dom Pérignon. Oh well. We'll go for the next best thing.

"How about the Chateau Margaux? I'm thinking about some bloody, rare beef for dinner tonight. That okay with you, love?"

Xavier blinked and swallowed so hard, she saw his Adam's apple jump.

"Fine," he said coolly, handing the wine list back to the waiter.

Zoe's eyes wandered back out through the window, taking in the picturesque winter scene. A city scene, she reminded herself.

Why do I suddenly feel so out of place?

The X-man had obviously regained his cool, calm demeanor. He cleared his throat and drew her attention. He was reaching under the lapel of his jacket, drawing out a small, velvet box that he laid on the table between them.

It was dark blue and wrapped in golden ribbon, sparkling as it caught the light from the candles.

Shit.

No, no. Regroup. Xavier is a smart choice. He's stable, and he's capable of taking care of me so that I'll never have to worry about anything ever again.

Anything *material*, that is.

The concierge had taken Zoe's coat at the door, but she'd forgotten she still wore her pale pink stocking cap. As cold and windy as it had been over these few days between Christmas and the New Year, a good, old-fashioned knitted cap was far from a rare choice. Apparently, in Xavier's world, it was a bit too practical.

He scooted his chair in closer to the table, leaning over to speak low so no one else would hear.

"Zoe, darling, your hat. Surely you don't intend to wear it

through dinner."

"Oh, I forgot all about it." She pulled it off, and then ruffled her short red wisps around her face with the other hand.

Xavier's eyes widened. "What the hell happened to your hair?"

Wow. The X-man said a wordy-durd. She racked her brain but couldn't recall ever hearing even one of the most banal curses cross his lips.

But it wasn't only shock she detected in his voice. There was something else, a tone that bordered on . . . scolding.

"This is the real me," she snapped back. "I've always been a pixie girl."

"Not since I've known you."

"That's because you've only known me for a short while. Post-trauma. Post-widowhood. Post huge-ass gash down the side of my face." She glared at him, daring him to react. "I'm over hiding what life's done to me, Xavier. I'm going back to the real me. If people don't like looking at my scar, they can turn the fuck away."

She plainly recognized the daggers in Xavier's eyes. He grabbed her wrist, none too gently.

"Keep your voice down, Zoe. You don't want to embarrass either one of us," he warned. "And keep your vulgar, Medina-inspired language to yourself."

He's hissing again. Just like the snake he is.

Fury flashed so hot in Zoe's chest she felt she could shoot flames if she opened her mouth.

At that moment the waiter arrived with the three-hundred-dollar bottle of wine. He presented it to Xavier cradled in a white cloth napkin, and then set it on the table and used a wine key to extract the cork. He splashed a taste in one glass and handed it to Xavier, who very appropriately swirled, sniffed, and sipped. After his nod of approval, the waiter poured a scant half glass for each of them, left the cork lying on the table near the bottle, and departed.

Center. Breathe. Don't let your emotions rob you of your ability to function.

Unable to look at him for fear of losing control, Zoe turned her attention back outside. She watched the clusters of skaters making their way, laughing and chatting, across the ice. A couple in the center drew her eye. The smiling mom and dad, both wearing their best Michelin-man parkas, flanked a tiny toddler whose bright pink snowsuit all but swallowed her. White, miniature skates slipped and kicked impatiently as they moved along the ice while her parents, with encouraging smiles, kept her safely upright.

"Zoe. Zoe, you haven't heard a word of what I've said."

She slid her eyes toward Xavier, who was glaring at her.

He pushed the velvet box toward her. "Open your Christmas present."

It wasn't an invitation, but a command.

Still, she could tell he was trying. The X-man's demanding, authoritative tone was lightly glossed over with something she was sure he thought of as tenderness. Unfortunately, the ruse wasn't very convincing.

Zoe gazed down at the box, knowing exactly what was inside. Some very expensive, diamond-encrusted engagement ring. A piece that probably cost more than her entire net worth.

A tiny, jeweled noose.

Diamonds are nothing but pretty rocks. Cold, hard stones. She lifted her eyes from the box to Xavier's icy, steely eyes. How fitting.

Stalling, her gaze drifted again to the window. That's when she saw them.

On the opposite side of the skating arena a raised platform held a special display for the holiday season. It was a forest scene, depicted in modern sculptures made of wire. Surrounded by various sizes of pure white Christmas trees posed a family of deer.

There were three of them. Clear, twinkling lights wove around the painted wire, sparking light through the ice that had formed over the tiny bulbs. Two larger, one small. A fawn lay curled in a froth of artificial snow. The largest carried a regal set of antlers. The doe had been rigged to move. Her head lifted from a grazing position and paused. Zoe could swear the animated sculpture was staring across the rink, through the window, and directly at her.

It was a sign.

Her mind whisked her back to the mountains flanking the big cold lake. Suddenly she was right there beside Jason on the four-wheeler, so close she could smell his scent. An imagined prickle of pine and dust tickled her nostrils. She itched to feel his taut, hard body under her arms again, like they did as they slipped and slid up the mountain trail.

The memory of that warm, sweet kiss, and all that had followed, gathered the muscles in her throat into a painful ball. Something inside her chest moved and cracked, like clay in an earthquake. Pain gripped her, and for a moment, she feared her heart might simply stop beating.

I need to get out of here. Now.

Xavier was in the middle of a sentence when she stood up, but since she hadn't been listening, she hadn't a clue what he'd been saying.

She reached forward and grabbed the wine in one hand, the cork in the other, and crammed it into the neck of the bottle. The waiter, seeing her rise, hastened to the table.

"Is something wrong?" he asked, glancing frantically

between them.

"No. Everything is absolutely wonderful." Her voice was so solid with conviction, even she was surprised. She pulled her stocking cap back down over her cropped hair. Bending, she picked up her oversized purse and plopped it on the seat of her chair.

"Xavier, I'm sorry. But I honestly don't give a shit what you're saying. Nor do I want your very expensive, generically prepackaged proposal." She nodded toward the box still sitting on the table. "I'm not a piece of chattel you can purchase. For any price."

His look of shock transformed his face into a caricature. If Zoe hadn't been suddenly filled with such urgency, his expression would have been hilarious.

But she'd wasted enough of her life on Xavier Le Blanc.

She picked up the Chateau Margaux and stuffed it into her bag at an angle. The neck stuck awkwardly out of the top, but she fastened the center snap of her purse, snugging it fast.

Good. Nice and secure. Shouldn't go anywhere.

"Please put the wine on my companion's bill," she said matter-of-factly to the stunned waiter. "I won't be staying."

Xavier was half out of his seat, expressions shifting across his face like dangerous shadows. First shock, followed by horrified embarrassment. Finally, fury.

"What the hell do you think you're doing, Zoe? Sit down, this instant."

The hiss had grown into a growl. And wow. Two wordy-durds in one night. I must really be important to him.

"I'm leaving, Xavier. I'd like to say it's been nice getting to know you, but it hasn't." She shrugged, lifting her hands. "I'm not even sure it's possible. To get to know you, I mean. Anyway, thanks for the wine."

She nearly knocked over the flabbergasted waiter as she

made her way to the door.

Chapter 20

By the time Zoe's taxi dropped her in front of her apartment building, fat snowflakes were wafting down between the closely packed buildings of Manhattan. She didn't remember hearing any warnings about storms. But then, she hadn't paid attention lately to weather reports, or news, or much of anything else. Zoe had merely been going through the motions of her life for the past few weeks. Or months.

Really, since the day she left Jason's hotel room in Albany last August. As if she'd left part of herself there.

As she rode the elevator to her floor, her mother's words echoed in her head.

If the rogue truly loves you, he'll find some way to make you believe it.

She snorted. Guess if she planned on waiting for that, Zoe would surely end up an old maid. Tears stung her eyes as she unlocked her door. Sure, she had choices. But she simply couldn't imagine a life as Mrs. Xavier Le Blanc. That cold emptiness, she knew, would be harder to bear than the pain she was suffering now.

Zoe flicked on the table lamp inside her door. The manila envelope was lying there, unopened. She slipped out of her coat and leaned her bag with the wine bottle against the table leg. Picking up the package, she noticed that, unlike the legal correspondences she'd received through Arlin for the sale of her property, the address on this package was handwritten.

In Jason's sloppy, loopy hand.

She carried it into her living room and flopped down on the carpet in front of her tiny, unadorned tree. The pine aroma permeated the whole room now, warmth having released the needles' spicy scent. Sitting cross-legged, her hands trembling a little, she studied the post office stamp.

December 21. So it *had* arrived before Christmas.

Zoe carefully fingered open the lip of the heavy yellow paper and reached inside. The bundle of papers wasn't very thick, maybe only twenty pages or so. But they were wrapped in white tissue paper, like any fine gift, a silk scarf or cashmere sweater. She laid the bundle on the floor in front of her and lifted the edge of the tissue.

The top sheet was a heavy, rough-textured slab of sketch paper, like the kind the street artists in Greenwich Village used for impromptu portraits. But this wasn't a portrait. Expertly rendered in what looked like charcoal and colored pencil, the image depicted Zoe's childhood cottage.

But there was no kudzu vine strangling the foundation. The clapboard siding was pristine white, the shutters a vibrant green. No boards obscured broken glass. New, multi-paned windows flanked both sides of the front door, which hung strong and square on its hinges. On its center hung an ivy and wildflower wreath.

The sketch depicted the cabin in full-front view, as though the artist was either standing waist-deep in the lake, or floating in a boat. The wide-planked porch, no longer sagging toward a broken piling, looked fresh and new. And on the glider off in one corner, the artist had sketched a soft, vague image of a little girl reading a book. A little girl with pixie-short, carrot-red hair.

Zoe brought her fingers to her mouth, and then swiped at

the tears streaming down her face. It was as though whoever sketched this had been there, twenty years ago, and caught her in a quiet moment during one dreamy summer at the lake. Recorded it in meticulous detail. Preserving her childhood.

Or, perhaps, resurrecting it from the dead.

Zoe stared at the sketch for a long time. What did this mean? Was it a cruel joke to taunt her? Or a loving gesture meant to bring her comfort for her loss?

There were more papers underneath the sketch, and Zoe carefully laid the image down beside her and picked up the sheaf of neatly typed, signed and stamped pages.

An architect's blueprint for a replica of her family cottage.

And a deed.

At first, Zoe was certain it meant Jason was signing the entire property back over to her. But as she scanned the pages more carefully, she realized there were two names on the legal document.

Zoe Anderson and Jason Rolland.

Without wasting another minute, she rose and grabbed an overnight bag. With her phone wedged between her ear and shoulder, she began stuffing the warmest sweaters and jeans she owned into the bag. The doorman was taking forever to pick up the phone.

"Arthur. Oh, I'm so glad you're still here. I need my car brought up from the garage. Can you bring it around front in about ten minutes?"

There was a long moment of silence on the other end. "Ms. Anderson, this is a pretty bad storm that's blowing in. Are you sure I can't call you a taxi?"

"No, thank you, Arthur. I doubt a taxi driver is going to want to make a two-hundred-mile drive tonight."

As soon as Zoe hung up, she dialed Jason's cellphone, but

it switched over almost immediately to voicemail. Her heart sank when a computerized recording told her the voice mailbox was full. She dialed the home phone then, but it rang and rang. After the fifteenth ring, she hung up.

Maybe he's given up on me. Maybe I'm too late.

The doorman had been right. The streets of downtown weren't too bad yet, since concrete and heavy Friday night traffic kept the streets warm and turned the snowflakes to brown mush. It wasn't until Zoe pulled her Cadillac out onto the New York State Thruway that she realized just how fast the fluffy white stuff was piling up.

She checked the digital numbers on her dashboard. 6:52 p.m. With any luck at all, she'd make it to Jason's cabin, even at a cautiously reduced speed, by midnight.

There were plenty of plows out, scraping the stuff off the pavement and dropping salt and sand in their wake. Each minute stretched out as though she were stuck in a time warp.

This is a freaking blizzard.

She could hardly read the road signs through the blowing snow, and there was no way she could get her bearings on how far she'd come, or how far she had to go. The storm had her GPS so confused, it sounded possessed.

She finally shut the thing off. Her fingers ached from clutching the steering wheel so tightly, as if that could somehow help secure her tires to the slick pavement.

As Zoe neared Albany, the snowfall lessened in its fury, and in places had stopped coming down at all. She breathed a sigh of relief and pushed her foot down on the pedal a little harder. 10:23 p.m. She might make it to Lake George before Jason's show ended after all.

That's when she punched the dial on her Sirius radio to the local station setting. Zoe knew, with the mountains challenging the signal, Jason's Lair reached only about a hundred-mile radius around the tower he'd erected behind his cabin. With any luck, she should be able to hear his voice any time now.

But as she turned onto the Northway and started climbing in elevation, the snow started coming down again. Thick, furiously swirling white flakes, some as big as coins, nearly obliterated her view of the road. Very few cars passed or flanked her on the highway now. And although she'd left the radio on scan, she heard nothing as it diligently panned through the frequencies. Nothing but white noise.

Exhaustion and fear clutched at her throat, but she fought back the tears. She was completely alone on this godawful journey, but the hope in her heart drove her on.

She pulled off at a rest area when her wiper blades got so caked with ice and snow, they screeched horribly as they scraped across the windshield. Sobbing in frustration, she banged the wipers again and again on the glass, desperate to break loose the frozen crust. She hadn't even taken the time to slip on her gloves. By the time she slid back behind the wheel, her fingers were so cold she couldn't feel them.

She wished the icy coating could do the same for her heart. She'd known how to make that happen once. But not anymore. Zoe dropped her forehead down on the steering wheel.

I'm never going to make it to Lakeview alive. But if I'm too late anyway, what does it matter?

She heard the roar of the snowplow then, coming up the deserted highway from behind her, south of the rest area.

Thank you, God.

Zoe shifted into gear and waited until the plow rumbled past the pull-off where she'd been parked. With perhaps a little more pressure on the gas pedal than needed, she fish-tailed down the ramp and snugged her car into the lane thirty feet or so behind the plow. Even through the thick haze of blowing snow, she could see the red and yellow blinking lights of the county vehicle.

Her radio continued to scan, and, able to relax a little now behind her blinking guide, Zoe turned up the volume. First, she heard soft music breaking intermittently through the static. The next time around the signal was stronger, clearer. She mashed the button to still the scanner.

The song ended and, finally, she heard him. His buttery baritone came vibrating through her speakers, and Zoe turned the volume up so he filled the space all around her.

"Hell of a storm hitting us up here in the lonely Adirondacks tonight," he said. "My advice to anyone out there who can hear my voice is to hunker down wherever you are, and wait it out. I've been advised that the Northway is closed for certain stretches over the mountain."

Zoe swore and snugged her car up a little closer to the plow. So close, she could hear the mixture of salt and sand pinging off her hood and windshield.

As long as I stay behind this plow, I can keep moving forward.

Music had replaced Jason's voice, and she ached to hear him again. It seemed he wasn't getting many callers tonight. Or maybe everyone with half a brain, at this hour, in this ungodly blizzard, had simply decided to turn off the radio and go to bed.

Except for Zoe. She glanced at the clock. 11:41 p.m. She should be getting close to the exit by now. She switched on her GPS, hoping the thing had resumed its sanity.

It had. The mechanical voice reported her exit was 1.5 miles ahead.

Please, please, please let the snowplow get off the same exit.

No such luck. The truck rumbled on up the mountain, and Zoe gingerly inched her car off the highway and down the ramp. There were tire tracks, but they were already filled with several inches of fresh snow.

Remembering what her father had taught her growing up, she pumped the brake pedal delicately. But there must have been ice underneath the harmless looking, fluffy white blanket, and the ramp was steep. As if in slow motion, her Cadillac began to slip sideways, and she panicked, slamming the brake hard. Her wheels locked, and she went into a spin.

Zoe had no idea if the car made two revolutions or ten. She clutched the steering wheel, squeezed her eyes shut, and screamed.

I'm gonna die, I'm gonna die.

She held her breath, waiting for the sound of impact, or to feel the jolt as her car careened off the elevated ramp and plummeted down into the woods below. But miraculously, neither happened. Slowly, almost gracefully, the car ended its pirouette and skidded to a halt with a soft thud, her rear tires jammed up against the plowed bank of snow.

Her breath was coming fast now, and she was shaking so badly she could barely hold the wheel.

I wonder if I'm stuck. I could die right here, freeze to death before anybody comes along to help me.

But when she tentatively pressed her toe on the gas pedal, her tires spun only once before they gained purchase. Slowly, she crept the rest of the way to the edge of Highway 9N.

Only a few more miles to go.

By the time Zoe's headlights finally slashed across the unlit sign for Lakeview Lodge, the red neon digits on her dash clock had flicked over from 11:59 to 12:00.

Jason stubbed out yet another cigarette butt in the

313

overflowing ashtray beside his switchboard. Not many callers tonight. He wasn't surprised.

This storm had blown in unexpectedly, changing course at the last minute to swing south from its original path toward Canada. So far, since midafternoon, almost a foot of snow had fallen. It was coming down so fast that the lone streetlight at the end of his driveway was little more than a glowing blur in the distance.

He raked a long, straggly strand of hair off his face and began shutting down the broadcasting equipment. One by one, he flipped the switches, extinguishing each group of blinking lights.

Sighing, and picking up his half-empty pack of cigarettes, Jason switched off the main power and the room went dark. He was about to turn away from the window when a flash of headlights caught his attention.

Who in hell would be crazy enough to be out on the roads tonight?

He squinted and leaned closer to the window, swearing when his own breath fogged the glass. He wiped it clear with his sleeve.

Some crazy loon was turning into his driveway. Surely, they had to realize the resort was closed. No lights were on except for his porch lamp, and the Closed for the Season sign had been in place for almost two months. He wondered how any vehicle, other than something as monstrous as his Hummer, could even make it in over the plowed bank on the side of the road.

But, Jason remembered, he'd gotten out there earlier. Before darkness fell, he'd cleared the entrance to the resort with his own plow. Knowing how much snow was expected that night, he hadn't wanted to struggle in the morning with an eight-foot wall scraped up by the county.

Maybe they're just turning around. Good move. The road north of Lakeview got steeper and curvier, and there wasn't anything much up there this time of year anyway.

But the vehicle didn't turn around. Jason couldn't make out what kind of car it was, but it wasn't a truck or SUV. The wall of snow on either side of the driveway, where he'd plowed earlier, came up nearly to the windows. Slowly, but quite determinedly, the car inched its way down the serpentine drive. He could hear the whine of spinning tires in the four or five inches of snow that had fallen on the pavement since he'd cleared it. Twice, he was certain the car was stuck.

Great. Just what I want to do tonight. Help some idiot shovel their car out of a snowbank.

Jason felt around on the counter for his cellphone. He knew a guy in town who ran a towing service year-round. He wondered if the number was saved on his contact list.

But his cellphone wasn't on the counter. He flicked on the small table lamp and scanned the room. He patted his jeans pockets. No phone.

Must have left it downstairs when I came up tonight. Oh well. Nobody of any importance ever calls anyway.

Jason switched off the light again and glanced out into the darkness. The car had made considerable progress, reaching the place where he had stopped plowing, and turned to clear a path up to his cabin. A beam of light crawled across the wall of snow as the car made the turn, skidding a good bit sideways, and then fishtailing up the last thirty feet.

Wonderful. Company. Why the fuck did I leave the porch light on?

But as the car crept up next to his Hummer and the glow of the porch light illuminated it, Jason could see a patch of dark paint through the snow heaped on the hood. He recognized the familiar shape. It was a burgundy Cadillac.

He raced down the two flights of stairs, reaching the door before the bell rang. Jason grabbed the knob, swearing when he pulled and realized it was still locked. He threw back the deadbolt and yanked the door open.

She was standing on the doorstep, bundled in a pink ski parka and matching hat. He blinked, unable to believe his eyes. She was looking down at her Ugg boots, stomping them one at a time on the top step like an angry little girl.

Finally, she looked up. Her eyes glittered under the lamp's glow, and her cheeks were flushed and freckled as ever.

"How in hell do you people drive up here in the winter, anyway?"

Jason blinked. Guess if he was hallucinating, the fantasy came with sound—and a temper.

"Four-wheel drive. And snow tires," he answered dumbly.

Her eyes narrowed. "Are you going to let me in, or keep me standing out here freezing my butt off?"

Zoe knew by his voice that the man standing in the doorway was Jason, but when she first looked up, for a split-second, she wasn't sure. This man looked much older. And scruffier. And way, way thinner. Like the homeless men she saw every day in the city.

His straggly black hair brushed his shoulders, and looked like it hadn't been shampooed in a month. White hairs sprinkled his full beard. Deep purple crescents hung under sunken, weary eyes.

But those eyes were still the same shade of impossible blue.

"What the hell happened to you?" she squeaked as she stepped onto the mat inside the door.

"What?"

Stomping the remaining snow off her boots, she unzipped her coat, staring at Jason in disbelief. "You look like a caveman. A starving one."

Jason had taken two steps back to let her in. Now he reached around her to shut the door against the blast of cold air. When he drew closer, she realized he smelled nearly as bad as he looked.

Maybe worse.

Zoe slipped her coat off and let it fall to the mat, and then stepped out of her boots before pulling off her knit cap.

Jason's lips crinkled into a smirk.

"What happened to your hair?" he asked as his eyes roamed over her face.

She perched her hands on her hips. "What?" she shot back.

The smile started in his eyes, and then warmed his entire face. "You look like a wood fairy."

Zoe sighed and closed her eyes, and then opened them, scanning the room behind him. Trash littered every countertop in the kitchen, the end table, the coffee table. The garbage can was overflowing, and the sink was heaped with dishes. It looked as though he'd had a party. A month ago. And hadn't cleaned up yet.

"Are you alone?"

Jason snorted. "Only for the last five months or so."

She blinked, one eyebrow twitching. He certainly didn't look as though he'd been entertaining much of late. God, how could anybody get close enough to be around him?

"The house stinks. And so do you, by the way."

Jason raked his hand through stringy hair and winced. "Gotten a little lazy lately. Nobody here but me anyway." He patted the pack of cigarettes in his breast pocket. "Started smoking again, too. That's probably what you smell."

He extracted the pack and a lighter, positioning a cigarette between his lips. He lit it, puffed a few times, then blew smoke back over his shoulder. "What the hell are you doing here?"

Zoe waved a hand in front of her face and coughed, but said nothing. She didn't know what to say. She obviously hadn't thought this far ahead.

Crossing her arms over her chest, she hugged herself. She was exhausted, from working all day to her final confrontation with Xavier to the grueling, terrifying drive up here. The shock of seeing Jason in this condition was the final feather that rocked her off balance. For a moment, her mind went blank.

Struggling to center herself, she drew in a deep breath. She would not succumb to the word scrambling again.

I may not know what to say, but I do know why I'm here.

Jason was still staring at her, his face sober now, his eyes narrowed, waiting. There was something in his gaze she couldn't quite read. Was it hope? Relief? Or anger?

"I left something behind last summer," she whispered.

A bitter-sounding laugh burst from him. "Picked a great night to come back for it." Jason took another puff on his cigarette, allowing the smoke to drift out of his nostrils, up and around his face in an eerie cloud. "I never found anything of yours here. You wiped yourself out of my life so fast, and so completely, I wondered sometimes if I'd created you in my mind."

"Jason," she breathed his name, loving the feel of it on her tongue. Loving that at last, they were again sharing the same air.

Even if that air was a little pungent at the moment.

He turned away from her, stooping to crush out the cigarette in an ashtray on the coffee table, one almost hidden amongst beer bottles and empty Styrofoam containers. He stood with his back to her, folding his arms across his chest.

"Why are you here, Zoe? To pour salt in the wound? To shove back in my face the Christmas gift you never even acknowledged?"

She crossed the room and laid her hands on his shoulders.

God, he's gotten thin.

She was shaking now, and her voice quivered. "Jason, I didn't get the package until tonight."

He turned around and stared at her as though she'd spoken in a different language. Her chest clutched to see sunken cheeks under the straggly black beard. The moment froze, and the drumming of Zoe's heartbeat, the blood rushing in her ears, was all she could hear.

But his eyes were cold, distant. Like a man she'd never known.

My God, I'm too late.

The thought gripped her, strangling her, threatening to take her breath from her lungs. There it was, the knife in her heart again, twisting and slashing her to ribbons.

Until he reached one hand forward to trace a finger gently down the scar on the side of her face. The shine glazing those ice-blue eyes gave him away.

"Not too late, my love," he rumbled, as though reading her mind, his voice thick with emotion. "Not yet. I'm not dead yet."

An hour later Zoe lit a candle on the freshly cleaned coffee table. She'd had to get creative to pull together an edible meal from Jason's depleted stores. The pound of hot dogs in the freezer, only slightly freezer burned, and the single can of beans hiding in the back of the pantry, would have to do.

Since there wasn't a clean dish left in the house, she

rummaged through the cabinets and found some china in a cupboard over the fridge. It had been carefully wrapped in a slightly yellowed, lace tablecloth. She carefully unwrapped two plates, rinsed them under hot water, and wiped them dry.

When Jason came thumping down the steps a few moments later, he'd showered and pulled his wet hair back into a band at the base of his neck. His red plaid shirt flapped open above worn jeans, and he was barefoot. He got as far as the bottom step and froze, staring at the plates on the counter.

Zoe studied his expression with concern. "Should I not have used the china?"

Jason swallowed, shook his head, and then pressed his fingers to his eyes. On a long, shuddering breath he said, "It was my mom's. It hasn't been out of the closet since I built this place."

"Jason, I'm sorry. I guess I should have asked you—"

"No." He swiped his hand down his face and crossed the room, taking her shoulders in his hands. He gazed down into her eyes. "I can't think of a better way for us to start our lives over."

They ate like starving animals, sitting side by side on the floor, off of delicate, flowered china, using the ottoman as their table. Zoe had never enjoyed hot dogs and beans so much in her entire life.

"It's amazing how much a bottle of three-hundred-dollar wine can improve a meal," she said with a chuckle.

"He was going to give you a ring." Jason's words were a statement, not a question.

"How did you know?"

"Tony and I still talk. Medina told him that Xavier flashed the thing around the office for a week before Christmas." His eyes strayed to her left hand. "I figured it'd be on your finger by now."

She shuddered. "Wasn't going to happen."

"Did you sleep with him?"

Her forkful of beans hung suspended halfway to her lips. She lifted her eyes slowly to meet his. "Did you sleep with Tracy after you and I were together?"

Flatware clattered to the plates as he pulled her to him, burying his face in her hair. He was trembling, violently. "No. Once I was with you that first time, Zoe, I knew you'd ruined me for anyone else." He choked on a sob. "No. I haven't been with anyone. Not since the first time with you."

She closed her eyes, a great wave of relief washing over her. "Nor I," she managed around the painful lump in her throat.

They sat that way for a long time, wrapped around each other, sobbing and rocking gently.

"I still can't believe you're really here," he murmured into her hair. "That this isn't all a wonderful, impossible dream. Or a cruel hallucination. I've been living in hell since you left, Zo."

She smoothed his hair and growled, "I didn't realize hell was this freaking cold. But I will tell you one thing." Pushing back, she gazed into his eyes. "I know I drove through hell to get here. There were a few times I didn't think I'd make it alive."

His brows knitted and he stroked her cheek, his expression full of questions. "Why tonight, Zoe? I mean, I thank God in heaven you're here, but what made you brave the trip now, of all nights?"

Leaning in, she placed a soft kiss on his lips. "Because I suddenly realized that this is where I belong. And I wanted to be back here with you, now, tonight, right away. I was terrified, so very afraid I'd waited too long. That you'd moved on and wouldn't want me anymore."

With a dark chuckle, he choked, "There was no moving on for me." His arms encircled her and he held her so tightly, she could barely breathe. "I was dying inside. Every day, every hour, every minute that went by, especially since I sent the package, and you didn't respond . . ." Another sob wracked his body.

"Hey," she whispered after a long moment, pulling away and framing his face with her hands. "The pain is all behind us now. We get to start over." Smiling, she ran a finger down his cheek and traced his lower lip with her thumb. "And I wasn't kidding when I said I left something behind this summer. It's something I just can't live without."

She kissed him again, slow and sweet this time, tasting him as she'd longed to for so very long. When their lips parted, she lifted his hand to press against her chest.

"Jason Rolland, I believe you still have possession of my heart."

Much later, in the dark, Zoe reveled in the feel of Jason's nude body spooned against her. They'd made love, dozed in serene comfort, and then started all over again. Now it was near dawn, though she knew it would still be hours before the weak winter sun would sparkle on the snow outside the window.

A window absent of the glow of street lamps and flashing neon signs. No horns honking, no sirens blaring. Outside this window, there was total blackness and utter silence.

She lay awake for a long time, listening to the only sound that made her world complete. The regular, even breathing of the man she loved.

Epilogue

The Big Haunt
Halloween, four years later

Jade stepped down off the stool, scowling at the grimy feather duster in her hand.

"Good thing we do this decorating thing once a year. It's the only way we get the grime out of all those high-up places." She turned to smile at Arlin as she handed him the packet of thumbtacks she'd been using to hang dancing papier-mâché skeletons, pumpkins, and ghosts from the open beams of the Boathouse Restaurant. "The tacks saved the day, though."

"Fact: tape doesn't stick well to dusty surfaces. Tacks do," he replied. His smile sent a flush washing over Jade like a summer breeze. He reached for her hand. "Come on. Let's sit down and grab a bite before any zombies start showing up."

Arlin pressed a warm hand on Jade's waist and they headed toward the big round table set up in the corner, flanked by six chairs and a highchair. Jade checked her watch.

"We're down to an hour until the doors open. Where is everybody?"

Before she finished speaking the side door opened and in strolled a monk. Jade stopped in her tracks and almost doubled over in laughter. Tony's Cheshire cat smile gave away his identity.

He'd pasted a circle of short, brown hair around his shaved head, giving him the perfect monk's tonsure. A huge, chocolate-colored robe covered his bulky mass to the floor, bound around the middle by a length of rope Jade would have bet he cut off the roll down in the boathouse.

"Brother Tony. So good to see you this evening. Took a night off from vespers?" Arlin struggled to keep a straight face as he shook Tony's hand, which made Jade giggle all the more. "And where's Sister Medina this evening?"

"She's helping get Tinker Bell dressed, I think," he said, glancing back over his shoulder. "Ah, but here comes the Captain."

And there he was, complete with billowing white sleeves and leather vest, his boots clunking in over the doorstep as though he wasn't quite sure how to navigate in them. He wore a red kerchief under a battered, three-cornered hat. A single strand of his long, black hair hung in a dreadlock dressed with beads. His short beard was split into two braids. A long, tangled feather earring brushed one shoulder, and he'd finished off the look with dark, smudgy liner encircling both of his pool-water blue eyes.

That, Jade was certain, had been at Zoe's insistence.

Jade shook her head as she folded her arms. "Perfect," she said, and then flashed him a grin.

Arlin reached forward to shake Jason's hand. "Welcome, Captain Jason. I'm pleased you've decided to join us this evening. No swashes to buckle? Damsels to distress?"

"Nope. I've got all the damsels I need. Distressing me," he said with a laugh.

Her brother eyed Jade up and down, and then Arlin. "What, no costumes for you two?"

Jade whipped out two masks from the pocket of her

apron, one black velvet, and the other bright red with feathery eyebrows. "Right here." She handed the black mask to Arlin.

The door swung open behind Jason, and in waddled a rather large nun. It took Jade a minute to recognize Medina without her billow of wild dark hair. Tonight, it was all hidden beneath a headdress made of cloth. A black veil flowed down over her shoulders. Essentially, every inch of her was covered from head to toe except for the now, even more rounded oval of her face.

But the yards of dark cloth flowing over her body couldn't conceal a very prominent, pregnant belly.

Tony went immediately to Medina's side, taking her elbow as she trundled in through the door.

"Come over here, Hon, and get off your feet." He led her to the nearest of the chairs flanking the round table. After making sure she was safely seated, he poured her a glass of water from the pitcher in the center. He ran his hand over her rounded belly as he rumbled a satisfied growl.

Jade perched on the edge of the chair next to Medina. "How are you feeling? Almost there, huh?"

She nodded. "I'm actually due tomorrow." She slid her gaze up toward Tony. "I had to do some fancy talking to get Daddy here to let me come to the party tonight. But the doctor says it'll be a little while yet. First babies, you know."

Jade patted the back of her hand. "Well, you get yourself something to eat, and head on back to your cabin anytime you're ready. We don't need you overdoing anything tonight." She rose and leaned over to plant a kiss on Medina's cheek. "We're all so happy for you. Both of you."

A squeal from the doorway made Jade spin around. A tiny, sparkling pink fairy child—complete with wings—came streaking across the space, headed in a beeline toward her.

She stooped to scoop her up before the sprite attached herself to her leg.

"And who do we have here? A butterfly? What sparkly wings you have." She grinned down at the toddler, whose fingers shot up to a quivering mouth. Fine, wispy curls of carrot-red hair swirled around her flushed face. Her plump cheeks sparkled with glitter, accenting her liberal sprinkling of pale freckles.

A shiver ran through her when she looked into Daphne's eyes. It never failed to amaze her. They were exactly the same shape and amazing color as her brother's.

The little girl shook her head slowly, her pouty lips puckering. Jade was afraid she might burst into tears. "I'm Tinker Bell, Auntie Jade. Not a bubberfly."

Jade patted her bottom. "Of course you are, baby. And a fine Tinker Bell too. Where's your mama at?"

"Wight dere." Daphne pointed with a chubby finger. Then she leaned close to Jade's ear and whispered, "She's kissing Daddy again."

A red-headed wood sprite in a lip-lock with Captain Jack Sparrow.

Not so unexpected, but a beautiful sight nevertheless. Jade's throat drew tight.

Zoe's curves were wrapped in a stretchy green garment patched with silken green and gold leaves. A circlet of matching vine perched atop her short, honey-red wisps. When the two lovers pulled apart, Jade spotted the tiny, sparkly leaves painted down the side of Zoe's face. They sprouted all along both sides of her pink scar.

She blinked back quick tears and glanced over at her man. "Uncle Arlin, can you please put Daphne . . . I mean, Tinker Bell, in her special chair? It's time we made a toast."

Minutes later, the group settled around the table scattered

with glitter pumpkins and ghost confetti. Claude came out of the kitchen carrying two bottles—one of Asti Spumante, the other of sparkling grape juice. He started around the table, filling flutes.

When he got to Medina's, he switched to pour from the sparkling juice bottle. Tinker Bell had her very own plastic replica of the adult's glasses, which Claude filled a little less than halfway with the bubbly, purple liquid.

Zoe held her hand over her glass when Claude lifted the Asti. "I'll take the other kind tonight," she whispered, sliding her eyes toward Jason with an impish grin.

Jade didn't miss the quiet exchange.

"No Asti tonight, Zoe?"

She grinned and shook her head, and then buried her face against Jason's shoulder. Jason cleared his throat.

"We discovered today you're going to be an aunt again, Sis."

A cheer went up around the table, and Tinker Bell, recognizing she was no longer in the spotlight, promptly turned her plastic flute upside down on her tray. Zoe leapt up, napkin in hand.

Jade chuckled. "You two are going to have your hands full, that's for sure."

Zoe shrugged, her hands busy sopping up spilled grape juice. "Captain Jason says he needs a first mate. Hopefully," she shot a glance at Jason, "he sent me some Y-squigglers this time."

Jason's eyes softened. "It doesn't matter. I'll take another mini-Zoe any day of the week."

When Zoe returned to her seat, Arlin raised his glass.

"Here's to all the health, good fortune, and love we've been blessed with over the past few years. And to the discovery of unexpected treasures," he paused and gazed at

Jade.

A warm wave washed over her as she planted a quick kiss on his lips. She turned and tipped her glass toward Medina, and then Jason. "To the taming of wild spirits." Pausing, she waited until Zoe's eyes locked with hers. "And to brand new beginnings."

They all sipped from their glasses, and then turned to kiss their sweethearts. Tinker Bell drummed away happily with the plastic glass on her tray in a thumping, cadenced rhythm.

A few hours later, the roar of laughter and music faded behind them as Jason led Zoe back to the cabin. Daphne had fallen asleep, her cherub's lips pursed as one chubby cheek rested on his shoulder. He handed Zoe the key to the gate, and she opened the lock.

The path to the cottage was paved now, colorful landscape lights accenting pruned vines and shrubs from the privacy fence all the way to the porch. The kudzu had been cleared away, along with any undergrowth where insects, vermin, or snakes could reside. Still brightly colored, fallen autumn leaves decorated the path like confetti. As they approached the steps, Zoe reached for the sleeping child.

"I'll get Tinker Bell to bed," she whispered.

Jason stayed behind on the lawn, gazing up at the replica of Zoe's childhood cottage. On the rebuild, they'd pushed it back from the original location, far enough away from the sandy beach to allow for a modest, safely fenced front yard. At first glance, the cabin appeared exactly as it had in the photograph, complete with wide, front porch, gingerbread trim, and a glider in one corner.

But when he'd rebuilt the cottage, Jason made sure it would stand up to the harsh Adirondack winters. A brick chimney hovered over the center of the family room where he'd installed a wide, fieldstone fireplace, perfect for hanging stockings on Christmas Eve. The original first-floor plan remained much the same, but a second story provided two additional bedrooms and a bath, each with dormers looking out toward the lake. Well-insulated and sheathed in vinyl siding, the house would stand up for many generations to come.

Many generations, he hoped, of he and Zoe's growing family. He was still standing there, his arms crossed, billowy white pirate's sleeves fluttering in the chilly autumn breeze, when Zoe came back out the front door. She paused on the steps.

"What?" she asked.

Jason smiled, twirling one side of his braided beard. "Do you miss the city, Zo?"

She lowered herself to sit on the top step and leaned forward, hugging her knees. "How could I possibly miss a place where you're not?"

"It's a different life for you here. I know you help run the resort, and do the part-time work down at the Women's Center, but—"

But she was shaking her head. "No, Jason. This is the life I'd always dreamed of. I'm exactly where I want to be."

He narrowed his eyes and raised one eyebrow. "It just occurred to me, Ms. Anderson, that you never did get back your right-of-way."

Zoe rose then, and closed the distance between them to wrap her arms around his chest. He rested his chin on her head, his fingers toying with the wisps at the nape of her neck. He reveled in the pounding of her heart beat against him, in rhythm with his own. The wind chased leaves across the grass. Water lapped softly on the sand behind them. Jason drew in a long, slow breath and closed his eyes.

Never, in his entire life, had he felt this complete.

After a long moment, Zoe tipped back her head, her green eyes glinting in the moonlight.

"It's occurred to me, Mr. Rolland, that you've forgotten I'm no longer Ms. Anderson. I'm Mrs. Jason Rolland. Now, and for the rest of time. And I have the only right-of-way I need." She reached up and tugged on his braided beard. "The one straight into your heart."

The End

A Note from the Author

Thank you for joining Zoe and Jason on their journey. I hope you enjoyed this, the first *Love at Lake George Novel*. Watch for *Anchor My Heart, Book II*, coming soon.

Please, take a few moments to leave a review on Amazon and Goodreads. Reviews are incredibly important to authors, and how our stories are able to reach more readers like you.

In addition to intensely emotional contemporary romance, I also write romance with a ghostly twist. Please check out my previous releases in the paranormal genre:

Phantom Traces

A geeky Goth chic, a sexy history professor, and a pipe-smoking, book hurling ghost. Put them together in a haunted library and...well... .

Hearts Unloched
~Chosen Runner-Up in the 2016 New York Book Festival~

A psychic interior designer reluctantly agrees to renovate a crumbling hotel on Loch Sheldrake, a lake rumored to have once been the mob's body dumping ground.

Remember: when you're in the mood for intensely emotional romantic novels, with or without a paranormal twist, think—

CLAIRE GEM

Made in the USA
San Bernardino, CA
16 January 2017